Horses of Tir Na Nog

A New Door Opens

Book One of the
Horses of Tir Na Nog Trilogy

By Bob Boze

Dedicated to Rio

First edition published October 2014
ISBN-10: 150286908X (Softcover)
ISBN-13: 9781502869081 (Softcover)
ASIN: B00OME9U24 (Kindle ebook)

Table of Contents

The Legend of Tir Na Nog

Tir Na Nog - Old Irish:

In Irish mythology, Tir Na Nog is widely known as an 'Otherworld' where sickness and death do not exist: A place of eternal youth and beauty where you will never grow a day older. It is a place where music, strength, life and all pleasurable pursuits come together; where happiness lasts forever and no one wants for food or drink.

--------//-------

Long ago on an isle of emerald green surrounded by a sea of azure blue, there lived a young man named Oisin.

Oisin liked to explore the moors with the Fianna, ancient warrior-hunters.

One day, when Oisin and the Fianna were out hunting, they saw an extraordinary sight - a beautiful young woman with long red hair riding on a spirited white horse. The sun glistened off the maiden's hair, casting a magical golden light.

The mare's movements were so fluid she appeared to float across the ground. As her rider brought her to a stop before the group, the horse's hooves struck at the field stones impatiently, sending small sparks into the air.

"My name is Niamh," the woman said in a voice that sounded like the music of a harp. "My father is the king of Tir Na Nog."

Oisin stepped forward from the group of hunters to welcome the rider. As his eyes met Niamh's, they fell in love.

"Come with me to Tir Na Nog," Niamh pleaded to her newfound love. After only a moment's hesitation, Oisin swung up behind Niamh onto the white horse.

Together, they crossed the sea to Tir Na Nog.

Having grown up on The Emerald Isle, Oisin would never have believed a more beautiful land existed. But as he gazed upon Tir Na Nog, he was stunned by the beauty around him.

In this magic land, Niamh and Oisin built a life together. They spent each day exploring Tir Na Nog with the white mare. Niamh and Oisin's love grew deeper as Niamh shared the beauty of her enchanted homeland.

Three hundred years passed as though it were but a single day. No one in Tir Na Nog ever grew old or fell sick. They lived in endless, youthful moments filled with happiness.

In spite of the beauty of the land and the deep love that Niamh and Oisin shared for each other, a small part of Oisin's soul knew loneliness.

Such feelings were unheard of in Tir Na Nog. But in spite of her efforts, Niamh was unable to ease Oisin's loneliness.

So when Oisin came to Niamh and told her of his desire to return to Ireland to see his family and the Fianna again, she could not hold him back.

"All right," said Niamh. "Return to Ireland on the back of the white mare. But, my dear, your foot must not touch the soil of Ireland."

Immediately, Oisin rode the white horse back across the sea to the land of his birth.

But as soon as the mare's hooves touched Ireland's soil, Oisin realized how much the land had changed. Oisin's family and friends had long passed away. Their grand castle was overgrown with ivy.

Oisin was so caught up in his quest to find his family and his grief at their loss, he forgot to care for the beautiful white horse. In spite of her hunger and fatigue, she continued to respond to her rider.

Finally, with a sad heart, Oisin turned the mare back toward the sea to return to Tir Na Nog.

Approaching the sea, he came upon a group of men working in a field. As the mare reached the group, her fatigue caused her to stumble.

Her hoof hit a stone. Oisin bent down to pick up the rock, planning to take it to Tir Na Nog. He was sure that it would ease his sadness to carry a piece of Ireland back with him.

But as his hand grasped the stone, Oisin lost his balance and fell to the ground.

Within moments, Oisin aged three hundred years.

Without her rider, the mare reared up and rushed into the sea, returning to Tir Na Nog and her beloved Niamh.

When the men in the field witnessed this, they were amazed. Not only had they seen a young man age before their eyes, they had also seen a tired old plow horse transform into a beautiful silver-white mare, who raced into the sea.

The men went to Oisin's aid and carried him to Saint Patrick.

When Oisin met Saint Patrick, he told Saint Patrick of his family and the Fianna, who had disappeared from Ireland almost three hundred years before. Then he told Saint Patrick of Niamh and the magical land of Tir Na Nog.

As Oisin ended his story, a great weariness swept over him, and he closed his eyes in eternal slumber.

Even to this day, the fisherman and lighthouse keepers still tell of foggy nights when the moon is full, and they see a shimmering white horse dancing in the waves along the shores of Ireland. Some say that the red-haired maiden who rides the horse still searches for Oisin.

Chapter 1 - Ella and Jewel

CJ sat cross-legged on the floor of the stall, her back leaning against the wall. "What a crappy day this has turned out to be, huh?" she said. CJ was no stranger to crappy days. Her life had been full of them, but this one had rapidly moved up the chart to become one of the worse. She had pretty much learned how to deal with 'normal' crappy days. After all, most of the time you could do something to help make the day better, and CJ had become a master at that.

No, it was the days where she had absolutely no control over anything that really got to her. Days where nothing she did or said made a difference and no matter how hard she prayed that the day would get better, it just got worse. She looked up at the ceiling and shouted at the top of her lungs "THIS. IS. SO. UNFAIR. I know you're listening up there. Why are you doing this?"

Before Kate left, CJ had promised her that she was okay. She could handle this. She had to. As his protector, CJ had promised herself she would be strong, wouldn't cry anymore, but the tears began to slide down her cheeks anyway. At barely a whisper, she added, "What on earth did he do to deserve this? What did he ever do to you? Or anyone else. You were supposed to help me protect him. Why didn't we protect him? I was supposed to save him. He doesn't deserve this." By then, the tears were streaming and she could barely see.

The anger left her, and pain took over. "Oh God, I promised you I'd keep you safe and look after you. Please, please don't leave me by myself again. I love you so much." Finally, sobbing uncontrollably, she completely lost it. With a loud clap of thunder, so too did the sky.

-----//-----

Today was Thursday, CJ's *easy day*. Not only would she have two volunteers to help her, it was also one of the two days of the week when Kate, the owner, would spend all day at the ranch.

Her morning had actually started out pretty good. She woke to find a note on her door from Kate, thanking her for doing such a great job the day before. It wasn't often Kate left a note. Kate never missed saying thank you, even if the person really hadn't done much, but a note was unusual.

As CJ reflected back on what should have been a normal, quiet Wednesday, she had to wonder how she'd actually managed to get through it. If any day had deserved a thank you note, yesterday had been it. There had been her usual 'morning chores,' which more often than not, ran way into the afternoon. On top of that, Kate had asked her to have one of the volunteers clean out the transit stalls and get them ready for the new horses being transported to the ranch by County Animal Services.

Only Shannon, the volunteer coordinator and trainer had shown up. She also informed CJ that she had a date to go clothes shopping with a friend and could only work until noon. *Great. So much for help.* She really couldn't get mad at Shannon. At least she had shown up, and CJ knew she would get as much done as she could before she left.

Later, when Shannon found out she and CJ were the only ones there, she said, "I'll call my friend and postpone our shopping trip so I can stay and help."

CJ's response was, "No way. You've already done more work than I could've hoped for. Go enjoy the rest of the day. Pick out something that makes you feel special whenever you wear it. Don't even think about wearing it to the ranch, though."

Shannon smiled at her. "Thanks. I'll send you a picture so you can see what I bought."

CJ shook her head. "Shut up, put your stuff away, and get out of here before I change my mind. Now go. Move it."

Shannon turned and headed for the storage shed with her wheelbarrow toolkit while CJ went to the hay shed.

How in the world was she ever going to get everything done before CAS arrived with the horses? Shannon—bless her heart—had finished her normal chores, then raked out both transit stalls, emptied, cleaned, rinsed, and refilled the water troughs, then made sure any *potholes* were filled in and tamped down. That left hay to be lugged and food to be readied. On top of all that, CJ still had the rest of her *morning chores* to finish, the most important of which was checking out each horse to see if anything 'abbynormal' showed up. As soon as the word entered her mind, she started chuckling.

CJ loved that term; abbynormal. *Young Frankenstein* was her favorite movie, and she would forever remember the first time she had watched it, especially the scene in the morgue. Seeing the brains floating in the lab jars and Igor (or was it Egor?) explaining to Dr. Frankenstein that the brain he had stolen belonged to someone named Abby Normal. She had laughed so hard that she missed the next 20 minutes of the movie. Even after she had calmed down, the brain in the jar would flash in front of her eyes, then she would snort and start laughing again.

Finally, her friend Beth, the drama queen, had turned off the movie, vowing *never* to watch another movie with her, which had just made CJ burst out laughing again. Even to this day, no one would watch the movie with her because she would start snorting before Igor left the castle, and by the time he got to the door of the morgue, she would be outright roaring.

CJ really didn't care what anyone else thought. The movie and that scene were therapy to her. Truth be told, she really wasn't sure how much of the movie she had seen, especially the parts following abbynormal. All she knew was whenever she was under pressure or really felt down, one of the three copies of *Young Frankenstein* she owned went into the DVD player, and by the morgue scene, she felt better and her side hurt.

The CAS pickup and horse trailer pulled up alongside her, and CJ snapped out of the trance she had been in. Laura, one of the rangers, got out and walked up to CJ. "CJ, are you alright, hon? Something must agree with you. You've got the biggest smile I've ever seen on you."

CJ started to say, "Oh, I was just thinking about checking all the horses to make sure they're normal," but before she could finish, a jar with a brain floating in it formed in front of her eyes and she broke up laughing. Not knowing why, Laura joined in.

Several minutes later, when she and Laura calmed down, Laura looked at her. "I don't know what we were laughing at, but I haven't laughed like that in I don't know how long." Over at the truck, Laura's partner Luke was laughing and hanging on to the truck's bumper to keep himself upright. As soon as CJ and Laura looked at him, they all burst into another bout of laughter. Minutes later, wet-faced and all hanging onto anything close by, Laura was the first to speak.

"Oh my God. What in the world were we laughing at?" Laura asked, still trying to calm herself and keep from snorting.

"If I tell you, you'll think I'm crazy," CJ said, shaking her head.

"You mean crazier than we think you are now?" Luke responded.

"I really have no idea what that was about, but it was probably a good thing to do before we open the back of the trailer," Laura commented.

12

CJ stared at her. "Oh no, how bad are they?"

"Not as bad as the last one. We've had these two over in the Bonita Animal Shelter for several weeks now, so we've had time to fatten them up a bit. The vet has also medded them up for some of the problems they have." Luke added, "You may have seen one of them on TV a few weeks ago. She was part of that band of horses that the news filmed running through the streets of Chula Vista."

CJ looked puzzled. "Oh? I thought they all got adopted out and found families."

"Yeah, that's what got reported by the news, but nobody wanted poor Ella," Laura explained.

"Ella?" asked CJ.

"We're not sure who named her. All the rest were either claimed by their owners or got adopted, but nobody claimed poor Ella and nobody submitted an adoption application for her. You'll kind of understand why when you see her."

"I'll never understand why," CJ said as the tears formed in her eyes. "So help me, as long as I live I'll never understand how anyone could do what they do to these wonderful creatures. Sorry, you'd think I'd be used to it by now."

"You never get used to it," Laura answered.

CJ wiped the tears from her cheeks and took a deep breath. "Moving right along. So who's the other one, and what's their story? Or do I want to know?"

"That would be Jewel. When you see her, it's not going to be obvious, but we actually fattened her up a bit since she's been in

13

our care. She came from an owner in the Tijuana River Valley area. Both Animal Services and TJ River Valley Animal Rescue tried to help them care for her. We even provided them with food to make sure she was getting the right diet, but for some reason, she was just not eating.

"Finally, with the owner's permission, we took her from them to see if they could do better at the Bonita Shelter. As you'll see, they were only partly successful. We hope you can work some of your magic and get her to eat."

Walking to the back of the horse trailer, CJ held her breath as Luke and Laura let down the ramp. Laura went up the ramp and backed Jewel out first.

As she came down the ramp, CJ stared in amazement. "Oh my God."

She continued to stare. *How can any horse be that thin and survive?* Jewel had to be at least three hundred pounds underweight, or more. She obviously hadn't been groomed in a long time. Her winter coat was all matted, and her mane just hung limply along her neck. She looked like a skeleton that someone had glued hair on.

CJ walked up to Jewel, leaned her head against Jewel's forehead, and whispered, "It's okay, sweetheart. You're home. You're safe now." She rubbed the bridge of Jewel's nose, then led her into one of the transit stalls. Next, she unhooked the lead from Jewel's harness, hung the food bucket on the railing so Jewel could get to it, pulled out a handful of food, and held it in front of Jewel.

Jewel looked at the food, then back at CJ, took a small nibble, another nibble, and finally finished what was left. She gently swung her head toward CJ's shoulder and nudged her. "Oh no, toots. I've got better things to do than stand here and hand-feed you." CJ pointed to the bucket. "This is self-serve, and you've got your very own bottomless buffet bucket, so go for it." Jewel looked at the bucket, back at CJ, then turned, stuck her mouth into the bucket, and began to crunch away.

Laura stood on the other side of the corral fence and shook her head as tears welled up in her eyes. "I knew it. If anyone could get her to eat, it would be you."

While the two of them were getting Jewel settled, Luke led Ella down the ramp and over to the gate of the other transit stall. CJ came out of Jewel's stall, closed and latched the gate, and walked over to Ella.

"You and I, missy, are going to become best of friends. Know why? Because we sorta have the same name. Yup. My middle name is Joella, and when folks aren't calling me CJ, I sometimes let them call me Ella."

She walked around Ella, checking her out, then turned to Laura and Luke. "Well, she's nowhere near as bad as poor Jewel over there, but she could stand to put on a few pounds too." Looking Ella in the eyes, she winked at her. "What do you say, sis, think we should fatten you up a bit? Trust me. You'll look a lot better in a bikini with a few more pounds on those gorgeous hips."

While Luke and Laura closed up the trailer, CJ led Ella into the second stall and hung a food bucket on the railing for her. She gave Ella a kiss on the nose and turned to leave the stall. As she walked toward the gate, she found Jewel staring at her from the next stall.

Not only was her food bucket completely empty but once Jewel knew CJ saw her, she started butting the bucket with her nose. "Okay, okay, I got the message. One more bucket coming up. I know I told you it was bottomless, but we need to go slow till your system gets used to eating normally. So two more buckets, then I'm closing the buffet line. Okay?"

As she went in to refill Jewel's bucket, Laura and Luke came over, and Laura asked, "Where is it?"

"Where's what?" CJ said.

"Your wand."

CJ scrunched up her nose. "What in the world are you talking about? I don't have a wand."

Luke smiled at CJ and said, "Come on, you can tell us. We promise not to tell anyone, Joella."

"Oh my God, as soon as I said that, I knew I'd live to regret it. Please don't ever, ever call me Joella. Ella is bad enough." She turned to Ella's stall and whispered, "I'm sorry, Ella, I really didn't mean that." She herded Luke and Laura to the other side of the trailer, out of sight and hopefully hearing range of Ella.

"Okay. What is with this wand thing? Did you two lose part of your brain matter during our abbynormal laughing spell?"

"Abbynormal?" said Laura. "What's with abbynormal? Now who's lost brain matter?"

Oh no, I've done it again. "This has to be the most nonsensical discussion I've had since my last discussion with myself. You go first with the wand thing, then I'll go with my abbynormal thing."

"It's simple," said Luke. "We just want to know where your wand is, so we know how you work your magic. Every time we bring a horse here, you pull rabbits out of hats, wave wands, or do whatever it is you do, and the horses smile and get better. So our question is very simple: Where is your wand?"

"Oh how much I wish that were true. How much I wish we could make all of them better. But thank you for believing in us so much." CJ smiled and looked around, obviously checking to be sure no one else was within hearing distance.

"You really want to know how we do it?" Lowering her voice to a whisper and leaning toward them, she said, "You're standing on the answer. This is Tir Na Nog. It's a magical place. It's the place, and the people."

Lowering her voice even further, she nodded over her shoulder and added, "And, FYI, I broke my wand on that elf over there by the big tree because he would only carry one bale of hay at a time." A second later, she broke out laughing as Luke and Laura turned to look at the big tree.

After CJ went through the *short version* of her love for *Young Frankenstein* and the abbynormal thing, Luke and Laura each gave her a long hug. They made sure the trailer ramp was secured before getting into the truck, waved good-bye to CJ and drove out the gate.

Standing there alone, CJ thought of the ten thousand things she still needed to do, just as Kate drove in.

Kate parked, got out of her truck, and walked up to CJ. "Well, I see our girls arrived. Oh my God. You poor baby, when was the last time anyone fed you, sweetie?" Kate added, looking at Jewel. "CJ, didn't you give her anything to eat? Her bucket is empty."

"Uh... this will be her third and *last* bucket. I don't want to overfeed her," CJ said, as she reached to refill it. "Luke and Laura said she wouldn't eat for her owners and at Bonita she just barely ate, but she's sure not having a problem here."

"Must be your magic working again, CJ."

CJ glared at Kate. "If you ask where my wand is, I'll hit you."

Kate looked at her and imitated the opening theme from *Twilight Zone* with, "doo, doo… doo, doo," while making air quotes with her index fingers. Then she turned and walked up the hill to the volunteer trailer.

What little was left of the afternoon flew by. CJ quickly made her abbynormal rounds, checking on everyone. Everyone looked good, no unusual behavior, and for a change, everybody was eating well. Especially Jewel who, once again, had emptied her bucket by the time CJ got back to her stall.

She opened the gate to Jewel's stall and went in. Stroking her nose, she leaned her head against Jewel's. "You do know I'm madly in love with you, don't you? Know why? 'Cause you make me look sooo good. They all think I have magic in me, but we both know if anyone's got magic, it's you." Jewel nudged CJ gently as she continued. "Whoever named you knew what they were doing. You're like a tarnished old ring, but not for long. Yup. We're gonna fatten you up, clean you up, then polish you till you're all bright and shiny and new.

"Follow me," she said to Jewel, as she walked toward Ella in the next stall. When they both arrived, CJ turned to Ella and said, "Ella, this is Jewel. Jewel, this is Ella." With her head between theirs, she hugged both of them. "I just know you guys are going to be best friends. And when I'm done with you, Jewel, you're going to sparkle and shine so much that everyone will need sunglasses if they get within thirty yards of you. Yeah. Even on a cloudy day. And Ella, you are going to look *sooo awesome* in that bikini, I'm going to make you. How 'bout yellow? Yeah, then everyone will need sunglasses for you too. Are we a team or what? Gimme five, girls."

Kate, who had obviously come back down and been watching, stood there staring at CJ with a smile from ear to ear. "And how exactly do you expect them to give you five?" As the words rolled off Kate's lips, each horse nudged the open palm of one of CJ's raised hands, then they all looked at Kate.

Kate shook her head. "I don't believe it. I don't believe it. I don't believe it."

Opening the stall gate, Kate entered, pulled CJ in, and leaned her forehead against CJ's. "I just hope you have some idea of how special you are, CJ. There is not a day goes by that I don't thank God for bringing you to us. I just wish it could've been under better circumstances, but I am so glad you found us and this is working for you."

"It's me that should be thanking you."

Kate put her arm around CJ's waist and steered her toward the gate. "You do know it's dark out, don't you? Not to mention your day ended several hours ago." As they walked up the hill, Kate added, "I just checked on Rio, and I'm worried about him."

"But I checked him a few hours ago and he was fine," CJ said.

"Calm down. I'm sure it's nothing to get all worried about, but do me a favor and keep an eye on him tomorrow?" She put her arm through CJ's as they headed up the path to the trailers.

CJ asked, "What did you see that has you worried?"

Kate shook her head. "You know, I don't know what it was. It's— it's just a feeling… It's weird. I was scratching his nose, and I got this weird feeling that something is wrong. I can't even tell you what to look for. Just keep an eye on him, okay?"

"You know I will. I've got to call it quits," CJ added, as she turned toward her trailer. "It's been a really long day. I hope I can keep my eyes open long enough to grab something to eat and shower. If you find me in the morning with my face in my cereal bowl or curled up naked in the corner of the shower, it's not because I went back to my old ways. It'll be because I fell asleep along the way."

"CJ, that's not even close to funny."

"Sorry. That's just my warped sense of humor."

"I'm used to you making light of your past, but I just can't wait for the day when you put your life on the street behind you."

CJ looked at Kate and shook her head. "Right. Like that's gonna happen. Kate, I know you mean well, and I love you to death, but I'll never forget my life on the streets. Too many people made sure that I wouldn't, and if I were to try, there's always going to be someone who'll be just too happy to remind me of what I am."

Kate looked at CJ. "God, I wish I could make your life better and help just some of the pain go away."

"You do, Kate. Every day," CJ whispered. Then she walked to her trailer and went inside.

Chapter 2 - Rio

CJ woke to the sound of her alarm screeching. Looking at the clock radio, she said, "So where's my coffee? A lot of good you are. Note to self: Self, get on Amazon and order blow-up, life-size Ken doll in boxers that gently nudges you with latte in hand each morning. Second note to self: Self, go for the twofer sale, add nighttime Ken with vibrator, wineglass, and no boxers.

"Oh my God, CJ, you sick puppy. You have so lost it," she mumbled to herself. With that, she pulled her nightshirt over her head, threw it on the bed, and shuffled naked and barefoot into the bathroom.

She took a quick shower, then pulled her hair into something resembling a ponytail before heading back to the bedroom. She pulled a sports bra over her head and stepped into a pair of plain-Jane, no-frills panties. *Okay, so much for the fancy stuff.*

Next, she slipped on a pair of well-worn but clean jeans and pulled a hoodie, which had obviously seen better days, over her head.

She checked herself in the dresser mirror, bowed, and said, "Okay, ladies and gents, let the ball begin." Smiling at the mirror, she added, "Oh damn, I forgot my slippers. Slippers... slippers, where are my slippers? Ah, there you are." She walked over to the door, picked up her rubber muck boots, then opened the door and went out.

As soon as she cleared the door, she looked up and said, "Uh-oh." The sky was already an ugly dark gray and getting darker by the minute. "Something tells me I really didn't need to shower this morning. Oh well, at least my hoodie will get washed."

She turned to close the door and noticed a note taped to it. Pulling the note off, she sat on the stairs leading up to the trailer, read the note, and smiled. She stuffed it in her pocket and pulled on her boots; all the while, her mind was racing through what she absolutely *had* to get done before it started raining.

Walking across to the volunteer trailer, CJ climbed the steps and went inside. After putting on a pot of coffee, she opened the closet, pulled out a yellow poncho, and slipped it over her head, then glanced in the mirror. "Oh, CJ, you're such a fashion statement. If your prince shows up today, he'll be so overwhelmed. Yeah, overwhelmed from laughing and throwing up. Good thing you have your slippers on. God, you looked better when you were on the street."

No sooner had the words left her mouth than she wished she had never said them. They were so untrue. She loved it here. She loved Kate, loved the animals, and the volunteers. Most of all, she loved her new life. She never wanted to even think about going back to living on the streets, sleeping in alleys, waking up high in sleazebag hotels, wondering who was lying next to her and trying to remember what they had done to her. Then wishing she hadn't, if she did manage to remember.

"Stop it. Stop it. Stop it. Pity party over. You don't have time for this. You need to check on Rio and then get your butt in gear." She filled her travel mug with coffee, grabbed her cell phone from the table, stuffed it in her back pocket, and headed out.

As CJ approached Rio's stall, she studied him. "You look okay," she said softly. She opened the gate to his stall and walked over to him. "Hey, Rio. How you doing, handsome?" She leaned her head against his and asked, "You okay, my handsome prince?" Rio's eyes met hers, and she immediately knew something was wrong.

She looked him over and checked every inch of him with her hands, all the time talking to him. "Okay, my love, what is it, huh? You can tell me. I promise not to tell any of the ladies, especially Deveny. You do know she madly adores you, don't you?"

He looked just fine, and she could find nothing wrong. His eyes weren't clear, but they weren't runny, swollen, or inflamed either. His nose wasn't running. She could find no lumps, bumps, bruises, sore spots, abrasions, nothing. She even took a stick and poked through the freshest droppings she could find. Nothing there either. Kate was right, though; CJ could feel it too. He just wasn't himself, and those gorgeous eyes were trying to tell her something.

"Okay, my love, it's going to start raining soon, and I don't want you out. I also want Dr. Hoover to take a look at you and see if she can figure out what's going on. So for now, we're going to get you out of the weather." CJ clipped the lead onto him, walked him out of the stall and over to one of the others with a covered shed at the back.

Once he was settled, she looked at him and said, "Okay, young man, I have work to do. You stay warm and dry, and I'll be back in a little bit." As she stepped out of the shed, she pulled out her phone and saw she had three and a half bars. "Thank you, Verizon," she said, looking up, then dialed the vet's office, followed by Kate.

"Hi, Kate, it's me. You're right. There is definitely something going on with Rio. I completely checked him over, and I can't find a thing, but something is very wrong and I'm really worried."

"I think you need to call Dr. Hoover," Kate told her.

"Just did. She's in surgery and can't get here till late this afternoon."

"How about Dr. Vreeland?" Kate asked.

"I asked if he was available, but he's out of town at a conference, along with most of the other vets in the area."

"I guess we'll just have to wait for Dr. Hoover. That's probably better anyway since she treated Rio when he first got here and knows him better than anyone else. CJ, I planned on coming out early today, but I've got some personal stuff *I have* to take care of. I'll try to get there as soon as I can. Any of the volunteers there yet?"

"Um, Shannon just pulled in, I think, and Christine is due a little later. The three of us can bang out what absolutely has to be done pretty quickly. Then I can spend some time with Rio before Dr. Hoover gets here."

"Okay, I'll be there as soon as I can, CJ." Kate hung up.

Shannon sauntered up. "You are not going to believe the sundress I found yesterday. Awesome doesn't even come close to describing it."

"So where's your phone?" CJ asked.

"Phone? Why do you need my phone? You lose yours or something?"

CJ stared at Shannon, shaking her head in disbelief.

Shannon smiled back. "Oh, you mean this phone?" She held up the screen with a picture of her in her new sundress on it.

CJ and Shannon were both laughing when Shannon asked, "Hey, is that Rio in there? What's up? Why is he over here? Is everything okay?"

24

"I'm not sure," CJ answered. "Kate and I are both worried about him. Dr. Hoover's going to stop by later to see what's going on with him. In the meantime, we need to get as much done as we can before the sky opens up and this place becomes its usual giant mud hole with Lake Gitche Gumee out there in the middle.

"I'll grab my stuff and get started doing the stalls on this side while you do the other side. As soon as Christine gets here, she can work on the back stalls. Whichever one of us gets done first can start on Deveny's corral and the arena. Then, if there's time, all three of us can tackle the sheep pens, goat pens, and chicken coops."

Shannon nodded. "Sounds like a plan to me. If there's any time left, we can all work on the turnout areas. If they don't get done before the rain gets really bad, it'll be a 'who cares' anyway. All that manure will just help the grass grow."

They both headed for the tool shed, put the tools they would need in a wheelbarrow, then assembled a third wheelbarrow kit for Christine. Shannon started toward the row of stalls on the left, and CJ turned toward the row on the right as the first drops of rain hit her face.

"Oh no, here it comes. Only do what you have to because we don't have much time left." Just as she said that, Christine pulled up in her truck. CJ looked up at the sky. *Thank you, thank you, thank you for getting her here early.*

Christine jumped out of her truck and said, "It's gonna pour like a race horse peeing after the race."

CJ smiled and pointed to the third wheelbarrow. "Your tools are over there, and you've got the back row of stalls. Only do what you absolutely have to because the race is almost over and the horse is about to lift his leg."

Puzzled, Shannon looked at CJ. "Horses don't lift their... leg," she said, then she got CJ's joke.

All three of them started laughing as they each headed to where they needed to be.

When they had finished their assigned row of stalls, CJ sent Christine over to work on Deveny's corral and the arena while she headed for the pens and coops. "Shannon, do me a favor, after you empty your wheelbarrow at the manure pile, can you go check on Rio for me? Then can you help me with the pens and coops?"

"No problem, be there in a few minutes," Shannon answered, before turning for the manure pile.

Ten minutes later, Shannon came into the sheep pen. As her voice broke, she whispered to CJ, "I think you need to come look at Rio. He's not good."

Together, they walked over to the stall that CJ had put Rio in. They entered and found Rio lying on the floor, not moving. "That's how I found him. He never lies down," Shannon whispered, as tears welled up in her eyes.

"Call the vets' office and see if they can get Hoover out here as soon as possible. Tell them it's an emergency. See if Christine is done and get her to help you with the pens, then both of you put all the tools away and come back here."

Shannon just stood there staring at Rio.

"Go." yelled CJ. As Shannon turned to leave, CJ called her back. "Hey, girl... I'm sorry I yelled at you."

"It's okay. Just make sure nothing happens to him while I'm gone," Shannon said, then turned and left.

CJ took off her poncho, sat down on the floor of the shed, and scooted toward the back wall. She picked up Rio's head, slipped under him, and lowered his head into her lap. Rio stared up at CJ with the one beautiful brown eye she could see. She felt like he was pleading with her, but she didn't know what to do for him. Just then, a large clap of thunder let loose, and it started raining.

Shannon and Christine came running into the shed, totally soaked. "How is he?" Shannon asked.

"Not good. I don't know what to do for him." As CJ said that, Dr. Hoover came through the doorway, followed closely by Kate.

As Dr. Hoover bent to look at Rio, another clap of thunder went off right over the shed and the rain came down even harder. "I'll move so you can look at him," CJ said.

Dr. Hoover held her hand up. "Stay. He's relaxed and calm, and I can check him just the way he is."

The vet checked Rio's eyes, nose, and neck, then opened her bag and took out her stethoscope. Just as she started to listen to Rio's heart, Rio look up at CJ, let out a deep sigh and closed his eyes.

"Do something," CJ yelled. "Do something. Oh God. NO," she screamed, as she rocked Rio's head in her lap. Shannon and Christine both broke into tears and hugged each other.

"I'm sorry, he's gone," Dr. Hoover said.

Kate just stood there, tears pouring from her eyes, feeling as helpless as everyone else. Finally she took a deep breath and

27

whispered to Shannon and Christine, "Why don't you two go up to the trailer? We'll be up in a minute." Lowering her voice even more, she continued, "Go on. There's nothing else we can do for him." Dr. Hoover put the stethoscope back in her bag, and she and the girls left as Kate turned to CJ, "CJ, honey, come on, let me help you up."

"No," CJ hissed, as the tears poured from her eyes. "I'm not leaving him." She rubbed his blaze and lowered her head till it rested on the top of Rio's. "He was there for me and Deveny when we both desperately needed someone, and I'm not leaving him now when he needs me."

"CJ, he's gone. He's on the other side of the rainbow bridge, in a much better place."

CJ looked up and whispered, "He's not there yet. His soul is still here, and I can't leave until his soul leaves."

Kate stared at her, shaking her head.

"I know you think I'm crazy, Kate, but I'm not. He's still here. His soul is still here, and he's worried about what will happen now that he's not here to protect the things he loved." She reached up and touched Kate's arm. "Trust me, I feel him. I swear it's true. I need to stay with him until he's sure everything is okay and he can leave. I need to be here, Kate."

She smiled at Kate and added, "Kate, I'm okay. We're okay. I just need to make sure he knows everyone he loves will be safe and we'll watch over them for him. Then he can join his friends and be at peace."

Kate swiped at the tears running down both cheeks, but as fast as she wiped them away, new tears replaced them. "Okay," she whispered. "He knew you were his protector since the day he got here and I guess now that means you get to make sure his soul gets where it needs to be, safe and sound."

Giving up on trying to keep up with the tears, Kate stood. "I understand. I really do. Take as much time as you need. We'll be up at the trailer when you're ready."

Stepping to the doorway, Kate turned. "Rio sure knew what he was doing when he picked you. You do know you're an angel, don't you? I mean a real, honest to God angel, and I sure hope you're around to watch over my soul when I leave this place. I love you, CJ."

After Kate left, CJ looked up at the ceiling and screamed at the top of her lungs, "THIS. IS. SO. UNFAIR." Taking a deep breath, she whispered, "Why are you doing this?" She had promised Kate that she was okay and could handle this. She had to. As Rio's protector, CJ had promised herself she would be strong, that she wouldn't cry anymore, but the tears had begun to slide down her cheeks anyway.

She added at barely a whisper, "What on earth did he do to deserve this? What did he ever do to you? Or anyone else. You're supposed to help me protect him. Why didn't we protect him? I was supposed to save him. He doesn't deserve this." By now, the tears were streaming again, and she could barely see.

The anger left her, and pain took over. "Oh God, I promised you I'd keep you safe and look after you. Please, please don't leave me by myself again. I love you so much." Finally, sobbing uncontrollably, she completely lost it. With a loud clap of thunder, so too did the sky.

Chapter 3 - Kitty Cat and Lizzy Lizard

Shawn pulled up to the stop sign and came to a halt. He couldn't help but think about what a great day it had been. He tried to think of when he had last taken time out for himself and couldn't remember. He needed to listen to Rick and Trish more often. They were right. Today had been just what he needed to clear his mind of work, and her. He had always loved his work, but lately it had become little more than an escape, a way to avoid thinking about her and how much he missed her. Funny, after all these months and all she had done, he still missed her. He didn't love her; he just missed her.

-------//-------

It was Thursday, the first day of his two weeks of vacation, and aside from his morning workout, his day had been free. That was, until last night's dinner with Rick and Trish changed things.

As he nursed a cup of coffee and rummaged through yesterday's paper, an article in the travel section caught his attention. He read the article banner out loud, "Julian, the perfect place for a day trip. So that's what gave them the idea to go back." Julian was where Rick and Trish were headed this morning to take the kids snowboarding.

During last night's dinner, they had insisted he join them. Even after pleading that he had a ton of stuff to do, they reminded him he still had several days to get everything done before leaving for New York and refused to take no for an answer.

Finally, Trish had leveled the ultimate threat. "I will never ever set you up with one of my friends again if you don't come and spend the day with us."

"Listen, I'm still recovering from the last time you set me up, so I'd be careful if I were you. You might just disappear in a snow bank and your body not found till the spring thaw," Shawn warned her.

"Hey, maybe we can just store her and the kids like that for a few days while we go up to L.A. for that hockey game she insists we can't afford," Rick threw in as he gave Trish a goofy grin.

"Ha, ha, and ha. Keep it up you two, and you'll both be wearing your Julian apple pie home tomorrow." Trish tried to look stern by scrunching up her face, but all it did was make everybody laugh, including her.

Ah, food. Even though Shawn loved Rick, Trish, and the kids to death, it was the food that ultimately caused him to give in and agree to meet them in Julian. Shawn's stomach actually rumbled as he remembered them telling him about this great little restaurant that had the world's best breakfasts and the pie shop with fresh, homemade pies that were to die for. Last night's description of breakfast had had him drooling, but the pie had actually been what tipped him over the edge. The thought of spending the day with them brought a big smile to his face, but throw in a great breakfast and fresh apple pie and how could anybody possibly resist?

Besides, when was the last time I actually spent some quality time with the girls? It seemed like they were still at school, busy doing homework, or already in bed whenever he got off and stopped by. If he ever had kids, he wanted them to be just like Lizzy Lizard and Kitty Cat, his nicknames for the two most precious and special women in his life. *Make that three, can't forget Trish.* Just the idea of spending an entire day with them had him grinning from ear to ear.

He closed the paper and walked over to the sink to rinse out his coffee cup just as the phone rang. "Hi, Rick," he said as he saw the picture of the couple kissing pop up on the screen.

31

"We're just heading out. You're still going to meet us up there, aren't you?"

"You bet," Shawn said. "My stomach started rumbling ten minutes ago just thinking about breakfast." Then he added, "Tell Lizard and Kitty to watch out. I dug out my super-duper surfboard, converted it to a snowboard, and I'm gonna beat the ski pants off both of them."

Shawn could picture Rick shaking his head as he said, "Uh, I'll tell them, but I don't think they're going to be very scared. I'll also warn them to make sure the stirrups on their ski pants are cinched up tight so you can't give them a wedgie like you did the last time you lost."

Shawn laughed as he remembered his last snowboard outing with the girls. The one where they had beat the pants off him, literally. They were almost halfway down the hill before he had gotten started. In the end, though, his empty snowboard had nearly beat them.

Once off the start line, his weight and gravity had been working in his favor, and he was gaining on them even though he was coming down mostly backward and mostly sitting on the snowboard. That was, until he scraped past a large bush, which had reached out and snagged his old-and-too-big ski pants. The pants had abruptly stopped, with him still mostly in them, while his feet slipped out of the bindings and the snowboard continued downhill, barely missing first place.

When everyone had rushed up the hill to make sure he was okay, they found him sitting with his soaking wet underwear stuck to his very cold, partially frozen butt and his ski pants down around his ankles. Snorting, Trish asked if he was okay while Lizard fell to the ground roaring with laughter.

32

Kitty was right behind her, and in between fits of giggling, kept yelling, "I'm gonna pee my pants, Mommy."

As Trish rushed the girls to the bathroom, Shawn realized everyone on the hill was pointing at him and snickering too.

The final insult had come at the end of the day, though. As they were leaving, a perfect stranger walked by the van and asked, "Aren't you the one who lost his pants to those two young girls in that race?"

Lizard and Kitty had fallen to the ground again laughing, then Kitty's face turned serious as she said, "I need to go back to the bathroom, Mom." To make matters worse, when Shawn reported to the fire station the next morning, there was not a soul who hadn't heard the story, at least three times.

Maybe challenging Lizard and Kitty again wasn't such a good idea. Worse yet, at ten and twelve, they were two years older than the last time and a *whole lot better* snowboarders now. Oh well, too late. The challenge had been thrown down.

At least the last time he had gotten some revenge by grabbing the back of their ski pants and giving them both a pretty good wedgie as they tried to beat each other to the van. This time, however, they would be ready. Especially after Rick told them to cinch up their stirrups.

Before leaving, Shawn turned on the local news channel. They were in the middle of the weather report, and he waited for them to cover the San Diego area. No such luck. San Francisco, L.A., Bakersfield, San Bernardino, everywhere in the state but San Diego. Judging from the weather map, it was raining everywhere but in San Diego proper, and the banner at the bottom of the screen predicted the storm was headed southeast.

Right. Every time they predicted a storm would move in from the north, it would hit Orange County, make a sharp left turn into Nevada and Arizona and miss San Diego completely. If the rain gods were really smiling that day, maybe Oceanside would get a few sprinkles. That's how it had been all year, LA, Orange County, and the mountains to the east would get drenched, and San Diego would sit there dry as a bone. For sure, it was going to be another bone-dry year and another really bad fire season.

Grabbing his keys, commuter mug, jacket, gloves, and his Old Navy watch cap, he headed out the door. After a quick stop at Starbucks for a decent cup of coffee, he worked his way to CA125, then headed north to Interstate 8. At the interchange, he took 8 east toward Descanso and the Julian turnoff.

Approaching the exit for CA79, he could just make out the snow-covered mountains off in the distance to his left. He exited onto 79, followed it to where it turned left, then drove the remaining fifteen miles into Julian. About halfway up, snow started appearing along both sides of the road. While the roads had been plowed, it was obvious the area had gotten a good foot or two of snow overnight.

At the stop sign on the south end of town, he glanced to his right at the large meadow where they would be snowboarding. The meadow was several hundred yards wide. Beyond the culvert along the road, it stretched over rolling hills for almost a quarter mile, up into the forest of snow-covered pine trees. On the right, close to the road, were several picnic tables with built-in benches and a snack stand that served coffee, hot chocolate, and fresh baked pastries on weekends. The entire meadow was covered with at least two feet of snow and had drifts that looked to be twice that deep. It looked like a scene right off of a postcard.

The best part was, since it was Thursday and the local kids were still in school, there was nobody there. He smiled, turned left, and headed into town. "Breakfast, here I come," he said out loud, as his stomach grumbled.

The plan was that they would meet at the restaurant in Julian for breakfast. Afterward, Rick and Trish would grab a couple of lattes and they would all head over to the snowboard hills and meadow just on the south end of town. While the kids beat the pants off Shawn, again, Rick and Trish planned on claiming one of the benches in the meadow. They would then spend their time watching the world go by as they sipped on their giant lattes and took in the beauty of the snow-covered mountains.

Shawn pulled into a parking space in front of the restaurant and parked right behind Trish's minivan. Rick, Trish, and the girls had obviously beat him to the restaurant. He saw them at one of the big tables in the back corner of the dining room as he came through the doorway. Liz and Cat spotted him before he even opened the door and they both jumped up as he approached the table. They ran up to him, one on each side, wrapped their arms around his waist and squeezed for all they were worth. Shawn put an arm around each of their shoulders and pulled them in as close as he could.

The girls started to pull away, but Shawn slipped his hands down to the middle of their backs and continued to hold them close. "Not so fast, I'm not done getting my hugs yet."

He turned and looked directly into Lizzy's eyes and said, "OH. NO." He lowered his mouth to her ear, looked around to make sure no one else could hear and whispered, "It's starting to show."

Liz looked at him with the most confused look he had ever seen. "What are you talking about?"

Lowering his voice even more, he said, "You know, the bump."

"What bump?" asked Cat, as she leaned toward Liz trying to see the bump.

"OH. NO. Not you too," he said, staring at Cat now. "Look, they're almost ready to break through the surface." He stared at Cat's face.

"What? Where?" they both asked, looking each other over, still totally confused.

By now Trish and Rick had both caught on. As Rick started laughing, Trish turned to Shawn and said, "You're so mean. Stop it. You're going to give them complexes."

"What are you talking about?" asked Liz, still running her hands over her lower back looking for the bump.

Trish started giggling and told Liz that she was rubbing her back looking for the bump that would eventually become her tail. "And Cat, I think your whiskers are about to sprout."

Liz and Cat both looked at each other, and before Shawn realized he was pretty much dead meat, they each grabbed a side and started tickling him.

"Oh God, stop." Shawn chuckled and moaned as he fell into a chair and tried to get them to quit.

Liz looked at him with zero sympathy. "You're so lame," she said, with a snicker. "And just so you know, my name's not Lizard. It's Liz. As in short for Elizabeth. And I am not going to grow a tail. Ever."

"Yeah. And just so you know, my name is Cat. That's C period, A period, and T period. Which is short for CAT."

All of a sudden, the girls realized the restaurant had gone completely quiet and everyone was watching them to see what would come next. They both looked at each other, smiled, and stepped closer to Shawn.

Liz kissed his cheek and said, "We love you, Uncle Shawn, but you gotta learn not to mess with Girl Power."

"Yeah", added Cat. "You're lucky we didn't use any of our ninja moves on you." And with that, everyone in the restaurant started laughing.

Trish came over, pecked Shawn on the cheek, and asked, "Are you okay?"

"Other than losing another battle to these two, I think I'm fine," he said, as they all got up and went back to the table where Rick was still laughing.

Rick, Trish, and the girls had already ordered, and the waitress came over to ask Shawn if he was ready. After writing down what he wanted, she turned and started to head for the kitchen. Suddenly, she stopped, turned around, and studied her order pad as if she had missed something in his order.

She looked straight at Shawn. "I know you from somewhere. Where, where, where? A ha, got it. You're the one who lost his pants up on the hill two years ago. You're actually quite famous around here, you know."

Shawn knew immediately he had been set up because Cat had started giggling before the waitress even finished saying she knew him from somewhere.

Breakfast arrived and they each dug in without waiting for the any of their side dishes to arrive. Shawn looked at the stack of blueberry pancakes on his plate and smiled. They had to be the biggest pancakes he had ever seen. There were three of them, overhanging the dinner plate by at least an inch on all sides, and each had to be over an inch thick. It also looked like an entire blueberry bush had sacrificed its life for each pancake, and oh God, they smelled amazing.

Drooling, he spread some butter on each one, poured a little bit of syrup over them, and cut a chunk out with his fork.

His eyebrows went up and through a mouthful of blueberry bliss, he mumbled, "These have to be the best pancakes I've ever had. Lizard… sorry, Liz, you want a bite?"

"Okay," she said, as she reached over and took the top pancake off his plate.

"Me too," said Cat, as the second pancake left.

He looked over at Rick and Trish who were both laughing and holding their sides. "Oh my God, if you could have seen the look on your face when Cat took the second pancake," Trish managed to spit out.

"I almost forgot I was sitting between the vulture twins. Don't you ever feed these two? Good thing I remembered and ordered a three stack with my eggs, hash browns and toast."

After coffee refills all around, Shawn turned to the girls and said, "I was hoping to get even on the slopes, but I was in such a hurry to see you that I ran off and forgot my snowboard. Guess we'll have to wait till next snow fall."

The girls looked at each other, then at Trish, who smiled and said, "We figured you would do something like that, so we brought one of the girl's old boards with us."

"Neener, neener, neener," Liz and Cat chimed together.

"Next excuse?" said Trish, as Liz stuck her tongue out. Then she added, "Oh, and we noticed you're wearing jeans, which means next you'll tell us you haven't replaced the ski pants you left on the hill last time. Not to worry, though. You can wear the extra pair that Rick brought. Have we missed anything?"

"Um, I'll never fit on one of the kids' old boards. I'm an adult."

"Well, that last part's debatable, but we figure you're not going to be on it more than a few feet anyway," replied Trish.

"And you'll be sitting on it, so it only needs to be big enough to hold your butt," added Cat, laughing.

"Ouch, you two, that hurt," Shawn said, trying to give them his most devastated look.

"We even scouted out a place with no bushes this time. And… it has a tiny little speed bump so you can do one of your famous flips that no one's ever seen," Liz threw in.

Trish looked at Liz and asked, "Honey, how's he going to do a flip sitting down with a death grip on the board?"

The waitress brought the check over and placed it on the table. She looked at Shawn and started laughing. "How were the pancakes?" she asked, then turned to Trish and the girls. "Thanks to all of you for making my day. I haven't seen anyone kibitz and laugh as much as you guys in a long time. You girls are so lucky to have such a wonderful family. When you grow up, just remember to pass all this on to your families."

As the waitress left, Liz turned to Trish. "That was really nice of her to say, Mom."

"Yes, it was, and don't forget what she told you. My fondest wish is that someday you two, your husbands, and my grandkids, will all be sitting in a restaurant somewhere, having as much fun as we did this morning."

She pulled both girls in and added, "You two need to promise me you'll never lose your sense of humor and you'll always be there for each other. No matter what."

"We promise," they both answered and squeezed her as hard as they could.

Shawn ducked into the bathroom to change into Rick's ski pants, which Rick had conveniently remembered to bring in from the van, while Trish and Rick ordered two large lattés to go. After leaving *way more than a good tip* on the table with the check, they all stood and headed for the door. As they did, the whole place broke out in applause. Smiling, they filed out, and Shawn, being the last in line, turned and bowed to everyone.

Chapter 4 - Snow, Thunder, and Lightning

They left Shawn's truck parked where it was, and all piled into Trish's van to head for the meadow. During the few blocks drive, Shawn tried again to get out of snowboarding by claiming to 1) have come down suddenly—like in the last minute or two—with the flu; 2) having injured ribs from the tickling bout—you'll be sitting down, so who cares; 3) not being able to remember his name or who he was—It's Sean spelled wrong and you're a senior dork; and finally, 4) who are you people, and why am I here?—We're your worst nightmare, and you're here to meet your maker. Now shut up and get your snowboard.

Oh, it was going to be a long and painful afternoon.

As Shawn and the girls trudged toward the middle hill with snowboards in hand, Rick and Trish cleared snow off of a bench and sat down. Rick looked at Trish and said, "Do you have any idea how lucky we are? Somehow we've managed to raise the two most wonderful kids in the world, and no one could ever ask for a better friend than Shawn. He absolutely adores the girls and they adore him."

Trish smiled at him. "What was your first clue? I just wish he would find someone who sees how special he is. My heart aches thinking about what Wendy did to him. God, he so didn't deserve that."

An angry growl slipped from Trish as she thought back to the night Shawn had knocked on their door looking like his best friend had just died.

Having no idea what was going on, Rick and Trish were surprised but glad to have Shawn spend the night. As soon as he arrived though, Trish asked where Wendy was and why he wasn't spending the night with her. Shawn suggested she put on a large pot of coffee, then sit down, because it was going to be a very long night. Once the coffee was poured, he went on to explain what had happened.

Hoping to bring his fiancée Wendy out of the funk she had been in the past two weeks, Shawn had managed to get off early. He had planned to surprise her with a great dinner, followed by a wonderful prelude of things to come during their honeymoon. But Wendy had ended up surprising him. He had walked into his condo to find her and Jenny, one of the EMTs from the station, sitting next to each other on the living room couch.

He wasn't surprised to find Jenny there. She, Trish, and Wendy were best friends, and she was going to be Wendy's maid of honor.

It didn't take him long to feel the tension in the air, then he noticed the stack of boxes. When he looked at Wendy and asked what was going on, Jenny suggested he might want to get a beer and sit down.

When he returned from the kitchen, Wendy explained that she was calling off the wedding. She told him she felt like she was constantly competing with Trish and the girls for his affection, and she just couldn't do it anymore. She felt like the three of them had spent the last six months undermining everything she did or said. And she had no intention of spending the rest of her life vying for his affection and attention.

It turned out that Wendy had been confiding in Jenny for almost a year, and they had started seeing each other, as often as they could, over the past six months. Adding that her 'last chance to run away with the girls' trip to Las Vegas had actually been a week spent with Jenny.

Wendy claimed the sex was just curiosity at first and she thought that spending time with Jenny would get it out of her system, but it had just the opposite effect. She realized she was in love with

Jenny and, unlike with Shawn, she didn't have to compete for Jenny's affection.

After getting over the initial shock, Shawn had thought back to the past six months. He'd sensed a change in her, but had no idea it was serious. He realized she was turning inward and every time he suggested they talk about it, she insisted nothing was wrong. He'd sensed her pulling away from Trish and her family too, but had no idea what was going on between them. Nor did Trish when he asked her. They had always been best of friends, and when Wendy had asked Jenny to be her maid of honor, it had shocked everyone.

Now, the pieces of the puzzle were starting to fall into place. The longer Wendy talked, the more Shawn realized she had fallen out of love with him months ago. Truth be told, he too had started to wonder if maybe they should put off the wedding until they could deal with whatever was bothering her. In the end, though, he had convinced himself it was just pre-marriage jitters on both their parts.

The more he thought about it, the more anger set in. Why had she waited till now? Obviously she hadn't planned on discussing any of this with him. If he hadn't surprised them by coming home early, she would've been gone when he got home.

Trying to keep his anger under control he had told Wendy, "I'm sorry you think Trish and the girls are competing with you. They're not. And most of all, I'm sorry you think they're trying to undermine you. They think the world of you and would never intentionally do anything to hurt you or stand in the way of our relationship.

"If you're really not in love with me," he explained, "we obviously shouldn't get married and need to call it off, but I think it's unfair of you to blame Trish and the girls. If anything, you should be blaming me for making you think you had to compete with them."

Suddenly, he had realized he couldn't deal with this anymore. He had to get out of there before he said or did something he would regret.

He told Wendy that, if she wanted, they could talk more in the morning. He would spend the night at Rick and Trish's, and Wendy and Jenny could stay at the condo for the night. They all agreed that calling off the wedding and dealing with everything else could wait till the next afternoon.

Around 3 am, he finished his story, and Trish—who had introduced him to Wendy—said, "Shawn, I'm so sorry," for the fortieth time.

Trish speculated that Wendy had realized a lot longer than six months ago that she was in love with Jenny and not with Shawn. She was also pissed as hell that Wendy was using her and the girls as an excuse for breaking up with him. Rick, on the other hand, just looked at him and said, "You do know that any other guy would have suggested that a threesome might be in order?"

Trish glared and shot daggers at Rick. "Don't even go there. When I'm done with the two of them, their only job opening will be as zombie extras on the SyFy channel."

After only a few hours of sleep, Rick and Trish got the kids off to school, then followed Shawn to the condo. Before they left, Trish had agreed to delay *offing* Wendy and Jenny until they dealt with cancelling the wedding. Turned out, offing them quickly became everyone's first choice after they arrived at the condo.

The door was locked, but Wendy and Jenny were gone. After a quick check, they found all of Wendy's things were gone. The two of them must have spent most of the night packing her stuff into their cars.

Five minutes later, Shawn received an alert from his bank, letting him know his checking account balance had dropped below the $50 alert level. Using his cell phone, he checked his checking and savings accounts only to find they both had a zero balance.

So much for moving everything into joint accounts several months ago. Shawn was absolutely livid, and Trish had gone ballistic, spitting out obscenities that neither Shawn nor Rick had ever heard before.

The police were called and took a report, but since Wendy was living in the condo and her name was on both accounts, there really wasn't much they could do. Later, Shawn would check with an attorney friend who told him it would cost more to pursue them than he could hope to recover. Not to mention, Wendy and Jenny had disappeared from the face of the earth.

The attorney advised him to cut his losses, be thankful most of the wedding expenses had been cancelled or prepaid and there hadn't been much left in either account when they had drained them.

The final straw had come a week later when Shawn remembered the college funds he had started for the girls several years earlier. He called the bank and the manager checked the accounts.

While he waited, his mind went back to the night Wendy had seen him transferring money from his checking account to the college funds and asked about the accounts. He explained that he had opened an account for each girl. He went on to tell her that neither Rick, Trish, nor the girls knew about the accounts and he planned to surprise each of the girls at the end of their senior year of high school.

"You're so wonderful." Wendy had told him. "Can I be a part of it too?" Sure enough, like a fool, he had put her name on the accounts.

Seconds later, the bank manager confirmed his worse fears, she had drained both accounts. He slammed the phone down and let out a string of curse words. How could he have been so stupid? How could he have been so trusting? How could he not have seen who and what Wendy really was?

He picked the phone back up and called the police who said they would amend the report but, again, there was little they could do. He hung up and murmured, "If I ever see you again, Wendy, I'm going to run your ass over and throw your body off the Coronado Bridge."

That had been a little over six months ago.

Trish looked up to check on Shawn and the girls and realized Rick was talking to her. "I'm sorry, hon, my mind was somewhere else. What did you ask?"

"I said... you're thinking about Wendy again. You've got steam shooting out of both ears."

"Sorry. I just can't believe how she totally ruined his life and he just shrugs it off and goes on as if nothing happened."

Rick shook his head. "Trust me, he hasn't shrugged it off. Inside he's really hurting, but he's getting better. I know he's gun-shy as hell right now, but I just wish someone would come along, recognize what a wonderful guy he is, wrap him in their arms, and love the bejesus out of him. He so deserves someone good."

"He's got us and the girls," Trish said.

Rick smiled. "He knows that. You three are the most special people in his life and always will be. God help anyone he finds if they don't adore the three of you the way he does. It will be the shortest relationship in the history of dating."

"Oh, hon, I hurt so bad for him," Trish whispered.

"You know what, Trish? Someone, somewhere will take one look at him, and before they even know it their life will be changed forever. And it'll happen when they least expect it."

Trish laid her head against Rick's chest and said, "God, I hope so and soon too." Looking up the hill, she added "That is, if the girls take mercy on him and he manages to survive the day."

Up on the hill, arms flailing, Shawn was making what he hoped would be his final 'race run' down the hill. As in all the other runs, the girls were light-years ahead of him. When he reached the bottom, he walked over to where the girls were standing in front of the bench, picked up Cat, set her aside, and sat down.

"Hey," she yelled. "Do I need to warn you again about my ninja moves? You are so lucky I knew you were there. You could've lost an arm or two if I'd had my ninja sticks."

"They're nunchakus not ninja sticks, dimple puss," Shawn said.

"My name is not Dimple Puss. And it's not Kitty."

Shawn smiled at her. "Yeah, Yeah, I know. It's Cat, C period, A period, T period, and that's short for CAT. I'll try to remember next time… Dimple Puss… uh, sorry… Cat."

"Okay, you two. It's getting late, and in case you haven't noticed, it's starting to snow again. We still need to stop and get pies before we head home, so let's head back into town," Rick said.

"Oh crap… I forgot my chains," Shawn said. "I need to get going before the snow gets too deep and I can't get out of here."

"Uh… did you remember to bring anything with you?" Liz asked. "You so need a girl in your life. Mom, can I go with Uncle Shawn? He really needs help."

"Catch me on the right day and he can have you. However, not today. Since you're only twelve, you'll just have to wait another six years. Then you can do what you want. Of course, by then he'll be old and decrepit and need constant care. You'll be so busy changing his diapers that you'll never have time to date and find a husband."

"Ewww," Liz said. Then added, "Sorry, Uncle Shawn, I'm not going home with you."

Shawn glared at Trish. "Thanks, I love you too. She'll never look at me the same after the diaper thing."

By then, the snow was really coming down. Everyone piled into the van and they drove back into town. They dropped Shawn off at his truck, then headed to the pie shop, promising to bring a pie home for Shawn.

Shawn checked his side mirror. When it was clear he made a U-turn and headed out of town. When he reached 79, he turned right and caught a glimpse of the now-empty meadow and hills they had just left. Everything was covered with a healthy dusting of snow. If there had been a horse and sleigh standing in the meadow, it would've made a great Hallmark card.

He was getting out just in time. Highway 79 was already covered with a good dusting of snow and it was rapidly building up on the tree branches overhanging both sides of the road. He took a deep breath to ease the tension. Another short five miles and he would be low enough that the snow would become wet slush, then rain another mile down. He loved the beauty of the snow, but without chains he was glad to be driving out of it.

Coming out of the hills just above the lake, the sky completely opened up and a horrendous clap of thunder let loose right above his truck. Man, he had just made it out in time. This kind of rain down here meant very heavy snow was now falling up in Julian.

His mind turned to Rick, Trish, and the kids. By that time, Rick had put chains on the van and, with any luck, was starting down out of the mountains. Rick, like Shawn, had grown up back east and was no stranger to driving in snow. But still, on narrow mountain roads with ice forming quickly in the shaded areas, even the most experienced drivers had to be really careful and stay alert. The last thing they needed was to be distracted while they were still on snow and ice. He would give them another thirty to forty-five minutes, then try to call them to make sure they were okay. By then, they should be just about to the lake, where he was now.

Fifteen minutes later, he rolled up to the stop sign where Japatul Valley Road ended and 79 made a sharp right.

-------//-------

A horn blew behind him and Shawn just about jumped out of his skin. He had no idea how long he had been sitting at the stop sign, but the guy behind him obviously thought it was too long. He checked to make sure it was clear and made a left turn.

After going about twenty feet, it dawned on him he had turned the wrong way, but the road had already narrowed and there was nowhere for him to pull over or turn around. If possible, it was now pouring even harder than it had been up at the lake, and his windshield wipers weren't even coming close to keeping up with it. In fact, he couldn't see a thing. Not even the side of the road.

49

He rolled his window down, found the double yellow line and used that to make sure he was still on the road and in his lane. He kept glancing up to make sure he wasn't about to hit someone or something, but it was a lost cause. All he could do was hope no one was as dumb as him and still out on the road in front of him.

Another mile and a half down the road and his engine started to sputter and run rough. *Great. Just what I need.* By then, his windshield had fogged up, and the wipers were going a hundred miles an hour but doing absolutely no good. To make matters worse, he still hadn't seen a place to pull over, much less turn around. Finally, off to the left, he spotted several very large trees and a gate set back from the road. The gate blocked a driveway that led into what looked like a ranch full of fenced off corrals and horse stalls.

Out of habit, he turned on his signal, not that anyone could see it, and pulled under the trees to the right of the gate. With the trees blocking most of the rain, he could almost see out the windshield. He reached over and turned on the defroster to try to defog the window just as the truck's engine died.

Crap, it was now almost dark. He had no idea where he was, other than in the middle of nowhere. His truck had died, he had no idea why, and the rain gods had decided to make up for three years of drought in the last thirty minutes. He turned the truck's ignition off, then back on, trying to restart the truck. Nothing. Not even a click.

Okay, time to call for help. He looked at the console tray where he usually kept his cell phone, but the tray was empty. *Great.* He was sure he had put it in the tray. It must have fallen out. He reached around under his seat. His hand hit something and it skidded across the floor mat toward the door. He opened the door so he could lean over and reach the floor, just in time to spot his phone making an escape for freedom. As it went over the doorsill, it started humming, then went silent after a barely audible splash.

Shawn straightened up and leaned out the door trying to see where the phone went. Just as he spotted it and reached toward the puddle, a clap of thunder and flash of lightning went off that he swore hit the truck. His wet hand slipped off the door armrest, and he joined his cell phone. Unfortunately for him and the cell phone, his hip landed directly on it making it very unlikely that Verizon would ever hear from it again.

Soaking wet, he picked himself up off the ground, glanced at the water sloshing around inside the phone's screen, and tossed it onto the passenger's seat. He reached in, turned off the headlights, pulled the keys out of the ignition, and searched his surroundings for any signs of life.

Just inside the gate, he saw what appeared to be a large corral. On the other side of the corral was a wide pathway with a row of stalls on each side. As best he could tell, the pathway wound its way up a slight incline, past some small sheds, and disappeared into a small grove of trees. Running down the center of the pathway was a torrent of water that passed through the left side of the large corral, under the gate, around his feet, and flowed swiftly into the overflowing ditch alongside the road.

The only light he could see was coming from a shed in one of the stalls on the right side of the pathway. He turned and looked behind him hoping maybe there were signs of life somewhere across the road, but all he saw was total darkness. The shed looked like his only bet for finding someone with a phone. Even if there was nobody in there, it would at least get him out of the rain while he plotted his next move. Not that getting out of the rain really mattered, since he was already soaked.

Given the shortest distance between two points is a straight line, he climbed the corral fence and headed for the pathway and the stall with the lit shed. As he crossed the corral, he realized that all of the stalls appeared to have one or two horses in them. Except the one with the light. Not only were there no horses in it, but the gate was open. His first thought was that the horse, or horses, must have gotten out. Maybe the thunder had spooked them and they broke through the gate and took off.

He stopped in front of the open gate and scanned the area. No loose horses in sight, and the gate looked undamaged. Someone must have left the gate unlatched, and the horses got out.

As he was looking around for escaped horses, he noticed two small mobile home-type trailers up the hill, just beyond the stand of trees. Not only was the porch light on in front of the closest one, but all the lights inside appeared to be on as well. *Think I'll head for the trailer. Hopefully there's a phone up there, and I can also tell them some of their horses escaped.*

Just as Shawn turned and started toward the trailer, someone in the shed shouted, "THIS. IS. SO. UNFAIR." He stopped and listened, but nothing else came from the shed. Whoever it was had sounded desperate… and hurt. He took a few steps toward the shed still listening. Nothing. The shed had no door, and he could make out something lying on the floor toward the back. It looked like a large brown blanket. The rain wasn't helping and nothing in there was moving.

All of a sudden, a voice said, "Please, please don't leave me by myself again. I love you so much."

Great, last thing I need is to get in the middle of a lovers' quarrel. Even though he was only a few feet from the shed, he turned intending to head back toward the trailer. Then, as if things couldn't get any worse, the heavy rain turned into a deluge.

Chapter 5 - A Door Opens

A loud clap of thunder went off directly over the shed. Shawn flew through the doorway. CJ looked up and screamed.

CJ put her hand to her chest and shouted, "You scared the living crap out of me." Then she quickly realized she had no idea who had just jumped into the middle of the shed. "Who are you? What do you want?"

Shawn looked down and saw that the blanket he had seen was, in fact, a horse. A very large brown horse. The horse's head was in the lap of a girl sitting on the floor. A very pretty girl. A very pretty, startled girl.

"Um, I'm sorry. I was on my way to the… uh… trailer and heard you yell out." At about the same time, he realized that the horse hadn't moved since he jumped through the door. *Doesn't thunder startle horses? The horse's eyes aren't open. How come they didn't open when I jumped into the shed? Don't horses at least look when people jump at them? Maybe the horse is asleep. But don't horses sleep standing up.*

A lightbulb lit, and two things popped into his head. He knew next to nothing about horses, but this horse looked… well… dead. He also realized that, other than the girl and the horse, there was no one else in the shed. If this was a lovers' quarrel, her lover was the horse.

"I'm really sorry I startled you. The thunder and downpour hit, and I just jumped in without thinking. Is everything okay?" He looked at the horse. "Is he okay? He hasn't moved."

"That's because he's dead," CJ whispered. "His name was Rio, and I'm waiting for his soul to leave."

CJ stared up at the guy, thinking, *why did I tell him that?*

"I'm so sorry. Did he get hit by lightning?" Shawn asked.

CJ continued to stare at him, then chuckled to herself. *Was this guy for real?* She started to ask, "Does he look like a crispy critter—" then stopped without finishing. *Oh my God, where had that come from? A minute ago I was bawling my eyes out over Rio dying and now I'm laughing and slamming this poor guy who feels bad because he's dead.*

"Now it's my turn to be sorry," she said. "He didn't get hit by lightning. I've been in here with him all afternoon. See? He's not even wet. And he's not smoking." *Stop. What are you doing? What in the world is wrong with you? It must be shock. That's it, I'm in shock.*

Shawn looked at her and smiled. "That was a pretty dumb question, wasn't it? I will not mention the soul-leaving thing, so that I don't look like a complete idiot. By the way, I'm Shawn... Shawn James," he added, as he stuck his hand out.

CJ took his hand in hers. "Hi, Shawn James, I'm CJ." Almost a minute went by before Shawn looked down. CJ followed his line of sight and realized she was still holding his hand. "Uh, I suppose you'd like your hand back, huh?"

"Not really," came his response.

This was completely unreal. *What is this, a high-school freshmen drooling over the football team quarterback?* No, that wasn't it. Something had happened when he jumped through the doorway. The minute she saw him, she felt... *relieved?* and... *safe? What idiot feels relieved and safe when a total stranger jumps through*

54

the doorway? And why am I so comfortable that I started kidding around with him before I even knew his name?

This was beyond stupid; it was insane. After everything that had been done to her, after all the counseling, after all the warnings, Shawn James jumps into her life, literally, and what does she do? *Gee, let's hold his hand, let's smile at him, and feel all warm and cozy. I know, let's kid around with him too. A little humor always loosens things up.*

Uh, think he might assume you're coming onto him? Nah... it's only been what, five minutes? How much coming on can you do in five minutes? Besides, I'm sure the dead horse's head in your lap will cancel out any coming on signals I've sent. If only my fangs were showing and blood and snot were dripping off my chin. Then for sure he would know I was seriously not coming on to him. 'Course, then he would probably figure out that he knew how the horse died and would be looking for fang marks.

"CJ? Are you sure you're okay?" he asked.

"Uh...Yeah. Sorry. I just drifted somewhere for a while. It's been a really long day."

Shawn was kneeling next to her. "Mind if I sit down? I don't think we'll be going anywhere for a while, unless we feel like swimming there." The downpour hadn't let up one bit while CJ had been off on her head trip.

"What did you mean when you said his soul hasn't left yet?"

"I thought you said you weren't going to go there," she questioned.

"Well, we can't go anywhere else, so I may as well go back to stupid questions."

"They're not stupid, and I'm really sorry if I made you feel like they were."

"How did he die?"

CJ looked at him and said, "No idea. Yesterday he looked fine. This morning, something just wasn't right so I put him in out of the weather and called the vet. By the time the vet could get here, he was already dying. Then he just closed his eyes and went to sleep."

"And his soul?" asked Shawn.

She looked at him. "It's still here. I know it sounds weird, but I feel it. He hasn't left, and I don't know why. I told him I'd take care of Deveny, his horse girlfriend, and make sure everyone was safe and loved. I don't know what else to do to make it okay for him to leave."

As CJ stroked Rio's head, Shawn looked at her and said, "Maybe it's not them he's worried about."

"What do you mean? I've covered everyone. Who's left?"

Shawn smiled and whispered, "What about you?"

She looked at Shawn. "Me?"

"You're the only one still here. You're the only one still caring for him. You're the only one making sure his soul gets set free." He touched her arm and added, "My money is on you."

CJ stared at Shawn, then looked down at Rio. "Is that it? Is it me you're worried about? It is, isn't it?" Her face turned into a giant smile. "Oh my precious guardian, I'll be fine. I promise you, I'll make sure nothing bad happens to me. No matter what comes up,

I'll think about what you would do before I do anything. I'll keep myself safe, and besides, I know you'll be up there watching over me."

She leaned her head against Rio's, looked at Shawn, and smiled. "He's gone," she whispered. "Thank you. Thank you so much."

"My pleasure," said Shawn. "It really wasn't hard to figure out. All I had to do was look at you to know who he loved."

At that moment, CJ knew a door in her life had closed and another had opened. And the new doorway had someone named Shawn standing in it.

They sat staring at each other for a few minutes before CJ asked, "Why are you here?"

Shawn started to respond with, "Well, I was on my way to the—"

"Yeah, I got that part, but I mean, why are you here, at the ranch? I've never seen you here before. Are you picking someone up?"

"No, actually, my truck broke down on the road out front, and this shed was the only sign of life so I headed for it. When I got to the open gate, I thought maybe the horses had gotten out. I saw the trailer and was just about to head there when I heard you and thought you might be in trouble. I came closer to investigate, the rain and thunder hit, scared the crap out of me, and I jumped in."

"Well, thank you for coming to my rescue, Shawn James. That was very nice of you. Not to mention brave."

Shawn chuckled. "Actually, I thought you were in the middle of a lovers' quarrel, and I had just decided the trailer was probably a safer bet when the sky opened up."

CJ smiled back at him. "I still think it was very brave of you, so thank you. My guess is you need a phone so you can call about your truck?"

"Yeah, my cell phone tried to float here on its own and might have made it if the current had been going the right way. I didn't help much by falling on it. About all its good for now is a mini fish tank for some very skinny fish."

CJ pulled her cell out of her back pocket and showed it to him. "I've got mine, but coverage at the ranch sucks and, with this storm, it'll be even suckier. Let's head for the trailer. There's a land line up there, if it's still working."

Shawn stood and helped CJ up. He took her poncho off the hook and held it so she could slip into it.

"Why don't you take the poncho? It'll help keep you a little dry," she said, pushing it toward him.

He shook his head. "Thanks, but I passed through *a little dry* an hour ago on my way to *soaked*. I'm now at *I don't get this wet when I take a shower*. If I hadn't fallen in the mud, I could skip washing everything when I get home."

CJ smiled. *Just like a guy.* Then she remembered her comment to herself this morning about her hoodie.

They stepped out into the rain as another clap of thunder hit. Heading to the front of the stall, CJ closed and latched the gate, then they started toward the trailer up the hill.

"You've sure got a lot of horses. Do people board them, then come here when they want to ride?" Shawn asked, looking around.

"No, actually they're all ours. Or at least they are now. This is a horse rescue," CJ replied.

"Rescued from what? Why would a horse need to be rescued?"

CJ raised her eyebrows and looked at him. "Don't get out much, do you?"

Shawn shook his head. "Guess not. At least not around horses. That was another stupid question, wasn't it?"

"No, and I'm sorry again if I made it seem like it was. It's just that I'd need a year or two to give you all the reasons why horses need to be rescued. Working here, you get to see the not-so-nice side of people and what they do when things get desperate." She saw the confused look on Shawn's face and added, "Subject for another time, Shawn James, subject for another time."

As they climbed the stairs to the trailer, she asked, "So what is it you do, Shawn?"

"Fireman," came his reply. "I work at the fire station in Bonita. And yes, people have horses there. I just have never had reason to be around them very much so I guess I'm pretty stupid when it comes to horse stuff."

CJ opened the door, turned, and looked at him. "You're not stupid at all. Sounds like you've just never had any reason to learn about horses. Come on in, and let's see if the phone's working."

The only person in the trailer was Kate, who stared at Shawn like his spaceship had just landed out front. "Are you okay, CJ? And you are?" Kate asked, looking first at CJ, then at Shawn.

"Hi, I'm Shawn," he said, as he extended his hand to Kate.

CJ added, "His truck broke down out on the road, and he came looking for a phone. Thanks to Shawn here, I'm okay, now. If he hadn't come along and figured things out, I'd still be sitting out there trying to get Rio to leave."

Kate stood there, looking back and forth between them, totally confused.

"You had to be there," Shawn said.

Kate shook her head. "I'm not sure being there would've helped, but I'm glad you're okay CJ. I was just getting ready to come down and check on you. Shawn, I'm sorry, but the phone is dead. Cell coverage is out too, and I suspect it'll be at least a day or two before the phone company even remembers we're here. All part of the joy of living in the middle of nowhere."

"Wow. My friends probably have the CHP searching the ditches between here and Julian looking for me. I was supposed to call them after I got on 8 so we could make sure everyone was okay. Any place close by that might have a working phone?"

Kate shook her head. "Closest working phone is likely to be at Viejas Casino. If power is out at the casino, Alpine's just a little farther up 8."

CJ realized both places were on Kate's way home and she might be thinking about offering him a ride. But neither of them could be sure he was who he said he was, where he came from, or anything else about him. For all they knew, he could be an escaped serial killer, and CJ wasn't about to suggest Kate get in a car alone with him. She looked at Kate, who seemed to be reading her mind.

"How about if I give him a lift down there and you can follow us, Kate? Once we find a place that he can call from, I'll head back and you can go home."

Shawn too seemed to realize what CJ was doing and turned to her. "Thank you. I know you don't know me, and I really appreciate your coming up with a safe way to get me to a phone. I can't tell you how much I appreciate it."

"One problem," said CJ. "You can't go like that. Your clothes are soaked, and who knows how long it's going to be before your friends pick you up. I've got a pair of extra-large sweats I kick around in that might fit you. Let me run up to my trailer and get them. The legs and arms might be a little short, but at least you'll have something dry to wait in." She turned and headed for her trailer, a little farther up the hill.

Kate stared at Shawn and said, "I don't know why she trusts you, but she does. I'm not so sure I'd be as trusting, but her instincts are usually pretty good, so I'll go with her plan. But. I'm going to warn you. If you even think about harming one hair on her head, I'll make sure you are drawn and quartered."

Shawn appeared totally confused. So Kate clarified it for him. "That's where I tie each of your limbs to a different horse and send them in four different directions. Got it?"

"Ouch," Shawn said. Then added, "Look, I understand, and I promise I would never do anything to hurt her, or anyone else for that matter."

"Good, because life has shit on her enough already," said Kate, just as CJ came through the door.

61

"Wow. Why is everybody so serious?" CJ asked.

"Oh, we were talking about poor Rio," Kate answered, glancing at Shawn.

CJ handed Shawn a pair of well-worn gray sweatpants and matching sweatshirt. "They're a little gross since I've been lounging in them all week, but they're a lot warmer and dryer than what you've got on. You can change in the bathroom, through that door."

Shawn stepped into the bathroom and closed the door. He stripped out of his dripping wet clothes, threw them into the shower, and pulled on the sweatpants. CJ was right. Other than the legs being about six inches too short, they fit him pretty well. He took his wallet out of his jeans and put it into the pocket of the sweatpants.

He picked up the shirt, brought it up to his nose, and took a deep breath. It smelled like fresh air, sunshine, and cookie dough with a light scent of lime bodywash and a trace of vanilla. Wow, if this was what CJ smelled like after a week of working on a horse ranch, what on earth did she smell like right out of the shower? He pulled the sweatshirt over his head, and like the pants, other than the sleeves, it fit pretty well. He smiled back at the mirror as he thought about what CJ must look like in the sweats. They had to swim on her. A picture of both of them sitting on a couch, with him searching through the sweats looking for her, popped into his head, and he started to laugh.

Shawn stepped out of the bathroom, held up his arms, and did a three-sixty turn.

CJ smiled at him. "Were you laughing at my sweats in there?"

"Actually, yes. I was trying to imagine you in them when this picture of me trying to rescue you before they swallowed you up popped into my head. Sorry."

"They are kinda ginormous, but they're great for slumming and they keep me nice and warm and cozy. Besides, they're so big that even if someone sees me in them, they don't really *see me*. I do have to be careful not to wear them outside on a really windy day though."

Shawn chuckled as he pictured her floating through the air in her sweats like the Pillsbury Doughboy.

"Thanks for trusting me with your treasured loungewear. I'll get them back to you as soon as I can, so you don't get cold. Can we get going? I'm sure by now my friends are worried sick."

"Sure, follow me. My truck's parked down by the entry gate."

Kate looked directly at Shawn and said, "I'll be right behind you, in case anything happens. Let's try the casino first. We should be able to tell if their power is on by the big sign on the freeway. If their sign is off, just keep going into Alpine. And don't forget, I'm right behind you."

"Yes, Mom," said CJ.

Chapter 6 - Sweats

As CJ and Shawn walked toward the entry gate to the ranch, she realized it had quit raining. "That's my truck right there, the white one." She pointed to her vehicle, but kept going toward the gate. "Go ahead and get in while I open the gate." After completing the task, she walked back, slid into the driver's seat, and started the truck. The engine sputtered, came to life, then died. She restarted it again. This time, it sputtered and finally roared to life. "Amazing. It usually takes at least four tries. You must be good luck, Shawn James."

They pulled through a gate onto the dirt driveway and turned left toward the main access leading out to the highway.

When they got to the second gate, Shawn said, "I'll get it," and started out his door.

"No way," yelled CJ. "Not while you're wearing my good loungewear. You stay here, and I'll get the gate. Those sweats are the only thing I have that'll fit you. If you fall in a puddle and get those wet, it's either you go naked or try to squeeze into a pair of my jeans. Either way, there's no chance you would get into the casino. So stay put."

"Yes, Mom. Maybe I should ride with Kate?"

"Trust me, you don't want to do that. She'll spend the whole trip telling you all the really nasty things she's gonna do to you if you're not nice to me."

CJ pulled through the gate, waited for Kate to pull through, then closed the postern. As they turned into the road, Shawn looked over at CJ and said, "She really loves you, you know. Kate, I mean."

CJ glanced at him and said, "Yeah, I know, and I love her just as much right back. If it wasn't for Kate, I'm not sure I'd be alive." Turning her attention back to the road, she went quiet, obviously not wanting to take the subject any further.

When they reached the interstate, she turned onto the west bound on-ramp and headed toward the casino and Alpine. She checked her rearview mirror to make sure Kate was still behind them, then glanced at Shawn.

"So Mr. Shawn James, tell me a little about yourself. Who are you, where do you come from and what, in God's name, brought you to the middle of nowhere on a night like this?"

"Wow, where do I start? Let's start by dropping the Mr. and the James, and please, just call me Shawn. Speaking of which, I don't even know your last name or what CJ stands for?"

CJ raised both eyebrows. "Nice try Mr.... ah, Shawn. We'll have no changing subjects in the middle of my interrogating you. And yes, you don't know my last name, will probably never know what CJ stands for, and if you were to accidentally find out... well, you'd find yourself being dumped in the bay, wearing a pair of cement galoshes. So back to you, and stick to the subject."

"Okay, okay, I got the hint. My initials are SNMIJ. And I'm proud to say that stands for—"

"Wait. Let me guess. Shawn. No Middle Initial. James. How's that for a lucky guess?"

"Oh, you are just too cute. Okay, I'll let the CJ thing go for now, but I'm not done." Adding under his breath, "Not by a long shot."

Shawn went on to explain that he was born and raised on Long Island in New York. He had joined the Navy shortly after graduating from high school and was discharged in San Diego after his last assignment on the aircraft carrier Ronald Reagan. Like his father, mother, grandfather, and many of his uncles, aunts, and cousins, he was a fireman and very proud of the family heritage.

Most of his family were with the FDNY in Manhattan, and two uncles, an aunt, and a cousin had been killed when the towers went down on 9/11. He had decided to stay in San Diego rather than return home because he loved the small town atmosphere and had actually made more friends in his short time out there than were left back home.

"Wow, your mom and aunts are firefighters?" CJ asked.

"*Were* firefighters. My mom and her sister, the one that died at the World Trade Center, were among the first female firefighters assigned to the FDNY in 1982. They both were with volunteer fire departments on Long Island before being accepted to the city's academy. My mom and dad are both retired now, but two of my cousins, who are sisters, are still active. One's an EMT in Manhattan, the other a firefighter in Brooklyn."

CJ listened quietly as he went on to talk about how he had joined Rick, Trish, and the girls up in Julian for the day. As he talked about their day, several things about him became obvious to her. Shawn James was as open and honest as they came. Maybe that was what she had sensed in the shed and why she had immediately felt comfortable with him.

She was also sure Rio had sensed it too. While it would sound stupid to anyone else, she was sure that had been part of Rio's knowing she was safe and it was okay to leave. Her mind drifted off... *Hmmm, is Shawn to be my protector? A girl could do a whole lot worse. Stop it. Once he finds out what I am, he'll erase*

66

me from his life like an unwanted text message. Bummer. She tuned back into what he was saying about his day with the girls.

The girls. That was the second thing she knew about Shawn. He loved Rick and Trish, but he absolutely adored their two girls. God help anyone who ever tried to hurt them in any way. *Yup, forget him being your protector, he already has the two of them to protect and you won't even come in a close third. Nope, if anyone is in third place, it is obviously Trish.*

How wonderful it must feel to be part of such a close circle of family and friends. The more she listened, the more she envied them. *What would it be like to be Trish or one the girls and be able to suck up all the love, warmth, and caring that just radiated from him?* But, she would never know, would she? *You're not even on the same planet, CJ.*

Shawn's raised voice brought her back to the real world. "The sign is on, and you're going to miss the exit."

She saw the sign for the casino just in time to turn onto the off-ramp. As they came to a stop at the bottom of the ramp, Shawn noticed a tear glistening in her eye.

"Are you okay?" he asked.

"Yeah, just something in my eye," she said. *You.*

She turned right and headed toward the casino. After pulling into the circular driveway of the casino and hotel, she turned to Shawn. "Run in and make sure they'll let you use a phone to call your friends. I'll wait here just in case you need to go to Alpine."

"Thanks, I'll only be a minute." He headed for the front door.

Two seconds later, Kate opened the passenger door, climbed in and asked, "You okay?"

CJ turned and nodded. "Yeah, I'm good."

"It looked like you two jabbered all the way here. I was sure you were going to blow right by the exit. So what's he like?" Kate asked, then added, "I've never seen you so comfortable with someone you just met. Especially a guy. What's with that?"

"He's just a really nice guy, Kate. This is going to sound stupid, but I trust him. I feel really relaxed around him. Even when he jumped into the shed, I wasn't scared. I somehow knew he wouldn't hurt me, no matter what. He's just a really, really nice guy."

"Wow, CJ, have you got it bad or what?"

"Yeah, lotta good it's gonna do me. His friends will come pick him up, they'll tow his truck tomorrow morning, and I'll never see him again. Speaking of which, where is he? See? He's already forgotten about me."

Kate just rolled her eyes. "Okay, Ms. Drama Queen."

"Please, Kate, don't try to force this to go somewhere. Even if he does like me, once he finds out what I was, I'm history. I can't take being thrown away again, and that's what he would do. That's what any guy in his right mind would do."

"CJ, no one is going to throw you away while I'm around. Anyone who doesn't understand how special you are has to be blind, dumb, and stupid, and I don't see Shawn as being any of those. I also can't help but notice the way he looks at you. Not to mention how you look at him. He is pretty nice eye candy, you know. And you're right. Where is he?"

The door to the casino opened. As Shawn came out, they both noticed the *way-too-short* pant legs and shirtsleeves of CJ's sweats on him and broke out laughing.

He opened the door on Kate's side. "What's so funny?"

"You. You're such a fashion statement in my sweats."

"Oh, you have no idea. Half the people in there think I mugged someone in the parking lot and stole their clothes. It took me twenty minutes at the hotel desk to convince them to let me a have a room for the night. I wouldn't be surprised if they post a security guard outside my room to make sure I don't attack any of the other guests."

CJ was surprised. "Weren't you able to get hold of your friends? I thought for sure they would come pick you up."

"I got hold of them okay. They had just gotten home and were actually on the phone with the CHP when I called. I didn't want them to have to drive all the way back out here to get me. Besides, I would just have to turn around and come back out tomorrow morning to get my truck. Staying here seemed to make a lot more sense. I'll find a tow company first thing in the morning and have them pick me up on the way to get my truck. By the way, where exactly is my truck? I mean what do I tell them so they know where to go?"

"Shawn, I have a better idea. There's a small garage in Guatay, just down the road from the ranch. Jim, the mechanic there, works on my truck all the time and he's really good. I can take a run over there first thing in the morning and see if he can look at your truck, then I can come pick you up. It will be a lot cheaper than getting it towed to Alpine and waiting the whole day while it gets worked on."

"I can't let you do that, CJ. You've already gone out of your way."

"I insist, Shawn. It's not a problem."

Shawn shook his head, "You're an angel. I'm going to owe you big-time for this, and I insist on paying you back. What time do you want to pick me up?"

"Let's say 10? That will give me a chance to get Jim over to your truck and my volunteers started on what has to be done at the ranch."

Shawn thanked her again, said good night to both of them, and started to head for the door to the casino.

"Shawn," CJ called out. "I think you should seriously consider using room service tonight. I'm not sure the dining room is ready for you in that outfit." Smiling, she added, "Sleep well. See you in the morning."

Laughing and shaking her head as she got out, Kate looked at CJ. "You are so bad. If that poor man has any brains at all, he'll catch a cab back to San Diego tonight so he doesn't have to deal with you in the morning. Trouble is, I suspect he's just as bad as you when it comes to teasing. Just another reason why you're so comfortable with him, I'm sure. Thanks for the entertainment. I'm going to head home. It's been a really long day for both of us. Thanks for being there for Rio. I'm sure going to miss him."

"Me too," whispered CJ. "Drive safe. I'll call you tomorrow and let you know how the day's going."

Sticking her head back in the truck, Kate said, "Oh, I forgot to tell you. Cell service came back on while we were on 8, so I called Gary and asked him to please deal with Rio's body. He promised he'd try to get there first thing in the morning. With any luck, he'll be done before any of the volunteers get there. You might want to time your trip to Jim's garage so you're not there too."

"Thanks, Kate."

Shawn watched CJ and Kate pull out, then went to the desk. "Is there any place I can buy some clothes?" The desk clerk looked at the clock and told him there was a men's shop directly across the way in the mall. He added that they should have closed five minutes ago, but if he hurried he might catch someone still there.

Chuckling, the clerk added, "Once they see what you're wearing, I'm sure they'll stay open to help you."

Shawn ran across the street and found the shop not only still open, but several customers inside. He quickly grabbed a three-pack of underwear, three-pack of socks, a pair of jeans, and a sweatshirt in his size, then headed for the dressing room. After changing into the clothes, he threw CJ's sweats over his arm and went to the cash register desk.

The clerk rang up his purchases, and Shawn asked the clerk if he would mind putting the extra underwear and socks in a garment bag. Shawn couldn't help but notice the clerk staring at CJ's sweats as if they were contaminating the store and knew he was about to ask if Shawn would like him to throw them away. Letting out a chuckle, Shawn informed him that they were 'on loan' from someone and he would be keeping them, thank you. He left the store and headed back to the hotel desk.

"Thanks," Shawn said. "I just made it."

The hotel clerk looked at him and said, "Would you like me to dispose of those for you?" He pointed to CJ's sweats.

71

"No, actually, is there any way I could get them laundered tonight? It's important, and I'll be willing to pay extra."

"I'm sorry but everyone from the laundry area has gone home."

The female clerk standing next to him said, "I think Cindy's still here. It's not her area, but let me see if she might be willing to wash them for you." She picked up the phone and, a minute later, said, "Cindy will be right down to get them from you."

Five minutes later, Cindy collected the sweats and promised she would have them delivered to his room in about an hour.

He opened the door to his room, walked over to the bed, and fell face first on to it. God, it had been a long day. After a minute or two and a loud rumble from his stomach, he got back up and searched the desk for the room service menu. He called in his order, stripped out of his new clothes, and headed for the shower. With the water as hot as he could stand it, he stepped under the stream, braced himself against the wall, closed his eyes, and stood there until he finally started to warm up.

In no time, the water worked its magic and his body relaxed, but his mind went straight to CJ. What was it about her that attracted him so much? She certainly wasn't drop-dead gorgeous, but she wouldn't have any trouble holding her own in a room full of pretty women either. As a matter of fact, her good looks combined with her girl-next-door appeal, would turn any guy's head.

But it was more than that. He absolutely loved her personality. She was funny, witty, and not short of anything in the intelligence department. She also radiated a genuine warmth and caring that he had rarely seen in anyone else. The thought that she was just plain comfortable in her own skin popped into his mind, but he had sensed there was something dark buried in there too. Kate's warning had convinced him he was right. CJ had been badly hurt somewhere in her past, and he needed to be careful. He needed to go slow and fine-tune his senses. Better yet, he needed to let her take the lead and not push himself on her.

Yeah, like that was going to be easy.

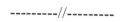

CJ opened the door to her trailer and, leaving a trail of clothes in her wake, headed directly for the bathroom and a hot shower. She stepped under the stream, braced her hands against the wall, closed her eyes, and hoped the smell of the ranch would wash off.

She also wondered what Shawn (who at that exact moment, was in the same pose in the hotel shower, thinking about CJ) was doing. What in the world was going on with her? She had never been like this with anyone. She just knew she was setting herself up to be hurt, but she couldn't help it. She was so relaxed around him. He was like the brother she never had. No, he wasn't like a brother. You didn't flirt with a brother, and brothers didn't cause the kind of feelings she had when Shawn was close. He was fun to be with and tease. Why did she like teasing him so much? And why did he put up with it?

She shampooed her hair with the cookie butter shampoo, then grabbed the bottle of lime body wash and poured some on her scrubby ball. As she washed, she wondered if he knew what she smelled like. What her hair smelled like.

She looked down at the foam circling the drain. *Right. You work on a ranch all day. What do you think you smell like? Horse shit and goat turds, dummy. And guess what, you loaned him your sweats so you can add BO to the formula. Probably should throw in a little hay smell, horse chow, and chicken feed. Oh, and let's not forget about the pee. We have horse pee, goat pee, burro pee, sheep pee, chicken pee, and dog pee. Oh yeah, he definitely knows what you smell like.*

After an extra long shower to try to make herself smell better, she stepped out and dried off. She reached for her sweats, remembered Shawn had them, and pulled her robe off the hook. She wandered into the kitchen, pulled a can of Franco-American Spaghetti-Os out of the cupboard and a beer out of the refrigerator. She put the Spaghetti-Os in a pot, set it on the stove to heat up, then popped the beer open and took a swallow.

Sliding her Kindle across the table, she opened the vampire book she was in the middle of and started reading while her gourmet Italian dinner heated. One beer, a bowl of Spaghetti-Os, four pages, and an hour later, she jerked her head up off the table and took herself to bed.

Chapter 7 - Deveny

At 9:55, CJ pulled in front of the casino and started to get out. Before she could get around the front of the truck, Shawn appeared on the sidewalk by the passenger door. She saw him and stuck her hand out to brace herself on the hood as her mouth dropped open. OH. MY. GOD. Was he hot. He had on a new pair of jeans that looked like they were custom-made for him and a light blue sweatshirt that hugged his upper body. Both left little doubt as to what great shape he was in.

Her gaze moved up to his face, and she was drawn to his brown eyes. *If he ever turns on the puppy-dog look, I'm dead meat.* There was nothing spectacular about any of his features, but the combination of his light brown hair, square face, slightly pointed chin, perfect nose, full lips, and olive skin all combined to make him unbelievably good looking.

CJ just stood there and stared. As she tightened her grip on the hood of her truck, her attention zoomed in on his lips. *Check that. Oh yeah, his lips are definitely spectacular. And they are screaming, "kiss me."*

Finally, Shawn said, "You might want to close your mouth before something flies in there."

"Ah, oh, wow. Do you clean up well," was all she could spit out.

"Glad you approve," he answered, smiling.

"Approve? I'm taking you home, locking you in my trailer, and never sharing you with anybody… ever."

The grin on Shawn's face grew bigger. "Uh, I've never been a boy toy before. Do I get a vote in any of this?"

"Nope," came her response.

They continued to stare at each other until CJ grunted and they both started chuckling. When their shared funny moment was over, Shawn said, "Thank you. That's the best good-morning greeting I've ever had. Has anyone told you you're fun to be with?"

"No. But I've been told I have a sick mind, in case you hadn't figured that out yet."

"Here, this is for you." He handed her the garment bag he had draped over his shoulder.

CJ opened the zipper, reached in, and pulled out a pair of men's jockey shorts. "How did you know?" she asked, waving the shorts around. "This was supposed to be my little secret." She pretended to glance around to make sure no one was watching. "Uh, I think you got the size wrong, though. I know I've got big hips, but these are going to take a lot of washings before they'll stay up."

Smiling, Shawn said, "Those are mine. The sweats are yours. And your hips aren't big."

Realizing he'd just told her she had his underwear, she stared at the top of his jeans. "Are you telling me you haven't got any underwear on in there uh… under there… under those? Of course you don't. There's no room in there for underwear."

Shawn broke out in a fit of laughter. He looked around, as if praying that no one else was watching all this, and told her, "You should have been an actress. Yes, I have underwear on. They came in a three-pack. You're welcome to the other two pair if you really want them. I'll even go across the street and exchange them for boy shorts in your size. Come to think of it, boy shorts would kinda go good with your sweats."

CJ's face went serious, and she stood up. She was getting way too personal and way, way too forward. If he didn't think she was a tramp before, she had certainly left no doubt after those comments.

Staring at him, she finally said, "Sorry, but they're not my color, and thank you for getting my sweats cleaned. We really should get going. Jim is working on your truck, and I need to check on my volunteers."

Walking back to the driver's side, she got in while Shawn hung the clothing bag in the back, then climbed into the passenger's seat.

Neither one of them said a word as they headed for the on-ramp to the interstate.

As she merged into the eastbound traffic, Shawn looked at her. "CJ, I'm sorry if I said something back there that offended you. I don't know why, but I'm completely relaxed around you, so I just spit out whatever comes into my head without thinking. I'm really sorry."

CJ looked over and smiled. "Do you read minds or what? I was just about to apologize to you for being way too forward for exactly the same reason."

Shawn let out a deep sigh. "Wow, I was so afraid I blew it big-time back there and you were never going to talk to me again."

"Like that would ever happen. Especially if you keep wearing those jeans. Oops, sorry, there I go again. I have to warn you, though, once the volunteers see you in those jeans and that sweatshirt... I will not be responsible for what happens. If you have time, I planned to give you a little tour of the ranch, but now, I'm not so sure that's a good idea."

Shawn smiled. "Thanks for the warning. I'll try to stay out of sight as much as possible."

"Don't you dare," she said.

They pulled up to the main gate, and Shawn noticed his truck was gone. "I thought you said Jim was working on my truck."

Looking totally unconcerned, CJ said, "He was. Maybe he took it to the garage or something."

"But he doesn't have the keys."

"Ah, yes he does. I gave them to him this morning."

Shawn looked very confused. "And how, pray tell, did you get my keys?"

"Um, out of your pants? The soaking wet ones you left in the bathroom, along with your shirt and underwear."

"Sorry," Shawn said.

"Don't apologize to me. Save that for the volunteer who found them there this morning. Then, good luck trying to explain why they were there. No matter what you come up with, it's not going to be even close to what she's already created in her mind. Especially when she gets a look at you in those… those jeans and that shirt." She burst out laughing, then added, "Strap in, Shawn James. Thanks to you, it's going to be a very interesting day at the ranch."

They drove through the gate and turned off the dirt road into the ranch. She parked the truck next to the volunteer trailer, and as they got out, Shannon came out of the trailer.

Shannon looked at CJ, then glued her eyes to Shawn as he got out of the truck. "Ummm, wow. We need... help... down at the stalls. The... uh... pump for... draining the troughs... isn't working. Uh... Hi, I don't think we've met. I'm Shannon," she added, as she held her hand out.

"Hi, I'm Shawn," he said, taking her hand. He glanced at CJ as she came around the back of the truck. "I can go take a look at it, if that's okay. I'm pretty good with electrical equipment."

"Thanks, it looks like they're at the stall Rio was in. I'll be down as soon as Shannon fills me in on what's left to be done."

Shawn glanced down, then up at Shannon, who was still shaking his hand. "Uh, can I have my hand back?"

"Sorry," she said as she took his hand in both of hers, pressed it to his chest, and patted it.

CJ just stood there with a giant grin, then looked at Shawn and said, "Told you."

Smiling, Shawn turned and headed for the stalls.

As soon as he was far enough down the hill, Shannon went off. "OH. MY. GOD. Who is that? Where did you find him? Can we keep him? Oh my God, oh my God, oh my God, is he ever cute. I think I creamed in my jeans while he was shaking my hand. Can we keep him? Please. Please. Please."

CJ started laughing. "Take a deep breath, Shannon. That's it, breathe in, breathe out. No, you can't keep him."

"Why, is he yours? Please tell me he's not yours. Please tell me he's a new volunteer. What days is he going to be here? I can change my days, you know. What days do I need to change to? Oh, I know, I can wear my new sundress with my boots. I'll bet he'll really…" She stopped in mid-sentence and looked at CJ, who was staring at her.

"Are you done yet?" CJ asked. "He's not a volunteer. He's a fireman, his pickup truck broke down out front, and we're helping him get his truck fixed at Jim's. As soon as it's fixed, I'm sure he's going to head home and we'll never see him again, so ogle while you can. Now, can we talk about the ranch?"

Reluctantly, Shannon quit pleading and filled CJ in on what chores were left. All the stalls and pens had been cleaned, everybody was fed, and they had finished draining and cleaning all but the last of the troughs when the pump quit.

"Wow, that's great, Shannon. I can't believe you guys got all that done. Thank you. Let's go see if Shawn was able to get the pump working."

As they walked toward the stalls, CJ asked, "Who showed up today?"

"Don't fall over, but everyone that was scheduled. Christine, Jasmine, and even Ami, *Ms. Personality*, decided to grace us with her presence."

CJ looked at her. "Oh great, just what I need."

When they reached the stall area, the pump was running and water was coming out of the drain hose. Inside the stall, Shawn was bent over the trough, trying to check the cord to the pump. On one side of him was Christine and on the other was Ami and Jasmine, all staring at his ass with their mouths hanging open.

80

Shannon, not to be left out, walked directly behind Shawn, pressed herself against his backside, leaned over the trough, and said, "Can I help?"

"Hey, you're blocking our view," Christine, Jasmine, and Ami all chimed in.

Shawn glanced over at Christine with a smile, making her realize they had just given away what they were doing. Quickly, she added, "Yeah, we need to see what he's doing in case it breaks again."

With Shannon still pressed against his back, Shawn looked up at CJ who had an *I told you so* smile on her face, as he said, "It was just a loose wire. Should be fine now."

Unable to move, he turned toward Shannon, almost kissing her because she was so close.

Shannon smiled at him and said, "Ah, sorry," then she stood up.

Shaking her head, CJ said, "Ladies, when you're finished refilling this last trough, you can all head home. And thank you for getting everything done; I really appreciate it." CJ hooked her arm through Shawn's and gently tugged him toward the stall gate. "Come with me, and I'll introduce you to my favorite girl, Deveny."

The four women watched Shawn and CJ walk up the hill toward Deveny's stall. Christine glared at Shannon and said, "Could you have been a little more obvious, girl?"

"Me? What about the three of you, standing there drooling over his ass in those jeans?"

"God, is he ever H.O.T.T," said Ami. Who then added, "What does he see in the slut?"

The other three stared at her. Finally, Shannon said, "You know, Ami, I don't know why CJ puts up with you. If you said that about me, you'd be fishing for your teeth in the trough."

Ami glared at her. "She puts up with it because she knows she's a slut. Once a slut and a whore, always a slut and a whore. And if you keep hanging around her and defending her, people are going to wonder if maybe you two have something going. It gets awfully lonely out here at night, and you're always the last one to leave, Shannon. You know, I've always wondered about that. I'm sure others have noticed it too."

Shannon's face turned beet red. She raised her hands and stepped toward Ami. Before she could get close, Christine stepped between them. "Enough, Ami. I think you've worn out your welcome, and we've had enough of your shit for one day."

Jasmine added, "Why do you come out here? You don't know anything about horses. Nobody likes you. All you do is cause trouble and make up shit about everybody."

Ami glared at the three of them. "I'll bet Shawn will like me, once he gets to know me. I've got it all over Ms. Blowjob up there. Once he finds out about her, he'll drop her like the piece of horse shit she is. That's when I'll be there to comfort him and show him what a real woman is like."

"Ah, excuse me while I go throw up," said Shannon.

"What do you smoke, Ami? It must really be some good shit if you believe half of what comes out of your mouth," added Christine.

Jasmine started shaking her head. "I'm out of here. I can't take any more of your foul mouth and asinine statements, Ami."

"Me too," said Shannon. "Why don't you go stand behind Milton Burro, Ami? He'd be happy to knock some sense into you. You coming, Christine, or are you going to hang with Miss Foul Mouth?" With that, the three of them left Ami standing there and headed to the volunteer trailer to sign out.

Shawn and CJ approached a fenced area up the hill, across from the pens. Standing toward the back of the large area was a beautiful gray mare, who stared directly at Shawn and wiggled her ears. Even though he knew nothing about horses, Shawn knew beauty and elegance when he saw it. And Deveny, if nothing else, had to be the most stunning horse on the ranch.

"God, she's beautiful," he whispered to CJ.

"Yes, she is," she whispered back.

"It's easy to understand why Rio loved her," he went on. "She's special to you too, isn't she?"

Tears welled up in CJ's eyes as she choked out, "Very. We kind of came from the same place so we understand each other." CJ looked up at Shawn, and behind the tears in her eyes was a sparkle he hadn't seen before. "For someone who doesn't know much about horses, you're pretty perceptive, Shawn."

"I'm a quick learner and, don't let this go to your head, but I've got a pretty good teacher too."

CJ knew she shouldn't, but she gently took his arm in both of her hands and leaned her head against his shoulder. "Thank you," she whispered.

"Pretty horse, isn't he?" came a voice from behind them. Shawn and CJ turned to find Ami standing there, staring at Shawn. "Hi, I'm Ami. We met down by the water thing, but I didn't get a chance to introduce myself." Then she pulled his arm out of CJ's hands and shook his hand. "I'm a senior volunteer here, and if there's anything you want to know about the ranch or horses, I'll be happy to show you around. I know CJ has a lot to do, so I'll take over and give you the guided tour."

Just as Shawn was about to say something, his truck drove through the gate and the horn blew. CJ rolled her eyes and thanked God. Jim's timing couldn't have been better.

"Sorry, Ami, we need to get Shawn to his truck so he can head home. Thanks for offering to play tour guide." CJ lowered her voice and added, "By the way, Deveny's a she."

With that, CJ took Shawn's arm and just about pulled him off the hill. When they were almost to his truck, Shawn looked at her and said, "What was that all about?"

"Oh, trust me, you don't want to know," she said.

As they walked down the hill, CJ's mind was racing. Things were going way too fast. She just knew a brick wall was going to jump up in front of her and she was going to run into it at full speed. She had no idea why she had hugged his arm and leaned against him up by Deveny's stall. All she knew was that it had felt so natural and she trusted him more than anyone she had ever met. When he was near, she felt safe and comfortable.

Why did she feel like she didn't need to keep her guard up, to protect herself, with him? For the only time in years, she was letting her guard down. Why did she think he would understand no matter what he found out about her? He would see her for who she was. He would understand that life had shoveled a pile of crap on her and it had almost killed her. But she had dealt with it and come out a better person. He would see that; she just knew he would.

But why? Why did she have all these feelings? He was a total stranger, for God's sake. He could have his pick of any woman on earth. What in the world made her think he would pick her? Rehab and therapy had rebuilt her confidence, but this wasn't being confident. This wasn't believing in herself. This was just plain stupidity.

What decent guy in his right mind would want her? She was bait for the perverts, not decent guys like Shawn. Shannon and Christine were much more his type. Even, God help him, Ami. Ami, who had just served notice on her up the hill, that she was taking a run at Shawn. Ami, who hated her, and would make sure no stone went unturned in revealing CJ's past.

Her mind screamed, *this is just plain stupid.* Was she setting herself up for a crash and burn, one that might destroy the person she had worked so hard to become? All of a sudden CJ felt exhausted.

Jim walked up and introduced himself, then handed Shawn his keys.

"What was wrong with it?" Shawn asked.

"It was pretty simple actually. The distributor cap was cracked and water got into it. The starter also had a loose wire and apparently got soaked. I would have had it back sooner, but I wanted to check and reset your timing before I returned it. Next thing I knew, it got real busy, and I just now got a chance to run it back. Sorry it took so long."

Shawn shook his head. "Are you kidding? I appreciate your coming over here, picking it up, and getting it fixed this quick. How much do I owe you?"

"Nothing. That new distributor cap had been sitting on my parts shelf for over three years now. I'm just glad to get rid of it. Besides, if CJ says you're special, then you're special, and we don't charge special people. Right, CJ?"

CJ pasted on a grin. She couldn't believe Jim told him she said he was special. "Right. I owe you, Jim."

Jim looked at her and said, "Yes, you do. You owe me a ride back to the garage."

"I'll run him back," said Shawn.

"No, you will not. You've been stranded out here all last night and most of today, and I'm sure you want to get home. I'll run Jim back. The garage is just around the corner. Come on, I'll open the gate for you."

As she turned to head for the gate, Shawn gently grabbed her arm and turned her around. "Are you trying to get rid of me?"

"No, no, not at all. I just thought you would want to get home."

"I do, but I'm not going to just run off without thanking you for all you've done or saying good-bye."

All of a sudden, her head started spinning.

"Are you okay, CJ?"

She pasted on a smile and shook her head. "Yeah, I just hate good-byes. That's all."

Shawn looked at Jim and told him they would be right back. Then he took her by the hand and led her toward the gate.

As soon as they were far enough away that no one could hear them, he looked at her. "I hate good-byes too. So let's not say them. I'm just going to say I'll see you soon, and I'd like that to be very soon, if you're okay with it."

Chapter 8 - The Longest Five Days Ever

CJ's mind raced. Why hadn't he just gotten in his truck and driven away? Why was he making this so hard for her? He was saying he'd be back, but then she would never see him again. If he did come back, Ami would make sure he knew every sordid detail of her past. Then it wouldn't be *see you soon*, it would be *good-bye forever*.

She knew he would never be back, and her heart was breaking as she turned away.

He gently turned her around and whispered, "You're worried I'm not coming back, aren't you? I promise you, I will." He paused. "Is it okay if I hug you?"

Afraid to look at him, she nodded. *Oh God, I can't do this. I don't want him to leave. I never want him to leave.* Laying her head against his chest, she tightly wrapped her arms around him as he gently pulled her body against his.

Jim walked slowly toward them. When he saw the sad look on CJ's face, he asked if she was okay. "It's been a long day, and she just lost her best friend," Shawn told him. "I'm going to take her up to her trailer then I'll give you a lift back to the garage."

He put his arm around her waist and turned her toward her trailer. CJ gripped his arm and hung on for dear life. When they got to the trailer, he helped her up the steps and she opened the door. He took her hand and led her back to the steps, gently pulling her down with him as he sat.

"Will you be okay?" he asked. She nodded and tried to smile. "I'm going to run Jim back, then I've got to go home. Okay?"

She nodded again, but still would not meet his eyes.

He tilted her chin up and looked into her eyes. "I really like you, CJ. I'd like to spend more time with you, so we can get to know each other better, if you're okay with that. I was thinking, I could come back out and maybe spend the day at the ranch helping you?"

Her eyes lit up. "Really?"

"Really." He smiled, then added, "But... I've got to go to New York for a few days. It's my parents' anniversary, and I'm flying out tomorrow morning to spend a few days with them. I'll be back Wednesday. How about if I give you a call when I get back, and we can work on a day that I can come out? Can I get your cell number?"

"Sure," she whispered, got up, went inside, and scribbled her name and number on a Post-it. Coming back out, she handed it to Shawn and added, "Will you call me? I mean, when you get there... so I know you arrived safe?" *God, that was stupid. Why did I just ask him to do that?* She tried to recover. "I'm sorry, that was stupid. You'll be busy with your parents and all."

Tucking the post it in his pocket, he smiled at her. "It's not stupid, and thank you for being concerned. I'll call you from JFK as soon as my feet are planted firmly on the ground. I gotta go, Jim's waiting. You sure you're okay?"

"Uh-huh," she said, nodding.

-------//-------

Shawn pulled into the parking lot of his condo complex. It was late; he was extremely tired and very worried about CJ. Things were happening way too fast, for both of them. His fear that something really bad happened in her past had once again been

89

confirmed by Jim, who had seen the look on CJ's face, and told him on the way to the garage that he would personally break both of his legs if he so much as thought about hurting her.

Jim will have to take a ticket. Besides, when Kate was done with him, he wouldn't have any legs to break. Or arms for that matter.

He unlocked the door to his condo, and just as he turned the light on, the phone rang. He walked over, picked it up, and found Trish on the other end.

"Are you okay? We've been really worried about you."

"Yeah, I'm good. I would've called you back, but my cell phone uh... went for a swim and I just now walked in the door. I had to wait for my truck to be fixed, and... I met someone."

After a very long pause, Trish said, "And?"

"And what?"

"Is she a she, and if so is she pretty?"

"Ah, I'm pretty sure she's a she, and yes, I think she's very pretty. And... I'm very tired, so the rest of your interrogation will have to wait until I get back from New York. As a matter of fact, if I'm lucky, it'll have to wait for a few days after that. I'm going to call her right after I get back and hopefully spend a few days at the ranch helping her."

"What? Oh, Shawn, she must really be special. She is special, isn't she?"

"Yes, Trish, very special," he whispered.

"Shawn, you can't do this to me. You can't leave me hanging like this."

He smiled. "Love you," he whispered, and hung up. It was nice driving Trish crazy for a change, and by the time he got back, she would be climbing the walls.

After hanging up with Trish, he showered and grabbed something to eat. He headed into the bedroom and packed his small wheeled suitcase. Next, he put his Kindle and a few items he would need on board into a carry-on and set everything by the door. He went into the kitchen, pulled a Post-it out of the holder on the serve-through, wrote PHONE, and stuck it on the top of the carry-on.

---------//--------

At 5 am, his alarm went off. He brushed his teeth, ran a comb through his hair, and dressed. At 5:30, the doorbell rang. With no one else to pick up, the shuttle dropped him off at the American Airlines curbside check-in at exactly 6. He checked his piece of luggage and headed for the Verizon kiosk in the terminal. By 6:45 he had his new smart phone and was sitting in the gate waiting area.

Pulling CJ's note from his pocket, he programmed her name and phone number into the phone. Since he didn't have a picture of her, he used a happy face and made a mental note to take her picture as soon as he got back. Next, he programmed in the numbers for his parents, Rick and Trish, the station, and a few other numbers he used often. Again, he made a mental note to take pictures for each. Just as he finished, they announced his 7:45 flight was boarding.

----------//----------

CJ opened her eyes and looked at the clock. 5:55. Trying to part the haze, she wondered, *Should I get another five minutes sleep or get up?* Just then the alarm went off.

"Ken?" she called out. "Where's my coffee? Oops… forgot, it's his day off." She smiled. "Maybe I could call Shawn. Bet he'd bring me coffee." She frowned as she remembered he was on his way to New York. "This is going to be the longest five days of my life."

Swinging her legs over the side of the bed, she stretched, stood up, stripped off her night shirt, and trudged into the bathroom to shower. Thirty minutes later, she walked over to the volunteer trailer just in time to meet Shannon coming up the hill.

"How did it go with Shawn yesterday?" Shannon asked.

"Good," CJ answered.

"Good? That's all you're going to give me? It went good? What the hell does that mean?"

"Good means good. It went… G.o.o.d. Good," CJ said, smiling as she went up the steps and into the trailer. She was driving Shannon crazy and loving every minute of it.

It was Saturday so more volunteers showed up than would have on a weekday. By 8 am, five volunteers had arrived, but for two of them, this was their first day at the ranch. That meant that only three would be helping CJ, while Shannon would spend her day training the other two. Even still, by 1:30 everything was done and CJ cut the three regular volunteers loose. A half hour later, Shannon finished her final lesson on how to build a wheelbarrow toolkit and cut the two newbies loose as well.

Shannon looped her arm through CJ's and they headed toward the trailers. "So how good was good? Are we talking kinda good, really good, or really, really good?"

CJ smiled and decided to let her off the hook. "We're talking really, really good... and then some."

"That's fantastic because in case you haven't figured it out yet, he really likes you."

CJ smiled at her. "That sure is a lot of reallys. If reallys count for anything, we'll likely be getting engaged when he gets back from New York."

"New York? What's he doing in New York?"

They reached the volunteer trailer and sat at the picnic table out front. "Visiting his parents for their anniversary. He flew out this morning." Just then CJ's phone rang.

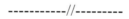

Shawn's flight landed right on time. They taxied to the gate, and as usual, he waited till almost everybody was off before he grabbed his carry-on and walked off the plane. He walked into the terminal and followed the signs to baggage claim. As soon as he came around the corner, he spotted his parents just outside the security barricade and waved. His suitcase was one of only three left on the carousel, and he walked over, grabbed it, and headed for his parents.

They met him just outside the barricade. He gave his mom a big hug, then hugged his dad.

"Long flight?" his father asked.

"Actually, it went pretty fast. I lucked out, and there was nobody in the center seat and the guy in the window seat wasn't a Chatty Cathy. So I buried myself in my Kindle, and before I knew it, we were landing."

"Let's head home. I'll bet you're starved. Your mom made one of your favorites, stuffed cabbage, and it should just about be done by the time we get home."

He kissed his mom. "I knew there was a reason I loved you. Can you hang on a minute? I need to make a call."

Stepping a few feet away, he pulled out his phone and punched the happy face icon.

-------//-------

"Hello," CJ said. Her face lit up. "Hi. You in New York? How was the flight? Did they feed you?" Her face scrunched up. "Oh... I didn't know that. I've never been on a plane, but is the food really that bad?... Uh-huh. What time is it there?... After five? You've got to be beat. I'm sure your parents are glad to see you... She made stuffed cabbage? Can you doggie bag some of it back for me?... Yeah, I understand. Enjoy your visit and tell your parents I said hi?"

She winked at Shannon and smiled. "Shawn? Thank you for calling," she whispered. "Call me when you get back?... Bye."

Shannon's eyebrows shot up. "He called you from New York? Wow, it really must've gone good."

-------//-------

Shawn hung up and stepped back next to his parents. "And CJ would be who?" his mom asked. "Are you seeing somebody new?"

"Not quite yet." He smiled. "But I hope to be soon. Let's get home. I'm starving." Then he added, "Oh, CJ said to say hi. And you need to make another batch of stuffed cabbage for me to take back to her when I leave."

"You haven't sounded this happy in I don't know how long. This is serious, isn't it?" his mom asked.

"I sure hope so," he said, as they headed for the parking structure and home.

-------//-------

In New York, the weather was unseasonably cold, and on Sunday morning it started snowing. That caused his parents to bring their anniversary party inside, which meant people were jammed into every available square foot of space in their small house.

Finally, his dad yelled, "That's it. We're taking the party to Jake's Bar down on the corner. Everybody out. We'll be down there in a few minutes after we clean up a little."

Shawn declined saying he needed to catch up on sleep. Instead, as soon as his parents left for the bar, he called CJ. It was her day off and he caught her down grooming Deveny. She finished Deveny while she talked to him, apologized for the noise and told him not to hang up while she rattled around in the tool shed. putting away the mat and curry combs. Finally, she reached the quiet of her trailer, or so he thought.

He heard a loud pop. "What are you doing?"

"Opening a beer. Want one?"

He went to the fridge, grabbed a beer, and told her, "Thanks. Got it." Then he headed into the living room, sat on the couch, and put his feet up on the coffee table.

"We had a slight change of plans here," he explained. "It started snowing this morning so, the party got moved to the corner bar. I'm surprised they didn't just hold it there to begin with, since everybody just about lives there. So, what's your day look like, and what did you do yesterday?"

When he finally stopped long enough to catch his breath, CJ jumped in. "What's going on?"

"Huh, what do you mean?" he asked.

"I mean, you've been jabbering since I said hello."

"Sorry."

"Don't be. I was bored out of my ass till you called, and I love talking to you. I just want to make sure you're okay."

He laughed as he realized he had been monopolizing the conversation. "I'm sorry. I guess I'm bored out of my ass too and needed someone to talk to."

"Well, I'm glad it's me. Do you think you should put in an appearance at the corner bar before your parents wonder where you're at?"

"Yeah, I made an excuse about needing to catch up on sleep, but you're right, I should put in an appearance, and soon. Another couple rounds of drinks and they'll forget I'm here and be trying to call me in Bonita."

The line went quiet, and for a second, she thought he had hung up. "CJ, is it okay if I call you when I get back from the bar?"

"Uh, sure, I'd love that, but are you sure you're going to want to?"

"Quite sure," he said.

"Okay, but if you get shit-faced and don't call, I'll understand."

"I'll call." Then he hung up.

Two hours later, CJ punched TALK and said, "Hello," before the first ring ever completed.

"What are you doing?" he asked.

"Ah, sitting in my sweats, drinking my second beer, and reading my vampire novel. How about you?"

"Wondering what you're doing."

"I just told you what I'm doing. Exactly how much have you had to drink?"

"I don't know. I'm not slurring my words, am I?"

"No, but you sound like you're about to go facedown. How about if you call me tomorrow and go get some sleep?"

"Okay," he replied.

"Shawn?"

"Yeah?"

"Thanks for calling me."

"You're welcome. Sleep well," he said and then hung up.

CJ turned off her Kindle, finished her beer, and turned out the light next to the bed. She broke into a big smile as she thought about Shawn. Two minutes later, she was sound asleep.

-----------//---------

Unlike New York, the weather in San Diego was its usual drop dead gorgeous, 72 degrees. CJ's days had settled into a very boring routine, with no new horses arriving and every day much like the last. At this rate, it would take forever for Wednesday to get there.

The highlight of her days were Shawn's calls. He called several times each day, and they spent hours filling each other in on the events, or lack thereof, of their day. She learned a lot about his family during the calls, and her envy grew as she realized how close they all were. During their Tuesday morning conversation, CJ suddenly realized how comfortable they both were talking about absolutely nothing. It also dawned on her that he would be home the next night and she would miss his phone calls.

--------//-------

Shawn too, had learned a lot about CJ over the past several days. Talking on the phone, rather than in person, had allowed her to open up and share some of her past. She still hadn't told him how she had gotten started on drugs or even if it was drugs. Nor did she tell him what had happened to send her to rehab, only that she had been in rehab and it had been the major turning point in her life.

During their conversations, she mentioned that the YWCA had taken her in and she had spent several months at Becky's House for Abused Women and Children while she underwent rehab and then counseling. After that, they had helped her find the job at the ranch while she completed counseling.

As she had gone through her story, Shawn pieced together what he was sure had happened to her. She had obviously been married and abused by her husband or if not married, then by her live-in boyfriend. That had likely led to drug or alcohol abuse and eventually landed her at Becky's House. Her story was not unique and one he had come face to face with on more calls than he cared to think about.

Chapter 9 - Welcome Home

The last five days had seemed like an eternity for both Shawn and CJ, but before either of them realized, Wednesday arrived. Shawn's parents dropped him off shortly after 10 am for his 12:30 flight out of JFK. As soon as his bag was checked, he passed through the security check and headed for his gate. He found a seat in the waiting area, pulled out his cell phone, and tapped the happy face.

CJ picked up on the first ring. "Shawn? Are you on your way home?"

"Not yet. I'm sitting at the gate waiting to board."

"What time does your flight get in?"

"Actually, there were no non-stop flights, so I'm going into L.A. Then I've got a connecting flight down to San Diego."

After a few seconds, he heard CJ take a deep breath. "Oh, I guess that means you'll be getting in pretty late?"

"No. Don't forget, I gain three hours coming back. Plus, my layover at LAX is just a little over an hour. So if everything is on time, I should get in a little after five. If I'm lucky and can catch a shuttle to the South Bay right away, I'll be home before seven."

"Oh." He could hear the disappointment in her voice. "I was hoping you would get in a little earlier and I would get to see you."

He smiled. "Me too... Hey, I've got an idea. How would you like to pick me up? I'll even take you to dinner." He could picture the smile growing on her face.

"I can do that. Where should I pick you up? What terminal and what airline?"

"Got a pencil handy?"

"Go ahead," she said.

"Okay, I'm on American Eagle, Flight 2624, due to arrive at 5:10. Oh, and I'll be coming into the commuter terminal."

Her voice lit up. "Got it. I'll be waiting." Then she added, "I missed you."

"Me too," he said.

"You missed you too?" She chuckled.

"Smart-ass. I'll see you in a few hours."

"Fly safe, Shawn," she whispered, then hung up.

Shawn's flight into LAX was only five minutes late, and his connection to San Diego left right on time. At exactly 5 pm, they touched down and quickly taxied over to the commuter terminal.

Walking through the door and into the terminal, he found her standing right in front with a smile that went from ear to ear, as she greeted him with a loud, "Hi."

He stopped in front of her. "You have no idea how nice it is to see you waiting for me. Is it okay if I kiss you?"

He started to bend down to kiss her when she said, "No."

Completely puzzled, he asked, "No?"

"You heard me. No. The person waiting always gets to kiss the person coming home, not the other way around. Don't you watch TV?" she asked. Then she pulled him into a long kiss.

When they finally broke off the kiss, he smiled at her. "Guess I need to watch more TV." She started to turn, but he pulled her back. "Wait." He kissed her again. "That's from my mom." Kissing her yet again, he said, "And that's from my dad." He kissed her again. "And that's from my brother." When they came up for air, he added, "Can't forget my cousin," and pulled her back in.

"I'm really liking your family," she finally mumbled. "And picking you up at the airport."

She reached over and took a small cooler out of his hand. "I can carry that for you. What's in it? Your lunch?"

"No, Your stuffed cabbage. My mom made a fresh batch last night and packed it for you just before I left. I think you already won her over."

"I haven't even talked to her, much less met her."

He put his arm around her waist and steered her toward baggage claim. "You don't need to; I already told her all about you."

"Do I want to know what you told her?"

Smiling, he added, "No, but it's all good."

They grabbed his checked bag and headed for her truck. As she pulled out of the lot, he told her to turn right on Harbor, then left onto Harbor Island at the next light. Once they were on the island, he directed her to turn left and go all the way to the south end.

As she pulled into the parking lot for Island Prime Restaurant, she glanced at him. "Shawn, I'm dressed in shorts and a plain old top. Everybody going in is all dressed up."

"Don't worry. You're dressed just fine. We're not going in there."

"What do you mean we're not going in there? There's nothing else here." Just as she said that, a couple stepped out of the bushes on a walkway at the far end of the building. Once she realized the walkway was there, she saw the sign for "C-Level Seating."

They headed for the sign and met the hostess at a small stand just inside the bushes. She smiled and asked Shawn if they would like to sit on the patio or inside. Shawn looked over at CJ, whose eyes and mouth were wide open.

"Do you want to sit inside or outside?" he asked her.

"Are you kidding? Who would ever want to sit inside?"

The hostess smiled at Shawn, then directed her next question to CJ. "Would you like to sit by the fire pit or next to the water?"

"Water," came CJ's response as she turned to take in the patio.

Her eyes were drawn to the fire pit that ran down the center of the patio and the mesmerizing flames dancing just above the top edge. On the left side was a row of tables against the fire pit, a small aisle, and a second row of tables against the bushes they had entered through. On the right side was another row of tables against the pit, another aisle, and finally, a row of tables against a rail right at the water's edge.

The hostess walked them to the far side of the patio and sat them at the last table in the row by the water. As she was sitting down, CJ noticed some steps just beyond their table, leading down to another patio. On the left side of the lower patio, set into the bushes, were what looked like two green and white striped tents that had been transported from an oasis somewhere in the Sahara.

"What are the tents for?" CJ asked the hostess.

"Oh, those are our private cabanas. If you have a function and don't want to hold it in the restaurant or on the public patio, we can set you up in one or both of the cabanas. Each one holds about twenty people, and you'll have your own private patio with one of the best views of San Diego Bay."

"Thank you," CJ mumbled, still trying to take everything in.

As soon as the hostess left, Shawn reached over and gently closed her mouth.

"Oh my God, Shawn. This place is unbelievable."

From her seat, CJ looked out at San Diego Bay. Directly in front of her, off in the distance, the Coronado Bridge sat spanning the channel leading to the South Bay area. To the right, across the bay, was Coronado Island and two aircraft carriers parked next to North Island Naval Air Station. To the left was the esplanade walkway, running alongside the harbor from the airport to the cruise ship terminal and the USS Midway Museum at the far end. Providing a backdrop to all that was the lit-up skyline of downtown.

Shawn sat next to her and pointed out the various attractions and areas of the city as she took everything in. Finally, she wrapped her arms around his arm and leaned her head against it.

She glanced up at him. "Thank you for this. I never knew any place like this existed."

"The view is gorgeous, isn't it? And the food and service are as amazing as the view. This is one of my favorite places, and I never get tired of coming here. Island Prime, the steakhouse inside, is excellent too, but I just can't bring myself to sit anywhere but the patio."

The waitress appeared, and they both ordered a Corona while they figured out what they wanted to eat. Several orders came out, and CJ commented, "Everything looks fantastic, but it also appears to be a lot of food. I have no idea what to order, and honestly, I'm not that hungry. I missed lunch and ended up nibbling on some junk food before I left because my stomach was grumbling. Sorry."

"Actually, I'm not very hungry either for pretty much the same reason. After gorging myself on my mom's food all week, my stomach started growling when they came by with the food cart, so I grabbed something. For a change, it wasn't all that bad. How about if we order a salad and an appetizer and split everything? That way there's not going to be a lot of food, and you'll get to taste several things. You okay with something a little spicy?"

CJ smiled at him. "Spicy works for me. You know, I could run out and grab your mom's stuffed cabbage, and we can ask them to heat it up."

Shawn laughed. "Uh... I don't think they would like that. Besides, that's *your* stuffed cabbage. She made it especially for you."

"I can't believe she did that. I know I'm going to like her when we meet." *Oh, great, CJ. Just invite yourself into his family, why don't you.* Trying to recover, she added, "I mean, if I get to meet her."

Shawn quickly let her off the hook. "Oh, you'll definitely meet her. Sooner, rather than later, if she has her way. She wants to be sure to give you all the *dirt* on me before I've convinced you of what a *nice* guy I am."

CJ hugged his arm tighter. "She's too late."

The waitress came back with their Coronas, and Shawn ordered the crusted brie appetizer and a Skirts on Fire salad, then told the waitress they were going to split the salad.

The waitress looked at CJ, then Shawn. "Great choices. The brie and Skirts on Fire are two of my favorites."

After the waitress left, CJ asked, "Why do they call the salad Skirts on Fire?"

"They lightly coat a skirt steak with spices and grill it. Then they cut it into thin strips and put it on top of a mix of salad greens and vegetables. Thus the name, Skirts on Fire. I love it. The spiciness of the steak adds just enough bite to wake up your taste buds, without being overly spicy or overwhelming everything else. The first time I had it, I was amazed at what a great complement the steak is to the greens and everything else."

CJ's eyebrows went up. "I never would have taken you for a salad kinda guy. You look more… meat and potatoes to me."

"You're right. I'm not a big salad fan, but I almost always order the Skirts on Fire salad when I'm here. It's such a fantastic combination and… it does have steak in it, so my Hunter-Barbecuer reputation stays intact."

106

Chuckling, CJ stared at him. "Hunter-Barbecuer?"

Grinning, Shawn explained, "Yeah, that's the modern equivalent of the hunter-gatherers from days of yore. Where have you been all your life? Didn't your parents ever let you out?"

"Actually, they didn't, but I somehow think it wouldn't have made much difference if they had." Now laughing, she added, "Days of yore? Hunter-Barbecuers? Did the oxygen masks drop during your flight and, by chance, you didn't get one? Or perhaps the igniter on your Weber grill didn't work and you inhaled too much propane? How about—"

"Okay, okay. I got the message. I've met my match... No pun intended."

They were both giggling like a couple of school kids when the waitress arrived with their order. She set everything on the table and smiled. "You two are having way too much fun over here."

CJ pointed at Shawn. "He started it."

"Oh, you both looked like you were holding your own to me," the waitress said, smiling. Then, she lowered her voice. "It's just nice to see two people laughing and enjoying each other's company, instead of sitting here texting or talking on their cell phones like two strangers. Enjoy your meal. I'll check back in a bit to see if you need anything."

The waitress had split the salad for them. CJ gasped. "Oh my God, that's half a salad? I'm never going to be able to finish all this."

While CJ dug into her salad, Shawn put some brie on a piece of toast and set it, along with some jalapeno jelly, on her side plate. "When you come up for air, try some of this."

107

"Mmmm… This is to die for," CJ mumbled through her third mouthful of salad. "You're right. The spices on the steak are wonderful, and it sets off the salad perfectly." Pointing her fork at her side plate, she asked, "What's the green stuff?"

"That's jalapeno jelly. Spread a little on the brie. It adds a little bit of sweetness and spice to the brie. Trust me, you'll like it."

"Yeah, if I can get my face out of this salad." She set her fork down and picked up the slice of toast with the brie on it. After spreading a little bit of jalapeno jelly on top, she took a bite. "Yum. This is unbelievable. I've died and gone to foodie heaven."

Shawn watched as CJ alternated between the salad and the brie, throwing in a *Mmmm.* each time she switched from one to the other. The only time she paused was to point out a very large ship rounding North Island and heading toward the bridge. "What in the world is that? It's mammoth."

"That's a car carrier. It's bringing in cars from Japan and headed for the dock in National City where a lot of the dealerships are. It's not unusual to see two or three of them unloading down there."

"Is that going to fit under the bridge?"

He smiled. "I hope so or we're going to have a front-row seat to a very big news story."

He looked down at her empty plates and added, "I thought you weren't going to be able to finish everything."

"Are you kidding? There was no way I was leaving any of that."

108

The waitress came by and asked if they were interested in dessert. They both passed and ordered coffee instead.

As they sat enjoying their coffee, CJ glanced at her watch and said, "Shawn, I hate to do this, but I have to get back. Kate had to go out of town so I'm in charge tomorrow, and I need to be up super early."

"I'd hoped we could spend a little more time together at my place before you had to drive back, but I understand. I've got some stuff to take care of tomorrow afternoon, but I thought I might spend the morning helping you at the ranch? That is, if you're okay with that?"

"Okay with that? Are you kidding? I'll take your company, and your help, any time. Actually, if you're only going to come out for the morning, I'll probably turn you over to Shannon, so she can train you. That is, if you don't mind? She can go over the basics and safety stuff with you and kind of show you where everything is."

"Sure, that's okay with me. Will I get to see you at all?"

"I've got a meeting with CAS, the Humane Society, the Viejas Fire Department, the Sherriff and Cal Fire to go over evacuation plans for both getting the horses out and boarding horses evacuated from other areas. It's going to take up pretty much my whole day, but I'll squeak out so I can spend a little time with you."

"I know how critical those coordination meetings are for making sure every possible scenario is covered during a wildfire, so don't worry about me. If you can get away for a minute or two during a break or lunch, that will be great, but I understand that the meetings come first." Smiling at her, he added, "Besides, I'm sure Shannon will take good care of me and keep me entertained."

"That's what I'm afraid of. Maybe I'll have Milton chaperone you two."

"Who's Milton?"

Laughing, she said, "You'll find out soon enough."

As they walked out to her truck, she took his arm again and laid her head on his shoulder. "I'm so glad you're back. I really missed you. And thank you for dinner and such a wonderful evening."

CJ dropped him off in front of his condo and after a very long toe curling kiss, she headed for the ranch.

Chapter 10 - Training Day

Shawn's alarm went off at 5 am. He smacked the off button, put on running shorts, a T-shirt, and staggered into the kitchen. While the coffee brewed, he laced up his running shoes. Carrying the mug into the bathroom, he brushed his teeth, ran his fingers through his hair, and headed out for his morning run.

He hadn't gotten a lot of sleep, and when he got back from his run he scared himself as he walked past the bathroom mirror. All night long he had tossed and turned as he wondered where their relationship was going. Every time he had dozed off, she would appear. Smiling at him with those sparkling hazel eyes, slightly pouty lips, barely turned up nose, and beautiful light olive skin; all framed by shimmering waves of dark brown hair.

After watching her at dinner last night, he realized he was mesmerized by her. Not only was she beautiful, she was extremely smart. She was also one of the most caring people he had ever met. And he adored her naiveté and childlike fascination with things he took for granted or didn't even notice.

As he stepped out of the shower he caught his reflection in the mirror. "Much better," he said and smiled because he was now sure he was in love with her. He also knew where he wanted their relationship to go and had a plan to steer it there. "Amazing what a shower will do," he said to the mirror.

At 6:30, Shawn turned off the highway, pulled up to the gate, and saw CJ standing inside the large corral near the entry. Their eyes met, and her smile spread from ear to ear. She waved, climbed the corral fence, and came over to unlock the gate.

After he drove through, she closed the gate, walked over, and got into the passenger seat. "Good morning," she said.

"Were you waiting for me?"

"Uh-huh. I didn't sleep much last night so I got an earlier start than I'd planned. Besides, I remembered that you couldn't get in, so I just putzed around in the turnout corral till you got here. Want some coffee? I just made a fresh pot," she said, before getting out and opening the second gate.

He drove over to the volunteer parking area and got out. "Coffee sounds great." Joining her, they headed up the hill toward the volunteer trailer.

Inside, CJ poured two mugs of coffee and handed one to him. "Shannon should be here any minute. All of the agencies are due around 7:30, and I've got a lot of handouts to collate and staple so I can't spend much time with you. Sorry." She stretched up and kissed him. "Thank you again for dinner last night." She kissed him again just as Shannon came through the door.

"Oops. Sorry. Want me to go out and come back in a bit?" Shannon said, laughing.

"No, we're done," CJ said.

Shannon looked at Shawn and raised her eyebrows. "I wouldn't be." She reached over and picked up the sign-in clipboard, scribbled her name, and looked at CJ. "You've got your emergency coordination meeting today, right? You need me to do anything other than my normal volunteer assignments?"

"Actually, I have other plans for you." She winked at Shawn, and Shannon noticed.

Looking back and forth between them, Shannon asked, "What? What are you two up to?"

"All the volunteers today are old hands, so dish out the assignments, then cut them loose on their own. I'd like you to spend the morning with Shawn. Show him where everything is and go over what needs to be done every day. Cover the rules and safety procedures with him. I need him to be trained just like a new volunteer. Oh, and you've only got him for this morning so don't worry about introducing him to the horses. I'll do that some other time."

"Oh, wow, this is gonna be tough. You trust me with him? Hell, I don't even trust me with him. You sure you want to do this?"

CJ looked at Shawn with a big smile then turned back to Shannon. "In case you haven't figured it out yet, I'm claiming him. So you mess with him, and I'll hurt you... bad. Understand?"

Shannon stepped back and saluted. "Aye, aye, *El Capitiana*. No messing with the boy toy. Got it." She turned to Shawn. "Follow me, mate... uh, matey? Pay attention, pass all your tests, and there will be an extra ration of gruel in your lunch bowl. Fail... and it'll be a flogging and the stocks for you." With that, Shannon turned and, doing her best peg-leg impression, limped and scraped her way to the door.

Shawn smiled at CJ, who shrugged and said, "See what happens when you spend too much time out here in the boonies? Good luck. See you later."

After another quick kiss from CJ, he followed Shannon out the door. He found her at the picnic table with two of the volunteers and the third walking up the hill. She told them all to go sign in and, after they returned, introduced Shawn. She gave each of them their assignments and explained that she would be giving Shawn a tour and initial volunteer briefing. Immediately, all three female volunteers offered to take her place.

"Sorry, he's mine," she said, sticking her tongue out.

113

The first half of the morning was spent with Shannon giving him the grand tour. She pointed out where everything was, what livestock they had, and where each was housed. Returning to the picnic table, she went over the safety rules, emergency procedures, and who to notify for each type of emergency making especially sure that he was aware of the rattlesnakes that resided on the ranch and what to do if an animal or someone were bitten. Just before they broke for a midmorning snack, she introduced him to Stanley, the ranch *guard dog*.

While they had been touring the ranch, Shawn noticed the various agency representatives going into the volunteer trailer. Just as he and Shannon came back to the picnic table, CJ led the group past them for a quick tour of the ranch.

As they filed past, someone called out. "Hey, Shawn. What are you doing here?"

Shawn stood up and shook hands with the Viejas fireman. "Hi, Jake. I'm getting trained." He turned, reached down and helped Shannon up. "Jake, this is Shannon. She's the volunteer coordinator and trainer here at the ranch."

Jake shook Shannon's hand, "Hi, Shannon. He behaving himself?"

Shannon nodded. "As best as can be expected. He's actually taught me a few things about safety and rattlesnakes."

Just then CJ came up, turned Jake toward the group, and looked at Shawn. "Stop distracting my meeting," she said. Then she winked at Shannon. "Only a half ration of gruel for him at lunch." Standing on her tippytoes, she gave Shawn a quick peck on the lips. "Behave yourself." Doing a princess wave at them over her shoulder, she led the group toward the stalls. As they left, Jake gave Shawn a big smile that pretty much said *guess we know why you're here*.

114

After sharing some chips and cheese bites with him, Shannon made a point of reminding him to be sure to bring snacks and a lunch with him next time. From there, they headed toward the supply shed.

Passing Stanley, sitting with his food dish in his mouth, Shawn asked, "Doesn't anybody feed him?"

"Only about five times a day," she responded. "Does he look starved to you? He would be as big as a cow if we filled his dish every time he thinks we should feed him."

Arriving at the supply shed, Shannon went over everything inside, then moved on to the tool shed. She explained what tools they had and what each was used for.

Catching the look on Shawn's face, she smirked. "I know this is pretty lame, but you would be amazed at what some of the volunteers try to do with tools sometimes. A lot of them don't know a pitch fork from a golf cart much less what each is used for." Laughing, she added, "Some of our best entertainment comes from watching a new volunteer try to pick up a pile of horse shit with a hay rake or pitch fork… especially if the horse has the runs."

For his final lesson, Shannon explained how to build a wheelbarrow toolkit. "It may seem stupid and simple, but believe me, when you're out in the back forty and someone didn't include something you need in your kit, you're not going to be a happy camper. You'll put on enough miles as it is without having to trudge all the way back to the shed for another tool every five minutes."

As they walked back toward the picnic table, Shannon added, "You probably know this, but I'll remind you anyway. It can be very cold early in the morning and scorching by noon out here so dress accordingly. I always recommend that people dress in layers as well as keep an old jacket or sweatshirt in their truck, along with other clothes they might need."

"Well, I'm done. Any questions?" she asked, as they sat back down at the table.

"You're amazing," Shawn said, then added, "The volunteers have no idea how lucky they are to have you training them. You may have learned a few things from me, but several things you covered I'm going to add to my safety lectures. If you're okay with it, I might even ask you to come join me? You would be great with the Bonita horsey set and the teen groups. Not only would you *wow* them, you might even find a few new volunteers for the ranch."

Giving him a big smile, she said, "I'd be happy to. I love doing this. I know I kid about people not knowing things, but honestly, that's part of what makes me feel so good when I'm doing this. If I can keep one person from getting bit by a rattler or passing out from heatstroke, I've done a good job."

"No wonder you and CJ get along so well. She's really lucky to have you helping her out here."

Shannon nodded her head. "Yeah, she's my idol. Some people may not think so, but I think she's the best."

He started to ask Shannon about her comment then thought better of it. It wasn't fair to pump her for information and put her friendship with CJ at risk. Changing subjects, he asked her about college, what she was studying and how long she had to go to finish. Just as she got started telling him about her major, CJ came out of the trailer.

She walked over and sat down next to Shawn. "You two all done?"

116

"Shannon is absolutely amazing," Shawn told CJ. "You're lucky to have her out here training your volunteers. I've just asked her if she would like to help me with some of my safety lectures, and she's graciously accepted."

CJ took Shannon's hand. "You don't need to convince me about how wonderful she is nor how lucky we are to have her. And I couldn't ask for a better friend." Turning back to Shawn, she apologized, "I'm sorry, but I need to get back in there. Any chance we can catch up with each other tonight? I don't know how long this meeting will go, but my guess is we'll wrap up no later than 6, and I could drive into Bonita right after."

"CJ, I would love to, but I've got a ton of stuff to take care of after being in New York all week. Then at 5, I've got to be at the station for the same kind of coordination meeting you're having. Ours will only be internal, so they can pass on what they came up with at the joint meeting Monday. Fire season, if there is such a thing anymore, is just about on us, and these meetings are critical for updating lessons learned from 2003 and 2007."

The disappointment on CJ's face was obvious and Shannon said, "I'll be happy to take your place in the meeting if that will give you two a little time with each other."

"Thank you, but I actually came out to tell you I want you in there too. The meeting is going really well, but we've had to scrap some of the old plans and come up with new ones and I want you to be a part of that. Shawn and I will just have to wait."

"Actually, we'll not be waiting too long. I planned on coming back out tomorrow when I can spend the whole day. If it's okay?"

CJ lit up with a smile. "Oh, Shawn, I'd love that." She bent over and kissed him, then pulled Shannon up. "Come on, girl. We gotta get in there. Put your thinking cap on because we can use all the ideas we can get and this is more your area than mine."

Shawn stood up, then turned to Shannon. "Thank you for being such a wonderful trainer, and I was serious about having you help me." He gave her a big hug. Before releasing her, he lowered his head beside hers and whispered, "It's not hard to understand why CJ adores you, and by the way, so do I."

He gave Shannon a quick peck on the cheek then Shannon took CJ's arm and the two of them disappeared into the trailer before he turned and walked down the hill to his truck.

Chapter 11 - A Day Off

CJ woke to someone knocking on the door and the sun blaring through the window. "Oh God, what time is it?" She looked at the clock and realized it was 8:15. "Oh crap." She grabbed her robe off the hook and slipped it on as she headed for the door.

She found Shannon, grinning from ear to ear, standing next to Shawn when she opened the door.

"I found him down by the gate when I got here. He was afraid to come up and wake you," she added.

"Oh God, I can't believe I slept this late. I should have had half the horses fed by now."

Shannon glanced at Shawn, then back at CJ. "I've got a great idea. Why don't you take the day off? If anyone deserves it, you do. I can't remember the last time you had a day off and enjoyed yourself. Besides, it's the perfect day. There are four volunteers scheduled, and even if only half of them show up, we can easily get everything done without you. Come on, CJ. Shawn? Can you take her somewhere far, far away and make sure she enjoys herself?"

Shawn looked at Shannon, then at CJ. "Honest. I did not put her up to this. But I'm seriously considering hiring her as my front man—uh, woman. I'm game if you are, CJ, but if you'd rather just sit around and relax or read, I'm…"

Shannon started shaking her head. "OH NO. If she does that, she'll be down in the stalls putzing around as soon as you turn your back. You need to take her somewhere else. Somewhere that will get her mind off this place for a while. Come on, you two. I'm offering you a mini vacation, for cripes sake. Please,

119

please, please? Shawn, just pick her up and stuff her in your truck the way she is. Even if she gets away, she can't run far in bare feet with only a robe on." She looked at CJ. "Okay, final threat. If you don't go with him, I'll go."

CJ smiled at Shawn. "You think maybe she wants me to go with you? Are you sure you're okay with this?" Without thinking, she blurted out, "I had to fill my tank the other night, so I'm pretty broke. That means you'll have to pay for everything and wait till I can pay you back for my share." *Oh God. You just told him you spent your last couple of bucks so you could pick him up at the airport. Great going, CJ.*

Shannon looked at her. "I'll pay for your share. Just *go*. Go shower, throw something on, and get out of here. I'll entertain him till you're ready. Come on, Shawn. I need you to lug some hay bales for me while she farts around getting ready."

Shannon turned and went down the steps while CJ and Shawn started laughing. "And I was wondering how I was going to ask you to go to lunch. Guess Shannon took care of that bit of awkwardness for me. CJ, are you really okay with this? We don't have to do this if you're not comfortable with it."

CJ turned serious. "I'm very comfortable with it as long as you are. Shannon's right. I really could use a day off. But. You have to promise me you'll let me pay you back for my share. Deal?"

"Deal. You can pay me back."

-------//-------

Shawn turned to follow Shannon. Knowing CJ had spent all of her money on gas to pick him up, having no intention of ever accepting money from her.

He joined Shannon down in the hay shed while CJ showered and got dressed. "You do know what you did was awfully nice?"

"I hope I wasn't being too forward in assuming you were okay spending the day with her."

"Are you kidding? Gee, let me see. You set me up so I can spend the day with the prettiest girl I've ever met and you want to know if it's okay? Someone would have to be deaf, dumb, blind, and stupid not to want to spend the day with her. I just hope I can make it a day she'll remember."

Shannon stared straight into Shawn's eyes. "Shawn, please be careful with her? Like I said yesterday, she's special. No, she's *very* special. I'm only twenty-three and she's just a few years older than me, but I don't think I'll ever meet anyone I'll admire more. It's not my story to tell and I'm sure she'll tell you when she's ready, but she has been through stuff most of us can't even imagine. Her life before coming here was a horror story that most women don't live through. One she almost didn't live through. But look at her. Somehow she came out of all that being the strongest person I've ever met. There's not an ounce of bitterness in her."

Shawn hugged her. "She's really lucky to have you in her life."

She laid her head on his shoulder, hugged him back, and whispered, "Why do you have to be so good looking… and taken? You wouldn't happen to have a brother in your back pocket, would you?"

While Shannon filled the color-coded buckets with the correct food for each horse, Shawn brought several bales of hay down on the golf cart and distributed them between the stalls. Locating them along the path, he cut the bands so Shannon could easily distribute the hay to each of the stalls.

Finally, he strung the extension cord to the farthest stall and set up the trough pump for her. As he bent over the trough to make sure everything was working, CJ walked up.

He sensed her before he saw her. Smiling, he looked up. He took in every inch of her, starting at her feet. She had on an almost new pair of light gray running shoes with dark green shoe laces and a pair of jeans that fit her perfectly. Not too tight, but tight enough that they left no doubt about what a great figure she had. Covering the top of her was a forest green and light gray hoodie that dipped low enough in the front to show off a bit of cleavage. The hoodie looked soft and cuddly enough to make him want to get lost in it, and the color brought out the green in her hazel eyes.

Her wavy brown hair was down and the soft natural curls made it glisten in the sunlight. As usual, she had on very little makeup, allowing the dark brown of her hair to perfectly frame her light olive skin.

Finally, he reached the feature that fascinated him the most. Her eyes. Those wonderful eyes with their flecks of gold, contrasting with her now sea-green irises. He had never seen eyes that sparkled like hers, and he was totally mesmerized by them. His face lit up in a smile. *She has to be the prettiest woman I've ever seen.*

CJ watched him checking her out, and when their eyes finally met, her eyebrows raised. "Do I pass?"

"Do you ever. I'm not sure about that top, though. It looks so soft, warm, and snuggly that I'm going to have a very hard time keeping my hands off you. I mean it. Consider yourself warned."

Turning serious, she stared at him. "Wow, so the top's the only reason you'd want to put your hands on me?"

He looked bewildered at first, then seemed to realize what she was doing. "Oh no you don't. You know exactly what I meant. I'm sure the body inside is much softer and more cuddly than the top, but since we'll be out in public, I'll limit myself to playing with the top." Then he added, "For now."

Shawn stood up, took CJ's hand, and gently pulled her toward his truck parked down by the ranch gate. She insisted on getting the gates as they left the ranch, and just as she was about to close the second gate, Ami pulled up.

Ami smiled at Shawn and yelled, "Hi, Shawn." Then turned toward CJ. "Well, are you going to open the gate or what?"

CJ shook her head. "You know, you really need to work on your manners, Ami." She opened the gate, and after Ami drove through, CJ closed it and climbed into Shawn's truck.

She reached over and gently touched Shawn's arm. "Before we go, thank you so much for doing this. I can't remember the last time I had a day off and actually went somewhere. But please, let's not spend a lot of money? I'm pretty broke right now, and I don't know when I'll be able to pay you back. A Big Mac and a walk in the park would be just fine with me."

Shawn couldn't help but stare. "You're amazing, you know that? Your only fun day ever and you would be perfectly happy with a walk in the park and a Big Mac."

CJ shrugged. "Simple things for simple minds."

"There is nothing simple about you, CJ, especially your mind. And I mean that in a good way. Look, I'll make you a deal. Today's on me. I know. I know. I promised I'd let you pay me back, and I will. You can spend a day introducing me to the horses on the ranch. Or you can cook dinner for me some time, how's that?"

She returned his stare. "Shawn, that's not the same, and you know it. But if you're willing to accept introductions and dinner as repayment, I'd be happy to be your guide and cook something for you. I'll warn you, though, I'm not the world's best cook. Actually, I think my cooking was the reason Pepcid AC was invented."

He put the truck in drive and pulled out onto the highway. "By the way, what gives with you and Ami? What did you ever do to piss her off and make her dislike you so much?"

"I'm here, that's what I did," she said. "Ami is a very confused seventeen year old with a lot of problems, so try to cut her a little slack, please? Shawn, there's a lot about me you don't know. Ami doesn't exactly see me as someone to look up to. She sees me more as a punching bag. Someone to take her frustrations out on. She's had a pretty troubled past, and if she can keep everybody's attention on my past, she thinks they'll forget about hers. She's really not a bad kid. Nobody's ever taken the time to try to understand her and help her, that's all. Anyway, subject for another day." A grin lit up her face. "Now. Where are you taking me for my fun day?"

As they entered the interstate, he looked over at her. "It's a secret, but I'll give you a hint. Do you like water?"

"Yes," she answered, "but I was hoping for a beer, actually."

He started laughing. "I meant water as in the ocean, but yes, you can have a beer."

"Yay! And yes. I love the ocean. That's that big thing with water and ships in it, isn't it?" He looked at her, and she stuck her tongue out at him. He responded by telling her she needed to be careful or McDonald's might just run out of beer before they got there.

Smiling from ear to ear, he thought about how much fun she was to be with. How he loved her teasing him and teasing her back. He had never felt so comfortable with anyone in his entire life, and she clearly felt the same about him. He had no idea why there was no man in her life, but was so very glad there wasn't. He also knew that he was going to do everything he could to make sure her day was special.

Heading west into San Diego, CJ listened while Shawn explained that he had grown up and lived close to one ocean or another all his life. He loved the water and couldn't fathom living inland and having to travel days to get to an ocean. Or worse yet, never having seen an ocean at all. The ocean was full of life and, like life itself, peaceful and soothing one moment and angry the next. Its waves were calming and beautiful as they rolled ashore. Even during storms, he would stand out in the rain and marvel at the beauty and power of the ocean. He compared it to many of the wild animals in the world, majestic and powerful, to be admired and respected, not feared.

CJ sat quietly, in awe of Shawn's love for the ocean. She so loved his analogy of the ocean being like a wild animal. She pictured herself watching a wild horse prancing in a field as he described the ocean's majesty, beauty, and the peacefulness of waves rolling ashore. Then she saw that same horse running flat out across a mesa as he described marveling at the power and beauty of a storm.

She smiled as she realized Shawn's oceans were her horses and her horses were his oceans. They were one and the same. No wonder they felt so comfortable with each other. They both marveled at and treasured the very same things. They just saw them in different media.

CJ realized she would never again look at the ocean without seeing it through Shawn's eyes. Now all she had to do was make sure he made the same discovery about her horses.

They exited the freeway and wound their way through an industrial area, finally turning into a marina. Shawn pulled into a parking space directly in front of the Galley at the Marina.

"God, this is gorgeous. Where are we?" CJ asked.

"We're at the Chula Vista Marina, and the Galley is another of my favorite places. It's not real fancy, but the food is great and service is always outstanding."

He walked around to her side of the truck, opened her door, and took her hand to help her out. As they came up the steps, the hostess had a big smile. "Hi, Shawn. Where have you been?"

Shawn smiled back. "Good morning, Linda. Linda, this is CJ. CJ, this is Linda. Any chance of getting a table out back, kind of away from everybody?"

"Nice to meet you, CJ." Linda winked before turning back to Shawn. "Sure. We're not very busy, so I'll put you down at the end and try not to seat anybody close to you."

Linda guided them past a large covered patio on the left, an open air bar on the right, and out onto another long patio overlooking the marina. She sat them at the far end, handed them menus, and took their drink orders. Less than five minutes later, she was back with two Coronas, two glasses of water, and setups for both of them. She explained that no one was assigned to this area so she would give them a few minutes, then be back to take their order.

CJ sat there, wide-eyed. In front of them was a small channel with multiple docks on the other side. Beyond that, she could make out the breakwater and an entrance to the harbor way off to the left. Within the marina, there had to be hundreds of boats of every size, shape, and description. White and sea blue seemed to be the colors of the day, along with nautical US and pirate flags. She was absolutely mesmerized by the fluttering flags and bobbing boats everywhere.

Shawn reached over and gently pushed up on her chin to close her mouth.

"Wow," was all she could say as he pulled his hand back. "Shawn, this is wonderful. The breeze smells so clean and fresh, and the gentle rocking of the boats and clanging of things is so relaxing. The view and atmosphere are to die for." She reached across the table and took his hand in hers. "Thank you for sharing another of your favorite places with me. Between this and C-Level, if I lived near here, I'd never eat anyplace else."

Linda came back, ready to take their order. To Shawn, she said, "I know… The jalapeno and jack burger with our homemade chips." She smiled at CJ. "He is like *so* stuck in a rut. He's going to turn into a jalapeno if he keeps this up. What can I get for you?"

CJ looked up at her. "You're going to hate me, but the jalapeno and jack burger sounds really good as do the homemade chips."

"Oh, these people with no class. I see he's already made you a Jets fan too," Linda mumbled, as she turned, leaving CJ totally confused.

Shawn pointed at her chest and said, "Your hoodie and your shoes. You're dressed in Jets colors, forest green and gray. Good choice, I might add." As they waited for their food, Shawn asked, "So what's Deveny's story? How did she get to the ranch?"

"Deveny, my sweet and wonderful Deveny," said CJ. "She was first seen near the desert, out in the middle of nowhere, by a rancher on his way home. He called a friend in the Department of Agriculture who had a team doing some work in the area near where he had seen her. The next morning the DOA team found her about two miles away, just wandering around. They don't know how long she had been out there without any food or water, but she was terribly emaciated. The poor girl was absolutely terrified, and it took several attempts before they finally calmed her down enough to get a lasso over her head. That's when they noticed what had been done to her. Whoever owned her had cut the brand out of her hide so she couldn't be traced back to them."

Shawn stared at her. "Who would do such a thing? I can't believe anyone could be that cruel."

"Now you know just *one* reason why horses need to be rescued," CJ said. "Anyway, a horse organization called the Return to Freedom Wild Horse Sanctuary stepped in and took her. If they hadn't done that, she would have ended up in a slaughter house, for sure. Since Return to Freedom couldn't keep her, they asked us to take her in, nurse her back to health, and provide a home for her."

CJ looked at the pained expression on Shawn's face. "I know. It breaks your heart to hear what someone did to her, but she's safe now and, as long as I'm alive, no one will ever hurt her again."

Just then, Linda arrived with their food. As she set the plates down, she glanced at Shawn, then CJ, then back at Shawn. "Are you okay?" she asked.

"Yeah," he whispered. "I'm okay."

Linda glanced back at CJ with an expression that clearly said, *if you hurt him, you'll have me to deal with,* then left.

CJ reached across the table and put her hand over Shawn's hand. "I'm sorry. Not a good subject for when we're supposed to be having fun."

Shawn stared at her and wondered how in the world she dealt with stuff like this and kept her sanity, not to mention her belief in people. "My God, she must be terrified of people after that."

"She was," CJ answered. "When we first got her, she would cower in the back of the stall whenever anyone got close. After working with her daily over the past couple of years, though, she's started to trust people again. I'm pretty sure it was a man that mutilated her because she's okay around women, but still goosey around men.

"Come on, let's eat. Our burgers are getting cold and I'm drooling just looking at these chips." With that, she picked up her burger and took a giant bite. After a couple more bites, a dozen chips, and several big swigs of beer, she set what was left of her burger down, wiped her lips with her napkin, and said, "This is to die for. I see why you're stuck in a rut, and if Linda thinks this is a no-class burger, then I'm glad I have no class. By the way, you do know she likes you? A lot."

Shawn shook his head. "Yeah, we actually dated a few times and she's a sweetheart, but nothing happened for either of us, so we're just good friends." Feeling uncomfortable talking about his relationship with Linda, Shawn asked, "How did Deveny get her name?"

"Her full name is Deveny's Ruckus. Ruckus for the uproar her heartbreaking story created, and Deveny for the brand inspector at the DOA who fought so hard to save her." She reached over, put her hand over his, and added, "There really are some good people out there too."

They finished their lunch and headed out. As they left, he asked her what she wanted to do next.

"Hey, you're the one leading this parade." She swept her arm toward the marina and added, "My day's already perfect."

Linda came out as they reached the stairs. "Bye, Shawn. Please don't stay away so long?" She gave CJ another wink. "You too, CJ."

Shawn opened her door, helped her in, then walked around to the driver's side. As he got in, CJ asked where they were off to next.

"Still like water?" he asked.

"Yeah, but I was actually hoping for a Margarita next." He just shook his head as he started the truck.

Getting on the 5 north, he drove toward downtown and got off at the airport exit. When they reached the harbor, he turned left, then parked directly in front of the Star of India, which was in full sail.

CJ, mouth wide open, stared through the windshield, taking in the massive snow-white sails that filled her view.

Shawn reached over and, again, gently pushed up on her chin.

"WOW." With a smile from ear to ear, she looked at him. "What is it?"

"Arrgh, matey. That thar would be a ship," he growled back. She reached over and punched him.

"I figured that much out on my own. What ship?"

Still smiling, he pointed to *Star of India* painted on the side.

"Oh Shawn, she's gorgeous. Can we go aboard?"

"Only if we hurry because our personal tour leaves in two minutes." Without even thinking about it, she leaned over and kissed him on the lips. Then she let out a big squeal.

At the gate to the gangway, Shawn flashed something at the ticket taker, and he ushered them through. Their guide was waiting for them at the top of the gangway. After introducing himself, he led them to the quarterdeck where he pointed out various features of the ship and gave them a brief description of the ship's history. He explained that she was the oldest active sailing ship in the world. She was built in 1863 and was one of the first ships to be built with an iron hull instead of wood.

He led them through various parts of the ship and went on to explain that she had initially been built to haul cargo between England and India and, later, was used to transport immigrants to Australia and New Zealand. During her first voyage, which took almost a year, her crew had mutinied, and during subsequent voyages, she had been severely damaged several times by cyclones, storms, and collisions. In total, she had sailed around the world twenty-one times, and volunteer crews still sailed her out into the ocean every November.

An hour later, he brought them back to the top of the gangway. He pointed to the steam ferry Berkeley, docked in front of the Star of India, then suggested they might want to wander through the museum inside and take in some of the other ships that were part of the Maritime Museum.

"Thank you so much," CJ said to their guide. "The ship and her history are fascinating. The picture you painted of immigrants spending almost a year on board before reaching Australia or New Zealand just blows my mind. I can't begin to imagine the hardships they must have endured in order to start a new life."

CJ and Shawn walked over to the Berkeley and into the museum located on her main deck. After spending close to an hour looking through the museum, they wandered over to the HMS Surprise where CJ latched onto another docent and milked him for every bit of information she could about the ship. Forty-five minutes later, it was obvious that the docent lived for this kind of thing, and he absolutely adored CJ and how she hung on his every word.

By 4 pm, they had added the steam yacht Medea, the B29 Russian submarine, the USS Dolphin Submarine, and the harbor pilot boat to their list of boats toured. By that time, it was also obvious that CJ had won the heart of every volunteer and docent at the museum. She had wooed every one of them with her unending curiosity and her ability to suck up every fact, story, and detail about the ships they could conger up.

Not once had her enthusiasm waned, as they went through story after story and fact after fact. And as each of them finished, she made sure she thanked them for their patience with her never-ending questions and for passing on not only their knowledge, but also their enthusiasm and passion.

Passing through the gift shop on the way out, Shawn pointed to the restrooms and told her he would meet her outside. When he came out, she was standing on the sidewalk, taking in every inch of the harbor that she could with her mouth hanging open again. He stopped less than a foot from her and stared, while slowly shaking his head.

"What?" she asked. Then she handed him a small bag from the gift shop and added, "This is for you." He opened the bag, reached in, and pulled out a small scale model of the aircraft carrier USS Ronald Reagan. "I'm sorry it's so small. I didn't have enough on me for the bigger one."

His grin went from ear to ear as he looked at her. "You are absolutely amazing. Do you know that there is not one single person on any of these ships that didn't fall completely in love with you this afternoon? You made every one of them feel like you had the most wonderful day of your life, thanks to them. Then what do you do? You spend your last few dollars on something that you knew would have special meaning to me."

He stepped closer, wrapped his arms around her, and kissed her gently on the lips. Her knees went weak as a fantastic tingle shot through her entire body, and he tightened his grip to keep her from falling.

He leaned his head back, then touched his forehead to hers as he whispered, "I have no idea why there's no guy in your life, but I'm glad there isn't. I'd like nothing more than to be that guy and see where this goes, if you're okay with that."

She looked deep into his eyes. "Shawn, I'm not what you think. I can't—" Just then, her phone rang.

Wow. Saved by the bell, she thought. She reached into her back pocket, pulled her phone out, and saw Kate's picture on the display. "I'm sorry. It's Kate, and I really should take it."

Shawn waited patiently while listening to her side of the conversation. It didn't take long for him to realize that Kate needed her back at the ranch for some kind of emergency.

When she hung up, she said, "I need to get back, right away."

"Is everything okay?" he asked.

"I don't know. All Kate said was the sheriff is there and they need me back as soon as I can get there."

Chapter 12 - Ami

CJ closed the gate after Ami drove through. As she turned to get into Shawn's truck, she didn't see Ami's hand come up and flip her off.

Ami headed for the ranch gate, and just as she reached it, her cell rang. "What now?" she answered, totally frustrated. She could sense the smirk on the caller's face, even over the phone.

"I told you to leave me some money."

"And I told you, I'm not a fucking bank," she shouted back.

"Listen, you're the one that wants me to get this stuff, and the shit doesn't grow on trees."

Ami ground her teeth. "How about you get one of those things called *a job*?"

"Up yours, bitch. I have a job."

"Right. How about a *real* job? Like one that pays in something other than a cheap high or quick hump?"

After a long pause, the person on the other end let out a deep breath. "Listen, I don't have time for this shit again. If you want the stuff, I need money."

"Alright. Alright. I'm on my way back." Ami turned the truck around, went back through the main gate, and headed home.

Six hours later she was back and in the mood to kill something or someone. Once again, she drove to the ranch gate, opened it, drove in, and parked in the volunteer parking area just inside. She got out and walked up the hill to the volunteer trailer.

As she got close to the trailer, Shannon came out and started down the stairs. At the bottom, she looked up, and noticed Ami and that the gate to the ranch was still open. "Ami, you left the gate open. Can you please go shut it?"

"I'm all the way up here already. Besides, I'm not staying long." With that, she disappeared into the trailer.

Shannon waited until Ami came back out. She told Ami they needed to talk and to have a seat at the picnic table. Reluctantly, Ami sat down.

"Look, I know you're not here because you want to be," Shannon began. "You've already been thrown out of two other court-ordered community service assignments, so this is like your last chance. If I were you, I would cut the crap, start obeying the rules, and treat everyone with a little respect. The gates get closed for a reason. If they're left open, the sheep and goats can just wander off the ranch. Then we've got to go find them and bring them back. It's not like we haven't got enough to do already without having to run around chasing after animals. And speaking of enough to do, where were you? You were supposed to be here this morning, and once again, everyone else had to pick up your chores."

Pasting on a big phony grin, Ami asked, "Are you done?"

"No," said Shannon. "As a matter of fact, I'm just getting started. I think everybody here has had it with your BS. We expect our volunteers to be here on time and do what they're assigned without us having to babysit them every ten seconds. We also expect them to work with each other. This isn't high school where you can bully your way through everything, and last time I looked, nobody died and left you in charge. So quit trying to force whatever you don't want to do on someone else and stop

135

demanding that everyone else has to do what you think needs to be done. You're not in charge. CJ and Kate are."

"So what's that make you? Aside from a big pain in my ass," Ami shot back.

Now it was Shannon's turn to paste on a big phony grin. "We went through all of this during volunteer orientation, where I'm sure you weren't paying attention to anything I said. I'm the volunteer coordinator and trainer. So it's my job to make sure you know the rules and follow them. I also hand out the assignments every day, so if you want every shit assignment that comes up, just keep giving me a ration of crap. I'll be happy to make sure you go home smelling nice and ripe every day."

Ami stood up, glaring at Shannon. She opened her mouth and started to say something, then closed it again.

With sheer hatred in her eyes, she stepped almost nose-to-nose with Shannon, completely invading her space. "If you ever threaten me again," she hissed, "I'll make you as lame as these dumb-shit horses and brand you so everybody knows you're my bitch." Reaching up, she grabbed Shannon's shirt then shoved her back.

-------//-------

Christine drove through the gate and wondered who had left it open. After parking, she started to walk back to close the gate, heard shouting, and turned toward the volunteer trailer. She looked up just in time to see Shannon go down.

She watched Ami walk over to Shannon, stand over her, and yell, "You want a piece of me? Come on, bitch." As Shannon tried to get up, Ami kicked out with her right foot and caught Shannon under the chin. Christine watched in horror as Shannon's head went back, slammed against the steel leg of the picnic table, then she slid to the ground.

Without even realizing it, Christine screamed, "What are you doing?" She started up the hill and reached into her back pocket.

Ami turned and looked down the hill at Christine. "You want some of this? Come on. I'll kick the crap out of both of you."

Oh God, Ami's gone crazy she thought, then looked over at Shannon and knew she was hurt and needed help. Realizing her phone was still in the truck, she turned and ran back the way she'd come.

Christine reached inside, grabbed the phone and dialed 911. Hearing nothing, she looked down, saw there were no bars showing and knew she was in one of the ranches many dead spots. She pulled her keys out, jumped in, started the truck and drove through the still open gate. When she got to the main gate, she skidded to a stop. Hoping to get a signal, she jumped out and looked up just in time to see a sheriff's car passing.

Yelling at the top of her lungs and waving her arms, she watched as the sheriff's deputy pulled into the turnout in front of the gate.

Jerking the gate open, she ran to the officer's window, and began yelling, "Please, you've got to help. We need an ambulance. Someone's being beat up. She's hurt bad. Please. She's going to kill her."

The deputy calmed Christine down and told her to move her truck and get in his cruiser. After pulling her truck to the side, she got in the sheriff's car, and they drove to the ranch entry gate just as Ami was trying to come out. The deputy stopped in the middle of the entryway and got out. He told Ami to park her truck, then told her and Christine to come with him.

As they walked up the hill, Ami grabbed the deputy's arm and pulled him around to face her. "She started it," she yelled. "I was just defending myself. She hates me. Everybody here knows it."

Christine shook her head. "That's not what I saw. You shoved her, then kicked her in the head when she tried to get up."

The deputy held up his hands. "Ladies, I'll get your statements after we get her some help and make sure she's okay." Then, he looked at Christine and asked, "Is that Shannon?"

She nodded and whispered, "Yes."

Bending over Shannon, the deputy reached for the button on his radio. "Dispatch, this is Jason. I'm at TNN ranch. I need fire and EMTs. I've got one female down with a head wound, and she appears to be unconscious."

The dispatcher responded, "Jason, any idea who it is and the extent of her injuries?"

"Yes" he responded. "It's Shannon. She has blood on the right side of her head, just above the ear, and is bleeding from the mouth. I'm not an EMT, Carol, but I think she'll be okay."

"Roger, Jason. ETA on fire is two minutes. We're lucky. We caught them on 8, heading back from another call."

"Copy, dispatch. ETA on fire two minutes."

He looked over at Christine and asked, "Where are CJ and Kate? Are they here?"

"I don't know," Christine said. "I just got here. I haven't seen them. They would've seen your car come in and come over if they were here, though."

"Thanks," Jason responded and got back on his radio. "Dispatch, this is Jason. It appears that both CJ and Kate aren't here. Can you notify them and ask them to come to the ranch?"

"Roger, Jason, already done. I just called Kate, and she's calling CJ now. Anything else I can do?"

"Not at the moment," he responded. "I think Shannon's starting to come around. I'll let you know how she is after the EMTs check her out. Don't worry, Carol. We'll take good care of your sister."

"Thanks, Jason," Carol responded.

And Ami mumbled, "Oh shit," under her breath.

Jason turned to Christine and tossed his car keys to her. "Do me a favor and move my car so fire and the EMTs can get in. Oh, and make sure we left the main gate open. Thanks." He pointed to Ami, then the picnic table bench. "You, young lady. Park your butt on the bench and don't even think about moving it till I tell you." Just then, a big pumper truck and EMT/Rescue ambulance from the Viejas Fire Department pulled through the main gate.

The pumper pulled past the gate on the road and stopped, leaving room for the ambulance to pull through the gate. The EMTs parked at the bottom of the hill just as Shannon coughed, spit out a mouthful of blood, and tried to sit up.

Jason reached over and gently held her shoulder so she couldn't sit up. "Stay put, freckles, till the EMTs check you out."

Shannon glared at him. "You call me freckles again, and you'll be the one that needs the EMTs. What the hell happened? The last thing I remember is going down, then the lights went out."

"I haven't taken anybody's statement yet, but Christine said Miss Personality over here pushed you, then kicked you when you tried to get up. From the blood on the leg of the table, I'd say your head bounced off that and out you went." Jason moved aside so the EMTs could check her out.

While the EMTs checked out Shannon, Jason took Christine's statement, which pretty much consisted of the same thing she had told him earlier. He then turned to Ami, who hadn't said a word since she sat down on the bench.

"Okay, Wonder Woman, let's hear your side of this."

"Up yours," Ami spat out. "I don't need to be Wonder Woman to take that bitch out. She started it. I was minding my own business. I just finished signing out, and she got in my face and shoved me. So I shoved her back. I can't help it if the dumb bitch lost her balance and slammed her ugly head on the bench. I just barely touched her. She's so retarded she probably just fell on her own."

Jason shook his head. "Okay, stay put till I tell you otherwise."

Jason went back over to Christine. "She claims Shannon pushed her first. Did you see Shannon push her?"

Christine shook her head. "No. All I saw was Ami shoving Shannon. If Shannon shoved her, it would've been before I got out of the truck or looked up the hill. But that's not like Shannon. It would really take a lot for her to do that."

Jason finished writing down Christine's comments and closed his note pad. He thanked Christine and walked over to where the EMTs were getting ready to load Shannon into the ambulance.

"How is she?" he asked them.

"Other than a nasty headache, I think she'll be okay, but we're going to run her to the ER just to be sure."

"Thanks, I need a minute with her," he said.

The EMTs walked back up to the picnic table to pack up the rest of their gear. Jason gently squeezed Shannon's shoulder. "You okay, freckles?"

Shannon rolled her eyes. "It's a good thing I'm strapped to this thing or you'd be gumming your food till your new teeth arrived. Stop. Calling. Me. Freckles."

"I've been calling you freckles since we were kids, and besides, I think they're cute."

"God, I hate you," she said.

Jason smiled. "Look, I need your side of this. What happened?"

"I'm not sure. Last thing I remember, we were arguing, and the next thing, I was going down. I think I was trying to get up when everything went black. All I know is my head hurts like hell and my mouth feels like the lacrosse team scored a goal in it."

"Ouch," Jason said. "Well, according to Christine, Ami shoved you, then kicked you in the mouth as you were trying to get up. But, according to Ami, you shoved her first and she was just defending herself. Oh, and... if you hit your head, you probably did it to yourself because you're a retarded piece of horse shit that nobody likes anyway."

Shannon started laughing. "How much of that is Ami, and how much is you?" she asked.

"Mostly Ami. A little me. Oh, and *I like you...* even if nobody else does."

Jason turned serious and asked her if she wanted to press charges against Ami. Then he bent over her and whispered in her ear, "I can take her in and beat her with a rubber hose till she talks." He looked around to make sure no one was near, then added, "Once we have her confession, she can disappear off the Coronado Bridge wearing a pair of cement shoes. Just say the word, freckles, and she's fish bait."

Shannon started laughing again then stopped. "Stop. Oh God that hurts." She looked at him. "Jason, seriously, what do you think I should do?"

"Honestly, it's your word against hers since Christine didn't see the start of it. But even if the charges are dropped, this will probably be the last chance she gets. Frankly, the juvi court has pretty much had it with her."

"Thanks, Jason. I really don't want to get her in any more trouble than she already is so I'll let it go. But I do need to talk with CJ and Kate about keeping her as a volunteer. The last thing we need is her beating the crap out of someone else."

Jason walked alongside the gurney as the EMTs took her to the ambulance. "I promised your sister I would let her know how you are. Okay to tell her you'll live?"

"Yeah. And feel free to tell her you did mouth-to-mouth and brought me back from the dead. That should win you a lot of points with her tonight. Actually, forget the mouth-to-mouth part. Just tell her you did CPR."

Jason smiled at her. "I might just do that."

As they loaded her into the ambulance, she yelled out, "Jason, how am I going to get home? Carol's on till midnight, and my truck's here."

"Don't worry. Let me see if Carol can catch Kate or CJ and have one of them meet you at the hospital. If not, I'm off in a few hours, and I'll come by and get you."

"Thanks. No wonder my sister really likes you. You're a good guy, Deputy Dawg."

Chuckling, Jason turned to walk back up the hill and pressed the button on his radio. "Dispatch, Jason."

"Go ahead, Jason."

"Carol, other than a nasty headache for a while, Shannon's going to be fine. They're running her to Scripps East County in El Cajon just to make sure. Can you see if you can catch Kate on her way out or CJ, wherever she is, and see if one of them can meet her at the hospital? She's still a little shaken up, and she's gonna need a ride home. If neither of them can do it, I'll be happy to go get her after I get off."

"Thanks, Jason. Let me see where Kate and CJ are."

Carol called Kate's cell, got her voice mail, and left a message. Then she dialed CJ who picked up immediately. "Hi, CJ, this is Carol at the sheriff's office. Can I ask where you are?"

"Sure," CJ replied. "We're about fifteen minutes from El Cajon, on our way to the ranch. What's going on, Carol?"

"Great, I caught you just in time. Can you detour and head over to Scripps East County Hospital? The EMTs are on their way there with Shannon."

143

"What? Is she okay?"

"She's fine. I don't know exactly what happened, but she was injured at the ranch. They're taking her to Scripps just to be sure everything's okay. I'd really appreciate it if you could be there for her. If I could ask another big favor, she'll need a ride back to the ranch too."

CJ took a deep breath. "Oh, Carol, you know I'd do anything for Shannon. God, I hope she's okay. I'll call you as soon as we know anything."

"Thanks, CJ. I've already called the hospital and asked them to call me as soon as they've had a chance to check her out. Jason answered the call at the ranch and he said it looks like she'll be okay, but I'll feel a lot better after a doctor looks at her."

CJ hung up and looked over at Shawn. "Can you get us to Scripps East County Hospital? Shannon's been hurt."

Shawn glanced at her. "Greenfield is a few exits up, and the hospital's right there. Is Shannon okay?"

"I'm not sure. That was Carol. She's a dispatcher with the sheriff's department and Shannon's sister. Jason, the deputy that answered the call at the ranch, said he was pretty sure Shannon would be okay, but they sent her to the hospital just to make sure."

"That's pretty much standard procedure," said Shawn. "Don't worry, the deputies deal with this kinda stuff every day. If he thinks she'll be okay, I'm sure she'll be okay."

CJ looked over and lightly touched his arm. "Thanks for doing this. You're probably right about Jason. He's actually Carol's boyfriend so I'm sure he'd be pretty certain before he told Carol her sister would be okay."

After Carol thanked CJ again, she hung up and dialed Jason's cell.

Jason answered on the third ring. "What's the matter, little girl, you break your radio?"

"Very funny," came her response. "I just wanted to make sure you knew how grateful I am for you taking care of my little sister, and I didn't think doing that over the radio was a good idea."

"Carol, I would have done the same for anyone. That's my job."

"I don't believe that," she said. "And even if I did, that doesn't make what you did any less special. You coming over tonight after I get off?"

"Of course, I plan on collecting my reward for saving freckles."

"Oh God, you didn't call her that, did you?"

"Yeah. I had to do something to wake her up. And yes, I'm still alive. But I'll be watching my back for the next several days."

"Jason?"

"Yeah?"

"I love you," she whispered. Then added, "You might want to pick up some whipped cream to put on your *reward*."

Chapter 13 - Frozen Yogurt Makes It All Better

They pulled into the hospital entrance and parked in one of the emergency-room-parking-only spaces. CJ got out without waiting for him to come around and open her door. As they walked into the emergency room, Shawn asked CJ for Shannon's last name.

"McClanahan," she said. "Shannon McClanahan."

With a big smile, Shawn said, "Wow. I'll bet she's Irish."

CJ snorted. "You are so... worldly. What gave it away? The red hair? The freckles? Or could it have been her first or last name?"

They went up to the reception desk. "Hi, I'm Shawn James with Bonita Fire. We understand the EMTs just brought a Shannon McClanahan in. Can you tell us what her status is?"

"Sure," said the nurse. "She came in about fifteen minutes ago. The doctor just had a quick look at her, and other than a good size lump on the back of her head and a few loose teeth, she should be okay. They did an MRI and X-rays of her jaw just to be safe, but he said to go ahead and release her. She's should be getting dressed about now and be out in a few minutes."

Shannon came through the double doors and spotted CJ and Shawn in the waiting room. CJ ran up, wrapped her arms around Shannon, and hung on for dear life. "Oh my God. Are you okay? I was so worried about you."

Shawn joined them, "You okay?" he asked.

"Yeah, I am now. Thank you both for coming to get me. I'm so sorry for screwing up your first date."

Shawn smiled at her. "You didn't screw up anything. We were just about ready to head back when we got the call that you'd been hurt and they were bringing you here."

Shawn gave Shannon a big hug. "I'm glad you're alright."

He started to let go and Shannon said, "No. Do not let go. Getting hugs from you makes getting my head bashed in almost worth it." She smiled at Shawn, looked at CJ, and whispered, "You sure he doesn't have a brother? He's gotta have a brother."

Finally, they released each other. Shawn took both of their hands and led them toward the door. "Come on, I've got an idea on how to make this all better." He opened the passenger side door, and CJ jumped in followed by Shannon. Shawn got in, started the truck, and pulled out of the hospital parking lot.

He made a right onto Main then another right onto Broadway. A few blocks later, he turned into a parking lot and parked in front of what looked for all the world like a big, white light house. Written across the front of the towering structure was, "The Yogurt Mill."

"Okay, girls. There is nothing better to cheer you up than frozen yogurt, and the yogurt here is the best. Plus it's on me."

CJ and Shannon squealed as both of them tried to get out of the door at the same time. Problem was, they both still had their seat belts on, so Shawn had no problem beating them inside. By the time they untangled themselves, got their seat belts undone, and got inside, Shawn already had his yogurt.

147

Both girls looked at the menu and said in unison, "Oh. My. God." They looked at each other with the biggest grins then they turned to Shawn and both said, "You're buying? Right?"

Before he finished nodding, CJ had ordered four flavors and about every kind of topping they had. Shannon followed with three flavors plus a double scoop of vanilla, then added M&Ms, Reese's Pieces, and chopped almonds.

As he paid for their yogurts, he turned to them. "Remind me never to take the two of you to dinner."

"Hey, this is yogurt. It's not fattening," mumbled CJ through a mouthful of everything.

"Right," he said, as he watched toppings slide onto the table every time either one of them stuck a spoon into their cup.

"God, I feel so much better," Shannon squealed, then added, "What was that about taking us to dinner?"

While they finished their yogurt, Shannon called Carol and let her know she had been released from the hospital and that Shawn was treating them all to yogurt. Then she filled Shawn and CJ in on her run-in with Ami. Afterward, CJ told Shannon all about her day as she kept looking over at Shawn beaming.

When she was done, Shannon looked at Shawn and said, "Thank you. I haven't seen her this jacked up in a long time." Realizing what she just said, she turned to CJ. "I'm sorry. Really bad choice of words on my part."

"Hey, it's okay," CJ said, as she reached over and put her hand on Shannon's arm.

Twenty minutes later, they pulled back into the ranch. Kate came out of the trailer and met them as they walked up the hill. "You okay, Shannon?"

"Yeah, I'm fine. But, you, me, and CJ need to talk about Ami."

"That can wait till tomorrow. How about if I drive you home? CJ can pick you up in the morning."

"Kate, honestly, I'm fine. Besides, tomorrow's my day off, and I don't want to have to come all the way out to the ranch to get my truck."

Shannon thanked Shawn and CJ, then left.

Shawn looked at CJ. "I'd planned on taking you out to dinner as part of your day out, but I guess that will have to wait."

"No way," said Kate. "You two go have a nice dinner. I've got plenty of paperwork to catch up on, and since I'm already out here, there's no time like the present. If you're not back when I get ready to leave, I'll lock up on my way out."

CJ looked at Kate. "Are you sure? I feel so guilty about everybody having to do all the work I should've been doing."

"Are you kidding? How many times have all of us not shown up when we were supposed to and stuck you with everything? Go enjoy dinner. I'll be fine."

Shawn thanked Kate, and CJ whispered in her ear, "Thank you. I love you." Then they headed for CJ's trailer.

When they reached the steps to her trailer, she turned to Shawn. "Thank you for asking me to dinner. I really don't want this day to end, Shawn."

149

"That makes two of us," he whispered.

"Let me grab a jacket then we can head out." Shawn waited by the steps while CJ ran in and got her jacket. She came out, locked the trailer door, and turned to him. "You're pretty special, you know that?"

"I hope so," he said, and then mumbled to himself, "I really hope so."

Chapter 14 - First Date

CJ insisted on getting both gates again. As she closed the second one, Shawn glanced into his rearview mirror and saw something move in the driveway down by the ranch gate. CJ finished running the chain through the gate and climbed back into the truck.

"Did you see something run across the road just now?" he asked her.

"No, I wasn't really watching. What was it?"

"I don't know. All I saw was a pretty big shadow in the driveway by the ranch gate."

"It could have been one of the mustangs in the pasture down where the driveway curves. Sometimes it looks like they're on the road, but they're actually behind the wire fence. Was it the size of a horse?"

Shawn shook his head. "I'm not sure. A little shorter maybe."

"Might have been one of the colts," she said. "You want to go back and check?"

"No, I'm not even sure if I saw something. It was probably just a bush being blown around by the wind."

Shawn pulled out onto the highway and headed toward 79. "So where are we going?" CJ asked.

"Well, the steakhouse in the casino looked pretty good the other night. Plus it's close so I thought we might give that a try."

"Oh, Shawn, no. I'm not dressed right, and that place is super expensive. I'm sure there's something in Alpine that would be more casual and cheaper."

"CJ, I've spent a wonderful day with a special person, and I want it to end with a dinner that's just as wonderful and special. Besides, the steakhouse is not formal. This is California. Nobody gets dressed up. If anything, you'll probably be overdressed compared to the shorts and tank tops most people wear into the casino and restaurant. Tell you what. Next time, I promise we'll do Big Macs and fries and use the drive-thru. Then you don't have to worry about being underdressed."

She hugged his arm and looked at him. "You're really spoiling me."

He pulled his arm, and her hands, in closer and whispered, "You deserve it."

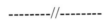

Kate went into the volunteer trailer, closed and locked the door, and headed into the bathroom. When she came out, she set her laptop on the table and pulled up the financial ledger for the ranch. Then she pulled a bunch of receipts out of her messenger bag and started to enter them into the spreadsheet.

An hour later, everything had been entered, and she started making a list of stuff she needed to pick up or have delivered for the following week. Finally, she pulled out her notebook with fundraising ideas and started to jot down some notes about an event idea CJ had mentioned a few days earlier. As she was writing, she thought she heard something outside behind the trailer. Then she heard Stanley, their big Great Pyrenees guard dog, bark once.

Stanley never barked at anything except mountain lions, and then he didn't stop till it was gone. She pulled the curtain back and looked out back, but it was pitch black. She listened carefully and watched for any kind of movement, but didn't see or hear anything. It certainly wasn't a mountain lion, and whatever it was, obviously wasn't worth a second bark from Stanley. She shrugged her shoulders then went back to jotting down notes.

After almost three hours, Kate had finished just about everything she could and packed her stuff into her messenger bag. She turned out all of the lights except the nightlight they always left on and headed for the door. As she pulled the door open and started down the stairs, Stanley barked once more, and something caught her eye in the direction of CJ's trailer. A shadow scooted from the trailer into a row of bushes out front, then disappeared behind the shed by the road. Stanley let out a grumble then went silent again.

"Thanks, Stanley," Kate called out. "Some guard dog you are." Shaking her head, she walked over to her SUV and got in. Two minutes later, she turned onto the road after having closed and locked both gates.

--------//--------

Shawn pulled into the casino parking structure and parked. He helped CJ out, and as they started to walk toward the casino entrance she reached out and took his hand. As they got closer to the door, she pulled on his hand till he slowed down then stopped and turned to look at her. He stared into the prettiest hazel eyes he had ever seen and started to smile. Then he saw the scared expression on her face.

"Are you okay?" he asked.

The look on her face scared him. "Shawn, why are you doing this? Why are you treating me like this?"

He felt his face scrunch up and he hoped it expressed just how confused he was by her questions because he was completely at a loss for words. "Did... I... do something wrong?" he said.

She continued to stare into his eyes and whispered, "No one has ever treated me like this, Shawn... and I'm so scared right now. I'm scared I'm going to disappoint you. I'm scared to death I'm going to screw things up and lose you."

Shawn reached around her with both arms and pulled her into him as she laid her head against his chest. He didn't say a word, he just held her tightly for the longest time. Finally, he whispered, "You've really been hurt in the past, haven't you?"

She tightened her hold on him, held on for dear life, and nodded against his chest. "Yeah," she whispered.

Shawn held her for a few more minutes, and neither one said a word. Slowly he moved his hands to her shoulders and eased her back a little so he could see her.

He gently lifted her chin so she was looking directly at him and said, "I'm treating you like this because you deserve it. I think you are one of the most wonderful people I've ever met and you deserve to be treated as special, because you are. And for the record, I'm scared too. I'm scared I'll do something stupid or push you too fast and you'll never want to see me again."

He took a deep breath and smiled. "CJ, I don't know where this is going. I know where I hope it goes, and I think you feel the same. I have every intention of spending as much time with you as I can, unless you tell me otherwise. I would never, ever do anything to hurt you. I would die before I hurt you and I would beat the crap out of anyone who did. Well, except for Ami, because I'd never hit a woman." His smile got bigger as he added, "But I would gladly hold her while you beat the crap out of her."

He tilted his head and looked into her eyes. "You're not going to lose me, and I can't think of anything you could do that would disappoint me. All you've done so far is impress the hell out of me.

He stood back and asked, "You still hungry?"

"Starved," she said.

He put his arm around her, pulled her close, and headed toward the door to the casino.

Once inside, she pulled on his hand and stopped him again. She looked into his eyes, smiled, and whispered, "Thanks." Then she stood on her tiptoes and gently kissed him on the lips.

They walked through the casino, hand in hand, and into the entrance to the Grove Steakhouse. As they approached the hostess station, the young woman at the station smiled and asked if she could help them.

Shawn smiled back. "Any chance of a very hungry couple getting a nice quiet table?"

"I think I can arrange that." She picked up two menus and a wine list and said, "Right this way please." She took them through a large open section filled with tables and directed them to a row of booths along the back wall. She extended her arm toward the far booth and smiled at them. "Is this okay? It's away from all the noise in the casino and the chatter of the main dining section."

"It's perfect," said Shawn.

"Any special occasion?" she asked.

Shawn and CJ looked at each other and both chimed, "Our first date."

All three of them smiled, and the hostess added, "You two make a really cute couple. I hope your first date turns out to be really special."

CJ looked at the waitress, then at Shawn and said, "It already is."

The hostess winked at CJ then told them their waitress would be Vicky and she would be right over to take their drink order. She placed a menu at each place setting, the wine list in the middle, then turned and left.

CJ slid into the spacious and comfortable booth that could easily have held a party of six. Shawn followed her as they slid around to the back of the booth. No sooner had they settled in when a busboy arrived and set an ice bucket next to Shawn's side of the table. Following close behind was Vicky with two champagne flutes and a bottle of champagne.

"Hi. So I understand this is your first date. On behalf of the Viejas Casino, we would like to help make this a memorable occasion. May I pour you each a glass?"

Shawn and CJ both chuckled, and Shawn nodded his head.

Vicky looked around to make sure nobody was listening, then whispered, "Actually, this was Irene the hostess's idea, but we have to give the casino credit since they're the ones that let us give their champagne away. I'll give you two a few minutes to look at the menu." She turned and started to walk away, then stopped and turned around. "Irene was right. You two make a really cute couple." Then she asked Shawn, "Do you have a brother?"

156

CJ was laughing so hard that half the dining room turned to look at her. "Your brother would certainly have no problem finding women with you around." Suddenly she went quiet and looked at him. "You do actually have a brother, right?"

He stared at her for a moment, then answered, "Yes. Why? Do you want to date him too?"

She took his arm. "I don't know. Is he as handsome as you?"

"More," he said. Then added, "Just remember you're going to have to fight Shannon since she has first claim on him. Oh, and did I mention he's only fourteen?"

Still holding his arm, CJ leaned against him, squeezed, and whispered, "I love you."

Realizing what she had just said, she gasped. "I... I mean I... I love you, not literally, but in other senses... ah, your sense of humor... your sense of honor." *Oh God. Keep digging, CJ. The hole's getting deeper. His sense of honor? His sense of humor? Great, now he thinks you think he's what, a funny knight? Just crawl under the table and escape when no one is looking.*

Shawn reached over and put his finger on her lips to quiet her. "It's okay, CJ. If you hadn't said it, I would have. We both feel it. I think we both felt it the minute I jumped into the shed. Let's just take this one day at a time. Okay? I think we both know where we would like this to go, but let's just get to know each other. If it's really meant to be, it'll be." He leaned over and gently kissed her on the lips, just as Vicky arrived.

"Are you two ready or did you need another minute or two?"

They both opened their menus and Shawn said, "Why don't you start us with an order of crab cakes and by the time you get back,

157

we'll be ready." He looked at CJ. "Are you okay with crab cakes?"

"I don't know, I've never had them."

He stared at her in amazement.

"Crab cakes are not exactly a fast-food item, Shawn. I know I'm embarrassing you. I can't even order from a menu like this because I don't know what half this stuff is."

"Okay, let's try a different approach. Do you like seafood?"

She stared at him. "I guess. I love fish tacos. Clam chowder's just okay. Oh, and I've had fish and chips once, which I really liked and frozen fish sticks from the store are just okay."

"How about French onion soup?" he asked.

"Nope, never had it."

"Wow, this is great. You're like a blank slate and I get to introduce you to all kinds of gastronomical delights. Are you okay with me ordering for you again?"

"Sure." She smiled and added, "If I throw up on you, it'll be a pretty good sign I didn't like what you ordered."

"I'm going to order totally different things for each of us. If you don't like what you have, we'll swap. How's that?"

"Okay, I guess. What if I don't like any of it?"

"Then I guess you'll starve, and I'll get fat. You'll be fine, stop worrying. Are you okay with steak? How about corn?"

158

"Steak? Who wouldn't be okay with steak? As long as it doesn't go *Mooooo Moooooo* when I cut it. And corn is good. I really like canned cream corn."

Shawn broke out laughing. "Can you do the *Moooo Moooo* thing a little louder? A few people in the casino didn't hear you."

"*MOOOOO MOOOOO*. How's that?"

Vicky came over and set the crab cakes in front of them. "I assume the *moo moo* was a hint that you're ready to order?"

CJ looked at her, said, "Moo?" and they all started to laugh.

Shawn placed their order. A Caesar salad and the ten-ounce filet mignon, done medium well for him, and French onion soup and salmon, done well for her. Then he added a side dish of creamed corn. Vicky nodded her approval, refilled their flutes, and went to put their order in.

He pulled the crab cakes in front of him, cut a small piece off one with his fork, and dipped a corner of it in the accompanying aioli sauce. Holding his hand under it so it wouldn't drip onto the tablecloth, he raised the fork to CJ's mouth. Staring at Shawn with her gorgeous hazel eyes wide, she opened her mouth, leaned forward, and dragged the piece of crab cake off the fork with her teeth.

Glancing down, Shawn made sure the tablecloth was covering his lap because he was about to cream in his jeans. CJ had to be the most amazing, sexy, and wonderful woman he had ever been with. He wondered how fast he could get a room and have the rest of their dinner brought up by room service.

159

Looking back up, he found CJ watching him with eyes that were about to pop out of her head. "OH. MY. GOD. This has to be the best thing I have ever tasted."

"I guess that means you like it?" he said as she reached over, picked up the dish of crab cakes, and pulled the one he had cut onto the plate in front of her.

As she spooned some of the aioli sauce next to the cake, she looked at him and said, "Do you want yours?"

He grinned at her and shook his head. "Go ahead and take both of them, but remember, there's still a lot of food coming."

She slid the other crab cake over to her plate and spooned the rest of the sauce next to it. Then she cut off a piece, dipped it into the sauce as he had, and raised it in front of Shawn's lips. He opened his mouth, and she slid the crab cake in, being careful not to stab him. He closed his mouth and she gently slid the fork out.

"That's it. That's all you get." Then she proceeded to finish off the rest of the crab cakes and sauce.

The salad and soup arrived. Vicky set the soup in front of CJ and salad in front of Shawn. She reached over, picked up the empty crab cake and appetizer dishes.

She looked at the dishes, then at them. "I was going to ask how the crab cakes were, but these don't even need to go in the dishwasher. What did you do? Lick them clean?"

After she left, CJ looked at Shawn and whispered, "Sorry."

CJ's eyes went to the steaming hot bowl of soup in front of her. "What's that white gooey stuff on top?" she asked, poking at it with her spoon.

"That's melted gruyere cheese. Be careful because it's going to be hot."

She took a spoonful of soup, blew on it, then tried to deal with the cheese strings after her utensil disappeared into her mouth.

"Ummm… ummm," she said, pointing to the strings of cheese. Shawn reached over and pulled on them till they snapped. He opened his mouth and dropped it in, then realized CJ was still saying, "Ummm… ummm… ummm," and pointing to the two large strings that had snapped up and stuck to her nose.

He started laughing then leaned over and came nose-to-nose with her. If possible, her eyes got even bigger, then crossed as he scraped the cheese off her nose with his teeth. "Ummm… good cheese. Great tasting nose.".

She pulled the spoon out of her mouth, swallowed, and pushed the bowl aside. "I think I'll pass on the soup." She looked around, then said, "It's really good, but I'm not sure I like sharing my nose with you in public." They both chuckled, and Shawn noticed her staring at his salad.

He pushed the salad plate so it was between them and said, "Want to share?" Before his hand was off the plate, her fork was leaving it with a hefty chunk of romaine lettuce and a crouton.

Vicky arrived once again with their entrees and the side of cream corn. She picked up the empty salad plate and still full soup bowl. She looked at CJ, "Was the soup okay?"

"The soup is really good, but dealing with the cheese is a bit of a challenge," CJ said.

Vicky smiled at them. "Looked like you two did pretty good to me. I even made a note to order French onion soup on my next date."

Lowering her head, CJ smelled the salmon. "This smells wonderful," she said, as she took a small forkful and slipped it into her mouth. With her empty fork in one hand, she raised both hands and started pumping her arms up and down as she stomped her feet on the floor. "Oh my God, oh my God, oh my God." She gripped the fork so the tines were facing down, wrapped both of her arms around her plate, then pulled it close as her eyes scanned the area. "Anyone that even looks at this plate is going to lose a hand."

Shawn chuckled. "I guess that means you like it and my steak is safe?"

"Actually your steak looks really good. Can I have a bite?"

"Sure, I'll trade you for a bite of your salmon."

She raised her fork. "Over my dead body. You toucha my salmon, I stabba you hand."

They nursed their way through the rest of the meal, alternately sharing bites of steak, salmon, and creamed corn with each other and savoring every bite. When they finished, Vicky cleared their once again *licked clean* plates. For dessert, Shawn ordered two Mexican coffees and a vanilla crème brulee with fresh berries for them to share.

CJ devoured most of the crème brulee, all the while flashing her doe eyes at him and explaining that it was a 'girly' dessert that he wouldn't like anyway. Each time his dessert fork wandered toward the plate, she would stuff a berry in his mouth and pull the ramekin closer to her. Finally, he just gave up and nursed his

162

Mexican coffee, which he kept safe by placing his body between it and her.

During their second round of Mexican coffees, he found himself staring at her. She was truly fascinating. So different from anyone he had ever met. She seemed so innocent and naïve, but he knew that she was much more than street smart and nothing escaped her. He also knew she could play him like a violin if she wanted, but he knew she would never do that. He hardly knew her, yet he trusted her in every way possible.

Shawn leaned over, intending to kiss her on the cheek, but CJ saw him lean toward her, turned, and tilted her head up so that their lips met. She reached around, put her hand on the back of his neck, and pulled him in to the kiss.

She held him there for the longest time, then leaned back and whispered, "Shawn, this is so wonderful. You're so wonderful. I will never, ever forget today."

He bent over and their lips met again. "You're amazing. You know that? I can't think of anyone I have ever been with who is so fascinating, so adorable, so caring, and so appreciative of every little thing I've done. It's easy to see why everybody thinks you're so special."

She stared into his eyes. "I'm not special, Shawn, even though you made me feel like it today. I'm not sure what you see in me, but please don't put me on a pedestal. If you do, I'll fall off, and I'm not sure I'd be able to get up again. It takes everything I've got to open myself to you, to trust you because I'm so afraid you'll walk away when you discover the real me. I'm broken, Shawn, and I'm not sure how well they glued me back together."

"Come on, let's get you back. It's been a wonderful but long and emotional day, and you're exhausted. We'll continue this conversation later, and I'll be happy to listen to you tell me all about the real you, but… I'm pretty sure I already know her.

Until then, just know that I would never betray your trust and I will never do anything to hurt you. Oh, and the only place I plan on walking is beside you."

They slid out of the booth and stood up, and CJ realized how totally exhausted she was. It was like her legs were rubber, and putting one foot in front of the other was next to impossible.

"You okay?" he asked.

"Yeah. I guess you were right about being exhausted."

He pulled her in close and kept his arm tightly around her waist as they walked through the casino, out into the parking structure, and finally reached his truck. He opened her door, helped her in, then reached across and buckled her seat belt for her.

"Anybody ever tell you you're cute?" she asked.

With little to no traffic, the trip back to the ranch went quickly. Neither of them spoke as they each reflected back on the day. When they got to the main gate, CJ jumped out, unlocked the gate, and opened it. After Shawn drove through, she closed and relocked it. She repeated the procedure at the gate to the ranch, jumped back into his truck, and directed him to the small driveway next to her trailer where he pulled in behind her truck.

"Buy you a beer?" she asked.

"One beer and I'll be out." He chuckled. "Besides, I've got a long drive back to Bonita."

She turned serious and looked into his eyes. "Shawn, please don't go. I don't want today to end. You've given me the most wonderful day of my life, and I can't think of anything I want more than to fall asleep in your arms."

"CJ, I didn't do any of this so I could sleep with you."

"I know."

He stared at her. "Are you sure you're okay with this?"

She nodded. "I've never been more sure of anything in my life."

He got out, and she slid under the steering wheel as he helped her out his side. He pulled her in close, and they walked up the steps and onto the porch of her trailer.

As she searched for her keys, he turned her around. "I need to say this before we get in there and passion takes over. I don't know what act of fate, magic, or the gods brought us together, but meeting you is one of the most wonderful things that's ever happened to me. If I never got to sleep with you, I would still feel the same way."

CJ could see the love in his eyes as tears welled up in hers. "Thank you," she whispered.

She knew she had to do something before she completely lost it. "Who said anything about passion… or sex? You already had your climax during my first bite of crab cake. All I planned to do is snuggle into those wonderful arms and that fantastic body of yours."

He shook his head. "You're so bad. Was I that obvious with the crab cakes?"

She smiled. "Ah… Yeah." She put the key in the door, turned the knob, and pushed the door open. She took his arm, turned him toward the door, then added, "If it makes you feel better, you weren't the only one that climaxed. Now, shut up and get in there so I can ravage you."

She followed him through the door, closed it, and stood staring at the lock.

"What's wrong?" he asked.

"I could have sworn I locked the door when we left, but when I went to unlock it just now, it was already unlocked."

"You did lock it. I watched you. Anyone else have a key?" he asked.

She looked at him, still puzzled. "Only Kate. But why would she have come in?"

"Don't know," he said. "Is anything missing?"

CJ turned on all the lights, looked around, then went to check the bedrooms and bathroom. "Nope, nothing missing that I can see. Hell, I haven't got anything worth stealing anyway. It must have been Kate. I'll have to ask her tomorrow what she wanted. So you want to be ravaged before or after your beer?"

He walked over, scooped her up, and carried her into the bedroom as she added, "I guess this means no beer?"

"No beer," he whispered as he kissed her ear.

Chapter 15 - The Morning After

CJ slowly opened one eye, looked around, and stopped at the clock. Was that a six or an eight? She blinked, tried to drag herself closer to the clock, and realized there was an arm around her. After another second, she remembered that the arm and the warm, cuddly body against her backside belonged to Shawn.

"WOW, it wasn't a dream," she whispered. Smiling, she pulled his arm tighter around her, snuggled into him as if she were trying to get into his body, and went back to sleep.

An hour later, her eyes flew open. Her bladder was about to burst. She carefully lifted his arm and slid out of bed. She shuffled naked into the bathroom and quietly closed the door. When she was finished, she tiptoed out, threw her robe around her, and went into the kitchen to put coffee on.

When the coffee was done, she poured herself a cup and sat at the table. God, her face hurt. Catching a glimpse of herself in the window of the oven door, she realized it was from the giant grin she couldn't get rid of. Her face wasn't the only thing that hurt, but none of the hurts were going to make her regret one minute of last night.

Shawn had been amazing. Not just amazing in bed, because he certainly was that, but also amazing in his concern for her. He had been so caring and so gentle. She could sense his understanding that she had been hurt before but didn't know how, so he had carefully read her every response and reaction before proceeding.

Not once had he embarrassed her by asking if what he was doing was okay. He just somehow knew if it was or not. In her heart, she also knew that if she had asked him to stop at any point, not only would he have stopped, but it would not, in any way, have changed his feelings for her.

She truly trusted Shawn in every way possible.

When it came to sex, he was more amazing than he had been in her dreams. Was that even possible?

She had let him take the lead and, at first, thought he was going to take *forever* just to undress her. But oh, was it worth the wait. Not only was he caring, gentle, and patient in his lovemaking, he was completely in tune with how to drive her absolutely crazy. When they came up for air, she had no idea how many times she had climaxed. Three times? Four? Hell, who cared. All she knew was when he finished, she was soaking wet, sore all over, and couldn't stop smiling.

After a short rest, filled with kissing, nibbling, and hugging, it was her turn. And gentle and patient were not part of her plan. She literally ravaged him. Over and over again. Each time different and each time with more passion. All she knew was they had both loved every minute of it. Another two? Three? Five? climaxes later and they both rolled over, soaked, panting, and completely exhausted. The last thing she remembered was him saying, "God, are you fantastic. Just give me a few minutes and…" Then she closed her eyes to the sound of him snoring.

Thinking back, she realized it had been over five years since she had slept with anyone. No wonder she had ravaged him. *It'll be weeks before he can walk right.*

She smiled. "Good job, CJ. Good job… You are soooo sick."

Shawn stepped out of the bedroom wearing nothing but a towel and a smile.

"Hi," she said. Then she patted the chair next to her, poured another cup of coffee and handed it to him as he sat down.

"God, am I sore," he said with a big smile. He bent over and kissed her, then added, "I think I used muscles last night that haven't been used in years, and *I know* you used muscles I didn't even know existed." He reached out, put his arms around CJ's waist, and pulled her into his lap.

CJ smiled at him, then turned serious. "Shawn, are we okay after last night?"

He looked straight into her eyes. "More than okay."

He pulled her in tight. "Look, this isn't the time, but we need to talk as soon as you're comfortable with it. I know you've been hurt, badly. I saw some of the scars last night. I also know you're worried that I'll find out about your past and dump you. Nothing... could be further from the truth. I have some suspicions, but no matter what you tell me about your past, it will not change my feelings for you."

"Shawn, I—"

He put his finger to her lips and quietly said, "Not now. I just want you to know that nothing you tell me will change how I feel about you. So stop worrying, but promise me we'll talk soon, so it isn't hanging over us. Okay?"

CJ nodded. "Okay."

"Now, if you'll feed me something, I'll see about giving you a hand today. That is, if you're okay with that."

"What?" she said. "I thought you were going back to Bonita?"

"I thought so too, till I saw you lock the gates last night," he said, smiling. "Actually, I'm off till next Saturday. I've got so much vacation time accrued that I'm about to lose some and they've been all over me to take it. So I thought, what's better than spending my remaining week here with you?"

CJ stood up, turned, pulled the bottom of her robe open, then sat down, straddling his lap. She put her arms around his neck and kissed him. "Oh, Shawn, I would absolutely love it if you spent the week with me, but don't you want to go someplace where you can relax and suck up sun? Working out here may be rewarding, but you already know it's no vacation."

"I just saw my family, and I'll get plenty of sun out here. Oh, and let's not forget the *fresh country air*. Besides, I can't think of anywhere I'd rather be than with you." He kissed her again. "I'd wade through waist-high horse poop just to be with you."

"That, my shining knight, is exactly what you're going to be doing. Now, come on and let's get you some breakfast."

CJ opened the refrigerator, pulled his mom's casserole dish out, and set it aside. "I assume leftover stuffed cabbage will not work for breakfast." She rummaged through the rest of the refrigerator and cabinets and set anything that looked like breakfast fodder on the table. "Okay, one and a half frozen waffles, one egg." She smacked something against the table. "I think this was a bagel at one time. About a bowl's worth of cereal, no milk, and if we chip the frost off this, I think we might find an Eggo."

Shaking his head, he looked at the pile of stuff. "I have an idea. Where's the closest place that might have something resembling food?"

CJ thought for a moment. "There's a little mom-and-pop country store and café on the right, just after the 79 turnoff. They'll probably be open early to catch some of the tourist traffic headed up to Julian or going back to San Diego."

170

"Good. Let's shower, you can get started out there, and I'll go get us something to eat."

Shawn scraped everything off the table into the trash can and put the casserole dish back in the refrigerator. "We'll also plan a shopping trip this afternoon to buy you some food."

"Picky, picky, picky," she said. "I'm headed for the shower."

"I'll join you in a minute."

"I think not," she said, as she walked back to the bedroom and disappeared into the bathroom leaving the door wide open.

Confused, Shawn followed her, pulled off his towel, and opened the shower door. To call her shower a very small closet would make it sound much bigger than it was.

CJ smiled at him and said, "Care to join me, sir knight?"

"I'll just wash your back while I've got the door open, then I think I'll wait till it's my turn."

After they had showered and dressed, CJ walked over to the volunteer trailer to see who, if anyone, was scheduled today while Shawn headed for the mom-and-pop place.

A little over an hour later, Shawn returned with enough takeout containers to feed six very hungry people. He set everything on the table in the volunteer trailer, went down to the supply shed, and started pulling CJ out the door as she yelled, "I'm right in the middle of filling the feed buckets."

"Tough. Your breakfast is getting cold. The buckets will still be there when you're done, and the horses aren't going to starve

171

while you eat." With that he picked her up, threw her over his shoulder, and carried her up to the trailer.

"Is this what you call a fireman's carry?" she asked.

"Yup. I'm a fireman and I'm carrying you. Next, you're gonna get a fireman's spanking if you don't eat your breakfast like a good little girl."

"Promises, promises," she said.

CJ was convinced that Shawn had ordered one of everything on the breakfast menu at the mom-and-pop café. That turned out to be a good thing, since they both ate like they hadn't eaten in a week. When they finished, they cleaned up, put what little was left in the refrigerator, and headed back to the supply shed.

Shawn brought hay bales over by the stalls while CJ finished filling the color-coded buckets. Next he went over to the tool shed and built two wheelbarrow toolkits just like Shannon had taught him. Finally, he threw the extension cord and trough pump into one and took each wheelbarrow down to the stall area. Just as he finished, CJ pulled up in an old golf cart with the back full of feed buckets.

As CJ started to lay out a plan of attack, Kate pulled into the ranch, followed by Melissa, a volunteer.

They walked up, and Kate introduced Shawn to Melissa, then asked, "So how was dinner?"

CJ's face lit up as she grabbed Shawn's arm and pulled him close. "He took me to the steakhouse at Viejas and it was incredible. Not only was the food out of this world, the people there were so friendly and gracious. I had crab cakes for the first time ever. I tried French onion soup, and we shared salmon, steak, and creamed corn. Yum. For dessert, we had Mexican coffees and shared a crème brulee. The hostess even sent over a bottle of champagne when we told her it was our first date."

She stopped and looked up at Shawn, "But... the most amazing part was the company. It was the most wonderful date I've ever had." Then she stood on her tiptoes and kissed him on the lips.

Kate smiled at them. "Wow, now I'm hungry."

"Oh, there's some leftovers from our breakfast in the fridge. If you want, help yourself."

"Breakfast leftovers?" Kate said, raising her eyebrows.

"Ah, yeah. Shawn ran down to that little mom-and-pop place and got us breakfast."

"I see," said Kate as she smiled at Shawn, who just shrugged and smiled back.

Kate turned back to CJ. "Have you had a chance to introduce Shawn to anybody yet?"

"Not yet. He's met Deveny, but we were just about to get started on my morning chores when you pulled in. I'd planned on introducing him to everybody else after I finished."

"Today's our light day, and Melissa and I can handle most of what needs to be done. How about if you two get Deveny and the left row of stalls, then you can introduce him to some of the other horses or take what's left of the day off."

CJ looked at Shawn. "Actually, he's taking the week off and wants to spend it here. I know, I know. I already told him he's nuts, but who am I to turn down such good-looking help? Anyway, I think we'll just work the stalls you mentioned, then

173

take the rest of the day off. He's already met Deveny briefly, and I'll need a whole day to explain Missy and Milton."

Kate smiled at Shawn again, and turned to CJ. "Do as little or as much as you want. Whatever doesn't get done, you'll inherit on Monday anyway."

"We'll start with Deveny," CJ said as they headed up the hill toward Deveny's stall with one of the wheelbarrows.

Like their prior meeting, Deveny stared at Shawn and wiggled her ears as they came up the hill. CJ turned to him. "This is twice she's done that with you. I think she likes you. Wanna go in and meet her?"

"Sure, as long as she's okay with it. How do you greet a horse anyway? Should I curtsey, bow, or what?"

"Just hold your hand out so she can smell it, and don't make any sudden moves until she gets used to you. She'll let you know when she's comfortable with you."

They entered the stall and slowly approached Deveny. Shawn held out his hand when they got close. Deveny sniffed it, then nudged it with her nose.

"What's that mean?" Shawn asked CJ.

"Wow. That means she's already got your number. She wants a treat." CJ pulled two carrots out of her pocket and started to hand them to him. "Try giving her one of these."

Deveny wasted no time intercepting the carrots as CJ reached out to give them to Shawn.

"Hey," Shawn said. "I was supposed to give you that."

Deveny looked at him and winked. Then she turned to CJ and lowered her head. CJ rested her forehead against Deveny's and rubbed the side of her head.

Shawn stood with his mouth open absolutely in awe of Deveny's beauty. Now it was CJ's turn as she reached over and gently pushed his mouth closed. "First rule on a horse ranch, keep your mouth closed at all times or something definitely will fly in there. Second rule, always watch where you step," she added, as she pointed to a big clump of horse turd on his shoe. She looked at Deveny. "He's new to horses, my love. Just be patient with him. He'll eventually figure things out."

No sooner did she finish her last sentence than Deveny took her nose and pushed hard against Shawn's chest. Catching him completely by surprise, he took a half step backward trying to keep his balance, but it was too late. Down he went, landing butt first in a puddle of horse pee. To add insult to injury, as he went down, he put his right hand out to try to lessen the fall and ended up completely burying his hand in a fresh pile of horse shit.

Deveny whinnied and bobbed her head while CJ laughed so hard she had to hang onto Deveny to keep from joining Shawn.

Kate and Melissa came running up the hill to see what all the noise was about. When they saw Shawn sitting in the middle of the corral, they both lost it. Shawn couldn't help but join them, and soon, they were all holding their sides.

CJ finally let go of Deveny and reached down to help Shawn up. As soon as she took his hand, Deveny put her nose on CJ's back and shoved. She landed directly on top of Shawn, and he wrapped his arms around her to keep her from rolling off. Nose-to-nose, he brought his head up and kissed her as they both lay there laughing.

175

Kate and Melissa came into the corral and helped them to their feet. Still laughing, Kate looked at them covered with everything a horse corral could offer and said, "I think Deveny is trying to tell you two something. Why don't you go get cleaned up and take the rest of the day off? I'll leave you a note letting you know if there's anything we don't get done."

Still unable to talk, CJ and Shawn laughed their way up the hill to CJ's trailer. Once on the porch, CJ told him there was no way they were going inside the way they were, so they both stripped down to their underwear then dashed inside.

CJ pushed him toward the bathroom and told him to yell when he was ready to step out of the shower. In the meantime, she pulled her sweats, a new pair of jockey shorts, and socks from the garment bag he had given her and took them into the bathroom. She pulled her sport bra off and stepped out of her panties just as Shawn stepped out of the shower.

"I don't have anything …" he started to say, as she kissed him on the lips, pointed at the pile of clothes, and slipped into the still-running shower.

After drying their hair and getting dressed, CJ brought their dirty clothes in from the porch. Shawn looked at her. "Our next stop needs to be my condo. I love your sweats, but not enough to be seen in public in them again. Besides, if today's any indication, I need to stash some clothes in your trailer or I'll spend next week driving home and back for clean clothes."

"Oh, but I love you in my sweats. And even better with nothing on. I have this all planned out. You only bring back one pair of shorts, one pair of jeans, and one shirt. Then, each night, you sit naked, and I watch you while we wait for your clothes to get washed and dried."

"No matter how many sets of clothes I have here, the last thing you'll have a problem with is getting me naked. Why don't you

176

throw our dirty clothes in with whatever you have that needs to be washed and bring everything with us. We can use the washers and dryers at the condo complex. I need to do a quick run to Vons for food then we can go do something or just hang at the condo while I cook up something for dinner."

CJ put the dirty clothes down, and her face turned serious. "Shawn, please sit?" He sat at the table and tried to pull her into his lap, but she refused and sat across from him. "This is so not fair. I'm supposed to be paying you back by making you something and giving you a tour. Instead, you're still paying for everything and spending even more money."

Her eyebrows went up as if she just discovered something. "I can't afford you, Shawn." She shook her head from side to side as she continued. "It's going to take me forever just to pay back my part of what we spent yesterday. I can't do this."

He took her hand and looked straight into her eyes. "I need to be honest with you. I never intended to let you pay me back, for anything. That's just not the way I was raised. I know you can't afford to pay me back, and even if you could, I wouldn't let you."

"But Shawn, that means I'm taking advantage of you and I can't do that. I will never do that. I spent three years of my life using people, doing anything I had to or needed to so I could to survive. I promised myself I would never do that again, Shawn."

She squeezed his hand so hard it almost hurt. "Please understand, I care for you so much. Too much."

Shawn stood up, and gently pulled her out of her chair and into his chest. "Are you done?" he whispered.

"Yes," she said.

"We need to have that talk. Today, so this isn't hanging over us. But, until we do, I need you to understand a few things." He sat back down and lowered her onto his lap, then lifted her chin so he could look into her eyes. "You're not taking advantage of me if I know what you're doing and agree with it. And how could you possibly be using me, if I'm the one suggesting what we do?

"I know your pride is hurt because you feel like you're not contributing your fair share, but that doesn't mean you're taking advantage or using me. You're not. Sharing is not about money. Sharing is about contributing in so many different ways, and while you may not realize it, you've already enriched my life by sharing who you are and what matters to you. Hell, if anybody's taken advantage of anybody, it's me. I've sucked up every bit of you I can. I've learned from you, I've admired you, and you've opened my eyes to things that were right in front of me but I never took time to see."

His face scrunched up, and he pulled her in close. "We need to get out of here. I love your sweatpants, but they're strangling me, and my voice is going to be four octaves higher if I stay in them much longer."

"Ooops. We can't have that," she said with a giant smile.

"How about if we head for my condo and we can continue this conversation as well as having the one I know you're dreading?" He turned her chin toward him. "Don't forget what I told you last night. Nothing you say is going to make me feel any different about you."

"I hope so but you might change your mind when you know some of the things I've done, Shawn. I wouldn't blame you if you never wanted to see me again."

"Come on, let's go. Please let me cook dinner tonight? I'm really a pretty good cook, you know."

She finally relented. "Okay, but you have to promise we'll come up with ways that I can contribute that makes us both feel good. Deal?"

"Deal," he said.

CJ loaded their wet, dirty clothes into her laundry basket, followed by the contents of her hamper. Next she grabbed the laundry soap, bleach, and softener, then added them to the basket. Shawn reached out and took the basket from her as they headed for the door. CJ locked the trailer while Shawn put the basket in his truck, then helped her in.

She slid in, and he asked, "Anything else you want to grab?"

"Just about everything I own is in the basket." She smiled and added, "I think I just figured out where the phrase 'I'm a basket case' comes from."

As usual, CJ insisted on getting the gates, and just before getting back in at the second gate, she called out and waved to Kate and Melissa.

They turned onto the ramp to 8 west. As he merged onto the interstate, "Just the Way You Are" by Bruno Mars came on the radio. He reached over, turned up the volume and started singing to her.

Shawn stopped singing and looked over at her. Her face was completely red, and she had the biggest, goofy grin he had ever seen. "What?" he said.

"You're embarrassing me. Nobody's ever sung to me before."

"Get used to it. This song describes you perfectly, and every time it comes on, I'm going to sing to you. Even when we're in public."

CJ reached over and pushed the center seat compartment up into the seat back. Then she unbuckled her seat belt, slid over, fished out the center seat belt, and buckled herself back in. Shawn put his arm around her and pulled her close.

She looked up at him and said, "The only thing amazing here is you."

Neither one of them said anything else for the rest of the trip as they enjoyed each other's company and the silence.

Chapter 16 - Cajun Food and Confession

Shawn pulled into his condo complex and parked. He walked around, opened her door, and helped her out. Then he retrieved the laundry basket from the backseat and steered her toward his condo.

He unlocked the door, opened it, and stepped aside so she could enter. She stepped in and her mouth dropped open. Again. She had expected a typical bachelor's condo—uninviting, beige paint everywhere, minimal furniture, tacky decorations, sports posters and stuff lying everywhere.

What she walked into was none of the above. Shawn's living room was stunning. Not only was it stunning, it was warm, inviting, and neat as a pin.

It was painted in two different light-brown tones, with a rust-colored accent wall on the left. The couch, love seat, and chairs all matched and were done in a beige and light-brown tweed. They also looked soft and comfortable enough to make someone never want to get up after sitting in them.

Mounted on the accent wall was a large, flat-screen TV with a built-in fireplace beneath it. A variety of brightly colored throw pillows, all in browns and rusts, adorned the couch, love seat and chairs. The coffee and end tables were a contrasting dark wood with dark brown glass inserts. Finally, a collage of several very nice paintings, all framed in dark wood, automatically drew your eyes to the far wall, as you took in the room.

"Oh, Shawn, this is… gorgeous. Did you decorate it?"

"Yes," he answered proudly, as he stepped in and closed the door.

"Would you like a tour?"

"Oh my God, yes," she said.

To the right of the pictures, on the far wall, CJ could see a serve-through, leading into what was obviously the kitchen. Shawn led her through the living room and past the serve-through, which had two cushioned bar stools at the counter.

The kitchen was painted in a very light green with dark wood cabinets and dark wood flooring. All of the upper cabinets had glass inserts instead of solid doors. The countertops and backsplashes were a gorgeous stark white quartz, which contrasted with the dark wood and helped brighten what, otherwise, would have been a very dark room.

Shawn flipped on the lights and the kitchen lit up like it was noon on a summer day. Twelve canned lights, installed in the ceiling, made sure that no corner went without light and under-cabinet lights gave the countertops a warm glow. All of the appliances were stainless steel and consisted of a french door refrigerator with a two-drawer freezer below, a five-burner gas cooktop, a double-wall oven, and a dishwasher.

From inside the kitchen, the cook could look out through the serve-through opening and see the entire living room. The two bar stools provided a great place for company to sit and chat with the cook, while dinner was being prepared. As in the living room, everything was in its place and the kitchen was absolutely spotless.

CJ was no cook, but she knew a gourmet cook's dream kitchen when she saw one.

Shawn reached out, took her hand, and led her back past the serve-through and down a hallway on the opposite side of the living room.

The first door to the right was what he described as the guest bath. The whole left wall was mirrored with a double-sink vanity below it. Beyond that was a separate room with a tub/shower and the toilet. Lining the wall opposite the vanity, were more cabinets than CJ had in her whole trailer. Once again, everything was in various shades of brown and the bathroom was spotless. On the counter was a basket full of anything and everything a guest might possibly need in the way of toiletries.

The next door on the right turned out to be the guest room. It was done in a very light shade of flamingo and contained a queen-size brass bed, a double dresser, and nightstand. A large walk-in closet was opposite the foot of the bed, and the far wall had a sliding door going out to a small patio. As with the other rooms, the bedspread, pictures, and other accessories matched or contrasted beautifully with the flamingo walls.

Finally, across the hall was a set of double doors leading to the master bedroom. As Shawn led her through the doorway, she came face to face with a massive California king bed with a very modern brass frame. On each side of the bed, there was a dark wood nightstand with a wall sconce above it. Behind the headboard hung a beautiful tapestry from the San Diego Zoo's Safari Park, depicting a variety of large African cats. Lighting up the tapestry were two small canned lights mounted in the ceiling.

Each wall was painted a different color in either pinkish orange or orange, and the wall behind the headboard was textured, using all of the colors on an off-white base. The result was nothing short of stunning, warm, and inviting.

At the foot of the bed was a six-drawer dresser and mirror, both in matching dark wood, and as in the guest room, there was a sliding-glass door on the far wall, which led to another private patio.

To the left of the dresser was a large walk-in closet and the entrance to the en suite master bath, which was almost as big as CJ's entire trailer. The bathroom, done in various shades of green, brown, and dark wood, contained a double-basin vanity that ran the length of the back wall and a small cushioned vanity bench against the front wall. To the left was a large European-style walk-in shower with a built-in bench and, to the right, a small room containing the toilet.

CJ sat on the cushioned vanity bench, and her eyes lit up. "I want to live in your bathroom. You could put twenty of my showers in your shower and not fill it. I can't even imagine what it's like to put your foot on the bench and be able to shave your leg without banging your head on the faucet.

"Shawn, your condo is unbelievable. Every room is so warm and inviting and the kitchen, oh my God. Anyone that cooks… would kill for a kitchen like yours."

Shawn's grin couldn't have gotten any bigger. "Thank you. I'm not sure my head will fit through the doorway after all that. I inherited most of my decorating skills from my mom, and thanks to her, everybody in my family is a *neat freak*."

CJ pasted on a big grin. "Gee, I never would have guessed."

He reached for her hand to help her up, but she put one hand under each thigh and sat there. "I'm not leaving. Please have the butler ring when my bath is ready." She glanced at the shower to her left. "Oh crap, no tub. Please have him ring when my shower is warm enough for my dainty tootsies."

Reaching down, he eased one hand out and pulled her up. "Sorry, but we need to go shopping if we want to eat. Oh, and today's the butler's day off so I'll be the one warming your shower for you."

"Oh goodie. Do we have to eat?"

He reached under her legs and scooped her up. She put her arms around his neck and kissed him as he carried her back into the living room and deposited her on one of the bar stools. While he went through the kitchen cupboard and spice cabinet to see what they needed to buy, he glanced toward the serve-through. He found her with her head on the counter and the side of her face pressed against the countertop. Her arms were stretched across the countertop and she had a death grip on the opposite side.

He walked over and found her with a serious frown on her face. "Are you okay?" he asked. He laid his head on the counter next to hers. Looking into her eyes, he asked, "What's wrong?"

Without lifting her head, she whispered, "Shawn, I don't ever want to leave here."

He slid his face over, kissed her gently, and said, "Funny, I was just thinking the very same thing. You walked in, and it was like everything I've done in here was so I could see your eyes light up when you saw it. You belong here, CJ."

A single tear escaped and ran down her cheek as she continued to gaze at him. "I am so hopelessly in love with you."

"Good, my plan's working." He kissed her again then asked, "Do you like Cajun food?"

She lifted her head then rested her chin on the counter. "Great, first you steal my heart, now you're going to kidnap my stomach. What is Cajun food?"

"Ah, you'll find out soon enough. Let's go shopping."

Shawn went into his bedroom, brought out the few items of dirty laundry he had and added them to CJ's laundry basket. He locked the door; then they headed to the laundry room where CJ sorted everything and got three loads of wash going.

After a short drive down Bonita Road, they pulled into a shopping center and parked in front of the Vons supermarket. Shawn came around to open her door, and as she got out, she looked across the street.

"Shawn, there's a couple of cowboys on horses across the street. Wow, the markings on that pinto are just spectacular."

He glanced across the street to the golf course parking lot. "Yeah, they're from one of the ranches down in Procter Valley at the end of Bonita Road. They walk their horses on the Bonita Social Circle all the time."

"What's the Bonita Social Circle?"

"It's a long story. Come on, let's grab a cart and get some food. I'll explain about the social circle while I'm cooking."

CJ followed him into the store, and thirty-five minutes later, they were in the checkout line. As they had wandered through the store, almost *everyone* they passed said, "Hello, Shawn".

When she asked him about it, he explained, "We shop here for the fire station so, between that and my personal shopping, I'm in here quite a bit." Then he added, "Besides, Bonita is a pretty small town and everybody knows everybody. Not to mention if you fart in public, the whole town will find out about it, before you got home.

They loaded the groceries into his truck and drove back to his condo. While Shawn unloaded everything, CJ walked over to the laundry room and put their wash into the dryers.

186

She came back into the condo and found him in the kitchen, singing at the top of his lungs to a New Orleans jazz CD. "Gotta get in the mood," he said, as he lifted her arm above her head and twirled her around.

After two twirls, he stopped her and pulled her arms and hands out so he could put stuff in them. He piled on two stalks of celery, an onion, one red pepper, one green pepper, a clove of garlic, and two sausage links. Then he turned her around and gently pushed her toward the serve-through counter, where two bowls, a knife, and cutting board awaited.

"You be the chopper and I be the cook," he said. "Wash your hands and start chopping, my fair maiden. It's time to earn your keep."

She watched Shawn drag out a large cast iron pot as he explained he was making a roux, whatever that was. As the roux browned, she chopped vegetables and listened as he explained about the Bonita Social Circle.

"There's a two and a half mile dirt path around the Chula Vista Golf Course and Sweetwater Park that everyone uses for walking, jogging, biking, or riding horses. Part of it runs behind our condo complex and another part runs alongside Bonita Road, across from the fire station.

"When I first got to the station, I couldn't help but notice that everyone in Bonita uses the path at one time or another during the day. I also noticed that people would often stop and chat with people they knew or say hi to people they didn't know, but apparently pass on the path every day. So one day, when we were washing the engine, I glanced over and commented that the social circle was much busier than usual, and somehow, the name stuck."

"That's cute. It also sounds like the perfect name for it." She carried the cutting board full of diced vegetables into the kitchen. "Where do you want them?"

"Perfect timing. Dump them into the roux, mix it up well, then you can slice up the Andouille sausage while I grill up some chicken."

"What exactly are we making?"

"Gumbo Ya Ya, with rice and greens."

"Oh, that really helped. I think I know what rice is, but with you, I'm not even sure about that."

She started slicing up the sausage as she watched him put the chicken on the grill. While the chicken was cooking, he stirred chicken stock into the roux mixture then added what looked to her to be some of every spice he had. Next he cut the chicken into one-inch cubes, put them on a plate, and brought it over to CJ.

He pulled out another large cast iron pot and set it on the stove. Glancing over to see how she was doing, he asked, "Done with the sausage?" as he put another onion, clove of garlic, and a package of bacon on the cutting board. CJ nodded and slid the sausage onto the plate with the chicken, which he moved over next to the gumbo pot.

"Okay, you're going to make the greens." He told her and gave her step by step directions. She diced up three strips of bacon, put it in a cast iron pot, and set the burner to medium. While the bacon browned, she diced up the onion and garlic. Next, she added both to the bacon fat, stirred everything till the onion was almost clear, then threw in the two packages of greens they had bought and stir it again till the greens were wilted. Finally, she added three cups of chicken broth, a pinch of red pepper, then put the lid on, turned it down to simmer, and let it cook.

As CJ put her preparation dishes in the sink, Shawn added the chicken and sausage to the gumbo, then turned it down to simmer so it too could finish cooking. With the gumbo and greens simmering, he set up the rice by putting more chicken stock in a pot, along with several pats of butter. Then he measured out the rice and set it next to the pot.

He reached over, caught CJ's hand, lifted her arm up over her head again, and twirled her around. "You were wonderful. Those greens are going to taste sooo good."

"A lot I had to do with it. My only claim to fame is I managed not to add my blood as seasoning when I diced up the veggies."

Shawn grabbed a bottle of red wine he had opened earlier, two wine glasses, then ushered CJ into the living room. He steered her toward the couch, and they sat down. "We've got an hour before all that's ready. How about we have that talk now and you can get rid of that big ugly gray cloud you think is hanging over your head."

CJ took a deep breath. She really didn't want to do this, but knew she had to tell him. If he found out from Ami or someone else, she might lose him before she ever had a chance to explain.

She crossed her fingers on both hands and held them up so he could see them. "I am terrified right now and hope to God you'll still want to be with me when I'm done."

"CJ, I—"

She leaned over and kissed him so he couldn't finish. "You have no idea how scared I am right now and how hard this is. Please,

189

just let me talk until I'm done. If you stop me, I'm afraid I'll completely lose it. Okay?"

Shawn nodded.

"From what you've told me about your family and friends, they all sound wonderful. Your family taught you all kinds of things, made sure you went to school, exposed you to different cultures, and supported you," CJ began.

"The only thing my parents taught me was to keep my mouth shut and do what they told me. If I didn't, they made sure I would remember their rules the next time.

"As long as I can remember, my mom was a drunk, and by the time I was a teenager she had added drugs to help her get through the day. My dad was even worse, when he was around.

"As for school, I didn't go much after grade school. On days when my mom was sober enough to drive, she might take me or she might not. Since catching the bus was a long walk, most of the time I just said screw it.

"My only friend was Fred. He lived next door, and his parents were just as bad as mine. The four of them would get together and wouldn't come down for days. By the time I was ten, I realized that Fred was the only one who understood me. He was the only one who didn't treat me like dirt, because he was dirt too. He was the only one I could trust and he was my best friend.

"The first time Fred and I had sex, I was twelve. By the time I was fourteen, we were doing it on a regular basis.

"Just before I turned fifteen, my dad walked in on us. He didn't yell, punch Fred, or beat the crap out of me. He just closed the door and left. Later that night, he came into my room and told

190

me that since I was already *broken in*. I needed to start servicing him whenever he needed me to.

"He was so high that night that oral sex was the only thing he could do. Even though I was the one doing all the work, right in the middle, he passed out. I was so terrified that I would be punished for not finishing. I ran next door and told Fred what had happened and begged him to help me. Our first thought was to kill my dad while he was still passed out, but neither of us had the courage.

"All I knew was that I would never let him put his hands on me again. So we both packed whatever clothes we could get in our backpacks, stole as much money and drugs from his parents and mine as we could find, and ran.

"We had no idea where we were going, we just ran. We caught a ride to the Ohio Turnpike and started hitchhiking west. All we wanted to do was get as far away as we could. I'm not sure how we ended up in San Diego. All I know is we spent ten days hitchhiking our way across country, going wherever anyone who stopped was going.

"Twice, the only way we could get a ride was by Fred telling them I would give them oral sex as payment. The first time I refused, but Fred told me he would give the guy a blowjob himself and leave me standing on the side of the road. I was so terrified of being left alone, I gave in.

"The second time, I didn't argue.

"By the time we got to San Diego, we were broke, had no drugs left to sell, had no place to sleep, and didn't know anybody. The first week we slept in Balboa Park, down in a canyon, and by the end of the week, we were starving. We tried stealing stuff but got caught all three times. The first two times we begged and they let us go. The third time, the store owner had two of his employees beat the crap out of us.

191

"By then, we were absolutely desperate, and Fred told me the only way we could survive is if I sold myself. It would only be till he found a job, and he promised he would find nice, clean guys. Besides, he would be there to make sure they didn't hurt me.

"The first guy was from out of town attending a convention. He treated me pretty good at first and even bought me dinner. Then he took me up to his hotel room, drugged me, and in between me giving him oral sex, he fucked me till I was so sore I couldn't walk.

"That was when I found out that I am one of those *lucky people* that become addicted after the first time. It took me the whole next day to come down, and as soon as I did, I couldn't wait to go back up. Fred quickly realized that as long as he kept me high I would pretty much do anything.

"In the following weeks, Fred gave up looking for a job and devoted his days to finding drugs, customers, and keeping me high. He bought me some nice clothes and peddled me near the nicer hotels around the Gaslamp Quarter.

"I'm told that went on for close to two years. Couldn't prove it by me. All I remember is being high twenty-four seven. When I did come down, I'd beg and do anything to get high again.

"At first, I would wake up in nice hotels with decent-looking guys. Fred would always be close by and waiting for me when they left. But as time went on, more often than not, I'd wake up in some sleazebag hotel with a guy or two that looked like they belonged in a horror movie. Soon, Fred was nowhere to be found afterward. He would drop me off and tell me where to meet him and God help me if I was late.

"Most of the time I was sore inside. But more and more, I'd wake up and have cigarette burn and bruises all over my body.

Apparently, strangling me while they fucked me was great fun because I often woke up with red marks all around my neck, and it was days before I could talk again.

"Finally, Fred sold me to three guys for a week. I don't think they had any intention of returning me, at least not alive. According to the police and doctors, they kept me just on the border of overdosing, then used me in any way they could think of. They fucked me every way they could and with anything they could. They beat the crap out of me whenever they felt like it, and when they finally got tired, they overdosed me and dumped me in a field."

For the first time since she had started her story, CJ lifted her head and looked at Shawn.

Tears were streaming down his cheeks.

"If you want to take me back now, I'll understand," she whispered. "I told you I was broken, Shawn. No man in his right mind would want me after what they did to me. After what I did to myself."

Shawn stood up and walked to the door. CJ's heart broke. She knew he would loathe her once he knew. What guy in his right mind, or any mind, would want to be anywhere near her? He looked like he was about to be sick. He was probably remembering last night, and the thought of having been inside her made him want to throw up. As soon as she left, he would spend hours in the shower, trying to wash away any trace of her.

CJ stood. "Let me get our clothes from the laundry room. It will only take me a minute to put my stuff in the basket and fold your things. Then you can run me back."

Shawn turned around and glared at her. "What happened to them?"

193

"Who?" she asked.

"Fred and the three guys."

"They caught the three guys. They were a rock group, in town for a gig, and decided they needed a little entertainment. They had kept me so doped up that I couldn't even identify them. Besides, it would have been my word against the three of them, and who was going to believe a whore? It wasn't like it was the first time I'd slept with more than one guy."

"And Fred?"

"I don't know. After the story hit the papers, he disappeared from the face of the earth."

Shawn wiped the tears from his cheeks and said, "Let's go get the laundry."

They walked over to the laundry room. CJ emptied the dryers, threw her stuff in the basket, and started to fold his clothes.

"Just throw it all in the basket," he said.

"Shawn, I'm so sorry. I should have told you before now. Before we got involved."

"It wouldn't have made a difference. What they did to you makes me sick."

As they walked back into the condo, she looked over at him. "I understand how you feel. Let me put your stuff in the bedroom, and I'll be ready."

"I need some air." he said as he walked back through the door and slammed it.

CJ whispered, "Oh God, I'm so sorry."

Chapter 17 - My Soul is Yours

CJ pulled his clothes from the basket, folded them, and took them into his bedroom. She set them on the dresser and started to leave; the last thing he needed was her invading his privacy. But she couldn't help it. Her hand reached down and pulled a drawer open.

She reached in and took a NY Jets T-shirt and held it against her nose. She closed her eyes, took a deep breath, and smiled. The shirt smelled just like him. Spicy, warm, friendly, inviting. He smelled so good. God, she would miss his smell.

Why had she told him? Why didn't she wait so she could have a few more days of being with him? He brought such joy and happiness to her life. She felt so safe with him, so wanted and happy. Why did she go and ruin that? Now he would hate her. Hell, he obviously already hated her. He couldn't even stand to be around her.

She needed to get out of here. Now. Before she totally lost it. Before she tried to defend herself or, worse, plead with him not to run, to be there for her. God, she needed him so badly.

"What do you think you're doing?"

CJ just about jumped out of her skin. She turned to find Shawn standing in the doorway glaring at her.

"I'm sorry. I was just putting your stuff away before we leave."

"And you were smelling my shirt, because?"

"Because I want to remember what you smell like."

"Why did you leave your clothes in the living room? And why would you smell my shirt when you've got the real me right here?"

CJ's eyebrows scrunched up, and she stared at him. "What— I don't understand? I need my clothes so… What do you mean, I've got the real you?"

"Me. See?" He held his arms out and did a three-sixty turn. "You can smell the *real* me anytime you want."

"But you hate me. I saw the look on your face. You wanted to throw up."

"CJ, what you saw was anger. What you saw was me wanting to go find Fred and those three guys and kill them with my bare hands."

"You don't hate me?"

He walked over, put him arms around her, and pulled her in. "I could never hate you. And I promise you… as long as I'm alive… No one. No one, will ever hurt you again."

CJ's head was spinning. Oh God, he didn't hate her. He wasn't running away. He wasn't throwing her away. He was standing right next to her, and he just promised to protect her. She leaned her head against his chest, and the tears poured down her cheeks.

He bent down, scooped her up as her chest heaved, and she sobbed hysterically. She wrapped her arms around his neck and bawled. God, how she loved him. She had never felt so safe, so protected. And she had also never cried tears of joy before.

He carried her into the living room and sat in one of the chairs, still cradling her in his arms. He pulled her even closer and whispered, "You're mine, and I have no plans of ever giving you up. I told you nothing you could say would ever make me change my mind, and I meant it. I could never hate you, CJ. I adore you, and I'm yours for as long as you want me."

She looked at him as the tears continued to pour down her cheeks. "I love you so much. I want you forever."

He tried to pull her in closer, as they sat there, neither of them saying a word. Finally, he gently lifted her chin and kissed her so tenderly that all the hairs on the back of her neck stood straight up.

"We need to go stir the gumbo, if it hasn't already burned."

With her still in his arms, he stood up. *How in the world does he do that?* He carried her into the kitchen. She reached down and picked up the serving spoon next to the gumbo pot. She put the spoon in, dragged it around the inside several times, then tapped it on the edge and put it back on the spoon rest.

She looked up at him and smiled. "Did I do good, sir chef?"

"You did outstanding. Still hungry?"

She wiped the last of her tears away and looked up at him. "Are you kidding? Crying's hard work. I'm starved." Then she hugged him even tighter. "I love you so much."

Shawn set her down and kissed her. "How are you at table setting?"

"What's that?" she asked, as she headed for the cabinet with the dishes in it.

While Shawn cooked the rice, CJ set up two place settings at the serve-through counter. Then, she went into the living room, retrieved their glasses, the wine bottle, and set them by their place settings.

She topped off their wine glasses, walked over behind Shawn, grabbed him around the waist, and peeked out at the stove. "Oh my God, does that smell good. How are my greens doing?"

He lifted the lid and wafted some of the steam toward her.

"Mmm," came her response.

"Wanna dish out the greens while I get the rice and gumbo?"

"Sure," she said.

They set out everything on the counter, and each took a stool on the other side. Shawn held up his glass for a toast, and she joined him.

"To the most wonderful person I've ever met. Thank you so much for being a part of my life." They clinked glasses as CJ's eyes just sparkled. She had never been this happy in her entire life.

Shawn put his spoon into his bowl of gumbo and rice and pulled out a spoonful. He carefully blew on it, then told her to open wide. He slid the spoon in, and she closed her lips on it as he pulled out the spoon. As she chewed, her eyes got as big as saucers.

"Oh Shawn, this is delicious. Oh, wow. I've never had anything like it. It's so thick, and there's a thousand flavors running around in my mouth right now."

He started to refill his spoon, but she yelled, "Wait." She filled her spoon with gumbo and rice from her bowl, blew on it, and told him to open wide.

They spent the rest of the meal feeding each other and laughing like two love-struck teenagers each time one of them missed the other's mouth. After seconds of everything, they rinsed off their dishes, put away what little was left, and started the dishwasher.

"Damn, I forgot to grab something for dessert," Shawn said.

She smiled and winked at him. "I already know what I'm having and I don't need to go to the store to get it."

They grabbed their glasses, another bottle of wine, and wandered into the living room. Shawn sat at one end of the couch, and CJ curled up with her head in his lap.

She wrapped her arms around his waist and squeezed. "I am the happiest person in the world right now. I have no right to be this happy, but I am and I don't ever plan to let go of you, Shawn James. You're mine, you're mine, you're mine," she squealed, and squeezed till he told her she was going to break a rib.

"Shannon and Kate were right," he said. "You're amazing. After all you've been through, you're not the least bit bitter. It's like everything you do is a new adventure, and you love everybody you meet."

"That's 'cos it is. I've never been anywhere or done anything, so it's all new to me. I think about the fact that I almost died without experiencing any of the wonderful things in this world and it makes me appreciate everything I see. I see things totally different now.

"And everyone I've met has been so amazing. Not only did they help me with my recovery, they opened my eyes to how wonderful and caring people can be. Every one of them treated me with nothing but kindness, starting with the firemen that found me naked and half beaten to death. They knew what I was, but they still had nothing but concern for me.

"I don't remember much about that day, but I remember them protecting me. I remember them telling me everything was going to be okay. Most of all, I will never forget the compassion in their eyes. They protected my dignity and made sure no one saw me naked. They didn't need to do that, but they did. I was just a thrown away piece of trash, but they still protected me. To them, I was a person. I needed their help, and they kept me safe and protected me so the doctors could make me better.

"Shawn, I hope I can explain this right. I treasure your love more than anything in this world. I treasure that you chose me. I treasure that I'm special to you, and most of all, I treasure that you're my own special hero. But I also realize that deep down, compassion and the need to protect are a part of your soul. It's who you are. It's why you are. It's why I felt safe the minute I met you. It's why Rio knew I would be safe and protected with you in my life.

"When I look into your eyes, I see so much love for me. But I also see the compassion of the firemen who found me, and I realize that you're not just *my* hero. You're a hero to everybody whose life you touch because you save them and protect them and keep them safe. That's what you do. You're one of them, Shawn. You're a fireman. You earn a special place in people's hearts because you save and protect them, no matter who they are. Not because it's your job, but because you care.

"Oh God, I'm just rambling, aren't I? Shawn, what I'm trying to say is that because you protect and keep others safe doesn't make me feel any less special. If anything, it makes me feel even more special. It makes me want to let everybody have just a little piece of what I have. I want them to know how special you are. I want them to know why I feel so very special to have you as mine.

201

"Shawn, they may not realize it, but those firemen who found me made me feel special too. They made me feel like a person. A person worth saving. A person with dignity who they needed to protect and keep safe."

She reached up, pulled his head down, and kissed him hard. "Crap, no wonder I'm so madly in love with you. I've got a fireman complex."

When Shawn's head came back up, he had a grin that went from ear to ear. "Everyone at the station is going to absolutely love you, but we're going to keep your fireman complex a secret. Okay? And, just so you know, I have no intention of sharing you, or myself, with anyone else. I found you, and I plan to keep you all to myself. I also have a plan to protect you and keep you safe; my plan is to spoil you so bad that nobody else will want you."

"Ooh. Spoil away, my handsome knight, spoil away." CJ yawned. "I think it's time for dessert. We can work on my spoil training too."

They both stood up. CJ collected their glasses and the empty wine bottle and took them into the kitchen. She rejoined him in the living room, and they walked hand in hand into the bedroom.

Shawn sat on the edge of the bed, pulled her into his lap, and they kissed. CJ leaned back and took his head in her hands. "Before I ravish you again... because it is my turn to go first... I need to tell you something. It's okay to be rough with me.

"I know you're being extra careful and worried because of what's happened to me but it's okay to let your passion out. Being in love is all about trust, and I trust you more than anyone in this world. I know you would never hurt me and I desperately need you to make mad, passionate love to me."

She kissed him on the nose then looked deep into his eyes. "I read somewhere that 'love is a single soul inhabiting two bodies.' I need you to search inside of me and find my soul, Shawn. And, when you find it, it's yours, to do with as you wish. It's my gift to you, along with my heart, which you already own."

Shawn stayed silent for the longest time. Finally, he pressed his lips to hers and his tongue forced its way into her mouth. He slipped her top over her head, must have noticed she had no bra on, and looked back up at her.

"They're all in the wash." She chuckled.

He stood her up, pulled her jeans and panties off, and laid her gently back on the bed. He slid his hand under her back and pulled a pillow under her hips. Bending over her, he gently kissed his way down to her belly button.

The last thing she really remembered was him kissing his way up the inside of her left thigh, as she completely turned herself over to him. Her mind relinquished all control of her body and went to a place it had never been before. A place full of pleasure and joy and love, while her body tried to suck in every ounce of him it could.

She never did get her turn. But she didn't need to. He brought her up then let her back down. Rough at first, then gentle the next time. Then he repeated it over and over again. When she thought he was finished, her mind had been cycled through so many feelings that it was about to explode. Her body had exploded. Over and over again, she had climaxed until she was totally exhausted. Until there was nothing left.

But he wasn't done. He reached deep once more and found another orgasm. Another wave of mind-blowing pleasure and love and tenderness passed through her as he again filled every part of her body with warmth.

In the end, she laid there totally spent. She was a pile of Jell-O with no bones. She couldn't even form a thought, much less a word or sentence.

All she knew was, she was hopelessly in love and she would never be the same. He had found her soul, several times over, and it no longer belonged to her. He wasn't her soul mate because there was only one soul now. Theirs. Her heart and soul were a part of him, and she knew he would protect them till his last dying breath.

She smiled as he pulled her close and kissed her.

"Your turn," he said.

"Hmmm," she moaned, as she curled into him and fell sound asleep.

Chapter 18 - Missy, Milton, and Horsey Talk

CJ woke to the smell of coffee and found Shawn sitting on the edge of the bed holding a coffee mug under her nose. "Wake up, sleepy," he said, as he kissed her.

She stretched her arms out and pulled him in. "Just because I haven't brushed my teeth yet doesn't mean you're going to get away without giving me my morning kiss."

He leaned in and kissed her again, his tongue finding hers. He leaned back. "Mmm, you taste good." He held up the mug. "Coffee?"

CJ stretched and took the mug. "What time is it?"

"It's 5. I thought you might want to get an early start back to the ranch. If not, you can curl back up and get another hour or two of sleep."

She put her arms around his waist and laid her head in his lap. "God, I would love to just curl back up with you, but I really need to get out to the ranch. Mondays, I'm usually the only one there."

"Well, today you'll have help. There's a new toothbrush on the counter and the toothpaste is in the top middle drawer. There's a scrubby ball, a bottle of your cookie dough shampoo, and lemon bodywash in the shower."

"Oh, Shawn, you really are spoiling me. But nothing will ever come close to last night." She pulled back the covers and swung her legs out. "Join me?"

"Of course. How else are you going to get your back clean? And front. And sides. And bottom."

She took his hand, and they marched naked into the shower. She handed him the scrubby ball and body wash. "You can start with the bottom," she said. "Nobody has ever washed my bottom before."

An hour later, they had finished showering, eaten two bowls of cereal, and were headed toward the 125. Shawn pointed out the fire station then CJ pointed toward the path across the road.

"That's got to be the Bonita Social Circle," she said. "I don't believe it. There's got to be eighty to a hundred people out there, and it's only 6."
"I told you, everybody in Bonita uses it. Most people try to get their run in before they head out to work. It's not unusual to see flashlight beams bouncing along in the dark at night, either."

"Do you run?" she asked.

"When I can."

"Can I run with you? When I'm here?"

"I would love to have you run with me, and I hope you'll be here every minute you can. If you want."

She reached over and took his hand. "I want."

There was next to no traffic going out of town on Monday morning. The same couldn't be said for going into San Diego. They were both glad they were headed east, not west.

At 6:30, they pulled up to the front gate, and CJ got out to unlock it. She opened the gate, Shawn drove through, she closed it, and

206

climbed back in. "That's funny. The gate was unlocked. The chain was pulled through and someone closed the lock so it looked like it was locked, but it wasn't snapped shut."

They drove up to the ranch gate and she hopped out once more to get the gate. As he drove through, he stopped next to her and rolled the window down. "Same thing," she said. "The chain was pulled through, but the lock wasn't snapped shut."

CJ looked over to where the volunteers parked and saw Ami's truck. She looked back at Shawn. "That's Ami's truck. How did she get in? She doesn't have a key, and she's not scheduled to be here."

--------//--------

Ami heard tires on the gravel and peeked through the curtain of the volunteer trailer. "Oh shit," she mumbled. She reached over, grabbed the baggie from the table, and stuffed it into the back of the drawer closest to her. She closed the drawer, put everything else back in the cloth bag with the peace symbol on it that she used as a purse. She pulled her sleeve over her knuckles, used it to wipe the table, then turned for the door.

As Shawn and CJ approached the trailer, the door opened and Ami stepped out.

Ami pasted on a big grin. "Hi, Shawn." She walked up to him, put her hand behind his head, pulled him into a kiss, then stepped back.

She twisted her shoulders toward CJ in kind of a half turn, then leaned back toward Shawn. "Wow, I'm glad I decided to come in today." She rocked toward CJ, took a step back, and tilted forward again. "Unfortunately I just got a call and my mom's sick so I gotta leave."

CJ stared at her. "Ami, how did you get in?"

Ami continued to swing her shoulders back and forth like she was dancing to some song that only she could hear. "Oh, the gates were open. Well, they weren't *open* open, but the locks were open."

She did another half turn back toward Shawn and smiled. "Well, gotta go."

"Ami, I don't think you should be driving," CJ said.

"Fuck you," Ami shot back, then marched off toward the parking area.

Shawn looked at CJ and whispered, "She's high on something."

"Tell me about it. She's stoned, and it's not even 7," CJ said.

Ami drove out and left both gates wide open.

"God damn it. I'm going to kill her with my bare hands." CJ said.

Shawn smiled and pecked her on the cheek. "I'll get the gates."

"Thank you. I'll meet you at the tool shed after I check the volunteer trailer." She reached up and pulled him into a kiss. A second later, her tongue found his, and what started out to be a short kiss turned into an 'I don't ever want you to leave' kiss for both of them.

"Mmm, much better than Ami."

She punched him in the arm. "Thanks. You better say that, if you value your life."

Shawn headed for the gates, CJ for the trailer. On the way back, Shawn jumped into one of the golf carts and drove over to the hay shed. After loading four bales of hay, he met her at the tool shed.

"Go ahead and run the hay over by the stalls while I finish getting the tools," she told him. "But, don't give anybody hay till I get there. Okay? I'll meet you down by the first stall, the one with Missy and Shakespeare in it."

He maneuvered the golf cart down to the stalls and quickly found the one with Missy and Shakespeare's names on the fence. He got out and walked over to the fence as a very small horse came up to the other side. "Hi there. And you would be?" he asked the horse.

"That would be Missy," came CJ's voice from alongside of him as she set the wheelbarrow down.

"She's just a pony."

"She's not a pony. She's full grown. She's..."

"Oh my God. You washed her and she shrunk," he said, before she could finish.

CJ chuckled. "She's a miniature horse, you dummy. And don't let her size fool you. She runs the ranch and rules the herd. We don't do anything without checking with her first." CJ reached up and scratched behind the ear of the red horse who came over and stood next to Missy. "And this gorgeous Arab gelding is Shakespeare, the love of Missy's life. One doesn't go anywhere without the other."

Shawn reached over and rubbed Shakespeare's nose. "I've heard of Arabian horses, but never knew what they looked like. I'll bet that bright red coat and his jet black mane and tail turn more than a few of the ladies' heads. He likes having his nose rubbed too. Don't you, fella?"

"Okay, time to start teaching you some horsey talk. The strip between his forehead and muzzle, nostrils to you, is his nose. A horse's nose can have different markings or no markings at all. The most common is a blaze, which is a wide white strip from his forehead to down over his muzzle.

"If the strip covers the whole width of his nose, it's called a bald, and if it's narrow, it's a stripe. If there is no strip but only a white patch on his forehead, it's a star and if there's only a patch on his muzzle, it's a snip. Got that?"

"Uh, sure. Is there going to be a test on this?"

"Pay attention." CJ giggled. "If a horse has a blaze, or other marking, you rub that, not their nose. So you would say, 'I rubbed the horse's blaze' not 'I rubbed the horse's nose.'"

"What if they have no marking?" Shawn asked.

"Then you're rubbing their nose. Oh, and never rub their muzzle. If you rub their muzzle, it's going to tickle them, they're going to sneeze, shake their head, and fling horse snot and slobber all over you. Got it?"

Shawn just stood there like a deer in the headlights.

Missy started whinnying and pawing the ground. "You're ignoring her," CJ said.

"Sorry, little girl," Shawn said, "Here, let me rub your—" He looked at her nose. "—blaze. So how did these two end up here? Were they raised together and that's why they like each other?"

"No. Missy came to us before Shakespeare, and she is about three years older than him. Like many of the other horses, Missy was abandoned, and when we first got her, she had major trust issues. She was also one of the first horses that we used operant conditioning and target training on.

"Operant conditioning is where positive reinforcement, such as praise and food rewards, were used to teach a horse to do something. For example, if you wanted to teach a horse to knock over a rubber cone with their nose, you would put a treat under the cone, then try to coax him to nudge the cone with his nose. When he finally knocks the cone over, he is rewarded with the treat underneath, as well as verbal praise. When this is repeated often enough, the horse learns to associate the command with the act of knocking the cone over and receiving the reward.

"Likewise, target training uses positive reinforcement and rewards, but adds a clicker to signal commands to the horse. Both of these methods help build a strong bond between the handler and the horse. And in Missy's case, dramatically increased her comfort level, confidence, and trust.

"In fact, Missy has gone from being a thirty-eight inch tall, shy, and withdrawn little girl to being a confident, bossy bitch, who is now perfectly comfortable running the ranch. And for Shakespeare, the love of his life who can do no wrong. In spite of her occasionally *pushy* personality, Missy has also won the hearts of everybody at the ranch with her playful antics and adorable good looks. Not to mention, those gorgeous brown eyes that simply melted your heart."

CJ glanced over to make sure she hadn't lost Shawn. "Shakespeare came to the ranch several years later. He was rescued by County Animal Services after the ranch he lived on went into foreclosure. His owners had simply left him and a ten-year-old paint gelding when they moved out. The paint found a happy home with a ten-year-old boy and several other horses. But no one wanted poor Shakespeare until CAS brought him here and Missy immediately claimed him as hers."

As part of Shawn's continuing 'horsey talk' training, CJ told him, "Shakespeare is short for a gelding and measures only fourteen HH, which stands for 'hands high.'

"Measuring a horse in hands goes back to ancient Egypt," she explained, "and has been used for centuries." Holding her hand up, she went on. "A hand is considered to be four inches, which is the approximate width of a male hand.

"When you measure a horse, you measure from the ground, just beside and behind a front foreleg, to the top of the withers, which is the fifth vertebrae. That's the part of the top line of the horse that does not change when the horse raises or lowers his head or drops or arches his back." Each time, she pointed out the place she was referring to.

"If a horse isn't an even number of hands high, then the remainder or partial hand left, is expressed in inches. So if a horse were seventeen and a half HH, you would say he was seventeen point two HH or seventeen hands, two inches, or half a hand, high."

"God, and I thought being a fireman was hard. So let me see if I have this right. You said Missy is thirty-eight inches high. So thirty-eight, divided by four, is nine and a half. That means Missy is nine and a half hands high or nine point two HH, right?"

"No," CJ said with a big smile.

"What do you mean, "no"? Nine point five times four is thirty-eight, right? And nine point five is nine hands, two inches. Right?"

"Right on both counts," CJ said, now laughing.

"So that makes Missy nine point two HH. Right?"

"Nope. Missy is a miniature horse."

"So what do you use? Midget hands?"

Smiling from ear to ear, she said, "No. Ponies and miniature horses are usually measured in inches, not hands."

"Oh, you're so going to pay for this tonight. By the way, what's a gelding?"

CJs started laughing again. "That's a male horse that's been castrated. He's had his testicles removed."

"Ouch. Why do they— Never mind. I don't want to know."

CJ took Shawn's face in her hands and kissed him. "I promise you will never be a gelding. I have a vested interest in your testicles and no one else will get near them while I'm around."

"Thanks, I feel a lot safer now. So what do you want me to do with all this hay?"

CJ laid out a plan. "How about if you do this row of stalls and I'll do the ones on the opposite side. Leave the hay for now and start with poop patrol." She pointed to the manure pile past the gate. "Run the wheelbarrows of poop over to the manure pile whenever the wheelbarrow gets full. While you're doing poop patrol, drain the trough using the pump, then clean it, refill the trough, and move on to the next stall.

"I'll drag the pump over to my side as we go so I can get the troughs over here. When we get to the end, we can both tackle the big corral then come back and distribute hay and the food buckets."

Two and a half hours later, as they finished the corral, a big burro with very large ears trotted up to the corral gate. CJ opened the gate and the burro trotted out like he was a dog whose owner was about to take him for a walk. He headed directly for Shawn. When he was right in front of him, he raised his head, brayed loud enough to be heard in the next county, then gently butted Shawn's chest with his nose.

"Shawn, this is Milton Burro. Milton Burro, this is Shawn."

Milton Burro brayed again. "I think he likes you." CJ chuckled.

The three of them walked back up to Missy and Shakespeare's stall. During the entire trip, Milton Burro never left Shawn's side. CJ was all smiles. "Yup, he definitely likes you. Your stalls look great by the way. Okay, I'm going to get the other golf cart and go fill the food buckets. While I'm doing that, you and Milton Burro can distribute hay. Cut the bales open and each horse gets a flake. *But* skip any horse that has a colored dot on the sign with his or her name on it. That's really important. Those are the horses that are on a special diet and don't get hay."

"Does Milton know who they are? In case I screw up? By the way, what's a flake?"

"When you break open the bale, it will kinda come apart in sections. When they make a bale, they build it in chunks. Each chunk, or section, is called a flake, and there's about eight of them to a bale. Anyway, each flake is just about the right amount for one horse.

"And yes, Milton Burro knows who they are and will likely head butt you if you screw up. Right, Milton?" Milton brayed again and nudged Shawn's arm.

Shawn glanced over to the stall next to them. "Since I'm starting right here, I see that Missy has a red dot on her sign, but Shakespeare doesn't. So that means I need to give Shakespeare a flake, but Missy can't have hay. How do I keep her from getting his hay?"

"That's easy. Since Shakespeare is much taller than Missy, you'll notice his hay tray is mounted much higher on the fence. So Missy, being only thirty-eight inches, can't reach it. These two are the only mixed pair, so in all the other stalls, either all the horses get hay or all are on special diets."

"Wow, you guys think of everything. How come Missy's on a special diet? She really looks healthy."

"She is now. But she has Cushing's disease, which is caused by a cancerous tumor in the pituitary gland. It's kind of difficult to explain, but it ends up screwing up their endocrine system and they can't regulate their body temperature. When we first got Missy, she was downing almost twenty gallons of water a day. Normal for a horse is five to eight, and don't forget, she's a miniature.

"We put her on meds as soon as the vets tested her and confirmed Cushing's. Now her health is back to normal, but she'll be on meds and a special diet for the rest of her life."

Shawn reached over and rubbed Shakespeare's nose. "You need to watch over her." Then he leaned forward and whispered in his ear, "I can see why you're in love with her; she's as cute as a button."

He broke open a bale of hay, and as CJ said, it split into eight chunks. *Oops, gotta remember, they're flakes, not chunks.* He put a flake's worth into Shakespeare's hay tray then drove to the next stall.

As he worked his way down toward the corral at the end, Milton Burro was always just off his left shoulder and never more than a step behind. Several times, he almost kissed Milton when he turned to the left. And each time, Milton would bray, bat his giant eye lashes then stare at him with the most gorgeous eyes Shawn had ever seen.

By the time they reached the corral at the end, Shawn was in love. Again.

CJ finished hanging the last feed bucket and came over and hugged Shawn. "I think he's in love with you," she said, nodding toward Milton.

"Good 'cause I'm in love with him. He's absolutely adorable. He had to be somebody's pet. I've never seen any animal so loving and trusting. Just look at those eyes." Milton brayed and leaned his head against Shawn's chest.

"Oh my God, I've been replaced by a eunuch," CJ cried.

"He's a gelding?"

"Uh-huh." She smiled.

Shawn leaned his head against Milton's forehead. "No wonder you're so sad."

CJ reached over and petted Milton. "Come on, big guy, time to return you to the corral."

She turned and walked over to the gate, opened it, and Milton trotted through.

"My God, he really is a giant puppy dog," Shawn said.

"Yeah, he's our off-site ambassador. We take him to almost all the fundraising events and people just love him. At our Christmas event at the Town and Country Hotel, we put a Santa hat on him, and everybody gets their picture taken with him. You're right, he had to be somebody's pet. We'll never understand why nobody claimed him or adopted him after he was found by CAS. But, you know what, we adore him and we're glad he's ours."

Shawn put his arm around CJ's shoulder and pulled her close. "Are we done?"

"Nope. But we're close. All we've got left are the coops and Deveny."

"Can I get Deveny?" he asked.

"Are you buttering me up? Okay, just let her smell you and get comfortable first. I'll start on the coops. When you're done pampering your favorite girl, come help me finish."

An hour later, Shawn ran the final wheelbarrow over to the manure pile and CJ put the last of their tools away. As they walked toward the volunteer trailer, CJ hugged Shawn's arm and rested her head against his shoulder. "Thank you sooo much. It's just 2.30, and we're done. If it weren't for you, I'd still have another four or five of hours of work left."

217

"The two of us put in close to seven hours each. How do you get everything done when you're here by yourself?"

"I don't. I get the important stuff done first, then do whatever I can till I run out of gas. Anything that I don't get done goes over to the next day when, hopefully, I've got a volunteer or two to help me."

She looked up at him just as they reached the trailer. "Anybody ever tell you you're amazing with animals? You've already won over Deveny. Milton Burro is madly in love with you. And, for someone that's never been around horses before, you're completely relaxed around them. That made every horse in every stall you worked instantly comfortable with you."

"CJ, you've only told me about how a few of them got here. But it doesn't take a mental giant to realize that none of them would be alive if it weren't for the ranch. And you know what? They know. All you need to do is look into their eyes. I may not know much about horses, but I know love and appreciation when I see it, and every horse in every stall I went in to just lit up when I came in. The eyes of every one of them said *thank you for caring about me; thank you for loving me.*

"They're all special, CJ. Each and every one of them. You know what? Deveny may be my favorite and Missy and Milton stole my heart first thing this morning, but every time I opened another gate, I fell in love all over again."

"Shawn James, you have to be the biggest mush muffin I've ever seen."

"You're going to think I'm crazy, but the reason they're all so comfortable with me was because Rio has been standing right next to me all day. I feel him, CJ. As crazy as that sounds. I never even got to meet him, but he picked me to be your protector, and every horse knows it the minute I walk into their stall."

218

"I know," she whispered, then pulled his head down and kissed him gently. "And I know why he picked you."

Chapter 19 - We Need A Dog

They entered the volunteer trailer, and Shawn headed for the bathroom while CJ checked for phone messages, special instructions from Kate, and tomorrow's schedule.

"Tomorrow looks like a pretty easy day," she said, as he came out. "Nothing special going on, no new horses arriving, and we'll have two volunteers to help in the afternoon. That is, if they both show up."

"Great. How would you like to meet Trish and the girls?"

"Oh, Shawn, I'd love to."

"There's this great little Mexican restaurant in Chula Vista, not too far from the condo. Rick is on shift today, but I can call Trish and see if she and the girls can meet us there." He reached into his pocket, pulled out his new phone, and dialed Trish. CJ could hear all three of them squealing after he asked if they wanted to meet her.

"I guess that means they're okay with meeting me?" CJ asked.

"Ah, yeah, I'd say so."

CJ locked up the volunteer trailer, ran over to hers, and grabbed a change of clothes to wear for dinner. After locking her trailer, they walked down to Shawn's truck. He took her clothes from her, and she went over to open the gate. Two minutes later, she snapped the lock shut on the last gate and hopped into the truck.

Shawn merged onto the interstate, and CJ reached over and turned the radio down. "Tell me about your job and the station. What's it like being a fireman?" Then added, "I mean... what do you do while you're waiting for something to catch fire or a damsel in distress to need rescuing?"

"Actually, we're more likely to be rescuing a damsel in distress than putting out a fire. About 80 percent of our calls are for medical aid of some type. That's why all of us are trained paramedics as well as firefighters. Accidents take up a good part of the remaining calls and fires, and snake removal make up most of the rest. Then there's the occasional cat in a tree or some other weird call.

"When we're not on a call, we do all kinds of stuff. Training is the biggest thing. Our training covers everything from refresher classes, sharing lessons learned with other departments, new equipment operation, briefings on new codes and laws, and reviewing coordination plans with other departments, the sheriff, and police departments.

"As you know, there's also the coordination meetings for brush fire season and staying current on who backs up who when engines leave the area. Since we're a small department with only one engine on line, we seldom get called out of the area. However, if engines from one of the stations near us leave, we help cover their calls till they're back. That's called a Move Up.

"If we're not training, there's equipment and station maintenance. That includes everything from mowing the grass and trimming the bushes at the station to washing the engines and making sure all our equipment is working and ready to go. We also do a lot in the community, like teaching classes on fire prevention, keeping people informed about the department, doing the Boot Drive, and other charity events. Finally, we're responsible for periodic inspections for all the businesses in Bonita to make sure they're in compliance with the latest fire codes."

"Wow, how do you have time for fires and damsel rescue?"

"I know you're only kidding, but our first priority is *always* people's safety. This is home for many of us, and even if you live somewhere else, this quickly becomes your second home. You spend half your life here, and you get to know everybody and everybody knows you. We're all too aware that our next call might be to a neighbor's house or our own house. Or the person you're trying to get out of that mangled car may be the kid across the street or the grocery clerk you said hi to this morning."

"Shawn, I'm really sorry. You know how I feel about firemen after what they did for me. I would never make light of what you do."

"Sorry, I didn't mean to lecture you."

"I understand. You weren't lecturing me. It's just that you're so passionate about what you do. I did a really lousy job of it, but that's kind of what I was reacting to. You treat what anyone else would consider the boring parts of your job with the same passion as the exciting stuff. Your face lights up when you mention washing the fire truck or teaching fire prevention or doing the Boot Drive, whatever that is."

"I guess you're right. To every one of us in the department, everything we do helps keep people safe and is a part of belonging to the community so it's all important. Even cutting the grass shows we take pride in our station and we're proud of our community."

"My hero. You're so passionate about everything you do. Even cleaning stalls at the ranch. It's who you are, Shawn. And, just one of the reasons why I love you so much."

They pulled into the parking lot of his complex and parked. CJ grabbed her clothes, and they headed inside so they could shower and change. "Do I get my bottom and other parts washed again?"

"Of course," he said, as they both stripped off their clothes and headed for the bathroom.

Forty-five minutes later, they were on their way to the restaurant in Chula Vista.

As they walked into the restaurant, two young girls ran up to them. "Hi, I'm Liz," one said.

"And I'm Cat."

"Pleased to meet you both. I'm CJ."

Each of them grabbed one of her hands and started to drag her off toward the tables in the back. "Oh, hi, Uncle Shawn. You coming?" Liz yelled back over her shoulder.

Trish stood up as they reached the table. "Hi, I'm Trish."

"Hi, I'm CJ."

Trish walked around to CJ, and CJ stuck her hand out. "We do hugs, not handshakes," Trish said, as she pulled CJ into a big hug.

CJ started to sit next to Trish, but the girls gently pulled her to the other side of the table. "We asked mom if we could have you sit next to us during dinner so we could get to know you. Is that okay with you?"

"Of course it is." She looked over at Trish and Shawn. "Guess you two are on your own."

Trish winked at the girls. "Remember what I said. You have to share. And you didn't ask Shawn if it was okay with him."

"Is it okay with you, Uncle Shawn?"

"Yeah, but I want her back before dessert," Shawn said, smiling at CJ.

"So where do you work?" Liz asked.

"And how did you meet Uncle Shawn?" Cat added.

"Well, I work on a ranch. A horse rescue ranch, actually. I'm kind of the caretaker there."

Shawn looked at the girls. "She's actually the manager of the ranch and a very good one, I might add."

"Wow, do you get to ride horses every day?" Cat asked.

"No, unfortunately, most of the horses are too old or have health problems so they can't be ridden. That's why they're there. When people find a horse that's been abandoned or an owner can't take care of their horse anymore, they try to find someone to adopt it. If Animal Services can't find anybody that wants to adopt it, they ask us. If we take the horse, we nurse it back to health and then provide it with a forever home."

"Does Uncle Shawn help with the horses? Is that how you met?" Cat asked.

The waiter brought over salsa and chips and told them he would be back in a minute to take their order.

"Well, yes and no. Your Uncle Shawn's truck broke down in front of the ranch in the pouring rain. He came looking for a phone so he could call for help, and that's when he met me. Then I had to loan him some of my clothes and give him a ride to a

224

hotel. The next morning, I picked him up at the hotel..." She looked across the table at Shawn then reached over and took his hand. "And that's when I fell in love with him."

Trish looked at Shawn. "You wore her clothes? I can't believe I missed that. Did you take pictures, CJ?"

She squeezed his hand and smiled at him. "No, I should have. He looked so cute in my sweats."

CJ turned back to Cat. "Anyway, your Uncle Shawn and I just started dating, and he's been coming out to the ranch to help me." She looked into his eyes and squeezed his hand even harder. "I know you're all very special to him, and I feel honored that he wanted you to meet me. And I *really, really* hope you like me because I know how important all of you are to him."

"I like you. A lot," Cat said.

"Me too," Liz chimed in.

Trish looked at CJ and smiled. "You had my vote as soon as you walked through the door. Anyone that can get him to smile like that has to be special." Turning to Shawn, she added, "Shawn, it's not hard to see why you're in love with her."

CJ lit up. "Thank you. I'm so lucky to have him in my life, and in case you didn't notice, I'm madly in love with him too."

Trish's eyebrows went up. "Oh, we definitely noticed, CJ."

The waiter returned and asked if they were ready to order. "Give us just another minute or two." Shawn told him then turned to everyone at the table. "Let me know when you're all ready, and I'll call him back over. Anybody want me to order for them?"

"No," Cat shouted. "You and Dad always order weird stuff. Like chili with cow brains and rattlesnake tacos."

CJ turned to Cat and Liz. "Can I order for you? It will be a good chance for me to practice my Spanish. Just tell me what you want and I'll order it in Spanish. Okay?"

"Cool," said Liz, then she and Cat told CJ what they wanted.

The waiter returned and asked if they were ready. Everybody nodded and CJ said, *"Tengo que lavar primero mis calcetines en el baño. Y ordenaré para las chicas después de que han tenido sus cigarrillos."*

She whispered to the girls, "I just told him I need to use the bathroom first then I will order for you." As she started to get up, Trish, the waiter, and everyone at the next table broke out laughing.

With tears streaming down her face, Trish reached out and pulled CJ back into her seat. "Um... CJ... my Spanish is not very good, but I'm pretty sure you told him you needed to wash your socks in the bathroom while the girls finish their cigarettes."

CJ snorted and turned red as she and everyone else roared with laughter. "Oh my God, I'm gonna pee my pants. I really need to go to the bathroom," she said, laughing as she stood back up.

"Wait, we'll go with you," Liz said as she, Cat, and CJ headed for the ladies' restroom.

Trish, in between fits of giggles, looked at Shawn. "Oh, Shawn, she's just adorable. There is absolutely nothing phony about her. I just think she's wonderful, and don't be surprised if we get to be good friends. The girls have already adopted her into the family."

"I hope so. She was so worried about whether the three of you would like her. By the way, nothing would please me more than the two of you becoming good friends. As for the girls, I think she won them over the minute she said hi to them."

"Shawn, the girls will love anybody you love. But don't underestimate them. They would bare their fangs in an instant if someone didn't treat you the way they feel you should be treated."

"I somehow don't think that's ever going to be a problem with CJ. She really loves you, Shawn. All she has to do is look at you and she lights up. Her face says it all.

"Let me translate for you, Shawn. She's thrilled you chose her and she wants to please you and everybody important to you, but she's not going to let that change who she is. She's telling you, *what you see is what you get and I'm so glad you like what you see. I'm all yours now and I'll always do my best to let you know you chose right.*"

Shawn bent close to Trish and pecked her on the cheek. "Thank you. How did you get to be so wonderful… and so smart?"

As CJ and the girls returned to the table, giggling, Liz announced, "Aunt CJ's socks are drying in the bathroom and we've finished our cigarettes so we're ready to order. Uh, Aunt CJ… I think we'll order our own food, though."

The next two hours were spent with everybody enjoying their dinner and laughing as CJ tried several times to practice her Spanish. When it was time to order dessert, Cat got up and switched chairs with CJ, in order to *return* her to Shawn, as promised.

While they waited for dessert to come, Trish asked CJ, "What did you do before you worked at the ranch?"

The table went completely quiet as CJ stared at Shawn with terror written all over her face.

"Are you okay, CJ?" Trish asked.

"Ah, yeah. It's just that my background is not a very good dinner subject and not one I'm sure the girls should hear."

Shawn kissed her gently on the lips. "If you're okay with talking about it, I think it's a good idea if they hear it from you rather than someone else. I know them pretty well, CJ, and I don't think it's going to make them think any less of you. But, it's your decision."

CJ looked at Trish. "God, I spent most of tonight hoping and praying this wouldn't come up. I so want to be your friend, and I hope you don't hate me for what I used to be. I'm not sure you want the girls to hear this because it involves some pretty ugly things."

Trish stared at her then looked at the girls. "CJ, they are growing up in a world full of ugly things, and I'm sure you'll put it in a way that will help them be aware and cautious of what's out there. As for hating you, I can't think of anything that could possibly make me, or the girls, hate you. You would really have to go some to undo the wonderful impression you've already made."

CJ whispered, "Thank you," and started telling her story. She repeated just about everything she had told Shawn, cleaning up the language and leaving out some of the more sordid details. But she also wanted the girls to understand what she had done and the consequences so they would never make the mistakes she had.

When she got to the part about getting hooked on drugs, she looked at Liz and Cat and directed the rest of her story to them.

228

She told them how getting hooked on drugs had made her lose complete control of her life. How the drugs took over, and no matter how hard she tried, she couldn't fight it.

She told them that no matter what anyone said, they needed to stay away from drugs. She explained that no matter how good they made you feel for a little while, they would end up stealing your dignity, your pride, and who you are. No matter how hard you tried, they would overtake everything important to you and become the only thing you cared about.

Finally, she pleaded with them to never do what she had done, to never turn control of their life over to someone else, for any reason. She also made them promise that if they ever wanted to try drugs, they would come see her first.

As she finished her story, she leaned her head against Shawn's shoulder, hugged his arm, and looked at Trish. "Now do you see why I'm so lucky to have him in my life? He looks at me and sees who I've worked so hard to become, not who I was. He treats me like I'm the most important person in the world, and he makes sure that I never forget how special I am."

"Oh my God, CJ, I'm so sorry you had to go through that," Trish said. "God, I admire your strength and courage so much. How can you have gone through all that and not be bitter? And thank you for the personal message to the girls about what drugs did to you."

Trish looked across the table at Liz and Cat. "I hope you both realize how much courage it took for CJ to tell us what happened to her. She hardly knows you, but she cares enough to put herself out there so you could learn from what she went through. And, I want to make sure you heard her say she'll *be there if you need her.*"

She reached over, touched CJ's arm, then slid her hand down to CJ's and clasped it. "I can't thank you enough for doing that."

229

Then she turned back to the girls. "I know you both love me, but trust me, there will come a day, soon, when you can't talk to me *because I'm your mother and I just don't understand*. When that happens, I want you both to remember your promise to CJ and talk to her. She's volunteered to be there for you and I can't think of anyone I would trust more to help guide you."

Trish turned to Shawn and CJ. "I can't tell you how happy I am that you two found each other. CJ, you're adorable and unbelievable, and in case you don't know it, you've just become part of the family."

The girls just sat there, not quite sure what to say. Finally, Liz spoke up. "Aunt CJ, I can't believe people did that to you. I promise, I'll never do drugs, no matter how cool everybody says it is. And Mom, I'll never stop talking to you. No matter what. I never thought about how much you and Dad love us until Aunt CJ talked about her parents."

-------//-------

Just as Liz was finishing, CJ got up and walked around the table. She lifted Cat out of her chair and pulled her in close before anyone realized that Cat was quietly sobbing. CJ gently guided her away from the table, and when they were out of earshot, she whispered, "It's okay, Cat. You're safe. I would never let anyone harm you or Liz."

Wrapping her arms around CJ, Cat whispered, "I need to talk to you."

"Sure. Right now?" CJ whispered back.

Cat kept her head against CJ's chest and nodded slightly, so that no one would see.

Holding Cat close, CJ looked back at everybody. "Girl talk," she said, and started to lead Cat toward a table on the patio.

"Wait, I'll go too," Liz said, as she stood up.

"I need a little alone time with Cat. Is that okay?" CJ asked.

Liz nodded and sat back down.

CJ led Cat out onto the patio away from everybody. As they sat down, the waiter came up and asked if they wanted anything. Cat wiped her eyes and asked for a Coke. CJ added a Corona Light to the order. She waited until the waiter was out of hearing range before she asked Cat what she wanted to talk about.

"I did drugs," Cat said, so low that CJ almost didn't hear her. She looked up at CJ, and pleaded, "Please don't tell anyone?"

CJ took her hand and pulled her close again. "It's our secret. You wanna tell me about it? Or do you want to just sit on it till you figure out what you want to tell me and what you don't?"

Cat looked up at her with total surprise on her face. "You're not going to yell at me or make me tell you where I got the drugs or why I did it?"

"Nope," she answered. "You'll tell me if, and when, you're ready. And I'll be there to listen whenever you're ready."

She gave CJ another big hug. "Wow, you're so cool, Aunt CJ. I guess I really should tell you now. I need your help so that I know what to do."

The next twenty minutes were spent with Cat explaining that she was being bullied at school by five girls in her class. The girls had formed a 'club', the sole purpose of which was to pick on and demean other girls. Two of the girls had been Cat's best friends all the way through grade school, but both of them had turned on her after joining the club.

After weeks of picking on her, her *friends* had given Cat a series of things she needed to do to become eligible to join the club. Included in that list was: smoking pot, doing ecstasy, giving oral sex to a boy of their choosing, stealing money from her parents, and helping post hate statements about others not worthy of being in the club.

She told CJ that she knew it wasn't right to do any of that stuff, but she was afraid of becoming an outsider that nobody wanted to have as a friend. So she agreed to smoke pot as the first step toward getting into the club. Now, they were pressuring her to do ecstasy, and they had already picked out who she was to give oral sex to.

"I'm so scared, Aunt CJ. I don't want to do any of the other things, and I don't want to be in their club. But if I don't or if I tell my parents or anyone else, they'll tell everybody that I'm a druggie and smoking pot, then nobody will believe me."

CJ pulled her in close and gave her a big hug. "Remember what I said about never letting someone or something take over your life? Well, that's what they're trying to do. But we're a lot smarter than they are. So let's see if we can come up with a plan to make sure their little club goes bye-bye. Are there any other girls, or boys, that they've bullied?"

"Yeah, lots of them… but they're all scared too."

"Okay, how about if we try this…." CJ spent the next ten minutes laying out a plan. Then the two of them refined it until Cat felt sure it would work and knew how she was going to implement it.

They got up, high-fived each other, hugged, then marched back into the restaurant.

"Wow. That was some girl talk, you two." Trish said. "Everything okay?"

Cat's face lit up as she looked up at CJ. "Aunt CJ is the coolest person in the world." Then she gave CJ another big bear hug.

They sat back down, and the waiter appeared with coffees, sodas, and two different dessert platters. CJ glanced at Shawn with a wicked grin. "Does this mean no dessert for me when we get home?"

"Plug your ears, girls," Trish yelled, as Liz and Cat both giggled.

An hour later, they finally relinquished their table and walked out to the parking lot. Hugs went around, then they headed for their cars. Trish unlocked her SUV, told the girls to get in, and that she would be back in a minute. She ran over to Shawn's truck and caught CJ just as he opened her door. She told Shawn to go ahead and get in as she pulled CJ to the back of the truck.

"Care to tell me what went on out on the patio?"

"Nope."

Trish smiled. "I love you. First night and you've won their trust and my friendship. Big-time. I meant what I said about being glad you and Shawn found each other." She pulled CJ close and whispered, "We're all in love with you. Thank you for talking to Cat. I promise, I'll not do anything to break the bond of trust she has with you." Then she turned and headed for her car.

CJ hopped into the truck, closed the door, and slid over next to Shawn. "Thank you so much. I love all of them."

"Yeah, I somehow think the feeling's mutual. Trish thinks you walk on water, and the girls absolutely adore you. I'm not sure what went on out on the patio, but it's obvious Cat trusts you. She came back a totally different girl. Hell, I could've just dropped you off and picked you up later, and nobody would have noticed I wasn't there."

"That's not true, and you know it. They love me because I'm with you, and I'm fine with that."

He leaned over and kissed her. "CJ, they love you because you're you. I had nothing to do with it. But I'm glad I didn't have to beat them up to make them love you. Mainly because they probably would have beat the snot out of me then fallen in love with you anyway."

They drove the short distance back to Shawn's condo. After he helped her out of the truck, she grabbed his arm and pulled him close as they went up the walkway. "I know I sound like a stuck record, but I love you so much. I have no right to be this happy and I keep pinching myself to make sure this isn't a dream."

He unlocked the condo door and pushed it open for her. "You have every right in the world to be happy, and I'm so glad to be a part of what makes you happy."

She headed for the couch and he for the kitchen. "Want a beer?"

"I'd better not," she said, as her stomach rumbled.

Shawn grabbed a Corona out of the refrigerator and joined her on the couch. As he sat down, her stomach rumbled again and her eyebrows shot up.

He looked at her. "Are you okay?"

"Yup," she said, then farted. "Oops."

She smiled at him, he laughed, her stomach rumbled and she farted again. Her eyebrows went up and she shook her head. "Wasn't me."

"CJ, there's only two of us here, and it wasn't me."

"It was the dog."

"I don't have a dog."

Her stomach rumbled yet again. "Yeah... well..." she snorted, then farted. "You need to get one."

The two of them broke out laughing with poor CJ unable to control her grumbling stomach... or her farts. "Oh God, please don't make me laugh anymore. It hurts. I'll never eat Chili Colorado again."

Shawn got up and headed toward the bedrooms. A minute later, he was back with a Pepcid Complete container in hand. "Here, take one of these."

"Oh God, I'm so sorry, Shawn. I know better. Chili does this to me every time." She chewed the Pepcid tablet and looked at him. "This is so embarrassing. I need to sleep in the guest room tonight." She kissed him, then got up and walked into the guest bedroom, snorting, laughing, and farting all the way.

She stripped and put her clothes at the foot of the bed. Sweeping the throw pillows off the bed onto the floor with her arm, she pulled back the covers and got into the bed as her stomach rumbled yet again.

Shawn finished his beer, got up, and walked into the guest room. He stripped and threw his clothes on top of hers and slid in next to her.

"You sure you want to do this?" she said without turning around.

"Uh–huh." He chuckled and put his arm around her.

"God I love you. But, if you value your life, don't squeeze."

She snorted, farted again, then snuggled into him. Within five minutes, they were both sound asleep.

Chapter 20 - She's Back

As soon as Shawn had pulled out onto the highway, Ami started her truck.

Sitting just around the bend in the road, she had been waiting for them to leave. *Finally.* As soon as they were out of sight, she drove up to the gate, got out, and opened it with her key.

Wrapping the chains at both gates to make it look like they were locked, Ami drove up the hill. She parked behind the row of bushes near CJ's trailer so her truck couldn't be seen from the road. Then, she got out and walked up to CJ's pickup.

She pulled on the driver's side door handle and the door swung open. Sliding into the seat, she took a baggie out of her cloth sack, opened the glove compartment, and stuck the baggie under a pile of papers and maps.

After closing the glove compartment and sliding out of the truck, she pulled out another baggie and put it next to the driver's seat so that it looked like it had slid off the center console. She closed the door to the truck, walked up to CJ's trailer, and unlocked the door with her keys. She checked the area again to make sure no one was around then reached in and turned on the lights.

Ami couldn't believe she had almost gotten caught getting the keys the other night. Parking all the way back by the mustangs, she had waited till CJ and Shawn pulled out before sneaking across the road and onto the ranch.

Discovering the extra set of keys hidden in the volunteer trailer had been almost a no-brainer. She knew they had to be somewhere that Kate or CJ could easily get to them. Somewhere out of the weather. That narrowed it down to the trailer or one of the sheds. There really weren't a lot of places in the sheds where they wouldn't be impossible to get to or easily discovered. So that left the trailer. And *bingo*, the first cabinet she checked had yielded the keys, hidden under some papers in a small metal case.

The spare keys were only there in case Kate or CJ misplaced their keys so the chance of them being missed, during the few days she would have them, was slim to none. Once she was done, she would return the keys, and no one would ever know they were gone.

What she hadn't expected was Kate to show up at night, especially on a day she wasn't even supposed to be there. Ami had found the keys and left the volunteer trailer just in time, only to be trapped; first behind the volunteer trailer, then alongside CJ's trailer as she tried to sneak back to her truck.

She had waited, thinking Kate would only be a few minutes inside the trailer. Realizing that Kate was taking much longer than expected, she finally decided to make a run for her truck and had almost gotten caught as Kate came out.

But tonight would be different. She had the ranch all to herself and plenty of time.

She also couldn't believe her luck when it came to Shawn helping her. He had shown up at the perfect time. Not only was he distracting CJ, she had been going into San Diego with him every night. That meant Ami had free run of the ranch to do what she needed.

Once inside CJ's trailer, Ami went over to the dining area. She picked up one of the bench cushions and started to put another baggie of drugs under the cushion. Then she thought better of it. *Too likely to be accidentally found.* She pulled the baggie back out and looked around, then her eyes lighted on the pantry cabinet. Opening the door, she was surprised to find next to nothing in the cabinet. *This is not going to work.*

She turned and scanned the rest of the kitchen. Her eyes came to rest on the small cabinet above the refrigerator. She walked over, opened the cabinet, and found it was full of Tupperware and empty plastic containers. *Perfect.* She emptied the left side, put the baggie in the far back corner, then put the containers back in front of it.

Next she headed into the bedroom. This one was going to be easy. She lifted the corner of the mattress and slid the last baggie to the middle of the bed. After lowering the mattress, she smoothed the sheets and blanket so no one would notice it had been disturbed.

She headed for the door and paused to do one final check to make sure no one would know she had been there. Just as she reached for the light switch, headlights panned across the front windows of the trailer.

"Oh crap," she whispered. She squatted so she was below the window, reached up, and pushed the lock button, then duck-walked to the hallway going into the bedroom.

Someone knocked on the door, and she almost shit her pants. "CJ, are you in there?" Kate yelled, then peered through the window. She knocked again, then after a minute, left and walked over to the volunteer trailer.

Ami waited till she heard the door to the other trailer close. She duck-walked back over to the door, raised up, and peeked through the curtains. Seeing no one, she quietly opened the door, crept through, pushed the lock button back in, and as quietly as she could, pulled the door shut.

Crouching, she headed for her truck, having no idea how she was going to start it and get out of the gates without being caught. However, that turned out to be a non-problem. No sooner had

239

she gone three feet when the door to the volunteer trailer opened and Kate stepped out.

Kate spotted her immediately. "Who is that?" she called out.

Ami stopped, bent over further, undid her shoelace, and started to retie it. "Oh, hi, Kate," she said, as she looked over. She stood up and added, "I was just getting ready to leave."

Kate walked over to her. "What were you doing in CJ's trailer? For that matter, what are you doing here at this time of night and how did you get in?"

"I wasn't in CJ's trailer, and I came back to get something I left here this morning."

"Ami, I just saw you coming from CJ's trailer."

"I wasn't coming from her trailer. I was alongside of it… taking a pee."

"Let me see if I understand. The volunteer trailer isn't locked and has a bathroom, but you decided to pee alongside CJ's trailer, because..?"

"I had to go. I wasn't going to make the trailer so I just squatted and went. You trying to tell me you never had to go so bad you couldn't make the bathroom?"

"Nice try, Ami. We're talking about you, not me. Now what are you doing here, how did you get in, and why were you in CJ's trailer?"

"I told you, I came to get something I forgot this morning, I got in through the gates, the ones that CJ must have left open. And I wasn't in her trailer."

240

"Then why are her lights on? Ami, I've completely had it with you. Your services as a volunteer here are no longer needed, and you're no longer welcome on ranch property. If we catch you here again, we'll call the sheriff and have you arrested for trespassing. Now, please leave before I change my mind and call the sheriff right now."

"You stupid bitch. You're the biggest asshole I've ever seen. You hire a druggie whore to watch over your precious horses that nobody gives a crap about anyway. Like I'm really going to miss shoveling horse shit for you all day. When I'm done posting what a crap place this is, nobody will want to volunteer here."

Kate held out her hand. "Just give me the keys you used to get in and get the hell off of my property."

"Fuck you. I don't have any keys." Ami turned and stormed off toward her truck.

-------//-------

Kate watched Ami drive through the last gate and, with tires squealing, turn onto the road. As expected, she left both gates wide open. She walked up to the road, closed and locked both gates, then walked back to the volunteer trailer. As soon as she inside, she went to the cabinet and checked to see if the spare set of keys were there. Not surprisingly, she found them missing.

Picking up the phone, she dialed CJ's cell and got her message recording. "Hi, CJ, this is Kate. I'm at the ranch, and I'll be back out tomorrow morning because we need to talk about Ami. I just caught her coming out of your trailer and found out she has taken the spare set of keys. I told her she was no longer welcome here so if she shows up before I get here, call the sheriff and have her escorted off the property. You might also want to check your trailer and make sure nothing's missing. Love you, and I'll see you in the morning."

241

Kate hung up and dialed Shannon's cell.

Shannon picked up on the second ring. "Hi, Kate. What's up?"

"Hi, Shannon, I know you're not scheduled to be here, but is there any chance you can meet CJ and I at the ranch tomorrow morning?"

"Actually, Yeah. I've got classes tomorrow, but they're all in the afternoon. What time do you want me there?... Is everything okay?"

"How about 8? And no, everything's not okay. I just caught Ami on the property, and she was in CJ's trailer... but... that can wait till the morning. It's late, and I feel bad bothering you and asking you to come out on your day off."

"It's not a problem, Kate. What in the hell is she up to? Is CJ okay?"

"Yeah, CJ's in Bonita with Shawn. I left her a message, but you'll probably get here before me so make sure she checks her trailer as soon as she can. Thanks, Shannon, I'll see you in the morning."

-------//-------

Shannon hung up and stared out the sliding door to the patio. She shook her head, got up, and walked into the kitchen to pull a beer from the refrigerator. She took two sips then reached for the phone.

"Hi, sis. Hey, I'm sorry to bother you, but is Jason there?... Can I talk to him for a second?"

A few seconds later, Jason came on. "Hi, freckles, what's up?"

"Hi, Jason. I'm sorry to bother you, but I need your help. This is probably nothing, but I've got a really bad feeling about something that's going on out at the ranch. Kate, CJ, and I are meeting tomorrow morning at 8. Is there any chance you can be there?"

"Sure, I'm on patrol tomorrow, so I'll just make sure I'm near the ranch around 8. Want to give me a hint as to what this is about?"

"Jason, I wish I could. I'm just worried about CJ. Something's going on with her and Ami, and I just have this really bad feeling that something's about to happen... I know I sound like a total nut case, but... I'm really worried."

"I'll be there. Get some sleep, and I'll see you in the morning."

Chapter 21 - Officer Clark and Buttermilk

At 7, CJ and Shawn pulled into the ranch and found Shannon standing next to her truck. "Hi, Shannon. What are you doing here?"

"Kate called me last night and told me what happened. She asked if we could all meet at 8, and since I couldn't sleep, I just figured I'd grab a latte and come over early. Kate also asked me to make sure you checked your trailer as soon as you got here. She's pretty sure Ami was in there doing something."

"Yeah, I listened to her message first thing this morning so we came straight out."

Shannon looked over at Shawn. "Hi, Shawn. Welcome to drama city." She turned back to CJ. "I hope you don't mind, but I asked Jason to come by. Kate's call really scared me last night, and Ami's just stupid enough to do... who knows what?"

"No. I'm glad you did."

"If Jason's coming out, you might want to wait till he gets here before you check your trailer," Shawn said, adding, "He knows a lot more about this kind of thing than any of us do. I'm sure he'll want to check for something that might tell us what she was up to."

Five minutes later, Jason pulled through the gate and parked. He got out of his cruiser, walked over, and gave Shannon a big hug. "You get any sleep last night?"

She shook her head no.

He turned toward CJ as she and Shawn walked over to him. "Hi, Jason. Thanks for coming out." She reached over and took Shawn's arm. "This is Shawn. Shawn, this is Jason." Then she added, "Shawn's with me."

"Gee, I never would have guessed. Hi, Shawn." He reached out and shook Shawn's hand then turned back to Shannon. "So what's all this about?"

Shannon and CJ started to explain what little they knew, just as Kate pulled in and parked. She got out and walked up to Jason and gave him a big hug. "I'm glad you're here. I called the station on my way out, but Carol said you were already here."

Kate spent the next ten minutes explaining what had happened the night before. She went on to tell him about finding the spare set of keys missing from their hiding place, which explained how Ami had gotten onto the ranch and into CJ's trailer.

"Did you find anything missing?" Jason asked CJ.

"I don't know. I haven't looked yet. Shawn thought it would be a good idea to wait till you got here before I went in. He thought you might be able to find something that would explain why she was in there."

Jason winked at Shawn. "Smart man. But I'm not a detective. I'm just a lowly deputy. CJ, you have any idea what she might've been doing?"

"No, I haven't got anything worth stealing."

"Okay, let's go have a look."

The five of them walked up to CJ's trailer, and she unlocked the door. Before she stepped in, Jason put his hand on her arm.

"After you go in, take a good look at everything to see if anything's been disturbed or moved. That may help us figure out where she was and hopefully, what she took or was doing."

CJ stepped in and moved to one side so everyone else could come in. She scanned the kitchen and dining area. She shook her head and told Jason that she couldn't see anything different, but she really hadn't paid a lot of attention when they had left yesterday.

She stepped into the spare bedroom, which had next to nothing in it, and told him nothing looked different. From there, they checked the bathroom and finally her bedroom, with exactly the same results.

Turning off her bedroom light, they all started to file out when she suddenly stopped. She turned the light back on and looked at the bed. "My bed's been messed with. I always do a military corner and tuck in the covers at the foot. A habit I picked up in rehab."

She walked toward the bed and pointed at the sheet and blanket neatly hanging free. "See? I know I tucked them in when I made the bed. I don't even think about it anymore. I just automatically do it."

Jason walked over, lifted the mattress, and carefully pulled the baggie out.

"Oh my God. Jason, that's not mine. I swear that's not mine." She turned to Shawn and looked into his eyes. "Shawn, it's not mine. Please, you've got to believe me. Oh God, I can't believe this is happening. Please, please believe me, Shawn. I would rather die than do drugs again."

Shawn put his arms around her and pulled her in close. "It's okay. I believe you," he whispered.

Jason came over to them and gently put his hand on CJ's shoulder. "I believe you too. If this was yours, you would have to be pretty stupid to lead us directly to your stash."

Shannon looked at Jason, then at Kate. "Why would she plant drugs in CJ's trailer?"

"Anybody got any ideas?" Jason asked. Everybody shook their heads that they did not.

"Okay," he went on. "I'd be willing to bet she planted more than just this one baggie. Let's each take a room and see what else we can find. Oh, and I don't think you need to tear the place apart. She obviously wanted this stuff to be found so it will be someplace relatively easy to find. Someplace where someone couldn't accidentally stumble on it, but easily find it if they were doing a search."

Shawn looked at Jason. "I'm going to take CJ outside. Let us know if you find anything else. We'll be right outside the door."

Shannon came over to CJ. "I know you wouldn't do drugs again, CJ. We all believe you and know they're not yours. And just so you know, I'm going to hunt that bitch down and kill her with my own two hands. I don't know why she's doing this, but she obviously knew this was the worst thing she could do to you. I swear I'm going to rip her heart out and shove it up her ass with my size-seven boot."

CJ hugged Shannon and hung on for dear life. "Oh God. Thank you for believing me." She glanced over at Kate. "Thank you *both* for believing in me."

Shawn pulled her back into him, and she completely broke down as he led her outside.

247

While Kate, Shannon, and Jason searched the trailer, CJ buried her face against Shawn's chest and sobbed.

After she calmed down, she looked up at him. "If it weren't for you being with me and the three of you believing in me, I'd just collapse in a corner and die. Why is she doing this?"

"I have no idea what Ami is up to. None of this makes a lot of sense, but you need to stop doubting yourself and start getting pissed at her. This isn't just about her not liking you. There's something else going on, and we just need to figure out what it is."

A minute later, the door opened, and Jason stepped out, waving a second baggie. "Found another one. It was in the cabinet above the refrigerator, hidden back behind all the storage containers."

Jason looked over at CJ's pickup. "I think I know what she's trying to do. Okay if I check your truck, CJ?"

"Sure," she said. "It's open."

He walked over, opened the passenger side door and lifted the handle on the glove compartment. As soon as the door dropped open, two maps fell out, revealing the baggie. Next he checked the door panel compartment, behind and under the passenger seat, then he walked around to the driver's side. He opened the door, checked the door compartment, looked under and behind the driver's seat, and found nothing. Before closing the door, he felt between the seat and the console and found the second baggie.

He walked back over to CJ and Shawn just as Kate and Shannon joined them.

"Everything was in a place where the cops would look first if they were doing a search of your truck or the trailer. It's rather

248

obvious that she wanted this stuff to be found. I'll bet twenty dollars that we get an anonymous call soon suggesting we search your truck and trailer for drugs."

"She's setting me up." CJ yelled. "Why is she doing this? If the police found this stuff and arrested me, how would that help her? I don't understand. I mean, aside from volunteering here, I don't even know her. I don't know anything about her."

"Take a deep breath," Jason told CJ. "Everything is going to be okay. Now that we know what she's trying to do, we'll be ready when she decides to call it in." He lifted CJ's chin and looked into her eyes. "CJ, we all know these are not yours. I don't know of one person that knows you that would believe for a second that you got back into drugs."

"Thank you, Jason. You hardly know me, yet you still believe me. I can't tell you how much that means."

"I deal with all kinds of people on drugs every day, CJ. Like most cops, I've gotten to be a pretty good judge of when someone is or isn't doing drugs. I would go to court and testify that you're not doing drugs. That's how strongly I feel that these are not yours."

"Wow. I don't know what to say. All of you put your faith and trust in me and *I promise* I will never betray that trust." She looked at Jason. "So what do we do now?"

"Don't do anything. The next move is up to Ami. I'm going to fill out a report on what happened last night and what we found this morning. I'll also talk to the sheriff and see if I can get some extra patrols past the ranch." Jason looked at Kate. "I don't think it's a good idea for her to be here alone, especially at night."

Kate looked over at Shawn, who raised his eyebrows and stuck his arm out. "Oh please," he said. "Someone twist my arm and force me to take her home with me."

Everybody laughed as CJ stepped inside his arm and wound herself into his chest. "How's that?" She bent her head back, and he bent over and kissed her lips. "Wow, Ami's not all bad. Thanks to her, I get to sleep with you every night."

She looked around at everybody, then back at Shawn. "Ooops. I guess our secret's out."

Shannon's eyebrows shot up as she shook her head and looked at Kate. "OMG. Did you know they were sleeping together?" She put the back of her arm across her forehead. "Our reputations shall be in ruins once the press gets hold of this. We'll all be branded with a big red A. Oh, Scarlett, I've got the vapors. Shawn, catch me. I'm about to pass out." Then she wound herself into Shawn's other arm.

Shaking his head, Jason looked at her. "Freckles, your brand is going to be DQ for Drama Queen. I'm beginning to think maybe I was wrong. You're *all* on drugs. And if you're not, you should be. I gotta go. Let me know if anything happens. I'll call you if I find out anything about Ami or we get any anonymous calls." He turned and headed for his cruiser.

Shawn caught up with him as he reached for the car door. "Jason, thank you so much for believing CJ and for everything you said to her. I don't think you'll ever know how much that meant to her. And me."

"Listen, I'm just glad you're here. I don't suppose I have to tell you that she really loves you... big-time. Shannon thinks you're pretty cute too. Any chance you have a brother?"

Shawn was laughing so hard, he didn't even get to say thanks before Jason drove off.

Kate looked around. "Okay, what do you say we forget about all this and get some work done? Our poor horses are all standing out there wondering where breakfast is. Before you all take off, though, Shannon, thank you for coming out on your day off, and, CJ, I do not want you here alone, under any circumstances. If you get out here and no one else shows up, you leave, then call me. Understand?"

Nodding her head, CJ said, "I understand."

"Good. I have to tell you, Ami scared the crap out of me when she went off on me last night. I don't know what she's capable of, but she's really scary. You getting hurt is not acceptable under any circumstances. If I have to, I'll chain you to Shawn's bed and bring someone else in here to watch the ranch until this is over. Your safety comes first. No matter what. Do I make myself clear?"

"Yes, ma'am."

"CJ, you and Shannon are like the daughters I never had. You two are the ranch. You two are the ones that make my dreams come true out here every day and I would never forgive myself if anything happened to either one of you. I love you both to death."

She smiled at CJ, who was snickering. "Chaining you to Shawn's bed was not much of a threat, was it?" CJ's grin went from ear to ear as she shook her head back and forth.

Shannon and Kate headed for their cars, while CJ and Shawn made their way to the sheds.

"Same plan as yesterday?" he asked.

251

"You just want Deveny. Okay, same plan as yesterday, but after we're done, I'm spending some time with my favorite girl. Oh, and don't forget to go get your buddy Milton. He'll be heartbroken if you don't take him with you on your rounds."

He walked over to the tool shed, built two wheelbarrow kits, and added the pump, hose, and extension cord to one. From there, he dropped one kit off for CJ and took the other all the way to the end by the large corral, then set the wheelbarrow off to the side of the pathway. As he walked toward the corral's gate, Milton let the world know that the love of his life was coming for him.

Once the gate was open, Milton trotted out, walked around Shawn, and laid his head against Shawn's left shoulder. "Yes, I love you too. But don't tell CJ," he added at a whisper.

From there, the two of them walked up the path toward the golf carts and the hay shed. As they approached CJ, she leaned back against the fencing in front of Missy and Shakespeare's stall. She crossed her arms and legs and shook her head as her gaze followed them all the way past her.

"What?" Shawn said.

Chuckling, she responded. "What a pair. You better be careful, Shawn," she said, then sang out, "Deveny's gonna get jealous. Deveny's gonna get jealous."

As if on cue, Deveny, who could see them from up the hill, whinnied.

"Oh, now you've done it. Come on, Milton."

The rest of the morning was spent cleaning their respective stalls, and at noon, they were joined by Jade and Christine, the two volunteers assigned for that day. Between them, they had

252

finished most of the stalls so they each turned their wheelbarrows and tools over to the two volunteers. CJ explained what was left, assigned each of the volunteers to an area, then turned to Shawn.

"Come on, I'll introduce you to some more of the horses."

He looked at Milton and said, "You okay with that?" Milton brayed his approval and the three of them headed for the closest stall. As they walked, he asked her, "Who's the big guy down at the end?"

"That's Officer Clark," CJ said.

"Officer, as in military officer?"

"No. Officer, as in police officer. He was part of the San Diego Police Department's Mounted Enforcement Unit in Balboa Park for almost five years. You'll love this. Prior to that he was an Amish cart horse in Clark, Missouri, which is where his name came from."

"Wow, bet that was a change. From Amish commune to San Diego. Talk about culture shock. So why is he here?"

"Well, at some point in his life, they think he sustained a neck injury that resulted in his developing what's called Wobbler Syndrome. The main symptom of which is he stumbles without warning. Obviously, that was not very safe for the officer riding him or for having him close to people in the park. It also meant that he couldn't be adopted out or sold as a riding horse. In the past, horses like him would have been put down. But, thanks to the officers who rode him and the SDPD, they arranged for him to live out his life here."

"So the SDPD pays for his retirement here at the ranch. How cool is that?" Shawn said.

"Unfortunately, no. The mounted patrol was eliminated in 2010 as part of the department's budget cuts, and there is no place in the PD's budget for horse retirement. Just like with retired police dogs, if their handler doesn't adopt them or they can't find a home for them some other way, they are put down."

"So you guys get to pay for all his food and medical care? For the rest of his life?"

"Yup. Some of the officers from his unit have donated toward his care, but we're still looking for someone to sponsor him. Actually, most of the horses here need sponsors."

They approached the next stall as a gorgeous yellow horse came up to CJ and stuck her head over the top rail. "This is Buttermilk," she said, stroking her forehead. "She's an Isabella Palomino that was part of a wild herd of mustangs up north, somewhere around Eureka. She was adopted out as part of the Bureau of Land Management's Wild Mustang Adoption Program. I'm not quite sure of her background, but I do know that at some point, her rider fell off her and shortly after that she ended up here.

"We think she has restricted vision on her right side, and her teeth are in really bad shape. Our vet thinks she may've been kicked in the mouth as a youngster. So our lovely lady gets her teeth brushed every week by one of our volunteers."

As CJ continued, Buttermilk sidestepped until she was in front of Shawn, who reached up and took over petting her.

"Right now, her coat is almost white, but as we get further into spring, it will turn a gorgeous, light yellow. I was also going to tell you that she's shy around strangers, but I guess we can skip that part since she's obviously already warmed up to you."

"Of course she has, I've cleaned her stall twice for her. She knows who to butter up, right, Buttercup?"

She lightly punched him in the arm. "You're impossible. It's Buttermilk, not Buttercup."

He looked at Buttermilk and whispered, "Let her think what she wants. We both know it's Buttercup, right, Buttercup?"

They strolled to the next stall. "This is King. King is an American quarter horse, and he's kind of our wild man. He was green broke, which means he has learned to be under saddle. However, we're still trying to evaluate how tolerant and responsive he is to a rider's commands. He also was previously housed in a large paddock and wasn't used to a daily routine.

"Since our horses are all housed in standard corrals, with regular handling and scheduled turnouts, the routine here is all new to him. Trying to get him used to a new lifestyle has been somewhat of a challenge, but he's really starting to come around.

"If you look at his back, you'll notice the curvature and hump of his spine, say compared to *your Buttercup* over there. That means he suffers from two spinal conditions. So he could never be adopted out as a riding horse, but he's smart and really picks up new things quickly, so we're working on a trick repertoire with him."

"How did you learn all this?" he asked. "Did you grow up around horses?"

"I never rode or even got close to a horse before I got here. Most of what I've learned has been from Kate, or Shannon and Christine, both of whom have been around horses all their lives. That, and just hanging around the vets and volunteers and asking lots and lots of questions. Pretty soon it starts to sink in and make sense. Heck, when I first got here, I didn't even know that there was a right and wrong side to mount a horse from."

"What do you mean right side and wrong side? Are you trying to tell me that horses are right or left sided?"

"No. I'm trying to tell you that all horses are trained to be mounted from their left side. If you try to mount them from the right side, they're likely going to start turning to try to get you to go to the other side. If they do that while your foot's in the stirrup, you're going to get hurt."

"I've seen how much you love these guys. I suppose after learning all this, you'll want to do something that keeps you close to them. Something like becoming a vet or a horse trainer."

"Actually, no. I love the horses and my life here has been amazing, but this isn't what I want to do for the rest of my life. I know what I do is important and makes a difference, but seeing what people have done to them really gets to you after a while. That and losing one you love and adore, like Rio, leaves a big hole in your heart that's pretty hard to recover from."

She looked up into his eyes. "To be honest, I'm not sure what I want to do with the rest of my life. I'm pretty sure I know who I want to spend it with, though. And... maybe, he'll help me figure out what I want to be when I grow up?"

He put his arm around her waist and pulled her in. "I can't think of anything I'd like better. For starters, though, I don't ever want you to grow up. I love the child in you, and I hope you never lose that. I love the way your mouth drops open and your eyes light up every time you see something new or experience something for the first time. You're like a little sponge. You soak up every drop of something and are absolutely amazed by things that most of us don't even notice. I don't ever want you to lose that quality. It's you. It defines who you are. How amazing you are."

Batting her eyes, her grin got bigger. "What I want to soak up right now, is you. How about if we get out of here?"

CJ started to turn toward the trailers, and her face ran right smack into Milton's nose. She stared into Milton's eyes. "Don't give me that puppy mule look. I'm taking him home with me. And no, you're not invited."

They walked Milton down to his corral where Shawn gave his nose a rub and CJ gave him a kiss on the nose before she led him through the gate and closed it. As they walked back up to the trailers, Milton started braying loud enough that everyone in Julian, fifteen miles away, could probably hear him.

When they reached the volunteer trailer, Jade and Christine were coming out. CJ asked if they had put everything away and signed out, which they had. She thanked them for all their help, wished them a good afternoon, and told them to close but not lock the gates.

Once they left, CJ said, "I've got to do a quick check of the stalls and sheds to make sure everything's closed and locked up."

"I can get that," Shawn said. "How about if you go grab some clothes and whatever else you think you might need, for at least the next few days. I'll go check the stalls and sheds and say a quick hi to Deveny."

Twenty minutes later, as they left, CJ snapped a new lock shut on each gate. Then she put the new key Kate had left with the locks onto her key ring. She put the old locks and key in the paper bag as they headed to Bonita and Shawn's condo.

257

Chapter 22 - Fate

Pulling into the complex, Shawn parked in one of his spaces. As he opened her door, CJ swung her legs out but stayed in the seat. She reached out, pulled him closer, and wrapped her legs around his chest.

"Can we spend a quiet night alone? I have some things I need to talk to you about."

"Sure. How about if I do Firehouse Italian tonight. That's simple and quick. Would you rather have spaghetti and meatballs or lasagna with meat sauce?"

"You pick. I like both so whichever one you would like is fine with me."

"Good, I'm in the mood for spaghetti. Let's get your stuff in, and I'll get the meatballs and sauce going. Once they're on, I need to run to Vons for some fresh-baked italian bread. You want to throw together a salad while I'm at the store?"

CJ filled her arms with the clothes she had brought, and Shawn grabbed the box containing some folded jeans, tops, bras, panties, her hair dryer, toiletries, makeup, and personal feminine items.

Once inside, she nodded toward the guest bathroom. "If you put that on the vanity, I'll put everything away in a minute or two." Then she turned and headed toward the guest room.

Shawn called to her, "What do you think you're doing?"

"Putting my stuff in the closet. Why? What's wrong?"

He put the box on the vanity, walked over to her, and steered her into his bedroom and into his walk-in closet. He reached up and slid everything on the left side to the far left. Then he moved everything on the right over to the newly emptied space. Finally, he took her clothes from her arms and hung them up on the now empty right side of the closet. "This half's yours," he said.

"I can't do that. This is your closet."

"This is *our* closet now." He looked at the eight or nine hang up items she had brought and laughed. "Your stuff does look kind of lost in here. How much is left at your trailer? Will this be enough room?"

She looked down at the floor. "I think it will be plenty of room. I brought everything I own."

He immediately realized she was embarrassed and tried to cheer her up. "Sounds like a shopping trip is in order pretty soon."

"Right," she whispered, as she turned, went into the bathroom, and gently closed the door.

He could hear her softly crying through the door. He went and got the box from the other bathroom and set it on the bed and gave her a few more minutes before he knocked. "Are you okay?"

She opened the door with a pasted-on smile, but as soon as she saw him, she broke into tears again. "I feel so out of place and helpless. I belong in a trailer, not here."

"You belong here with me and nowhere else. I'm sorry, I didn't mean to be so insensitive and embarrass you."

"It's not your fault I don't have anything."

He lifted her chin and smiled at her. "Okay, what do we do to get you out of this downer mood?"

"How about if you pick me up and carry me into the kitchen while I shower you with kisses? That will cheer me up. With luck, we might even manage to have dinner. Or not." He picked her up, and she hugged his neck. "I'm sorry. I try to stay positive, but every now and then, my life jumps up and slaps me in the face. Usually, when I least expect it."

She kissed him and added, "Thank you for sharing your closet with me. While you're at the store, I'll hang up my bras and thongs. That will help fill up my side and give you something to think about while you get dressed each morning."

He kissed her back as he set her down in the kitchen. "You do that and neither one of us may ever get dressed again."

Opening the freezer, he pulled a baggie of frozen meatballs out, put them into a bowl, and put the bowl into the microwave to defrost. Next he removed a storage container full of marinara sauce from the refrigerator and put it into a pot to heat.

"Wow, I could have done that. I thought you were going to make everything?"

"I did. It's all homemade. I made everything the other day. Cooking for myself every day is a pain in the neck. So I usually make a week or two's worth of meals and freeze or refrigerate them. Then each night all I have to do is pull out what I want, defrost it, and heat it up."

She bent over and started hunting through the kitchen trash can. He watched for a second then asked, "What are you doing?"

"I'm looking for the Spaghetti-Os can."

"Cute. Real cute." He chuckled. "Where did you say you were eating tonight?"

The microwave dinged. He took the meatballs out and put them into the sauce. "Okay, I'm going to run up and get the bread. Be back in a few minutes." He pecked her on the cheek and headed for the door. "Don't cut yourself on the Spaghetti-Os lid," he called back over his shoulder.

She stuck her tongue out. "Cute. Real cute," she said. "Who did you say you were having for dessert tonight?"

Shawn had no sooner left when the phone rang. CJ let the answering machine pick it up.

The female voice at the other end said, "Shawn, please pick up. It's important. If you're there, please pick up."

CJ hesitated. After a few seconds, she realized the caller sounded desperate to have Shawn pick up and thought it might be an emergency.

Reaching down, she picked up the phone from its base, pushed TALK and said, "Hello?"

After a very long pause, the woman on the other end said, "Who is this?"

"This is CJ. Shawn just ran to the store. He should be back in just a few minutes. Do you want me to tell him to call you right away?"

"Hi, CJ. This is Kim, Shawn's mother. I just wanted to see how he's doing... actually, how you're both doing."

CJ kept quiet. Poor Kim had obviously been surprised when CJ answered the phone, and she wasn't quite sure where to take the conversation from here.

Finally, CJ decided to take the lead. "Shawn said he had told you about me when I picked him up at the airport. Oh… and gave me the stuffed cabbage. Thank you so much. It was wonderful of you to do that and it was absolutely delicious. It's not hard to figure out where Shawn's cooking skills come from."

Kim laughed. "You're welcome, and I expect you to return my casserole dish in person. To be honest, I actually called to grill him and see how things were going with you two."

Just then, Shawn walked through the door. CJ pointed at the phone and mouthed, "It's your mother."

"Put her on speaker," he told her. CJ pushed SPEAKER. "Hi, Mom. Have you and CJ been having a nice chat?"

"Actually, I just called so we've only had a chance to say hi."

"I'm making spaghetti and meatballs for dinner and had to run out for bread," Shawn said. "Why don't you two talk while I put the water for the spaghetti on and stir the sauce?"

CJ felt really uncomfortable. She had no idea exactly how much Shawn's mother knew about their relationship or if he had told her that CJ would be staying with him for a few days.

From the silence, Kim sensed CJ's unease and realized that Shawn had unintentionally put her on the spot. "I'm sorry, CJ. Shawn obviously didn't tell you that he's told me all about you and that you're staying with him." She laughed. "Oh, he also said that he's madly in love with you."

Kim continued, "We don't keep secrets in our family, CJ. We raised our kids to be open and comfortable with talking to us about anything. We trust their decisions, and while we might offer an opinion, we try not to pass judgment. So if my son says he's madly in love with you, you must be very special, and I can't wait to meet you."

"Thank you," CJ replied. "I'm looking forward to meeting you too."

Just then Shawn walked over and sat next to CJ on the arm of the couch. He put his arm around her waist and pulled her close as she looked up at him and smiled. "She is special, Mom, very special, and I know you'll think so too, as soon as you two meet."

"I'm sure you're right, and I can't wait to get her alone for a few minutes and tell her some of the horror stories about trying to raise you."

Still looking at Shawn, CJ raised her eyebrows. "Oooo!... Dirt on Shawn, I can't wait."

"So Shawn, when *are* we going to meet CJ?" his mom asked.

"Soon, Mom. Very soon." He pecked CJ on the cheek. "In the meantime, there's something you can help me with. I planned to ask her during dinner, but since we have you on the phone, you can help me convince her, in case she says no." He looked into her eyes and asked, "I'd like you to move in with me. That is, if you would like to."

CJ choked up, but had a big smile as she nodded and hugged him.

"I take it from the silence that she said yes?" his mom said, then added, "I trust both of you to be careful with each other, but you might want to slow things down a little? Give your minds a chance to catch up with your hearts. Get to know each other. Put the lust aside for a while?"

CJ smiled at him and shook her head *no* for the last suggestion.

"Listen, I'm going to let you two go have your dinner. Shawn, I know I don't have to remind you of this, but I will. If you hurt her, you'll have me to deal with. CJ, the same goes for you. Be careful with my son's heart. And CJ, I can't wait to meet you. You two have a wonderful evening. Love you."

As soon as his mom hung up, CJ pulled him down onto the couch. "Are you sure you want me to move in with you?"

He nodded. "Very sure."

"Shawn, can we talk for a few minutes before dinner? It's really important."

"Sure, I haven't put the pasta on yet, so we're fine. Before you start, though, can I take a minute to tell you something?"

She nodded in response.

He turned to face her and took both of her hands in his. "I know that by moving in with me, you're putting yourself and everything you have in my hands. I will never for one second forget the trust you have in me, and I will never do anything to lose it.

"You also need to know that I want you to move in with me so we can spend more time with each other. I'm not trying to get you out of the trailer because I'm embarrassed about where or how you live. If I thought my moving into the trailer with you would be better, I'd do it in a minute. I want to be with you, and

264

it doesn't matter to me where. You mean the world to me, CJ, and I want to spend every moment I can telling and showing you how special you are."

"Thank you. For understanding the trust I'm putting in you and I know that works both ways. But there's something you need to know."

She stopped and took a deep breath. "This is all going so fast that my head is spinning... but I don't want it to slow down. I never imagined I would find this kind of love and warmth, and every night I say a prayer of thanks that I get to give all my love to you."

She squeezed his hands and looked into his eyes. "But the one thing I can never give you, Shawn, is a family. When they found me, I was so damaged inside that they had to do a hysterectomy to keep me from bleeding to death. So I can never have children."

She paused, took a deep breath, and went on. "It's obvious how important family is to you and how much you adore Cat and Liz, so you have to know how broken I really am. I'm sorry, Shawn. I would've told you sooner if I'd known things were going to move this fast."

He pulled her closer. "Thank you for telling me. You know?... I guess I really haven't thought much about having kids. I honestly don't know if I want kids or not. How about you? Do you want kids?"

She looked at him, completely puzzled. "Shawn, I just told you, I can't ever have kids."

"Haven't you ever heard of adoption?" came his response.

Her smile lit up her face. "God, I love you. Thank you for that," she whispered. "You are the most wonderful person in the world. I can't wait to meet your family. Especially your mom and dad, so I can tell them what an amazing son they raised."

He put his arms around her neck and pulled her into a long kiss. "Um, you can tell them, but they're going to think you're crazy and I brainwashed you. How about if we eat? If we both weren't so starved, I would have suggested we go straight to dessert."

"Maybe we should *unwrap* dessert before we sit down to eat? Kind of like an *incentive*?"

"Oh....you're soooo bad."

She batted her eyelashes at him. "That's what makes me soooo good."

They both got up and went into the kitchen, where Shawn put the pasta on and CJ built a salad. An hour later, they were still sitting at the serve-through counter, taking turns feeding each other the last of the meatballs and spaghetti. CJ got up, kissed him on the cheek, and started to clear the counter just as his phone rang.

Shawn saw it was Trish and put her on speaker. "Hi, Trish."

"Hi, Shawn, is CJ there?"

"Sure, hold on, she's got her hands full of dishes." He took the dishes from her.

"Hey Trish. What up?

"Hi, CJ. I forgot to ask you the other night, but Thursday is the Boot Drive and I wondered if you wanted to join us?"

266

"I'm sorry... what's a Boot Drive?"

"It's where the fire departments raise money for the Burn Institute. The firemen stand on the corner at major intersections with a fireman's boot and collect money from people driving by. Wives and girlfriends are invited to help, and I thought you might want to join our group, pass the boot, twirl signs, and collect a few bucks. What do you think?"

"Uh... sure. Actually Thursday is my day off at the ranch, and yeah, I'd be glad to join you." She looked at Shawn and asked, "Can I borrow one of your boots?"

Laughing, he said, "Sure. I should warn you, Trish has a reputation for turning the Boot Drive into a *girls' fun day out event*. They always end up raising more money than any other group, but... I'll let her explain how they manage to do that."

CJ turned back to the phone. "Okay, I got a boot. I'm in."

"Good. First thing we need to do is go shopping tomorrow night, so we've got something to wear. What time should the girls and I pick you up?"

"Uh, what's wrong with jeans and one of my tops?"

Trish laughed on the other end of the phone. "CJ, we need eye-popping, car-stopping clothes. This is fundraising we're doing. Besides, it's supposed to be in the low eighties on Thursday. Definitely not jeans weather."

"Uh... okay, I guess. We should be back from the ranch by 6, but we'll need some time to eat before you pick me up.

"Let Shawn play bachelor for the night. We'll pick you up at 6 and grab something to eat at the mall. See you at 6."

CJ pressed OFF and looked at Shawn. "Why am I getting the feeling that the Boot Drive is going to be an experience I'll never forget?"

Smiling, he said, "Oh, you have no idea. You *will* have fun, though. Trish will make sure of that."

CJ raised her eyebrows. "Are you going to be okay playing bachelor and eating by yourself?"

"Sure. I'll just open a can of Spaghetti-Os. I think I'll go whole hog and do Spaghetti-Os with meatballs."

"Don't you dare have Spaghetti-Os without me!"

"Okay, okay. I'll do beans and hot dogs."

"Ugh! Gross. I'm glad I'm not going to be here. Are you going to be on the corner with us tomorrow?"

"Rick and I will be on a corner, but not the same one you'll be on. If Trish does the same thing she did last year, there will be three or four of you at the intersection and believe me, you'll have no problem getting people to donate."

They headed into the living room and curled up on the couch. "Oh joy, I can't wait. Am I being set up?" she asked.

"No, Trish wouldn't do that to you. Trust me, it'll be a fun day that you'll enjoy. The Boot Drive has gotten to be kind of a tradition for us. Afterward, Rick and Trish will pick up the girls, and we'll meet them somewhere for dinner. You should feel honored that she asked you to join them. She never asked Wendy. Or, if she did, Wendy never helped her."

"What did she mean *twirl signs?*"

"You know, like the guys on the corners that advertise new homes, restaurants, and other businesses by twirling and tossing a sign to attract attention."

Panic set in. "I can't do that. I spent two years in grade school trying to be a cheerleader. All I ended up doing was constantly dropping my baton and tripping over my own feet."

Shawn laughed and pulled her closer. "Trust me. Trish has this all figured out. You'll do fine. Now, how about we unwrap dessert?"

Twenty minutes and a lot of wandering hands—on both sides—later, he picked her naked body up and carried her into the bedroom. He pulled back the covers, gently set her on the bed, and slid in next to her. Once he was settled, she rolled over onto him, straddled his hips, and took him into her.

Two hours later, exhausted, she laid her head on his chest and stayed perfectly still. "I can't remember what life was like without you. I just want to stay like this forever."

Shawn could feel her smile as she snuggled her ear into his chest and tucked her arms under him.

Then she fell asleep, listening to his heartbeat.

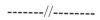

CJ woke at 4 am, still partially on top of Shawn. She looked up and saw the biggest smile she had ever seen on him.

Reaching up, she pushed his hair away from his eyes, laid her head back on his chest, and asked, "Feel like a run?"

"Sure," he said.

She sat up, straddled him, and kissed his nose. "Stay right where you are. I gotta go pee, then I'll get us coffee. Your job is to lay there, smile, and look cute. Be right back." She got up and padded naked into the bathroom. When she was finished, she walked back to the bed, bent over, kissed him, and reminded him not to move.

"Sorry, but I've got to go too," he said. "Okay, but I want you in bed when I get back with coffee. Understood?"

As he walked into the bathroom, he responded with, "Yes, your cuteness."

CJ turned the coffeemaker on and pulled two mugs out of the cabinet while it heated the water up. She loaded a K-cup into the holder, pulled the lever down, and pushed the *big boy's mug* button, as Shawn called it. Repeating the process a second time, she then grabbed both mugs and padded back into the bedroom.

Shawn lay there looking cute and laughed as she came back in. "What a way to wake up."

She set the mugs on the nightstand, sat on the edge of the bed, and snuggled up to him. "I'll be getting your coffee every morning for the rest of your life, my fine knight. That is, if you wish it."

He pulled her close and whispered, "You are absolutely adorable. And, yes, I wish it."

After brushing their teeth, they both put on shorts, T-shirts, and running shoes, then finished their coffee and headed for the door. They walked around to the back gate of the complex and stepped onto the Bonita Social Circle.

At mile two, Shawn took her hand and steered her across Bonita Road and into the side entrance of the engine bay at the back of the firehouse. As they entered, the four firemen and two EMTs all stopped what they were doing and stared at CJ.

Finally, Victor, one of the EMTs, looked at Shawn and said, "Wow. Did you find her on the track? Looks like I need to start running in the morning." He reached his hand out to CJ and added, "Hello, I'm Victor."

Just as CJ finished shaking Victor's hand, Rick came up, put his hand out, and said, "I'm Rick, you must be CJ."

As CJ shook Rick's hand, she said, "Hi, Victor. Hi, Rick. Yes, I'm CJ."

Rick turned to Shawn. "No wonder you decided to burn some of your vacation hours."

The rest of the crew came up, and Shawn introduced each of them to CJ. As he finished, the station chief came through the doorway and into the engine bay. "CJ, this is Tim, our chief."

Tim shook her hand. "CJ. It's a pleasure to meet you." He smiled at Shawn. "It's not hard to see why you wanted time off." Turning back to CJ he asked, "Is he treating you good?"

She took Shawn's hand and looked up at him. "Very good. He's spoiling me rotten. And I love every minute of it."

"We're just finishing our run before we head out to the ranch," Shawn said. "I wanted to let you know I'll be back for my shift on Saturday. Oh, and CJ will be joining Trish for the Boot Drive tomorrow."

Tim smiled at CJ. "Thank you, CJ. The Boot Drive is one of our biggest fundraising events, and since the wives and girlfriends started helping, we've more than doubled the amount we raise each year. We really appreciate their help, and we're glad to have you join us." He turned back to Shawn and Rick. "With CJ joining Trish and her crew, this should be a banner year."

Shawn gave CJ's hand a squeeze. "Well, we need to go get showered and head to the ranch. We'll see all of you tomorrow morning for the Boot Drive."

As they turned to leave, Rick looked at them. "Can I talk to both of you for a minute?"

The three of them walked through the open bay door and stopped just outside, out of earshot of the others. Rick turned to CJ. "You're Cloris Cole, aren't you?"

CJ went completely white. How did he know who she was? Oh God, was her past coming back to haunt her? How did he know her name? Nobody knew her name. Nobody.

Shawn saw her turn white and asked, "Are you okay?"

Taking a deep breath, she nodded. "Yes." Absolutely terrified of the answer, she finally asked Rick, "Hav... have we met?"

"Kinda," Rick said. "I was one of the firemen that found you five years ago."

CJ's hand went to her mouth. "Oh my God." She just stood there, staring at him. Her hand started shaking and lower lip started quivering.

Shawn put his arm around her and pulled her close as Rick continued. "I'm sorry. I didn't mean to shock you. Trish only told me your name was CJ, so I didn't realize it was you until you walked in with Shawn. I'm so sorry about what those men did to you, and I'm glad to see you've recovered."

Turning to Shawn, he said, "Our crew kind of adopted her that night." Then he turned back to CJ. "We kept track of you up until you left the hospital and went into rehab. After that, we deliberately lost track of you, once we knew you were okay. We figured that keeping in touch with you would be invading your privacy and only remind you of that night.

"Listen, I'm sorry I shocked you. I'm just glad to see you're okay. I can't believe you two found each other. I know he's my best friend and I'm more than a bit biased, but you couldn't have found a nicer guy. You two go on and get out of here. We'll have plenty of time to talk later." He turned and started to walk back into the station.

CJ took another deep breath, then called out, "Rick. Wait." She ran after him, threw her arms around his neck, laid her head on his shoulder, and whispered, "Tha-Thank you... for saving me."

As they walked back to the condo, CJ squeezed Shawn's hand. "Do you believe in fate?" she asked.

"I do now," he said.

Chapter 23 - Let's Go Shopping

Shawn and CJ's day at the ranch flew by. The usual chores of cleaning and refilling the troughs, raking stalls, and hauling horse poop to the manure pile took up most of their day. Feeding and checking to make sure everyone was okay wrapped up the afternoon. Four volunteers had shown up, so CJ assigned two of them to brush and groom the horses, a treat for both the horses and the volunteers.

No new horses were scheduled to arrive, and with all the help, everyone finished early. After thanking them, she cut the volunteers loose two hours early then took Shawn up the hill to introduce him to the wild mustang herd.

As they walked hand in hand back down to the trailers, CJ asked him again, "Are you sure you're going to be alright with 'baching' it for dinner? I can stay if you want then meet them later."

"Go enjoy your evening with Trish and the girls." He looked at her. "Are you okay for money?"

She nodded her head. "Yeah... I can't spend much, but I should have enough. Thank you for asking."

When they got to the trailer, CJ sat at the dining table and pulled out the volunteer schedule while Shawn used the bathroom. She checked the schedule to make sure Kate would've enough help on Thursday. Finally, she wrote a note to let Kate know that all the chores had been completed and the horses had been groomed.

Leaving the trailer, Shawn steered her toward the picnic table out front. He sat her on the bench, then straddled it, facing her. "I just want to take a minute and let the world slow down a bit. It's so peaceful and quiet out here." She leaned into him and put her head on his shoulder as Deveny, watching them from her corral, whinnied and nodded her approval. "I'll bet you're going to miss this," he said.

"If I stayed out here, I'd miss being with you a hundred times more. You're giving me the best of both worlds. I get to be with you, yet I'm less than an hour away from the ranch." She put her arms around him, pulled herself in tight and whispered into his chest. "I had no idea how lonely my life was out here until you came along. I don't ever want to wake up again without your arms around me, and I'm not sure I could get through a day without you being a part of it."

They sat in silence for several minutes, the wind in the trees the only sound. Finally, he kissed the top of her head. "Guess we better head back. Is there anything else in your trailer you want to grab before we go?"

She smiled. "Everything I want to grab is right here in my arms." Suddenly, she jumped up and yelled, "Let's go. I've got some serious shopping to do for tomorrow."

All the way back, CJ jabbered excitingly about her upcoming shopping trip. She jumped out of the truck and ran for the door as soon as they pulled into Shawn's parking space.

"Last one into the shower makes dinner tomorrow night," she shouted on the way. She got to the door and screeched to a stop.

"Looking for these?" Shawn said, as he dangled the keys to the condo by her ear.

"Damn. That was about dumb. Guess I'll be making dinner. Since you'll miss out on Spaghetti-Os tonight, what's your pleasure, my knight? Meatballs or meat sauce?"

"Ugh. How about a big salad and garlic bread? You're pretty good with greens." He handed her the keys. She unlocked the door, turned, and handed the keys back to him.

"They're yours" he said, pushing her hand back. "You're now officially my roommate, as well as my lover, my confidant, my soul sharer, my trusted sidekick, and the most beautiful woman in the world."

She stretched up and kissed him. "Trusted sidekick?" She held her hand up, palm out, and said, "How... Kemo Sabe."

He smiled and smacked her palm. "How... about... we go shower? Princess Spaghetti-Os."

He put his arm around her shoulder, and she put hers around his waist as they walked through the door, then into the bedroom. They stripped out of their ranch clothes, and he followed her to the shower, pinching her behind as she stepped in.

"Cute butt."

She turned, wiggled her eyebrows and handed him her scrubby ball.

An hour later, CJ kissed him and swung her legs over the side of the bed, then laid her head back onto his chest. "Have I ever told you I love you?" She reached back, took his hand, and pressed it to her breast. "Can we continue this when I get back?"

"You bet. As soon as you're done modeling whatever you buy for tomorrow. Now get your butt moving before Trish and the girls catch us both naked."

Three minutes later, CJ was pulling up her jeans as the doorbell rang. Shoes in hand, she headed to the door. "Did we interrupt something?" Trish asked.

"No, I was waiting for you," CJ answered.

"Uh-huh," Trish responded. "With your jeans unzipped and your blouse misbuttoned? Not to mention the canary feathers hanging out of your mouth. Good thing the girls waited in the car, or I'd be doing Sex Education 101 with them."

Trish glanced over CJ's shoulder as Shawn walked up behind her. "I promise we'll get her back soon so you two can pick up where you left off." She looked down at Shawn's jeans. "In the meantime? You might want to zip up so something doesn't catch a cold while we're gone."

CJ leaned her head back and Shawn kissed the top of her head. "Busted," he whispered.

As they walked to Trish's SUV, Trish took CJ's arm. "I'm sorry. I shouldn't tease you two like that, but I couldn't resist."

CJ smiled at her. "Totally our fault. Next time we'll leave a bit more time… or we'll just leave you standing outside till we finish getting dressed."

The girls hopped out, and each of them gave CJ a big hug, then they all piled into the SUV and Trish headed for the Plaza Bonita Mall. She turned into the third entrance and found a parking space in the first row, directly in front of Applebee's.

"Wow. Front row. I can't remember the last time that happened." They all piled out and started toward Applebee's and the mall entrance. "Since we're right here, why don't we eat first and then head for the shops?"

Forty-five minutes later, they headed into the mall and ducked into the first women's shop they came to. Five shops later, while Trish had found everything she needed, CJ had looked at or tried on dozens of items. All had been too revealing, didn't appeal to her, or were too expensive.

Getting discouraged, they walked across the aisle and into the Slinky Kitten. Each of them went in a different direction, hoping to find something that would work for CJ. Ten minutes later, Cat, Liz, and Zoey, a sales clerk, approached CJ. Cat was waving a pair of white shorts, and Liz had a dark blue scoop-neck top.

"You gotta try these," Cat and Liz said.

CJ took both items and headed for the dressing room. Several minutes later, she stepped out and everybody agreed they were perfect. That was, until CJ looked at the price tag on the shorts.

"Oh my God. One hundred twenty-three dollars. There is no way. That's pretty much my wardrobe budget for the year," she said. She looked at the tag on the top, and it was seventy dollars. "I'm sorry," she said to Zoey. "I love both pieces, but they're completely out of my price range."

Zoey checked the tag on both the shorts and the top and looked at CJ. "I have an idea. Don't move. I'll be right back." A minute later, she came out of the stock room with a Slinky Kitten bag and handed it to CJ. "Go try this stuff on and see if it fits while I make a phone call."

Back in the dressing room, CJ opened the bag and found a pair of white rolled shorts, almost like the one hundred twenty-three dollar pair she had on; a watermelon-red scoop-neck T-shirt with elbow-length puff sleeves; a V-neck short-sleeve top with shoulder cut-outs in army green; and a pair of multi-color beaded thong sandals.

She absolutely loved everything that was in the bag. All of the items were exactly what she would've picked out, and they were perfect for tomorrow. Next, she checked each of the items for price tags, but nothing was marked. She shrugged. *What the heck?* CJ changed into the shorts and tops, and found that everything fit perfect. Even the sandals.

She stepped out of the dressing room, wearing the shorts, watermelon top, and sandals and collected ooh's and ah's from everybody. Zoey asked if the other top fit too, and CJ nodded.

"Everything fits perfect, including the sandals," she said. "I'm almost afraid to ask. How much is this stuff? Nothing is marked."

"I don't know how much it is," Zoey said, as she smiled at CJ. "All of this stuff was stolen from somewhere several weeks ago. The police picked up two girls for shoplifting at the Chula Vista Mall and found this stuff in one of our bags in their car. They returned it to us, but it's not our merchandise and we have no idea whose store it came from. When I saw you in the shorts and top, I remembered this stuff and thought it might fit you."

"That's great, but how much are you going to charge her for it?" asked Trish.

Zoey looked at Trish, then CJ and smiled. "I just talked to my boss. Do you think *free* is within your budget?"

"What?" all four of them yelled.

"Oh no. I can't let you do that," CJ said.

"Sure you can," Zoey responded. "Look, we can't sell it, so my boss said to just give you whatever fits. It's either that or we throw it away."

"Oh my God. I can't believe this. Are you sure? These should be yours. You should take them, not me. You never even saw me before, and you're giving me a whole wardrobe. Oh my God. Am I dreaming?"

Reaching over, Zoey lightly pinched CJ's arm. "No dream. They're way too small for me so I guess you're just going to have to take them." She stopped for a moment, then smiled. "I'll tell you what; the girls told me you're doing the Boot Drive with the Bonita Fire Department tomorrow, and that's what the clothes are for. So… I'm adding a condition. You have to put five dollars in the boot for me. That will make us even. Okay?"

CJ gave her a big smile. "I'm putting twenty dollars in the boot for you, first thing. More if I have it. Thank you. I still don't believe this is happening."

Trish thanked Zoey too. "That was awfully nice of you. Can I get a business card with your boss' name on it? We want to make sure he knows that the Slinky Kitten now has four new customers, thanks to you. We'll be sure to check here first whenever we're shopping for clothes."

The four of them left the store and headed out to the parking lot. After they were all buckled into the SUV, Trish looked over at CJ in the passenger seat. "That was unbelievable." Looking up, she added, "Someone up there loves you."

CJ smiled at her. "It's Shawn and Rio. They're my lucky charms."

Trish smiled back. "Who's Rio?"

"He's responsible for Shawn and I meeting… It's a long story, best told over a few drinks when we can spend some girl time together."

Reaching over, CJ put her hand on Trish's arm and turned to look at the girls in the back seat. "Thank you all for being so accepting. I can't begin to tell you how welcome you've made me feel."

Liz said, "You're welcome."

"Let's get you back," Trish added. "Tomorrow will be a long day. How about if I pick you up at 5:45? We want to catch as many people on their way to work as we can. The girls already made up the signs so all we need to do is stop by the station and grab our boots. That should put us on the corner by 6."

"I don't know if I'm more excited or nervous," CJ told Trish.

"You'll do fine. It's for a very good cause and a lot of fun. Everybody knows about it, and you'll be amazed at how supportive people in San Diego are. Every year I'm blown away by how much we collect."

They pulled into the condo parking lot. CJ leaned over and gave Trish a big hug as both girls jumped out and came around to her door. She collected her bags, stepped out, and put her arms around Liz.

As she turned and pulled Cat in, she said, "How's our project going?"

Cat's grin spread from ear to ear. "Wow. Aunt CJ, I'm the coolest person in my school. Oh, and you need to watch the news on KUSI tonight."

CJ looked over at Trish, who just shrugged. "Don't look at me. All I know is we all need to watch KUSI at 10."

281

As Trish and the girls left, CJ waved good-bye. Reaching into her purse, she took out the key to the condo that Shawn had given her. She looked at the key and smiled as a wave of warmth swept through her. *My own key. He gave me my own key.* Just as she was about to push it into the lock, the door opened.

"Hi. I thought I heard you," Shawn said, as he reached out and pulled her into him.

She laid her head against his chest and whispered, "I'm the luckiest girl in the world, and I am so in love with you."

"Well, I'm glad because I love you too, but what brought that on?"

She looked up and tucked herself against him as tight as she could. "You, Trish, the girls, Rick, Kate, Shannon, the sales clerk at the store, all of you. I had no idea that I could ever be this happy. I never thought I would be a part of so many wonderful people's lives. Most of all, I never thought the most amazing guy in the world would be all mine."

He picked her up, and she wrapped her arms around his neck. Nudging the door closed with his foot, he carried her over to the couch. "Wow. That must've been some shopping trip."

"You have no idea. Wait till I tell you what happened and show you what I got. Before I forget, though, we need to watch the 10 pm news on KUSI, so I better hurry."

Picking up the remote, Shawn turned the TV to KUSI as CJ pulled her top off. She kicked off her shoes, unbuttoned her jeans, and stepped out of them. Reaching into the bag, she pulled everything out as she told him the story of the stolen clothes and how the sales clerk had given her everything for free.

Shawn stood there watching her in nothing but her bra and panties as she pulled the puff-sleeved watermelon top over her head. Reaching back to pull the waves of her long brown hair through the scoop-neck, she realized Shawn was staring at her.

"What?" she asked.

"Do you have any idea how gorgeous you are? If I were the sales clerk at the Sleazy Kitten, I would have given you the whole store."

CJ broke out laughing. "It's *Slinky* Kitten, and you are never, ever allowed to work there. I have absolutely no intention of sharing you with all the pretty girls who shop there. Your being a fireman is bad enough."

She stepped into the shorts and wiggled them over her hips before pulling the zipper up and buckling the dark brown belt that came with them. After she slipped on the sandals, she put her arms out and did two full turns.

"What do you think?" she asked.

"I think you're unbelievably hot. Maybe we should skip the Boot Drive and spend the day here."

"Oh, no, no, no. I promised Trish I would help her, and I can't go back on my promise, as tempting as your offer is." She walked over, sat in his lap, and put her arms around his neck. "Besides, it would take her a fast two seconds to figure out what we were up to and be beating down the door."

She kissed him, then added, "And thank you for the compliment about being gorgeous. Have I told you lately how much I love you?"

He kissed her back. "Uh, about five minutes ago, but I never get tired of hearing you say it."

Suddenly, she jumped up and pointed at the TV. "Oh… Oh… turn up the sound. That's Cat."

On the TV screen was a picture of Cat shaking hands with the school's principal. The banner below read: BULLYING IN SCHOOLS BECOMING A NATIONAL PROBLEM. As the sound came up, the news anchor was saying "—and this young lady decided to do something about the problem at her school. She started an anti-bullying club—" The anchor looked down at his notes. "—that now has over five hundred members. That's three-quarters of the school's students, all of whom have vowed to help stop bullying at their school."

"Oh my God. Go, Cat. I'm so proud of you," CJ shouted at the TV.

The news anchor went on. "Her efforts have already caught statewide attention. The school's principal and counselors have asked her to work with them to put together a plan that—"

"Your phone. I need your phone," CJ yelled to Shawn. He picked up his phone from the coffee table, punched the icon for Rick and Trish, and handed it to CJ.

"Hey, Shawn," Trish's voice said.

"I need to talk to Cat," CJ shouted into the phone.

"Ah, hi, CJ, I take it you watched the news. Just a minute. I'll put her on."

"Hello, Aunt CJ," Cat squeaked into the phone.

"You are awesome. I am so proud of you."

"Thank you, Aunt CJ, but it was your plan."

"No. You did it. You own this, not me. You took the idea and ran with it. You made it happen. You're my hero. You're everybody's hero, and I am so proud of you."

CJ could sense Cat choking up from being the center of attention. Suddenly, Trish's voice came back on. "We're all a little overwhelmed right now so it's a little hard for us to talk. CJ, none of us will ever forget this night. We will never, ever forget what you did for our daughter." She too started to choke up but managed to squeak out, "I knew you were special. I knew it. I just had no idea how special… I gotta go before I cry. Thank you." And she hung up.

Shawn hugged her.

"I didn't do anything. I made a suggestion. She turned it into reality," she whispered.

"Right. You'll never convince them of that. You won their daughter's confidence and helped her with a problem she obviously couldn't go to her parents with. Now she's helping others." He held her face between his hands and gently kissed her. "You're contagious. You meet people, they fall in love with you, and they become better people."

"You're adorable, but none of that's true. I'm just me." She rubbed his nose with hers.

He raised his eyebrows. "Come with me, my princess, and let me show you just how special and contagious you are." Before she could answer, he picked her up, carried her into the bedroom, and began removing her clothes.

Chapter 24 - The Boot Drive

CJ wanted to get a run in before Trish picked her up for the boot drive so Shawn woke her at 4 am. That way they would have plenty of time for their run, a shower, a quick bite, and getting dressed.

As usual, he woke her with a kiss and coffee in hand. She stared at him through sleepy eyes. "You are so much better than a Ken doll. My God, you are spoiling me so bad."

"Great, my plan's still working."

They both slipped into their running clothes and shoes and headed to the social circle for their run. Forty-five minutes later, they were back, and after stepping out of their running gear, they headed for the shower.

CJ handed him her scrubby ball with a stern look on her face. "No messing around. After the Boot Drive, I'm all yours... to do with as you please," she said.

At exactly 5:45, Trish knocked on the door. When they reached her SUV, Trish introduced CJ to Gwen and Donna, both wives of Bonita firemen, then they followed Shawn in his truck to the fire station.

Once there, they collected their boots, and Trish started going over who would be where. Finally, she looked at CJ. "If you need to go, go now because we'll be out there for a few hours."

"Nope, I'm fine."

They all walked over to Trish's SUV, and Trish pulled out one of four 2 foot by 3 foot oval signs and handed it to CJ. "These are the signs we'll be using. Compliments of Liz and Cat."

Across the top of the white sign was a row of cartoon kids. Beneath that:

CAMP BEYOND THE SCARS

FIREFIGHTER
BOOT DRIVE
All proceeds benefit the Burn Institute

Each line was in a different dark color, and a bright red two-inch border ran around the edge. On the back were three handles. In the center was a single handle on a shaft that allowed the sign to be spun. To the left and right were two draw-pull type handles, either of which could be used to hold the sign with one hand, leaving the other hand free to hold the collection boot. Or both handles could be used to *wiggle* the sign to attract attention.

CJ stared at the sign. "These are unbelievable. Who came up with the idea?"

"That would be Liz. She got all the artistic talent in the family. The rest of us can't even draw recognizable stick figures." Trish chuckled. "Cat helped her, but all she had to do was use the colors Liz told her and stay within the lines."

Putting her arms around Trish, CJ gave her a big hug. "Your family is amazing."

Just as they were about to get in the SUV, Shawn came up with Gwen's husband. Shawn pulled two Bonita Fire Department helmets from behind his back and put one on each of their heads. Gwen's husband did the same with Gwen and Donna.

287

"There you go. Now there's no doubt you're with the fire department," Shawn said.

"Trish, there's also been a change of plans. Since your group always manages to collect way more than the rest of us, we decided to split you up. That way we'll have two of you at each end of town rather than all of you on the same corner. Gwen, you and Donna will be in front of Jack in the Box on the corner of Willow and Bonita Road with EMT Victor."

Looking at CJ and Trish, Shawn pointed behind them. "You two are on the corner of Central and Bonita Road and EMT Rachel will join you. Both Rachel and Victor will have radios so we can all stay in contact."

CJ pushed the bill of her helmet up and turned around. She held her hand above her eyes and looked at the corner of Bonita and Central, one short block from the fire station. "All the way down there? I'm not sure I can make it."

"Oh, my poor princess." He kissed her, then smacked the back of her helmet. "Get your butt moving before I pick you up and carry you."

Trish smiled and raised her hand. "You can carry me."

They all laughed then collected their signs from Trish's SUV. Victor pulled up in the ambulance, and Gwen and Donna put their signs in back and jumped into the front next to him while Trish and CJ headed to their destination.

When they got to the corner, CJ looked at Trish. "Wow. Tough duty. Right in front of Starbucks."

Rachel, dressed in her EMT uniform, walked up a short time later and introduced herself to CJ. She shook her head at them.

288

"There's no way I can compete with you two in this uniform," she said, and crossed to the opposite corner of the intersection.

For the next three hours, they stood on the corner, spinning, twirling, and wiggling their signs as commuters stuck their arms out with handfuls of cash. At one point, for some unknown reason, donations slowed down even though traffic hadn't. To juice things up, CJ and Trish, both in shorts, started hip-bumping while they wiggled their signs high over their heads. Within minutes, donations picked back up.

After three and a half hours and four *long* treks back to the fire station to empty fire boots overflowing with cash, they headed toward Starbucks. Rachel met them at the door and all three of them went in.

"You rock," the girl behind the counter yelled as she held her open hand up and everyone in the sitting area applauded.

They each high-fived the girl's open palm and said, "My manager said whatever you want is on us. Oh, and this is from us," she added, handing Rachel three five-dollar bills.

To both baristas and their manager, Trish said, "Thank you so much."

"What can we get you?" Melinda, the barista asked.

"I'll have a Grande Latte," said Trish.

"That sounds good," added CJ.

"Me three," said Rachel.

"Pastries, anyone?" Melinda added.

289

"I'm good," said CJ.

"Me too," Trish added with smile that said *that's the last thing I need.*

"I'll take one of those," Rachel said, pointing at a chocolate chip muffin.

"On second thought, make that two," CJ threw in.

After collecting their lattes and muffins, they headed out to a table on the patio. Before they could sit down, the manager came out and stood close by. "Thank you so much for helping with the Boot Drive. My nephew was badly scalded in a kitchen accident when he was three, and if it hadn't been for the Burn Institute, I'm not sure how our family would have gotten through it. If you want anything else, don't be bashful. It's the least we can do to say thanks."

No sooner had the manager left than several customers from inside and other patio tables came over. Each handed money to one of them and thanked all three for helping with the drive.

Rachel commented to CJ and Trish, "With all the bad stuff I see on my job, it's things like this that make me realize there's still a lot of good people in the world. And, speaking of good people, thank you both for spending your day helping us with our drive."

As they were about to leave, Melinda, the young girl who had waited on them, came out, her shift obviously over.

She walked up to CJ, bent over, and slipped several dollars into her hand. "This is from Carly, the other barista, and me."

"You already gave us money," CJ objected.

"No, actually, that was from Juanita, our manager. She said to hang onto our tips and she would give you money for all of us. She even made sure we gave you three fives so it looked like we each put in five dollars. She's like that, always doing stuff for us, but we still wanted to each give you something. Please don't tell her. We wish it could be more, but tips today weren't all that great." She gave them a *see ya around* wave, then walked to her car.

"That was unbelievable," whispered Rachel, as she swiped at a tear making its way down her cheek.

The three of them walked back to the fire station, each of them turning in another completely full boot. Rachel checked in with the dispatcher to let her know she was back in the station, while CJ and Trish went to the lounge to wait for Shawn, Rick, and the others.

Rejoining them, Rachel sat across from CJ and gave her a big smile. "CJ, I know I just met you and I probably shouldn't say anything, but Trish will tell you, I'm not bashful about speaking my mind."

"Bashful?" said Trish, looking at CJ. "If you look it up in the dictionary, you will not find Rachel's picture within a hundred pages. But *brazen*, now that's a different story."

"Okay, okay, don't get carried away, Trish. Look, CJ, you need to know that everyone at the station thinks the world of Shawn. And all of us girls think you're the luckiest girl in the world. Next to Trish, that is."

"Thank you. Flattery will get you everywhere," Trish threw in.

Rachel continued, "I was at the station when you were found so I know what you've been through. And just so you know, everyone at the station kind of adopted you. Helping with your recovery kind of became our project."

Frowning, she added, "Maybe project's not the right word. All we knew was that finding you like that woke something up in all of us. Hell, you could've been the wife, sister, or some relative of anyone of us."

CJ turned to Trish. "You knew? You knew all along who I was?"

"No," whispered Trish, as she reached over and took CJ's hand. "No. Everyone knew about them finding someone, but no one at the station ever said who you were or gave any details. All anyone ever said was that they had found a girl that had been beaten and dumped in a field. I never connected the dots until you told your story to us at the restaurant. Even then, I wasn't sure you were the one they had found."

"How many people know?" CJ asked Rachel.

"Well, actually only two of us, now. Rick and I. We're the only ones still here. Everyone else has retired or moved on. CJ, you need to know that everyone of us did everything we could to keep your identity a secret. Like I said, we kinda adopted you. The last thing any of us wanted was the people who did that to you finding out anything about you."

A puzzled look came over CJ's face as she struggled to remember something. "Oh my God. You sat with me in my hospital room, didn't you?"

"Yeah, that was me," Rachel answered. "I'm surprised you remember. You were so out of it most of the time." She smiled at CJ, then looked over at Trish. "You're not going to believe this, but it was me and Jen."

Trish's eyes flew wide open. "Jenny? The one that Wendy ran away with?"

"The same. The chief back then would only let the two of us go check on CJ. Because of what happened to her, he didn't want any of the guys there." Looking back at CJ, she continued, "The two of us took turns checking on you. We would each spend a few hours with you, either reading to you or telling you about our day. Of course, we left the bad stuff out. That's the last thing you needed to hear about."

Tears were running down CJ's cheeks as she asked, "Why? Why would you do that? Why would you and Jenny spend hours reading to someone like me? You had to know what I was, what I did?"

"I can't speak for Jenny, but like I said, finding you woke something up in all of us. For me, no matter what you were or what you did, you didn't deserve what had been done to you. I also realized that it could just as easily been me lying there after being picked up in a club, then drugged, beaten, and raped. And if it was me, I knew I would've wanted someone to care. Someone to care enough to spend a few hours, to sit and read to me or tell me about their day."

Her mind in total overload, CJ sat staring at Rachel. Trish squeezed her hand. "Are you okay?"

"No... No, I'm not okay," CJ whispered.

Just then, Shawn and Rick walked in. Shawn took one look at CJ, walked over, and lifted her out of the chair and into a hug. "What's wrong?"

"Please take me home?" she whispered.

293

Shawn looked at everyone. "Please excuse us. I'm going to take her home and let her get some rest." He led her toward the front door of the station.

Just as he pushed the door open, she said, "Wait, I can't leave like this." She took his hand and led him back to the lounge. Walking back in, she put Shawn's arms around her waist and pulled him tight against her back. She looked directly at Rachel.

"You're right, Rachel. I *am* the luckiest girl in the world. Not only because Shawn loves me but because of all the wonderful people in the world who care about me. Right now I'm completely overwhelmed and I need Shawn to take me home, but I can't leave without each of you knowing how much you mean to me. Thank you all for being in my life." She turned in Shawn's arms and looked up into his eyes. "Take me home?"

-------//-------

They drove back to the condo with CJ's head against Shawn's arm, neither one of them saying a word. As soon as they were inside, he pulled her into him. "Are you okay?"

Nodding her head against his chest, she softly said, "Yeah... I'm getting there."

"Want to talk about it?"

"I should but... maybe later. Right now, I just want to be held and loved. And fed? Being emotional makes me hungry." Looking up into his eyes, she smiled. "I am so in love with you. I am so in love with life... I'm just rambling like a mad woman, aren't I? I guess I do need to talk."

She took his hand and led him over to the couch, turned him around, and pushed him down. She sat on the floor in front of him, pulled herself between his legs, and laid her head on his thigh.

"This is going to sound crazy. I think I just realized that I almost died. I mean, when I was listening to Rachel, I *really realized* that I almost died. Until today, it never sunk in that if it hadn't been for a few people, I would not be here. I would've led my very short life never having known happiness. Or love. I wouldn't have contributed anything. I wouldn't have been remembered by anyone. I would've died, never having done anything to be remembered for.

"I would've missed everything. I would never have gone to the ranch. The horses would never have become a part of my life, and I would never have become a part of theirs. I would've died and never been able to help them.

"And people. I would never have met all the wonderful people who have come into my life and care so much. Rick and the other firemen and EMTs who came to my rescue. All the people who rescue the horses and other animals that can't defend themselves. Kate and Shannon and all the volunteers who care for the horses and make them feel wanted and loved. Zoey, the sales clerk who found a way to help me get clothes she knew I couldn't afford. Juanita, the manager at Starbucks, who donated to the Boot Drive for the two baristas so they wouldn't have to give up their tips. And Carly and Melinda, the two baristas who gave us their tips anyway then apologized because it wasn't much.

"Then there's Rachel and Jenny, the EMTs, who I just found out spent hours in my hospital room talking and reading to me while I recovered. Most of the time I didn't even know they were there, yet they still came to make sure I was okay and spent time with me."

She looked up at Shawn, tears slowly running down her cheeks.

"Oh God, Shawn, I realized I would never have met you. I would never have felt the warmth of your touch, known the security of being in your arms. I would never have known what love is, what it's like to be loved, what it feels like to have you make love to me.

"If I had died, I would've missed all of that. I would never have had a life. All of a sudden, it's like this big neon sign lit up in my head: **You almost died. You came close to never experiencing life and love.**"

She wiped away the tears and smiled.

"I think I now understand the look in the horses' eyes when they come to the ranch. Their eyes are saying, *'I almost died and you saved me. You took me in and nursed me back to health and made me feel wanted. You gave me life and love and I will never forget you.'*

"I'm just like the horses, Shawn. I almost died, and so many wonderful people saved me. They nursed me back to health and made me feel wanted. Then you stepped into my life and gave me the most precious gift of all… your love."

Shawn gently helped her up and into his lap. She stretched her legs out onto the couch and curled into him. Pulling her in tight, he kissed the top of her head, rested his chin in her hair, and took in the scent of her. For the next five minutes, they hugged each other, neither of them saying a word.

Finally, she whispered, "Didn't know you were getting a basket case, did you? I don't know why I keep breaking down like this. I try to be strong. Honest. Right now, you've gotta be wondering if my moving in, or even being with me, is such a good idea. If you want to change your mind, I'll understand."

Shawn stayed quiet for the longest time, then finally said, "Nice try. You're not getting out of cooking dinner tomorrow that easily."

She looked up into his eyes. "Damn," she huffed, then reached up and pulled him into a long kiss and whispered, "I love you."

He pushed her hair from in front of her eyes then ran his fingers through the soft curls till they reached the end. "You're as far from a basket case as anyone could be." He moved his hand back up and did it again but stayed quiet, his chin resting on the top of her head.

She could feel his warm breath softly stirring her hair as her head gently rose and fell with his chest. For a moment, she wondered if he had fallen asleep. Curled into him like this, she certainly could. She actually found herself wishing he was asleep, wishing he wouldn't say another word. If he did, it would break the magic spell that was wrapping them in a moment she never wanted to end. As if reading her mind, he turned his head and laid his cheek on top of her head as he pulled her tighter into his arms.

For the next fifteen minutes, they sat like that—wrapped in each other's thoughts, neither one of them saying a word. Finally, he lifted his head and rested his chin back on the top of her head.

"Have I told you how much I envy you? You've been through things most people would never have survived, and you came out the other end the most wonderful person I've ever met. You summoned all the strength and courage in you, pushed aside anger and the ugliness and cruelty of what had been done to you and fought for your survival.

"Then I came along, and for some reason that I will forever be thankful for, you put your trust in me. You paved a small path through the shield of bravery and courage that you built to protect you, and you let me walk through. After everything that's been done to you, you had the courage to trust me with your heart and soul.

"And today, you were brave enough to lower the shield again and finally let in the reality of what actually happened to you. CJ, you're not a basket case. You're the bravest person I've ever known. And I'm so grateful to have you in my life."

"Thank you," she whispered, not looking at him. "I don't feel very brave or courageous. Right now, I just feel… worn out."

Shawn lifted her chin and looked into her eyes. "Trish is expecting us to join the group for dinner. You okay if we beg off?"

"Thank you… I wasn't sure how to tell you I really don't want to go. It's been a very long day. I'm completely worn out and I don't want to be a downer at their celebration."

"I'll give her a call."

"Thanks, but I should be the one to call. I need to thank her again for inviting me and tell her what a great time I had, as well as apologize for leaving the way I did."

"You call, and I'll go round up something for us to eat."

Just as CJ finished her conversation with Trish, Shawn set down a big tray of *grazing* food and two Coronas, a lime slice stuffed into each bottle. Before the tray even hit the table, CJ reached over and grabbed two chunks of cheese, a broccoli floret, and a handful of chips.

"God, am I hungry," she mumbled through a mouthful of chips.

While CJ washed the chips down with a big swig of beer, Shawn turned on the TV. A weird creature with tentacles and the head of a shark, swallowing a paddle boat with two people in it, filled the screen.

CJ almost choked on her beer, laughing. "What the hell is that?"

Shawn punched the INFO button on the remote. "Octoshark," he read. "It's a full one and a half stars and just starting."

They both curled up on the couch, and CJ scooted into his arms. "I'd rather do this than party, anytime. Octoshark... it just doesn't get any better."

Chapter 25 - Stanley, Ace Watch Dog

Friday morning and their run came early. They had wasted away what was left of the previous evening watching Shark Week movies on the SyFy channel. It turned out to be just what they needed to shed the seriousness and drama of the morning and afternoon. At one point, CJ actually rolled off the couch she was laughing so hard. Later, neither of them could remember exactly what had caused them to crack up. Shawn voted for Dynoshark ripping off Hipposhark's dorsal foot. But CJ insisted it had to be when Roboshark tore Transformoshark's steering wheel off, causing him to go in circles and self-destruct.

All they knew for sure was that making love later proved impossible. Each kept blaming the other every time they tried to get serious and ended up giggling, snorting, and roaring with laughter. They finally completely gave up when CJ tried to do her fish-mouth imitation then got mad because Shawn completely missed the *let's try oral sex* connection. Not only did he miss the connection, he was laughing so hard at her that he almost rolled off the bed.

Somewhere around midnight, they fell asleep in each other's arms with swollen eyes and sides that hurt from laughing so much.

The next morning, dressed for their run, they hit the social circle. An hour and a half later, they pulled into Starbucks for drinks before heading to the freeway and the ranch.

No sooner were they in the door when Melinda yelled out, "Hi. You two are up early." She looked at CJ's eyes, then whispered, "Looks like you got to bed late too."

CJ looked at Melinda through half-shut eyes and said, "You have no idea. I think we watched every Shark Week movie the SyFy channel had yesterday."

"Oh, I love shark week," Melinda said. "Did you see when Roboshark ripped off Transformoshark's steering wheel and he spun himself into a pile of junk? Or how about when—"

"Stop," CJ yelled, as she and Shawn started laughing. "Don't go there. The reason our eyes look like this is from laughing so much. Do. Not. Get. Us. Started. Again."

Melinda desperately tried to keep a straight face as she made their lattes, but every time she made eye contact with one of them, all three started laughing again. Finally they said good-bye to Melinda, collected their lattes, climbed back into Shawn's truck, and headed for the ranch.

By now they had comfortably settled into a routine. So when they reached the ranch, CJ went into the volunteer trailer to check for messages and Shawn headed for the tool shed to assemble their wheelbarrow toolkits.

As he approached Deveny's corral, he glanced over to say good morning to her. It took him several seconds to realize that the corral was empty and the gate was open. He looked around and finally saw Deveny, standing with several other horses way down by the turnout corral. Just then, CJ came running up to him with her cell phone in hand.

"Just a minute, Jason," she said into the phone, then looked at Shawn. "Somebody completely trashed the volunteer— Oh, my God. Where's Deveny?"

"She's down there," Shawn answered, pointing toward the turnout corral.

"That's Officer Clark next to her," CJ said as she looked around. "Somebody let all the horses out. Oh my God, if any of them get out to the road, they'll be hit. Shawn, we have to find them."

"It'll be okay. Both gates to the ranch were closed when we came in so they're all probably on the ranch somewhere. We'll find them. Is that Jason from the sheriff's department?" he said, pointing at the phone.

CJ nodded then spoke back into the phone. "Jason, someone's let all of the horses—" She looked over at the pens. "—and other animals out too. I've got to go. We need to round them up so they don't get hurt."

She nodded as she listened to Jason. "Sure, we'll be here. I'll call Kate and Shannon." Listening again, she kept nodding as if Jason could see her. "Oh, so you'll bring her with you? Great. Jason, thank you so much."

Punching END, she turned back to Shawn. "Jason's on his way. He'll call Shannon and bring her out with him."

"I'll go down and start rounding up horses while you call Kate."

"Shawn, thank you. I don't know what I would have done if you weren't with me. See if you can find Missy. She'll help you. Believe it or not, she really does run the ranch, and all the other horses will listen to her."

She tapped Kate's picture on the phone, then continued, "Don't try to put them back in their stalls. Have Missy help you herd whoever you can into the turnout corral so we know where they're at. We can sort them out later. Oh, and don't worry about the other animals. They're used to roaming around the ranch and will not try to get out."

Kate answered, and CJ responded, "Kate? This is CJ." She mouthed, "I love you" to Shawn, then explained to Kate what had happened and that Jason and Shannon were on their way.

She listened for a minute, then added, "Kate, please don't drop everything and rush out. The last thing we need is you getting into an accident trying to get here. I know you're worried, but I think we have everything under control. Shawn's herding the horses into the turnout, and Shannon will be here any minute to help. Besides, by the time you could get out here, we'll have everybody back where they belong."

After listening and nodding her head a few more times, she told Kate, "I understand. Look, I'm going to go down and help Shawn. As soon as we get them corralled, I'll do a head count and make sure everybody is here and okay. As soon as I'm done, *I promise* I'll call you. Till then, just stay put. Okay?"

Looking up, she saw Jason's cruiser pull through the second gate. Shannon didn't even wait for the car to come to a complete stop before she jumped out. Running right past CJ, she headed for the turnout, so she could help Shawn.

"Kate, I gotta go. Jason and Shannon are here. I promise I'll call you as soon as I account for everyone. I know you're worried, and I'll call the minute I know everyone is alright. Gotta go."

CJ turned to Jason. "Thank you so much. God, I can't believe this. Who would do this?"

Jason raised his eyebrows. "People do crazy stuff, CJ. Why don't you go down and help them, and I'll go look through the trailer. Is your trailer trashed too?"

She shook her head. "I don't know. I haven't made it that far."

While Jason turned and headed for the trailers, CJ took the path between the stalls on her way to the turnout. Looking down the path, she realized that only the stalls on the left were open and empty. Everybody on the right was still in their stall and the gates were closed. Those stalls bordered the ranch entry, which was probably why they hadn't noticed anything as they came in.

She took a quick inventory of the right-hand side as she walked, making sure the horses that belonged in each stall were in fact in there. She also checked to see that everybody looked okay. Once she reached the end, she opened the gate on that side of the turnout and went in.

Shawn and Shannon were just closing the gate on their side as Missy *bossed* the last horse into the corral. CJ did a quick head count and realized someone was missing. She recounted and discovered all the horses were accounted for, but one of the burros was missing.

She walked over to Shawn and Shannon. "All the horses are here, but we're short one burro."

Shawn took in the whole corral. "Where's Milton?"

CJ smiled at Shawn. "If someone's gotta be missing, I'm glad it's Milton. Not only is he *street smart*, he loves you. Call him."

Shawn stood there staring at her.

"Go ahead. Call him," she said.

"Milton. Where are you, buddy?" Shawn yelled out.

Within seconds, loud braying came from the hill beyond the trailers. "See? Told ya. He's up by the mustang herd." CJ smiled, then went serious. "Oh my God, the mustangs."

304

All three of them ran up the hill. As they approached, there they stood, inside the open gate with Milton in the entry, blocking anyone from getting out. As soon as he saw Shawn, he started braying again.

"Well, don't just stand there. Tell him he did good," CJ told Shawn, as they all started laughing.

While Shannon secured the gate and made sure all the mustangs were accounted for, Shawn led Milton back down the hill and CJ called Kate. "Hi. You can breathe again. Everybody's accounted for, and nobody appears to be hurt. Turns out they only opened about half the stalls. I'll do a more complete check on everybody a little later just to be certain everyone's okay.

"I haven't completely checked the rest of the livestock yet, but they all appear to be okay. Oh, and Stanley, *our ace watchdog*, was sitting there waiting for breakfast as we ran by so I'm sure he's okay." She listened for a moment, then laughed. "Yeah, I know, Stanley only does mountain lions. I'm surprised he didn't con whoever did this into feeding him breakfast."

She listened again as she walked toward the trailers. "I'm on my way there now. Jason's checking them out, but I haven't had a chance to talk with him yet. All I know is the volunteer trailer was a complete mess when I walked into it this morning. I'm not sure about my trailer, but I'm looking at it now as I walk past. The front window is broken, and the curtains are gone. Other than that, I can't tell what else they did.

"I still need to check the supply and tool sheds too, but I didn't see any obvious damage as I went by." She listened again. "Yeah, I'd bet money she had something to do with this too, but what can she possibly gain by trashing the place and letting the horses loose? None of it makes any sense."

Jason came down the stairs of the volunteer trailer just as CJ reached them.

"Oh, hang on, let me put Jason on." She mouthed, "Kate" to Jason and handed him the phone.

"Hi, Kate. I heard what CJ said about none of this making any sense, and I'm going to add to the mystery. Whoever did this totally trashed both trailers, but did next to no damage. I mean they threw stuff around, took the curtains off the windows, emptied cabinets, but broke next to nothing. The only thing broken is the front window in CJ's trailer and that looks like it was an accident. Whoever did this is trying to send a message, but I'll be darned if I know what it is."

Jason handed the phone back to CJ. "Kate, we'll finish checking all the animals and clean up what we can. Once we're finished, I'll call and update you on everything."

After she hung up, she and Jason went through both trailers. As she scanned both trailers, she realized he was right everything that wasn't attached had been overturned, scattered, or dumped on the floor, but other than the window, nothing was broken or destroyed.

When they finished touring the trailers, they walked down to the turnout. Shawn was just coming out with Deveny on a lead, about to head for her corral. "Other than being a little spooked, they all seem to be okay," he told CJ. "Shannon got me a lead and showed me how to use it so I'm taking the horses that are comfortable with me back to their stalls. She'll take the others. I actually think we have a pretty good handle on things."

CJ put her arms around Shawn's waist and looked at Jason and Shannon, who had just walked up with Simone. "You three are my heroes. When I first realized what had happened, I almost lost it. All I could picture was these guys getting off the ranch and being hurt or injured. Here we are, not even two hours later,

306

and all the animals are safe and accounted for. Thanks to you. I can't thank you enough." She hugged Shawn tighter and looked up into his eyes. "You, I can... but that will be later."

Shannon looked at them and laughed. "You two need to get a room. Come on, Simone. Good thing you've got blinders on. It's getting X-rated around here." She led Simone toward her stall.

By noon, all the horses were back where they belonged. Jason had finished his incident report and left, and CJ and Shannon had checked all of the animals. While Shawn started on their daily tasks, CJ phoned Kate to update her.

"Everything is fine," she reported. "Other than the mess in the trailers, there is no sign of damage anywhere, and nothing is missing."

"Thank God. CJ, I can't thank you and Shawn enough for being there and taking care of everything. And Shannon too. She's as amazing as the two of you. CJ... can I ask a big favor? Would you mind staying till I can get there? I really need to talk to you. I've already arranged to get off at 3, and if it's the usual Friday-light traffic, I should be there by 4 at the latest."

"Sure, not a problem. I have some stuff I need to talk to you about too. I was going to wait till Sunday, but we can do it tonight if you're okay with that."

"I somehow get the feeling we're both going to be talking about the same thing, but if not, tonight's as good as Sunday. See you in a couple of hours... Oh, can you ask Shannon to stay too? She really needs to be a part of this discussion."

CJ yelled over to Shannon, "You okay with staying late?"

"Sure," she yelled back.

307

"We're on. See you in a bit," CJ told Kate.

By 3 pm, all the chores were finished and their tools put away. Everyone had been fed, watered, and Shannon and Shawn had set out to brush Deveny and Missy: Missy, as a reward for helping round everyone up and Deveny, because Shawn insisted she had been traumatized by the day's events and he needed to spend time with her.

Shaking her head, CJ smiled at him. "Like you need an excuse to spend time with her. She has you so wrapped around her hoof. You better take Milton in there with you or there will be hell to pay. And don't forget, he would love a little grooming too."

Turning, she started up the hill. "I'll try to put the volunteer trailer back together as much as I can before Kate gets here. Have fun, you two."

At 3.45, Kate pulled through the second gate, parked next to the trailer, and set a cooler on the steps. She walked over to Missy's stall just as Shannon finished brushing her and was putting things away.

Reaching through the fencing, Kate rubbed Missy's blaze. "Missy. You look gorgeous."

She looked at Shannon. "Can I get you to join us up at the trailer?"

"Sure," Shannon said, as she exited the stall and closed the gate.

Kate put her arm through Shannon's as they started up the hill toward Deveny's corral. They stopped right in front of Stanley, who sat watching them.

Kate turned and hugged Shannon. "Have I ever told you how wonderful you are? There is no way I can thank you enough for your help today. Not to mention the training you've done with the volunteers and the fact that you're always the first one to jump in and help. But..."

Shannon's eyebrows went up. She stared at Kate with a totally puzzled look. "Am I about to be fired?"

"Hardly." Kate laughed. "But... I do need to make some changes. That's why I asked you all to wait for me. Let's go collect Shawn, and I'll explain as soon as we get to the trailer."

She turned to Stanley. "But first, I need to talk to *our ace watch dog* here." She put her hand under Stanley's chin and looked right into his eyes. "And where were you while all this havoc was going on?" She rubbed behind both of his ears and continued. "Stanley, your job involves more than chasing away mountain lions and bobcats."

Stanley looked up at her, tilted his head to the side, and stood up. He yawned, stretched then turned and walked over to the plastic food dish in front of his doghouse. He picked up the dish, walked back in front of them, and sat down. Staring at them, he opened his mouth and let the food dish drop onto Kate's foot.

They both chuckled. "Guess we know where his priorities are," Shannon said. "Good thing whoever broke in didn't have treats with them. He probably would have helped them open the stalls."

Shannon picked up his dish. "Go collect Shawn," she told Kate. "I'll feed him, then meet you up at the trailer."

Kate watched Shawn grooming Milton as she approached Deveny's corral and broke out laughing. "You should see the look on his face," she called out to Shawn. "He looks like he's died and gone to grooming heaven. Look at him… He's got a giant smile on his face and he's in a trance."

Shawn walked around in front of Milton, pushed part of his mane aside, and looked into his eyes. "Just ignore her. You look very handsome. Come on, let's get you back so all the girlie asses can see how good looking you are."

"Girlie asses?" Kate said, laughing so hard she had to hang onto the fence rail.

He looked at Kate and smiled. "That's horsey talk for female burros." He looked back at Milton. "I don't think her momma ever let her out much. She certainly hasn't spent much time around a ranch, has she?"

Laughing even harder, Kate managed to squeak out, "If you two can stand to be apart for a while, please join us up at the trailer. Now if you'll excuse me, I'm going to go throw up."

She and Shannon reached the trailer at the same time, and Shannon asked, "What's so funny?"

"Shawn," she said. "One week on the ranch and he has totally lost it. What do they call it? Valley fever? Thanks to him, Milton is going to be impossible to live with, and he's got Deveny prancing around like a princess whenever he walks by. If he spends any more time with Missy, I'm selling the ranch."

Red faced and snorting, they both entered the trailer. "What did Shawn do now?" CJ said.

"He is so good for you," Shannon said.

"Yeah... if you don't mind sharing him with Milton," Kate said. Laughing, she added, "Oh, CJ, he is such a find, and I couldn't be happier for you."

Just then Shawn walked in. All three of them looked at him and lost it. "What?" he said.

CJ walked over and hugged him. "Nothing," she said. "It's a girl thing."

Chapter 26 - Another Door Opens

After they all calmed down, Kate asked them to take a seat. She pulled four Coronas and a lime out of the cooler she had grabbed off the steps as she came in. "I think you all deserve these," she said, passing a bottle to each of them and the opener to Shawn. She sliced up a lime, put the slices on a plate, took one, and passed the plate to Shannon.

Kate shoved the lime wedge into her bottle and took a sip as she leaned against the counter. "CJ, I've given this a lot of thought, and I don't want you staying out here anymore."

"Am I being fired?" CJ asked, as she looked at everyone else.

"Not unless you want to be?" Kate said. She turned, glanced at Shawn, then back at CJ. "Look, it doesn't take a mental giant to see how much in love you two are, and I couldn't be happier for you." She paused. "It also isn't hard to figure out that your life has taken a wonderful turn and I'm going to lose you soon, which I suspect is what you wanted to talk about. Correct?"

CJ nodded. "It's not because of the ranch... I love the ranch and so does Shawn, But I want to be with him as much as I can. I feel really guilty, but I *have* to be with him as much as I can and I can't do that living out here." She took Shawn's hand, squeezed it, and looked at him. "He's my life now, Kate. He's everything I ever hoped and wished for and—"

Kate cut her off. "CJ, you don't need to explain. But I've got a ranch to run and horses to take care of. And you're the last person in the world that I need to tell, *they come first.*"

"I know," CJ whispered. "I feel so guilty leaving you after everything you've done for me. I... I planned to stay for as long

312

as it takes to find somebody else, but I don't know if you're okay with that. I want to give you as much time as possible to—"

"CJ, stop," Kate whispered. "I'm not mad. I'm not disappointed with you. I think this is the most wonderful thing in the world for you. I've prayed for the last five years that someone would come along and carry you off to live happily ever after. Now someone has, and I couldn't be happier for you. I also couldn't have wished for someone better than Shawn. He adores you." She smiled at Shawn. "Plus, he knows what I'll do to him if he does anything other than treat you as special as you are.

"I really want to make this a win-win for everybody. But to do that, I need to know what you want to do." She looked over at Shannon, then back to CJ. "You've long since paid me back for taking you in, and now I owe you the right to choose what you would like to do. I would love to have you stay on as manager, if that's what you want. But under no circumstances are you living in the trailer by yourself. It's just not safe."

"I want to stay on as manager, I really do, but my life has taken a different turn, Kate. I need to go be with Shawn." CJ smiled at him. "I've discovered a whole new world out there, thanks to him. Not because he wanted me to leave this one, but because he knew I've only seen a fraction of what life is about. Now I need to go explore. I need to go explore with him by my side. I need him to teach me about the world so I can discover who I am and what I'm capable of.

"I'll stay on as long as you want, until you find another manager. I'll even help train them." She looked over at Shannon. "But I think the best manager you're ever going to find is already here."

Kate looked at Shannon too, then asked, "What do *you* think?"

"Who, me?" said Shannon, looking around.

They all started to laugh as CJ said, "Earth to Shannon... Earth to Shannon... Do you want to be ranch manager? Over."

Shannon looked at each of them like a deer in the headlights. Finally, she turned to Kate. "Uh... I'll have to have my people get with your people to look over the papers so they can advise me... but... until then... HELL YES." She jumped up and hugged Kate, then everyone else as she sang, "I'm gonna be a manager... I'm gonna be a manager."

Kate looked at her sternly. "Managers don't go around singing, 'I'm gonna be a manager', Shannon."

"Oh, sorry."

"They go around singing 'I *am* a manager, I *am* a manager.'" When everybody quit laughing, they all congratulated Shannon.

Turning serious again, Kate added, "Shannon, I don't want you to feel like an *also ran*. You've always been my choice to replace CJ when she left. I owed it to CJ to make sure she knew she was welcome to stay if she wanted to before I offered you the job. I need to make sure you know that and your feelings aren't hurt."

"Are you kidding? I could have been twelfth in line, and I'd still be happy to take the job." Looking at CJ and smiling, Shannon added, "The person who trained me taught me that life is like choosing up sides in dodge ball. When you get picked isn't important, as long as you get picked. From then on, it's up to you."

"Oh God. And I was hoping CJ's little quips would leave with her," Kate mumbled. "CJ, I'd like you to stick around as long as you can to help train Shannon in the things she's never done. Are you okay with doing that?"

"Sure. I'm yours for the next couple of weeks while I try to organize my life. Actually, after that, I'd like to stay on as a volunteer if I can. I'll probably only be able to work one day on weekends. Is that okay?"

"As manager," Shannon piped up, "I'll have to have my people—"

Kate shook her head. "As owner, you're welcome here any time, any day. And feel free to ignore the manager and her people... whoever they are."

CJ pulled her keys out of her back pocket and removed the secondary key ring with the ranch keys. "I better give you these," she said, handing the keys to Kate.

"No, I want you to keep them. That way, when your new life gets busy and you forget about us, I can use the *I lost my keys* excuse to call you."

"Kate, no matter how busy my life gets, I'll never forget you or the ranch."

Passing out another round of Coronas, Kate said, "I need both of you to help me with something else. You too, Shawn, if you're willing. As I said, I don't think being out here at night is safe for a single young woman. However, I still need someone here at night to keep an eye on the place. So I placed an ad in the local paper for someone to move in as caretaker, in exchange for free room and board and a small stipend.

"I received *a lot* of responses, which I've narrowed down to the one that I think is the best fit. I would really like all three of you to talk to them and tell me what you think. He's an ex-marine, discharged here, and his girlfriend flew out to join him in hopes they would settle down in San Diego. Since then, life has been taking dumps on them.

"I ran a background check and they both came back clean. No drugs, never been in trouble with the police, not even a speeding ticket. Just two young people, down on their luck, and needing a break.

"They're both from Georgia and were raised on farms, so they're used to living out in the country. Both farms had a variety of livestock, as well as horses, so they're already accustom to most of the daily rituals of life on a ranch.

"His name is Rob and hers is Linda, both in their late twenties. I've met with them twice, and I fell in love with them during our first meeting, which is why I would like the three of you to meet with them. I'm afraid I may be biased by their situation." She looked at CJ and smiled. "Although the last time that happened, it turned out to be the best decision I ever made.

"They have agreed to be available to meet with all of you sometime this weekend, if you're okay with that."

"Today's my last day off," Shawn said. "I need to be back on duty tomorrow morning for the start of my go-around, but I'm off on Sunday."

"What's a go-around?" Shannon asked.

Shawn started to answer, but CJ jumped in. "Wait, I got this. Shifts at the fire station are twenty-four on, twenty-four off for four days. Then he gets four days off. Pretty cool, huh? Anyway, the four day on/off period is called a go-around."

Addressing CJ and Shannon, Kate asked, "Are you all okay meeting with them on Sunday?"

"Sure," everyone responded.

"Good, then I'll set it up for 10 am?" All three of them nodded. "I'd like Shannon to take the lead at the meeting since they will be reporting to her as ranch manager. Actually, Shannon, it's going to be your decision as to whether or not they get the position. You already know how I feel, so get everybody's input and, if you all like them, tell them they can start on Monday.

"You might want to use CJ's trailer for the interview so they can see where they would be living. CJ, can you spend tomorrow putting it back together? That way, Shannon can meet with *her people* and *play* manager tomorrow and you'll be close by… just in case she needs rescuing."

"Now, for the big surprise," Kate said. "Guess who else applied?… Ami."

"What?" all three of them shouted.

"Shawn, if you want to pass on being involved in this drama, I'll understand, but CJ and Shannon, any suggestions?"

"Actually, I do," said CJ. "I'm almost positive she was behind what happened last night, but for the life of me, I can't figure out why. How about if we call her in for an *interview* and see if we can find out what she's up to?"

Shannon stared at CJ. "How about if we invite her in and just punch her lights out?" Then, she looked around. "I know, I know, I'm a manager now, I have to exhibit restraint and patience. So I'll invite her in and hold her while our new volunteer, CJ, beats the crap out of her. How's that?"

Snickering, Shawn turned to Kate. "I think CJ has a good idea. A lot of what Ami has done seems to be directed at CJ. She's also been careful not to be very destructive. It's all been kind of *fluff*

317

and puff? You know, a lot of noise and arm waving without much damage."

"She has to know things are changing at the ranch," he went on. "We haven't exactly kept CJ staying with me a secret. But even if she didn't know, your ad confirmed she's not living in the trailer anymore. If she thinks CJ's out of the picture, or leaving, maybe she'll divulge what she's up to during an interview."

"You're right," Kate whispered. "Let's get who we're really going to hire out of the way first. Then I'll set up an interview with her for some time next week. She knows my schedule and days off so I'm thinking Thursday would be good. CJ, I don't want you there. As a matter of fact, I don't want you there either," she added, looking at Shannon.

"Let her think CJ left and I'm without a manager and have nobody to keep watch over the ranch at night. That might just get her to spit out what she's up to."

Kate looked at all three of them. "I have a few more things to say and then you can all get out of here. CJ, I knew this day was coming, and in some ways, I've dreaded it. I could never have asked for a better manager… and friend." She turned to Shannon, then back to CJ. "You two have been an amazing team. CJ, you embraced Shannon the minute she came to the ranch. You two gladly shared everything you could. You helped and supported each other regardless of whose job it was. And I've no doubt Shannon will carry on that tradition with Christine, who I hope will become our volunteer trainer.

"There have been so many times that, if it weren't for you two, I'm not sure the ranch would've survived. You've both hung in there through the good and not so good times and I can never thank either of you enough."

She turned to Shawn. "You're next. You've won the heart of one of the most wonderful people I've ever known, and I'm so happy for both of you. You two are so right for each other it's almost sickening. Take her hand and go show her the world. She's spent her time here giving her love and kindness and support to our horses. Now it's time for you to pour every bit of love and kindness and support you can into her. Not only is she deserving of it, like everything else she does, she'll return it tenfold."

She smiled at CJ, who was gawking at Shawn. "You're the luckiest man in the world, Shawn. And you, CJ... you chose well."

They drove back to Bonita in silence with CJ sitting next to Shawn, holding his arm. She had thought this day would be sad, but it wasn't. She looked up at him and knew: Another door in her life was opening, and once again, someone named Shawn was standing in it.

Chapter 27 - Food Truck Friday

Returning to the condo complex, Shawn pulled in and parked, then walked around to her side. As he opened the door, she swung her legs out and said, "Let's go celebrate?"

"I thought you'd be sad."

"So did I, but I'm not. Shawn, a new chapter in my life started today. You're going to think I'm crazy, but something weird happened in the trailer. Once I knew Kate and the ranch were going to be okay without me, I realized the ranch is not my life anymore.

"At first I was scared, but a wave of energy wrapped itself around me and I knew I was going to be okay. Better than okay. Then I looked at you, you smiled at me, and I knew that tomorrow and the next day and the next and every day after are going to be the best days of my life. Crazy, huh?" Her face lit up. "But you know what? Crazy or not, I can't wait to get started on the rest of my life, Shawn. And I want to start by celebrating with the most important person in my new life. You."

"I've got just the place to celebrate. Let's go get changed." He lifted her out of the truck, and they started toward the condo.

Coming up the walkway, CJ playfully bumped his hip with hers. "Hey. Know what?" she said, as she stepped in front of him. "I love you," she whispered and pulled him into a long kiss.

Midway through the kiss, one of Shawn's neighbors passed on the sidewalk. He laughed, then said, "Get a room you two." Without breaking from the kiss, they both waved, neither one of them caring if he was still watching or long gone.

Finally making it inside, they showered and both put on jeans. CJ slipped into the army green V-neck top with shoulder cutouts, which was part of the free clothes she had gotten from the Slinky Kitten, while Shawn put on a Chargers T-shirt.

CJ looked at him. "Uh… I hope there's no Jets fans where we're going."

He smiled at her. "We're headed into Charger country, darlin'. Besides, I actually root for both teams, as well as the Saints."

"Sounds like you can't make up your mind who to root for." She grabbed her denim jacket and headed into the living room as she yelled back, "Okay, let's go. I'm tired of waitin' on ya. I got places to go, people to see, and partying to do."

Shawn grabbed a leather jacket and was right behind her.

She looked at him. "Where are we going?"

Ten minutes later, turning north onto Interstate 5, Shawn finally said, "Some friends of mine own a wine bar right by the airport called 57 Degrees. That's where we're going."

Scrunching up her face, she grumbled, "A wine bar? I thought we might get something to eat and maybe go to a club for a little dancing afterward? Besides, I didn't think you were really into wine."

"I'm not, but this is not your average wine bar. You'll see when we get there. If you don't like it, we can go someplace else, but I somehow don't think that's going to be an issue."

They took the Washington Street exit to the end, turned left, and crossed under the freeway. When the light changed, he made a left onto Hancock, and CJ spotted 57 Degrees on the right. Just

321

as he turned, someone pulled out of a parking place right in front of the entrance.

Pulling into the space, he looked at her. "Wow. That's never happened before. You're my lucky charm."

CJ glanced at the patio out front and noticed a line at a table next to the front door. She looked at the glass-fronted building beyond the patio and, through the open doorway, saw the largest bar she had ever seen. Shawn opened her door as she stared in amazement.

"This is a wine bar? Shawn, it's huge and look at the size of the bar inside."

"I told you it's not your average wine bar. Oh, and that's less than half of the bar. It's round so you can only see one side of it from out here." He took her hand and walked her to the end of the line. "Okay, payback time. You can pay the cover charge."

She grinned at him. "Thank you. It's about time you let me pay for something." She dug into her purse and pulled out her wallet as they edged their way to the table.

When they finally got there, the guy at the table said, "Two of you? That will be four dollars."

CJ stared at him. "Fo-four dollars? You've got to be kidding."

The guy looked at her. "It's the best deal in town, lady."

"Oh... oh no... I wasn't complaining."

Handing him a twenty, she turned to Shawn. In her best high-pitched, pissed-off voice, she sneered. "Think you're a smart ass, don't you. 'Oh... you can get the cover charge, CJ. It's part of payback.' I am going to hurt you when we get home. Bad."

Just then, a cute blonde, slightly older than CJ, ran up. "Oh, no, no, no, no, they don't pay. They're good friends." She pulled the twenty out of the man's hand and gave it back to CJ.

CJ looked at Shawn and said, "Now you're definitely gonna die."

The blonde smiled at CJ and stuck her hand out. "Hi, I'm Carolyn."

CJ looked at Carolyn, shook her hand, and said, "Hi, Carolyn, I'm CJ, Shawn's future widow."

Laughing, Carolyn looked at Shawn. "Oh, I like her already. Did I hear 'when *we* get home'? Is there something I should know, Shawn?"

Carolyn took CJ's hand and pulled her toward the entrance. "Come on, I'll show you around, and while he's trying to figure out if you're going to kill him or just maim him, we'll get you a gallon pepper jar and a Post-it note."

Totally puzzled, CJ asked, "A pepper jar and a Post-it?"

"Yeah... you know, so you can make a collection jar to put on the bar. To help you pay his funeral expenses? Or hospital bills... depending on how bad you decide you're going to hurt him. A lot of our female patrons will be very sympathetic to your cause."

Shawn joined them, and CJ's smile turned to a snort, followed by roaring laughter when she looked at him. She hugged Carolyn's arm. "Oh, I love you. We're going to get along so well." She turned back to Shawn again. "And you… you're going to be *so* sorry the two of us ever met."

As her laughter subsided, CJ's eyes took in the inside of the wine bar. To nobody in particular, she said, "This place is massive." Slowly turning to her right, she noticed a large open area filled with dozens of wine racks. Toward the front, three guys were playing eight-ball at a pool table. In the adjacent blocked off area were four couples playing some kind of bean bag toss game.

Against the far wall, she noted the entrance to the restrooms. To one side of the entryway was a piece of artwork that looked like a space capsule, which then drew her eyes to the walls filled with colorful art.

Turning toward the massive bar, she saw, as Shawn had suggested, it was easily four to five times bigger than she'd first thought.

Suddenly, her eyes went wide and she turned to Carolyn. "I'm going to need more than one pepper jar."

"No problem." Carolyn chuckled.

Beyond the bar, her attention was drawn to the floor-to-ceiling windows that were the back wall and a set of glass doors leading out to the parking lot. To the left and right of the doors sat large, padded booths close to the bar and, farther out, bar-height tables surrounded by bar stools.

As she looked into the parking lot, a colorful Southwest Airlines 737 taking off from San Diego International Airport caught her eye. The plane disappeared into the clouds and her gaze lowered to the parking lot where food trucks lined the perimeter.

Glancing back to the airport, she could see almost all of San Diego Bay, with Coronado Island and Point Loma looming in the background. Next, her attention was drawn to the left where the cruise ship terminal and the USS Midway sat, with the picturesque skyline of downtown San Diego as a backdrop.

"Oh my God, this view is to die for," CJ said.

"You should be here on a holiday evening when they have fireworks out on the bay," Carolyn said, then added, "There's almost nothing blocking our view right now, but unfortunately, some of the airport construction will change that."

CJ smiled at Shawn. "Guess we know where we'll be on the Fourth of July."

She turned back to Carolyn and asked, "What's with all the food trucks?"

Carolyn's face lit up. "This is third Friday food truck night. On the third Friday of each month we bring in gourmet food trucks. It's the only time we have a cover charge, but for two bucks, you can stake out a table, then go and grab whatever type of food, or foods, appeal to you. If you can't find something you like when all the trucks are here, it probably doesn't exist. Oh, and there's even a boutique truck or two if you would rather shop than eat."

Just as CJ was about to respond, "Testing. Testing. One. Two" came through the speaker system. Looking to the left to see where the voice was coming from, she saw a cluster of deli counter display cases. Surrounding the cases were several groupings of couches and lounge chairs and more bar-height tables. A sign on one of the counters announced a variety of paninis and cheese plates that they served when the food trucks weren't there.

Still searching for the source of the voice, she turned toward a large open area in the front, obviously set aside for dancing. Close to her, she noticed more couch groupings and, finally, against the front wall, a band setting up and testing their equipment.

As she watched the band, people going in and out of a door on the far wall caught her attention. Peering through the doorway, she could see a large patio filled with outdoor lounge furniture. Outside, she saw someone waving at her. It took her a few seconds to realize it was Linda from the Galley.

She waved back and turned to Shawn. "Look; there's Linda out on the patio."

Shawn smiled. "We use third Friday food truck night as an excuse to get together. I suspect we'll find half of the department out there, along with their wives or girlfriends. Linda became part of the group when we were dating and still comes every third Friday, even though we're not seeing each other anymore."

A good-looking guy came up behind Carolyn, put his arms around her waist, kissed her neck, and looked at CJ. "What do you think?" he asked. Before CJ could answer, Carolyn butted in. "This is my fiancé, Mike. Mike, this is CJ."

"Hi, CJ," he said, as they shook hands.

"This place is absolutely amazing. I know where we're coming... every chance we get."

Mike smiled at her. "Are you kidding? Up until recently Shawn practically lived here. Now I see why he's been among the missing lately. I need to steal Carolyn for a while." He went on, "A couple just came in and they want the cost and details for holding their wedding reception here. She does all the event planning and knows everything by heart. If I do it, they'll be celebrating their second wedding anniversary by the time I figure out what to charge them."

326

"This would be wonderful place for a wedding reception," CJ said.

Mike hugged Carolyn. "Since we moved in here, Carolyn's been working her butt off to book private events. One of the reasons for picking this place was to have more room for wine sales and private wine storage. But we also wanted enough space to start doing private events.

"When we first moved in, we were rattling around in here like two BBs in a box car. Slowly, she added the patio furniture, the couch and table groupings, then the deli counter so we could serve paninis and appetizer platters. Finally, the dance and game areas went in. The nice thing is, other than the deli counter, we can move everything around so we can adapt to each event. That also allows us to easily do multiple events. We can set up the patio area for one party, have something else going in the back, and two more events up front."

As CJ's gaze met Carolyn's, not only could she hear the pride in Mike's voice for what Carolyn had accomplished, she could see it in Carolyn's eyes.

"It's taken five years," Mike went on. "But thanks to her, more and more people are booking their events here. Now, you name it, we do it. Weddings, receptions, bar mitzvahs, birthday parties, company functions. Hell, even the Navy is starting to hold some of their functions here. Just last week, we did two promotion ceremonies."

Carolyn jumped in. "Don't forget about the welcome home party for the USS Pickney. As big as it is in here, they just about took up the whole place with almost three hundred sailors, wives, and friends.

"But, it's not just me." Carolyn continued. "Mike is the one that came up with the third Friday food truck idea, and look, it's not even 7 and we're packed already. And, how many times have people come in for Food Truck Friday and ended up booking an event, like the couple waiting right now?

"He's also the one that designed the giant bar. When he first told me what he wanted to do, I laughed and told him it was so big nobody would want to sit at it. Now it's the center piece of our business. It's like a giant magnet that pulls people in. Because it's so big, people aren't in each other's space so they feel comfortable socializing. It's the first place people are drawn to when they walk in, and it's always full."

"What a great team you two are," CJ said.

Shawn reached down and took CJ's hand. "Let's let these two go help the couple waiting." To Mike and Carolyn, he said, "We'll be out on the patio with the group. Come join us when you can."

"We'll be out in a little while then you can fill us in on you two," Carolyn said, winking at CJ.

As they walked out onto the patio, Rachel and Linda both rushed up to CJ and hugged her. "I'm really glad you came," said Rachel.

"Me too," added Linda.

Rachel and Linda each took one of CJ's hands and pulled her away from Shawn and over to a large group standing toward the back side of the patio as Linda shouted, "Everyone. This is CJ. Shawn's girlfriend." Then Rachel recited everybody's name as she pointed out each of them.

"I'll never remember everybody," CJ whispered to Rachel. The guy next to her whispered, "Don't worry. We're all used to answering to 'Hey you' whenever we get a new member in the group." Putting his arm around Linda, he said, "By the way, I'm

Jack, Linda's boyfriend. And, no, I'm not a fireman." Smiling at Rachel, he added, "or an EMT."

Shawn came over, said hi to everybody, then took CJ's hand. "Let's get something to eat. I'm starved."

"Me too," she said.

They excused themselves, walked out into the parking lot, and started down the line of trucks. CJ read the names as they went. "Two for the Road, American Gourmet Comfort Food" was the first truck. Next in line was "Not So Fast, Paleo and Gluten Free," followed by "Crab Cakes 911, Crab Every Which Way," and on and on they went: "Super BBQ," "New Orleans Cajun," "Chop Sooey," "Taco Machin," and "God Save the Cuisine."

In the middle was "Lil Miss Shortcakes," and at the end by the doorway, "Stop Shop & Roll, Clothing Boutique" and "Ing's Bling, Jewelry and Accessories."

When they reached Lil Miss Short Cakes, CJ looked up at Shawn. "I have no idea if I should go for gourmet, the healthy stuff, skip the food and go right to cupcakes, or just say the hell with eating and shop. I'm sooo confused."

Shawn laughed. "You don't have to do it all in one trip, you know. Let's grab something to eat. Then we can come back out and grab some dessert. I suggest we do a little dancing in between. That way, maybe, our seat belts will still fit. If you're still standing after all that, you can shop."

"Just like a guy. Put the shopping at the end. How about if we shop first, run the stuff out to the truck, then worry about eating?"

"Here's the keys to the truck. You shop, I'll eat, and let me know when you're ready to dance."

She pulled him in close. "I was just kidding."

"I know," he said with a big grin. "You were just stalling while you figured out which trucks you were going to hit."

"Think you've got me figured out, huh?"

"I hope so or I'm really in deep doo-doo. Which truck you want to hit first?"

"Let's start with God Save the Cuisine; I'm in a British mood. Then we can work our way back."

Three trucks later, they walked back onto the patio with their arms full of food. They added their food to the other containers already on the table in front of the big outdoor sectional.

"Feel free to grab anything that looks interesting," Shawn said to no one in particular.

"How many are you two eating for?" asked Linda, as she grabbed a potato pierogie.

Shawn went into the bar and grabbed two beers and dragged Carolyn back out with him. Mike joined them a few minutes later, only to have both of them summoned by one of the female bartenders just as he reached them. Shawn and CJ spent the next hour talking with Bert, a fireman from the station, and Jack and Linda. Soon they were joined by Rachel, Jim, a fireman from Chula Vista, and another couple that wandered over to join the conversation.

When Shawn went for two more beers, CJ excused herself to go get rid of one. As she headed back toward the patio, Carolyn came up, put her arm around CJ's waist, and steered her toward the bar.

They took the two seats near the bar's entry, and Carolyn turned to CJ. "I can't tell you how glad I am that Shawn brought you tonight. The rumors that he was seeing someone have been flying, and we've all been wondering when we were going to get to meet you."

"Do I pass?" CJ said.

"Oh, CJ, this isn't a test. I'm sorry if it sounded like that. Shawn aside, I liked you the minute we met, and I hope we become good friends. I'd be lying if I told you we weren't all worried after what Wendy did to him. But the minute you two walked up, it was obvious to me that you're the best thing that's ever happened to him. CJ, he's been more comfortable and laughed more with you tonight than I've ever seen him do before. And based on how fast everybody accepted you into the group, I'm not the only one that really likes you."

She took CJ's hand. "So, my new friend, if there were a test, you passed it with flying colors before you ever said a word to any of us."

Shawn came up. "There you are. I thought I lost you." He set the second two beers on the bar, gently pulled her off the bar stool, and bowed. "May I have this dance, milady?"

CJ curtsied. "Of course, my fair knight."

As Shawn led her toward the dance floor, Carolyn called out, "Oh yeah, you two are definitely made for each other."

They danced to the next five songs then Shawn headed out to Lil Miss Shortcakes for some cupcakes while CJ went back to the bar. When he returned, he had a six-pack of cupcakes. He gave one to CJ, one to Carolyn, one to the female bartender, and took one for himself.

"The other two are for whoever wants them," he told the bartender. Before he could swallow the last bite, CJ was pulling him back toward the dance floor.

They danced till just after midnight, then headed for the patio to collect their jackets and say good night to everybody. On their way out, they detoured to the bar to say good-bye and trade hugs with Carolyn and Mike, before heading to the truck.

Shawn opened her door, and she jumped in. She swung her legs out, put them around his waist, pulled him in, and gave him a long kiss. "Thank you for tonight. You do know that everybody in there adores you? Even your ex-girlfriend. Linda actually pulled me aside and said she was thrilled we were together and she had never seen you so happy. That was right after Carolyn told me pretty much the same thing."

She squeezed tighter. "You're pretty special, Shawn James, and I'm the luckiest girl in the world because you're all mine. And I have no intention of sharing you with anybody."

Kissing him again, she added, "I'm pretty sure it's your turn. So how would you like to take me home and make mad, passionate love to me?"

Chapter 28 - Win Big and Go Home

Shawn and CJ were both up at their usual 5 am and finished with their run by 5.45. As they stepped into the shower, she asked, "What time does your shift start?"

"Eight am," he answered. "What time do you need to be out at the ranch?"

"I'm actually not sure. We didn't really discuss when Shannon was going to take over, or did we and I missed it?"

"Nope. If it got mentioned, I missed it too. I assume you would like to get out there before 7 so you can be there before the volunteers. How about if you drop me at the station right after we shower, then take the truck and head out to the ranch? But it's going to cost you a latte."

"Oh, Shawn, that's going to put you at the station at least an hour and a half before your shift. I can wait and..."

"It's not a problem. I've got plenty of paperwork I can catch up on. Besides, it's just for today. Tomorrow, when we go out to interview that couple, you can bring your truck back afterward."

"Thank you. You want me to stop by the station when I get back to see if you need anything?"

"We're pretty self-sufficient at the station, but I'd never pass up the opportunity to collect a kiss should you find yourself in the neighborhood. Why don't you see how you feel? If you're tired, just head straight home and give me a quick call when you get there so I know you're safe."

"Hi. You two are up early for a Saturday. You both working?" Melinda said, as they came into Starbucks.

"Yeah, I've got to drop him off at the station, then head out to the ranch."

"Oh, you work on a ranch? Wow, how cool is that. I've wondered what living on a ranch would be like," Melinda said, as she made their lattes.

"Actually, it's a horse rescue ranch, and I'd be glad to take you out there someday."

"I'd love that," Melinda said, as her eyes lit up.

CJ dropped Shawn off and, after a very long kiss, headed toward 125 and the ranch.

She and Shannon arrived at the gate to the ranch at almost the same time. After parking their trucks, they headed toward the volunteer trailer arm in arm.

"I'm so glad Kate chose you to be manager," CJ said.

Shannon turned and smiled. "Yeah, I was hoping I'd get your trailer too. Then all I'd have to do is wait for some knight to come riding in and carry me off, like Shawn did with you." She hugged CJ's arm tighter and laughed. "Guess I'm just destined to be an old maid. Look at me, twenty-three and still a virgin. Well, sorta. For the past three weeks anyway."

Stopping, CJ said, "Wait." She bent over, partly stuck her finger down her throat, and made throwing up sounds. Standing back up, she said, "There, that's better," as Shannon punched her arm.

Heading into the trailer, Shannon stopped and pulled CJ around so they were face to face. "I'm going to really miss you. Please promise me we'll spend as much time together as we can? I know it's going to be crazy for both of us for a while, but you'll always be my best friend and my big sister."

She looked into CJ's eyes. "I don't ever want to lose you, CJ."

"You couldn't lose me even if you wanted too," CJ whispered.

"Wait a minute. What if I change my mind someday?"

CJ laughed. "Tough shit. You're stuck with me, little sister. Now, let's go find you a knight."

"Can we start with Shawn's brother?"

"He's fourteen, Shannon."

"So I'll wait."

The two of them were laughing so hard they had to hang onto each other to keep from falling over. Just then, Christine walked into the trailer. "Oh God, Ami was right about you two," she managed to get out before she started giggling.

A half a box of tissues later, Shannon told CJ, "There's no time like the present for Christine and me to start our new jobs."

"I agree, I'll go straighten up my trailer and clean out what little is left of my stuff. How about if we all meet in about an hour and I'll go over some of the bookkeeping stuff I need to pass on?"

Opening the door to her trailer, she shuddered. "Oh my God, what a friggin' mess." She went into the spare bedroom and got several boxes. First, she cleaned up the glass from the broken

335

front window. After sweeping the shards into one of the boxes, she carefully removed the remaining pieces from the window and walked the box down to the dumpster. Next, she cut a piece of cardboard and taped it into the window opening, then rehung the curtains.

Since all of her clothes and most of her toiletries were already at Shawn's, she decided to attack the two easiest rooms, her bedroom and the bathroom, first. She stripped the bed, folded all the bedding, and put it into a box. To that, she added a wayward pair of socks and two pair of thongs that she found behind the bottom drawer of her dresser.

"I wondered where those went," she said, as she put them in the box. Her one and a half sets of bathroom towels went in next and filled the box, which she ran out to the truck.

The next box collected what little was left of her bathroom toiletries and personal grooming items. Then it was off to the kitchen. Setting the partially filled box on the kitchen table, she noticed a small stack of mail in the middle of the table. She pushed it to the end of the table, intending to put it on top once the box was full. As she pushed the pile over, the top envelope, which was upside down, fell over the edge.

CJ bent over and picked up the envelope. The logo on the back flap looked familiar, but there was no company name or hint as to who it was from. She turned it over, and stamped above her name and the ranch address was "Personal and Confidential" but still no clue as to who it was from.

She started to put it back on the pile but paused. *Bet it's one of those, "You've just won a free cruise to the Bahamas. Just send forty thousand dollars to cover shipping and handling", and don't hold your breath waiting for the tickets.*

"May as well sort out the junk mail rather than lug it all back to Shawn's," she said out loud.

336

Pulling the pile over, she sat down and picked the envelope up again. She loosened the corner, ripped the flap open, and pulled out the single sheet of paper inside.

Shannon and Christine heard the first blood-curdling scream, stopped what they were doing, and looked at each other. "What was that?" Shannon managed to get out before the second scream. They both dropped their tools and ran to CJ's trailer.

They burst through the door just as CJ let loose with the third scream, followed by, "OH MY GOD, OH MY GOD, OH MY GOD, OH MY GOD. OH. MY. GOD."

Shannon ran over to her. "Are you okay?"

CJ nodded but said, "NO," and handed Shannon the sheet of paper.

"OH MY GOD, OH MY GOD, OH MY GOD," Shannon yelled.

"Will you two quit oh my goding and tell me what's going on."

Shannon handed Christine the sheet of paper.

"OH MY GOD, OH MY GOD, OH MY GOD," Christine yelled.

The three of them hugged each other and started jumping up and down and turning in a circle.

Finally, Christine broke away and read the letter out loud.

Dear Ms. Cole

It is our pleasure to inform you that you have been selected as this year's recipient of the YWCA Becky's House Four Year Scholarship Award for Women.

This scholarship program was established solely for battered and abused women and is intended to pay any and all financial expenses associated with obtaining a four-year degree of your choosing at San Diego State University (SDSU). That is to say, this is a full-ride scholarship covering tuition, books, lab fees, and all other fees associated with obtaining your degree.

In addition, our benefactors have established a separate fund from which you may draw a monthly housing allowance and a monthly stipend which may be used, as you see fit, for food, clothing, and other necessities.

Please contact the YWCA office at SDSU at your earliest convenience for the complete details of your award and instructions for setting up your trust accounts.

With our sincerest congratulations

"Yada, yada yada," Christine said.

CJ sat back down and stared at them in complete shock.

Shannon's grin covered her whole face. "Oh, CJ. This is fantastic. When did you apply?"

CJ just continued to stare at her.

"Uh…. Earth to CJ? When. Did. You. Apply?"

Finally CJ's mouth moved. "Five… no, four years ago?" She shook her head. "They only pick one person each year, and I thought if you didn't get it, that was it. I had no idea they carried your name over. Oh my God, what do I do now?"

Christine chuckled. "Let's see? Call the YWCA office at SDSU, pass go, collect two hundred dollars, and go to school?" She walked over, pulled CJ up, and wrapped her arms around her. "I'm so happy for you. You deserve this more than anybody I know."

Shannon laid her head on CJ's shoulder. "Breathe, CJ. That's it. Another one?"

All of a sudden Shannon lifted her head, looked around, and ran to the refrigerator. Opening the door, she looked inside. "Shit." She turned and ran out the door.

Three minutes later, she was back with three Coronas in one hand and a lime in the other. "Time to celebrate." She pulled a bottle opener out of one drawer and a knife out of another.

She sliced the lime up, opened the bottles, jammed a slice in each, handed one to each of them, and raised her bottle, "To our student-to-be."

They all raised their bottles, clanked them together, and took swigs. "What are you going to study?" asked Christine.

"I'm not really sure… but I've got a couple of ideas." Then she smiled. "And I know this really wonderful guy who said he would help me decide."

The three of them finished their beers, and CJ's breathing returned to something resembling normal.

"Okay to leave you alone to finish? You promise, no more screaming and scaring us out of ten years' growth?" Shannon asked.

CJ smiled. "I'll promise, but I haven't finished going through the mail yet."

"If you win anything else, I will personally kill you and claim it was mine," Christine said, as she and Shannon went out the door.

Sitting in silence, CJ looked at the letter again and shook her head. "Shawn, how am I going to tell you about this?" she said, then thought, *I can't just drop by the station and say, 'Look what I won.' His mind will be on this and not his job, and I don't want him getting hurt because I distracted him. I'm going to have to wait till tomorrow.*

She finished going through the mail and found she hadn't won or been awarded anything else. Walking into the second bedroom, she got another box and set it next to the half-full box from the bathroom. As she cleaned out the kitchen cabinets, she separated things into the two boxes. The things she was sure Shawn didn't have and thought they could use went into the half-full box. Everything else went into the new box.

After she put the *take-home* box in her truck, she set the *giveaway* box on the porch and went back inside. Clearing out what little there was left in the refrigerator and freezer, she made another run to the dumpster. Even though it was clean, she washed out the casserole dish Shawn's mom had sent the stuffed cabbage in again, and put that in the truck.

Grabbing her phone, she ran through her contact list until she got to the ranch handyman. She selected his number and punched send. When he answered, she said, "Hi, Rich, this is CJ. Any chance of having you come out to the ranch to replace a broken window and rekey a lock?" She nodded. "Sure, Monday will be fine." She gave him the dimensions of the glass, told him they would need three keys for the rekeyed door, then thanked him and hung up.

After going back inside, she wiped down all the cabinets and countertops, then made sure all the dishes, pots and pans, and everything else that had been in the trailer when she had moved in were in there original places. Cleaning the bathroom was next, followed by a quick dusting, then she vacuumed up all the cobwebs and finished with the furniture and floors.

Locking the trailer, she took the giveaway box into the volunteer trailer and sat at the table. A few minutes later, Shannon and Christine finished putting everything away and joined her.

"How did it go?" CJ asked.

"Pretty good. Everybody looks good, and they're all eating well," Shannon answered.

"Good. Shannon, I've got Rich coming out on Monday to replace the window and rekey the lock on my trailer." She pushed the box toward them. "If there's anything in this box that either of you want, it's yours. Whatever is left, I'll leave for the new tenants.

"You two want to spend a little time going over some of the administrative stuff? Also, do either of you have any questions or anything you want me to go over?"

"Yeah," answered Christine. "Who's responsible for ordering stuff and making sure it gets delivered?"

"Good question. Actually everybody is, but Shannon will have ultimate responsibility for making sure everything gets ordered and delivered. When I first got here, it seemed like we were always out of something. In some cases, critical items like medication the horses needed. I also noticed that the prior manager was the only one who could order and take delivery of stuff, and he wasn't always *on top* of things.

"So I set up what I like to call my check, check, and triple-check system, which Shannon helped me with. You want to explain it to Christine, Shannon?"

"Sure. As you know, there are two clipboard stations. One here in the volunteer trailer and one down in the supply shed. When anyone, volunteers included, notice something getting low or about to run out, they enter it on the supply status sheet. If it's getting low, they enter it in the "Low" column and note about how much is left or "don't know" if they don't know. If we're almost out of it, they enter it in the "Out" column and do a judgment call in the note column as to whether there's "a little left" and if it's "critical" or "desperate.""

CJ jumped in. "No matter what anybody enters, it's never to be questioned. The whole purpose is to make sure everybody takes ownership in making sure we have what we need. I would much rather find we actually have more of something than find out they weren't sure and it didn't get ordered because they didn't want to get yelled at. So everybody has to be comfortable with writing down anything they think is needed." She smiled at Shannon. "Sorry, go ahead."

"Actually, that was a great lead in to the second check and triple check. Christine, you're now the second check, and I'm the triple check. It's your job to check the lists at the end of each day and

342

let me know what's been noted. I'll check all entries by going over the inventory and delivery history, just to make sure it hasn't already been ordered, just came in and didn't make the supply shed yet, or got put in the wrong place and is here somewhere. If it hasn't been ordered, I'll order it and note the scheduled delivery date in the "Due In" column on the status sheet. That way everybody knows it's been ordered and on its way. If it's already been ordered and here, we'll hunt for it.

"Likewise, when it comes in, you or I will sign for it and make sure it gets stocked, then update the supply sheet with the date it was stocked. Whatever you do, don't sit on stuff. Make sure it gets put where it belongs as soon as it comes in. What happened before was the prior manager would put it somewhere *till he got around to putting it away*. That ended up with stuff, delivered but nobody knew where it was. Finally, when you're all done stocking it, be sure to drop the signed delivery slip in the accounting in-box.

Jumping in again, CJ added, "Since we're a nonprofit, it's really important that Shannon, and sometimes Kate, get as much time as possible. If we don't have the funds or an item is donated, like expensive medications for example, they may have to scramble to get the stuff here. So make sure you stress to everyone that they let you or Shannon know whenever they think something needs to be ordered. Likewise, if there is something we don't have and they think we should, I want them to feel comfortable in suggesting we look at ordering it.

"Christine, aside from making sure stuff gets ordered on time, I tried to create a system that allows everyone to feel like they have some ownership in making sure things run smoothly. I think it's really important that they feel like they're more than just free labor. I want them to know we value their suggestions and opinions just as much as we value their passion for the horses and their donated time."

"Wow," Christine said. "You two really put a lot of thought into things. I hope I don't disappoint you. I'm not very good when it comes to being creative."

"You'll do just fine," Shannon said. "Besides, sometimes our creativity backfires. Like when we decided to hold staff meetings to solicit suggestions." She and CJ looked at each other and started laughing.

"Oh, yeah. We'll never do that again," said CJ.

"Why?" asked Christine.

"Because we learned, when you surprise people and they haven't had time to think about things or it's an area they know nothing about, they come up with some pretty weird stuff."

Chuckling, Shannon said, "Yeah, like the woman that suggested we give the horses chocolate milk during the day to keep them cool and hot milk before bedtime to help them sleep. She said it worked really good with her kids, and if we got a couple of cows, the milk would be free."

Laughing, CJ added, "When Shannon asked about the chocolate milk, I couldn't help bursting out with, 'How now, brown cow,' and the woman just nodded her head."

Even though she could hardly talk, Shannon went on. "How about the high school student who said he would have his science class convert a Robovac to scoot around the corral, pick up all the horse shit, and take it to the manure pile. All we had to do was promise to give him some advanced funding and sign a contract to buy the first ten prototypes."

CJ jumped in again. "I'll never forget his face when he saw how much Officer Clark expelled when he took a dump."

Snorting, Shannon added, "Or, when he saw Missy with the runs."

By now, all three had tears running down their cheeks. "Oh God, please don't tell me I'm in charge of suggestions," Christine said, holding her side.

When they finally regained their composure, CJ said, "Why don't we call it a day and finish up on Monday. Before we lock up, let me make a quick call. Don't go anywhere." She stepped outside, made a phone call, then came back in. "Christine, are you okay with coming back tomorrow morning at 10?"

"Sure," Christine answered.

"Good, we're going to interview a couple that Kate is looking at for caretakers on the ranch, and Kate and I think it would be a good idea if you were there too."

Knowing it was CJ's idea and she had just run it by Kate for her approval, Christine smiled. "Thank you."

"You're welcome," came CJ's response. "You two are going to make a great team. I couldn't be leaving the ranch in better hands."

They did another group hug, and Shannon locked up after they headed through the gates.

Chapter 29 - Surprise! Surprise!

Shawn came through the front door and found CJ standing just inside with a cup of coffee in her hand. "Hi."

She smiled, handed him the coffee, and gave him a big hug and a kiss. "How was your shift? How many damsels did you guys save?"

He smiled. "Zero damsels. One pissed-off road rage guy who missed the other car, but found a *big* tree. One rosy boa rescue. A kitchen grease fire and a domestic call where the guy's wife caught him cheating with the golf pro and liked to beat him to death with his five iron. She said she used the five iron because blood would have lowered the resale value of the four hundred dollar driver she bought him for Christmas. Overall, just your typical day at the station."

Laughing, CJ laid her head against his chest and wiped her tears on his uniform shirt. "And I thought we had fun at the ranch yesterday. Is this what I have to look forward to when you come home?"

He kissed her. "Pretty much."

"Before you shower and get changed, I have something to show you. But you need to be sitting down." She steered him toward one of the bar stools at the serve-through, eased him onto the stool, slid the letter off the counter, and handed it to him.

As he read the letter, his face took on the biggest grin she had ever seen. His eyes went back to the top of the letter, and he read it again. Finally, he looked up at her. "I am so proud of you. CJ, this is wonderful, and the timing couldn't be more perfect. You never mentioned that you applied for a scholarship."

346

"Well, I sorta applied, and I didn't. I applied over four years ago, before I left Becky's House and came to the ranch. But I didn't get it and I didn't know they kept my name in the hat until I found this yesterday morning while I was cleaning out my trailer. I thought it was junk mail at first and almost threw it away."

She put her arms around his neck and kissed him. "This is a dream come true. Now I really need to get my butt in gear and figure out what I want to do. Can I run something by you? I want to be sure your feelings are not going to be hurt."

He smiled. "Since you're asking my opinion, I doubt my feelings will get hurt."

"You don't even know what I'm going say."

"Actually, I think I do."

"Okay smarty. You first."

"You're going to ask me if I would be okay with you asking the girls to help you decide on a career. How's that?"

"Ho-how... how did you do that? Uh, know that?"

He pulled her closer, kissed her ear, then whispered, "You asked me in your sleep the other night."

"Oh God, I talk in my sleep?"

"Yup, you sure do. And I promise, I'll never tell anybody what else you said. Or... about you drooling on your pillow."

"You're just pushing my foot... aren't you?"

347

"You mean pulling your leg, don't you?"

"Yeah, that too. Shawn, do I really talk in my sleep? And please tell me I don't drool? Oh God, this is embarrassing."

"You only talked a little, and you only drool after eating chili and drinking Corona."

She reached over and punched his arm. "If you ever tell a soul, you'll wake up a gelding."

"Ouch."

He pulled her into another kiss. "I'm perfectly fine with you asking the girls to help you. I know you're toying with doing something techie and what I know about the cyber world wouldn't even be a drop in the bucket compared to them." He pushed her back slightly. "Do I have to tell you that asking them to help you is going to make their heads so big they'll be lucky if they can get through the doorway?"

"Thank you. I adore them as much as you do. They're also both extremely smart and, like most kids today, totally up to date on some of the areas I've been thinking about."

"Okay, that was easy. Let me jump in the shower, and you can tell me about the rest of your day on the way out to the ranch. By the way, we might also want to think about what questions we want to ask this couple and jot them down."

CJ filled him in on her day, which took a fast five minutes, then went on to write down some questions they might want to ask. Arriving just before 10, they joined everybody in the volunteer trailer. Five minutes later, Rob and Linda knocked on the door.

CJ opened the door and invited them in. One step inside the doorway, they couldn't help but notice everybody sitting in the dining area and looked at each other. Shannon immediately picked up on their concern that they were about to be skewered and grilled by the group, so she asked CJ to leave the door open.

"Let me go around and tell you everybody's name then let's all go out to the picnic table?"

She introduced herself to Rob and Linda first then went around the room. She got to Kate last and, smiling at her, apologized for taking over.

Kate told Shannon, "You're doing just fine. As a matter of fact, I've already talked with them several times so I'm going to let all of you chat while I go check on the volunteers. Call me when you're done."

They all filed out and sat at the table, while Kate headed for the supply shed. Once they were seated, Shannon went around the table again, repeating each person's name and telling them who they were and what they did on the ranch. When she got to Shawn, she explained, "He's a fireman, a volunteer at the ranch, and—" CJ gave him a big hug. "—CJ's boyfriend."

When she finished, she told them, "Kate's gone over your background, but I would appreciate it if you could tell everyone where you're from and why you're interested in being caretakers at the ranch."

Rob looked at Linda. "Why don't you go first?"

Linda smiled, then turned serious. "I have to be honest with you. The thought of being caretakers never occurred to us, but when we spotted the ad in the paper, we thought, why not?" She glanced over at Rob and continued, "Kate called us in for the first interview and we liked her immediately. Plus, the more she

349

talked about the ranch, the more it seemed to be a perfect fit for us.

"We were both raised on farms in Georgia, and although neither farm raises horses, both farms have working horses and a variety of livestock on them. So we're very familiar with caring for horses and other livestock." She glanced back at Rob. "We also know it's hard work and we're not afraid of getting our hands dirty."

"And everything else," Rob threw in.

Rob took over. "Look, we're not going to lie to you and tell you that this is our dream job and where we want to spend our lives. It's neither. But we both realize how much the ranch and these horses mean to all of you. If you do offer us the position, we'll treat the horses and the ranch as if they were our own for as long as we're here. That's the way we were raised. We just need someone to give us a chance, and if you do, we would be forever grateful."

Linda added, "I'm sorry. I hope we don't sound like we're begging for handouts. We're not. Our pride is hurting a little right now from not being able to find jobs. We were taught to work hard, earn what we need, and help others. But we can't do any of that unless someone will give us a chance to get our feet on the ground. I promise you, if you give us the position, you will never regret it."

Shannon looked across the table at them. "No one here thinks you're begging. We all know how hard things are in the job world right now. Plus, Rob's recent discharge from the military and both of you being so far away from home has to make it really hard on you.

"Could I ask both of you to go inside the trailer for a moment so we can have a quick discussion? There's fresh coffee and Cokes and some lemonade in the refrigerator. Please help yourself. I

350

promise this will not take long and one of us will come get you in just a little bit."

Rob and Linda went inside, and Shannon looked around the table. "What's everybody think? Do we want to ask them any other questions?"

CJ smiled at her. "They had my vote when they said they would treat the ranch and horses as their own. It's your decision, but I'd hire them in a minute."

Shawn nodded. "I agree with CJ. There's no doubt in my mind that they will work their butts off. Plus, their background is ideal for living out here and caring for the animals."

Shannon turned to Christine. "You and I will be working with them the most. What do you think?"

"I agree. I really like them and I have no doubt they will work hard and get along fine with everybody."

"Good, then it's settled. Shawn, since you're closest, would you go get them?"

Everybody came back to the table and sat down. Shannon looked at Rob and Linda and smiled. "I think it's time we gave you two a tour of your new home."

Tears welled up in Linda's eyes as she hugged Rob, then turned to Shannon. "Thank you. Thank you so much. I promise all of you that you will never regret giving us this chance."

CJ took Linda's hands in hers. "We're glad that we can help. I think we all knew you two were going to be a perfect fit the minute we met you."

Looking around, Rob asked, "Don't you need to discuss this with Kate before you offer us the position?"

Shannon smiled at him. "Are you kidding? She would have hired you after the first meeting. She just needed to make sure all of us were in agreement, which, like CJ said, took a fast two minutes. So welcome aboard."

Shannon scanned the group. "Does anyone have any questions?" CJ's hand shot up. Shannon pointed at her. "Yes, you in the corner. What's your question?"

"Um... I was wondering when you wanted Rob and Linda to move into my... uh, their trailer and if they needed any help? Oh and don't forget, Rich will be out first thing tomorrow morning to replace the glass in the front window and rekey the lock. Other than that, my stuff is out, it's all cleaned and move-in ready."

"Good." She looked at Rob and Linda. "Actually, you can move in starting tomorrow morning. Also I want to let you know that you have the whole week to get settled. The only thing we would like is that both of you get with Christine sometime during the week to get trained. I know Kate covered this with Rob and Linda, but since the role of caretaker is new, let me go over what's expected of them for everybody else's sake.

"First, the intent is that one or both of them be on the property when no one else is scheduled to be here. We want to make sure someone is present on the ranch at all times or as much as possible. That's especially true at night. But I have to add that we don't want Linda to be out here by herself. So, if for some reason, Rob can't be here and Linda would be alone, we expect her to notify Kate, Christine, or myself. One of us will then either stay out here with her overnight or lock the ranch up and make arrangements for her to spend the night somewhere else.

"Second, in return for the stipend, we would like one or both of them to assist with the horses whenever and as much as they feel comfortable with. Their schedule will be their own and how much time they put in will be up to them, but we would hope they would jump in and help on days when we're short on volunteers."

She looked over at Rob and Linda. "We know that one or both of you will be job-hunting, and our first priority is going to be getting you settled and giving you time to find jobs. So I'll be as flexible as I can until at least one of you finds something. Kate also asked if all of us would keep an eye out and let you know about any job openings that might be of interest to either of you."

CJ nodded, then added, "What all that means is, you've been adopted into the ranch family and all of us will do everything we can to help you get settled and find jobs."

She glanced over at Shawn, who added, "If you two need anything we can help with, just ask."

Linda stood there, shaking her head. "You guys are unbelievable. We haven't even started and we already feel like part of the family. This is so much more than we ever could have expected. We owe you so much."

Shannon smiled. "The only thing you owe us is your promise to help someone else once you're on your feet. That's the way it works around here."

Shawn stood and helped CJ up. "We need to take off. Rob and Linda, do you two need help moving your stuff? We've got two pickups, and we would be happy to help you bring your stuff out."

"Thanks. I think we've got it covered. We don't have a lot to begin with, and a friend has a one-ton van that he said we could use. CJ, will you be out here tomorrow? If so, we would really appreciate your going over stuff about the trailer. You know, where the gas, water, and electric shut-offs are. Quirky little things we might need to know, like you have to flush twice, the oven is ten degrees higher than what you set it at… anything like that you can think of."

"Sure. Shawn goes back on duty at 8 so I plan on being out around 7 or 7:30." Turning toward Shannon and Christine, she added, "Jot down anything you might want me to cover tomorrow since I don't know if I'll be out during the rest of the week. I plan to stop at SDSU one day and get the ball rolling. I suspect I'll also need to spend a day with a counselor deciding on my major and signing up for classes."

She took a deep breath. "Other than that, I'm available."

Shannon laughed. "Right. Listen, you do what you need to and don't worry about us. We'll muddle through on our own. If not, we'll do a 911 to you."

Turning to Rob and Linda, CJ added, "You two are going to fit in so well. Please, please, please, if you need anything just ask."

Linda smiled at her. "CJ, I know I keep saying this, but I still can't believe how welcoming you all are. We've been doing odd jobs through the Hire-a-Vet website, and everybody in San Diego has been terrific. That's one of the reasons we would like to stay here. But *all* of you have gone so far beyond anything we ever expected. Then you turn around and the only payback you want is for us to help someone else? You all put southern welcome and friendliness to shame. You've also confirmed our decision that this is a wonderful place to raise a family."

On the way to their trucks, Shawn turned to CJ. "What would you think about inviting everyone from the ranch to join us at 57 Degrees for the next Food Truck Friday?"

"I think they would all love it," she answered. "I also think we're going to end up being very good friends with Rob and Linda."

"Now who's reading minds? I was thinking the very same thing as we were talking with them."

Chapter 30 - Pizza Night

Entering the condo, Shawn turned to CJ. "How would you like to call the girls and see if they want to spend the night? We can send out for pizza, throw together a salad, and you can talk to them about helping you with your career plans."

"Oh, Shawn, I think that would be great. You sure you want to spend the night with three girls jabbering all night? I was actually thinking about talking with them on a night you were on duty, but I'd love you to be part of the discussions, if you're okay with that?"

"I hardly ever get any time with them, and I'd love to be a part of your discussions." He handed her his phone. "Go ahead and call them. Oh, and ask what kind of pizza they want. We can pick them up and get the pizza on the way back."

He handed her his phone, and she tapped the picture of Rick and Trish. "Hi, Shawn," Trish answered.

"Hi, Trish. It's CJ. I have a favor to ask."

"Sure, what do you need?"

"Any chance on borrowing your daughters for the night?" She could see Trish's smile through the phone.

"Uh, I'll waste time asking, but I think we both know what their answer is going to be. How long you want them for?"

"All night? Is that okay with you?"

"Oh, they are going to go nuts. Sure you don't want them for the week?"

"Uh, I think one night will work for now."

"Okay, hang on. Oh, CJ? Hold the phone away from your ear."

She heard Trish ask the girls if they wanted to do a camp over with Uncle Shawn and Aunt CJ. A minute later, the screams died down. "Okay, they're all packed and waiting by the door," Trish said, laughing.

"We were planning on pizza, so can you ask them what they want on theirs?"

Trish yelled, "What do you two want on your pizza?"

"Oh my God, pizza. I want mushrooms and pepperoni with extra cheese," CJ heard Liz yell.

"Me too. Oh, and sausage," Cat added.

"You get that?" Trish asked.

"Yup, sausage, pepperoni, and mushrooms with extra cheese," CJ answered.

"CJ? I don't want to rush you, but they're going to pee their pants if you don't get here soon."

"We'll be over as soon as we call the pizza order in."

"Thanks for taking them for the night. Rick and I will be forever grateful for a night alone."

357

CJ hung up. "Shawn, how hungry are you, and what do you want on your pizza?"

"I'm starved and good with anything except anchovies and pineapple."

"Me too." CJ tapped the pizza picture on the phone and ordered a large deluxe and a large sausage, pepperoni, and mushroom, both with extra cheese."

After calling in the order, they jumped into Shawn's truck and headed for Rick and Trish's. As they turned into the driveway, the front door flew open. The girls, with overnight bags in hand, charged out and were waiting on the side of the driveway before the truck came to a stop. The back door opened and the bags flew in, followed by the girls.

"Okay, we're ready," they said, as their seat belts snapped shut.

Trish walked over and leaned on Shawn's windowsill as CJ leaned over. "Okay if I drop them off tomorrow morning on my way out to the ranch? Will seven be too early?"

"No, that's fine," Trish said, as Liz yelled from the backseat.

"Aunt CJ? Could we go to the ranch with you?"

CJ raised her eyebrows as she looked over at Trish. "I'm okay with taking them out to the ranch if you're okay with it."

Trish smiled. "I'm actually a little jealous."

"Well don't be. Come with us. Instead of dropping them off, we'll pick you up. How's that?"

"You sure you want to drag all of us out there with you?"

"I'd love to have all of you come out with me." She turned to the girls.

"You two want to run back in and grab some old jeans, T-shirts, and closed-toe shoes that you don't mind getting dirty?" Before she could finish, the girls were out the door, bags in hand. Less than five minutes later, they and their bags were back in the truck.

Shawn leaned his head on the steering wheel and mumbled, "It's going to be a very long night."

Trish leaned in and kissed him on the cheek. "It'll be okay, big guy." She looked over at CJ. "See you at seven?"

CJ patted Shawn on the head and smiled at Trish. "See you at seven."

They picked up the pizzas and headed back to the condo. Once inside, Shawn put the pizzas in the kitchen, and the girls put their bags in the guest room, then joined Shawn and CJ in the living room. They sat on the couch and looked over to find Shawn and CJ staring at them.

Liz and Cat looked at each other, then back at Shawn and CJ. "What?" they both said.

"What are you two up to?" Liz asked.

Shawn looked at the girls. "CJ needs your help. I'll let her explain while I go dish out the pizza and salad. Everybody want salad?"

They all nodded and Shawn headed off to the kitchen.

"I just found out that I won a scholarship to SDSU."

Liz jumped up, came over, and hugged CJ. "Wow, that's so cool, Aunt CJ. What are you going to study?"

"Well, that's what I need your help with, trying to refine my career goals and what I should major in."

Liz and Cat both stared at each other, confused. Finally, Cat spoke up. "You want us to help you decide what to take in school?" She turned to Liz, then back to CJ. "Aunt CJ, we don't know very much about college."

CJ smiled at Cat. "I know that, sweetie, and I wouldn't expect you to for at least a couple more years. However, you both know a lot more than I do about the internet, social media sites, and the dangers young people face today. And that's kind of what I'm thinking of doing and where I need your help."

A second later, Shawn set plates, forks, and both pizza boxes on the coffee table, then returned a few minutes later with four salads and napkins. "Okay, who wants what to drink?" They all put their orders in and he headed back to the kitchen.

"Do you just want to specialize in the internet or Facebook or Twitter?" Liz asked, reaching for a slice of pizza.

"Well, I know there are Social Media Safety Consultants that counsel and teach people about things to be careful of on websites like Facebook and Twitter, but I would like to cover more than just that."

Shawn returned and set everybody's drink in front of them. "You know, I just thought of something. Just before my last deployment on the Reagan, one of the sailor's wives came on board and gave a briefing on ways to keep your family or significant other safe while you're deployed. I remember being extremely impressed with her and how much thought had gone into her presentation. She covered not only internet safety, but a lot of things most of us had never thought about.

"For example, those family decals people put on the back window of their car with mom, dad, the kids, and pets all holding hands. Or, worse yet, the ones with everybody's names under them, or dad with a sailor's hat on, or there's a "Navy Family" bumper sticker. All that could tell a potential thief or rapist who everybody is and even the dog's name. They could also get an idea of the kids' ages and when they were likely to be in school. All they would need to do is watch for a few days to see if dad was deployed and know exactly when to break into the house.

"She also talked about other things like bragging to the grocery clerk about not having to buy beer because your husband's deployed; telling the hairdresser, and everyone else, your boyfriend's ship will be on maneuvers for the next two weeks; or explaining to the teller at the bank that you finally got the six months' back pay the government owed you."

CJ's smile got bigger. "I'm liking this. That's exactly what I was looking for. Issues, other than the internet or social media. So I want to look at not only social media safety but also other safety areas unique to a group like military families or females."

"Wait, what about single guys?" Shawn asked. "They need to be aware of stuff like cougar attacks, pissed off ex-boyfriends, and the hazards of sending nude pictures too."

All three of them looked at him and spit out, "Cougar attacks?" at the same time.

"Yeah, you know, when an older lady takes advantage of a younger guy in a bar without him realizing it?"

361

CJ smiled at him. "Like that's gonna happen a lot. But you're right. Boys and men are victims too, and I need to think about things that are unique to them."

They all went quiet as they munched on either pizza or salad.

Finally, after swallowing her last bite from her slice of pizza, CJ spoke up. "Okay, so here's what I see so far. We need to summarize what we just said and come up with a name or title for what I want to do. Second, I need to go to SDSU and see if I can match all this to a curriculum or field of study they have. Or at least get as close as I can, because I get the feeling we've covered a lot of areas. What's everybody think?"

Shawn nodded. "You're right. That covers a lot of territory. Liz, can you jot down what we said so we can see if we can put a name to it?"

"Already did, Uncle Shawn. She wants to counsel people on safety awareness for the internet, social media, families, singles, and military deployments." Smiling at Shawn, she added, "Oh, and specialize in cougar attack awareness and defense to keep all those young guys at the bars safe."

Shawn looked at them, stuck his tongue out, and gave them all a big raspberry.

Cat's hand shot up. "Aunt CJ, can we add harassment and abuse to that? I mean, that's what they were doing to me and the others at school. Since I've been helping the principal, I've learned that it can happen to anyone, anywhere—schools, businesses, teachers, boyfriends and girlfriends, ex-husbands and wives. Even people that don't know who's harassing them or why, like the crazies that make random calls at midnight, then hang up."

CJ nodded. "Good addition, Cat. Anything else? Anybody? Okay, so what have we got, Liz?"

"Safety awareness, abuse, and harassment counseling related to the internet, social media, families, singles, businesses, schools, teachers, and the military."

Shawn smiled. "I've got a title suggestion. How does 'Social Safety Counseling for Individuals, Families, and Businesses' sound? The social part of it kind of keeps you out of the hazmat, physical safety area."

Everybody nodded their agreement.

Liz handed CJ a sheet of paper with the summary and Shawn's suggested title on it.

"This is fantastic, you guys. I'm really excited about this. What does everybody think?"

Shawn raised his eyebrows. "I think it's great, but before any of us say anything else, *you* need to tell us if this is what *you* want to do."

"I can't answer that… yet. I love the general idea, and I think it covers so much that it will allow me a wide variety of areas to pick and choose from or specialize in. However, a lot is going to depend on what they have to offer at SDSU. Right now, I don't know much about a lot of these areas, so I'll need to get the right classes to learn enough to be able to advise people."

She smiled at them, held up the sheet of paper, and added, "So… next stop… SDSU and see what kind of a curriculum I can match up to this."

"Aunt CJ," Liz chimed. "A lot of what's been brought up is really just common sense. I mean, it's things that people should know but don't think about before they go and do something. I know that Facebook, Twitter, and the internet are all new to you,

363

but not posting stupid stuff on them is just common sense. It's really just things people need to be reminded of."

Cat jumped in. "Hey, when we were putting together our anti-bullying club at school, we did what the teacher called brainstorming, where everybody just shouted out their ideas on things we could do."

Liz looked at her. "Thanks, Cat. Why don't we make a game of this? Everybody just shout out ideas on what CJ can teach people about, and the one that has the biggest list wins."

Shawn smiled at them. "How did you two get to be so smart? You're right. She can use the list to eliminate things she's not interested in and bounce what's left against the curriculum classes to make sure they cover what she wants. For anything not covered by classes, we can even help her find another way to learn about it."

"Wait," CJ said. "This is supposed to be a fun night for you guys, and we're spending all of our time on my problem. How about if we finish our pizza and salad and Uncle Shawn can break out his PS3 and we can shoot some zombies? Or... we can turn on the SyFy channel and see what the creature of the week is?"

Liz looked at her sister, silently asking what she wanted to do. "I vote for the list game," Cat said. "Besides, I already started my list from our brainstorming at school, so I know I'm going to win."

CJ glanced over at Shawn, who just shrugged. "Okay, I tried," she said.

Sneaking a peek at Cat's list, Liz watched as Cat finished filling up one side of the page, turned the sheet over, and added several more things. "Holy crap," she yelled.

"Told ya," Cat said.

"We better start thinking of stuff," Shawn said, looking at CJ.

"Why?" she answered and added, "We don't stand a chance of even being *also rans* with these two."

After writing down everything each of them had come up with, there was no doubt Cat had won, and everybody congratulated her. Liz then proceeded to cross out duplicate entries, using Cat's list as the base. When she had finished, CJ's list had two items left and Shawn's had been reduced to only things pertaining to the military or businesses.

While Liz copied everything over to a final list, Shawn and CJ stood up and started collecting dishes. "Well, that was fun. Who wants ice cream?" Shawn asked.

Everybody's hand shot up.

CJ dished, then carried Cat and Liz's ice cream out to the living room. She sat down and took her dish from Shawn as he joined them.

"Thank you guys soooo much. This is really going to help me choose a major and classes. And, honestly, up until the list, I wasn't all that sure that this was what I wanted to do. Now my mind's going a thousand miles an hour, thinking of things I need to study and ways I can help people."

Shawn hugged her. "I guess that means we did good?"

"No, you all did amazing," CJ said. Looking at her watch, she added, "We should think about getting to bed. We've got an early wake-up tomorrow morning."

This time, the girls collected the dishes, rinsed them, put everything into the dishwasher, then headed for the guest bathroom. "We'll be in in a minute to read you a bedtime story," Shawn said.

"Our parents quit reading us bedtime stories when we were five years old, Uncle Shawn," Liz said.

"Okay, we'll be in to tuck you in and say good night. How's that, *Ms.* Liz?" Shawn said, throwing a wink at CJ.

As Shawn started the dishwasher, CJ came up and wrapped her arms around him. "They are nothing short of adorable. I hope they have some idea of how much they helped me tonight."

He smiled. "Oh, I think they know how much they contributed, and I think they really appreciate you asking for their help. And please don't tell them they're adorable. Their heads are big enough already."

They wandered into the hallway just as the girls came out of the bathroom. After they climbed into bed, Shawn kissed each of them on the forehead, said goodnight, and headed for the master bedroom.

As he closed the double doors, CJ sat on the edge of the bed next to Cat. "Thank you two for all your help tonight." She reached over and swept the hair from in front of Cat's eyes.

Cat sat up and wrapped her arms around CJ's waist. "Aunt CJ, is Uncle Shawn going to marry you?"

Caught by surprise, CJ stared at her then finally said, "I hope so. Some day."

Liz smiled from across the bed. "We hope so too."

"Get some sleep you two," CJ whispered, as she gently closed the door.

CJ stepped into their bedroom, eased the door shut, and leaned back against it. "Are you okay?" Shawn asked from the bed.

"I'm so much more than okay." CJ nodded. She headed into the bathroom, stripped out of her clothes, brushed her teeth, and joined Shawn in bed.

She laid her head on his chest and curled into him. "Thank you," she whispered.

"For what?" he whispered back.

"Just thank you," she said, as she snuggled her face into his chest and tightened her arms around him. Shawn couldn't see her face, but he knew it had a big smile on it and she was already sound asleep.

He whispered in her ear, "I love you," then fell asleep with a smile that matched hers.

Chapter 31 - Ranch Tour Day

Shawn and CJ woke to a quiet tapping on their door. Glancing at the clock first, Shawn looked down at CJ. "It's four thirty," he whispered.

"Think they're anxious or something?" she whispered back at him.

"Nah, whatever gave you that idea?"

"Uncle Shawn? Aunt CJ? Is it okay to come in?" Liz asked through the door.

Pulling the sheet up over them, CJ said, "Sure, come in."

Liz opened the door, and Cat entered the room with a tray containing two cups of coffee, cream, sugar, spoons, and two toasted bagels, heaped with cream cheese. As Cat handed the tray to Shawn, CJ looked over at him.

"I think we might want to keep these two. What do you think?"

"Yeah, I could get used to this. But I think this is more for you than me and they're trying to tell you to get your butt in gear."

CJ looked at Cat's wet hair. "Did you two shower already?"

They both nodded.

"What time did you get up?"

"Um... three. We didn't want to be late." Liz smiled.

"You do know we're not picking your mom up until seven, right?"

"Yeah. But we didn't know how much time you needed to get ready."

"...and you didn't want me to be late," CJ added. "Okay. Go grab something to eat while I shower and get ready."

"Uh, we already ate," Cat said.

"Okay then. Go... and do... *something* while I get ready," CJ said, shaking her head.

After they left and closed the bedroom door, Shawn burst out laughing. "Sure you want to keep them?"

CJ kissed him. "If we do, I'll never be late for anything, that's for sure."

They finished their bagels and coffee and headed for the bathroom. By 6 am, everybody was dressed and ready to go. Shawn handed CJ the keys to his truck. "Let me have your keys. My truck has the crew cab, so the four of you will have more room than in yours. I may as well go in early rather than stand here all dressed up with nowhere to go."

"I'm going to miss you. Stay safe, my knight," CJ said.

Shawn hugged each of the girls, gave CJ a long kiss, told them all to have a great time, and headed out the door. "Okay," CJ said, looking around. "Think your mom might be up yet?"

Liz nodded. "We called her while we were waiting for you. She's all ready."

369

"Then I guess we're off," CJ added, shaking her head again.

They pulled into Rick and Trish's driveway just as Trish was locking the front door. She walked over, climbed into the passenger seat, and smiled at CJ. "Welcome to my world. What time did they get you up?"

Smiling back at her, CJ responded, "Uh… that would've been four thirty… and… a nap will definitely be in order this afternoon. At least they brought coffee with them."

"Yeah, I trained them well." Trish chuckled.

"Speaking of coffee, how about a stop at Starbucks? It's not like we don't have a little extra time or anything." CJ grinned at Trish, then added, "Starbucks it is."

As the four of them entered Starbucks, they found Melinda sitting at a table by the door reading something on her Kindle. "Hi, Melinda," Trish said.

"Oh, hi Trish. Hey CJ. You guys get earlier and earlier."

CJ looked over at Cat and Liz and mumbled, "Not by choice." Looking around, she added, "You are open, right?"

"Oh, yeah," Melinda said. "Today's my day off, and I woke up early and couldn't fall back asleep. Since I had nothing planned for today, I figured I might as well come get a latte, catch up on some reading, and watch the world go by."

CJ smiled at her. "Want to join us? We're headed out to the ranch."

"Are you kidding? I would love that. Are you sure? I don't want to be a bother."

"No bother. I'm going to be giving Trish and the girls the grand tour, and we would love to have you join us. By the way, these are Trish's daughters. This is Liz and this is Cat."

Melinda said hi to both of them, and Liz came over and stood next to CJ. "We would all love to have you join us, and there's plenty of room in the truck."

Melinda smiled at Trish, then turned back to Liz. "Well, thank you. How could I possibly refuse an offer like that?"

"You okay with getting a little dirty or do you need to run home and change?" CJ asked.

"Nope, these are my knockabout jeans and T-shirt, so I'm fine. And thank you again. I really appreciate this."

Trish and CJ grabbed lattes and croissants for themselves and juice and pastries for the girls, which Melinda insisted on paying for. Piling into the truck, they headed to 125 and the ranch.

CJ pulled the truck into the volunteer parking area and the back doors flew open. "Wait," she yelled before anyone could get out. She twisted around in her seat and looked at the girls. "This is a working ranch, and we have rules that we need to go over with all of you. But first, we've a lot of rattlesnakes out here." Pointing to the volunteer trailer, she added, "So we're going to *carefully walk*, *not run*, to the picnic table up in front of that trailer. Once we're all up there, I'll introduce you to everybody and we'll go over the rules. Okay?"

Everybody nodded and carefully got out of the truck. As always happened after her little speech, nobody moved until CJ came around and took the lead. Just as they reached the table,

Shannon, followed by Christine, drove onto the ranch and parked.

As they walked up to the trailer, Shannon took in the crowd at the table, smiled, and asked CJ, "You earning extra money by giving tours now?"

CJ smiled, then looked at everybody at the table and whispered, "Don't tell them I gave you all a discount on the night tour of the ranch, okay?"

"Hi, everybody. I'm Shannon and this is Christine. CJ, you want to introduce everybody?"

"Sure, this is Trish. Her husband Rick works with Shawn, and these are her daughters Liz and Cat. And this is Melinda, she's a barista at the Starbucks in Bonita. Everybody, this is Shannon, she's the ranch manager, and this is Christine, the volunteer coordinator and trainer for the ranch."

Cat looked over at CJ, puzzled. "Aunt CJ, I thought you were the ranch manager?"

"Well, I was until I decided to go back to school. So now Shannon's taking my place and Christine is taking Shannon's place. Christine, I was just about to go over the safety rules with everybody, but since you're here, would you like to do the honors?"

"Sure, it will be good practice for me. Let me go sign in, and I'll be right out."

Christine came back out and sat down at the picnic table. "Okay, this is a working ranch, and the very first thing I want to remind you of is that, even though many of the animals here are tame and some were trained, most of them aren't used to having people around. Especially strangers. I don't want you to be afraid of them. But I do want you to respect them. They are big and they weigh a lot, and when they move, they may not realize you're there. So it's up to you to pay attention to them. Always be aware of where they are and just use common sense when you're in with them.

"Make sure they can see you at all times and that you're not in a blind spot. The best way to do that is to stay in front of them. Also don't go running up to them. Hold your hand out and let them smell and get to know you. Let them get comfortable with you before you approach them or try to pet them. Finally, if one of us gives you a treat to feed them, hold it in the palm of your hand with your hand out flat." Demonstrating, she added, "This way they can't accidentally bite you, thinking your finger is a carrot.

"I assume CJ already told you about the rattlesnakes. It's almost spring. It's been hot the past few weeks, and that means the babies are hatching, so keep your eyes open and watch where you walk. The babies are much worse than the adults. An adult will try to avoid humans, and if it bites you, it will strike and then take off. But the babies don't know any better. They will bite and hang on while they continue to pump venom into you. So the smaller the snake, the more you want to stay away from it.

"If you see a snake, what should you do?"

Cat's hand shot up. "Stop, don't move, and yell SNAKE as loud as you can."

Christine smiled at her. "Very good. Who taught you that?"

With obvious pride, Cat said, "My dad. He's a fireman."

"Okay. That's all the really important stuff. Since this is your first time out here, I don't want any of you going anywhere

without one of us with you. Not even to the bathroom. Got it?"
She looked around, and everybody nodded.

She smiled at everyone, then added, "I hope I didn't scare anyone. This may not be new to some of you, but I need to make sure everyone is super aware of where you're at and what you're doing so you don't get hurt. Trust me, by the end of the day, you'll all be old hands and almost everything I mentioned you'll do without even thinking about it. Oh… and by the way, the bathroom is in there," she said, pointing at the trailer.

Shannon stood up. "Okay, ladies, let's go meet some horses."

As Shannon led the group toward Deveny's corral, CJ walked over to Christine. "That was amazing."

"Thanks." She glanced toward Shannon and the group, then smiled at CJ. "I had two amazing teachers."

Slipping her arm through Christine's, CJ steered her toward the group. "Come on, we can't let Shannon have all the fun."

Approaching the group, CJ noticed Trish hanging back and waiting for them. As they came along side of her, arm in arm, Trish smiled at them. "I know we just got here, but I am already impressed beyond words. You three are the greatest team I've ever seen. You're like three sisters that have spent their lives working together and helping each other as you grew up. The pride you three have in each other is obvious."

Looking toward the group, she went on. "I know Cat and Liz noticed it. I looked over and the two of them were staring at the three of you like you were all goddesses." She looped her arm through CJ's free arm. "I so hope my girls grow up to be like you three."

Shannon turned to see Trish, CJ, and Christine, arm in arm, approaching Deveny's corral. Feigning tears, Shannon spit out, "Now I'm really jealous. What am I? Chopped liver?"

"Come over here," CJ said. Then added, "Everybody. Group hug."

After a very long group hug, Shannon ushered all of them toward the gate of Deveny's corral. "Okay, why don't we break into groups? Unfortunately, Christine and I have work to do—" She stared at CJ. "—unlike some people we know. So whoever comes with us will have to help with the chores."

CJ stuck her tongue out at Shannon as Cat and Liz ran over and yelled, "We'll help."

CJ looked at them and mumbled, "Traitors."

After breaking into teams of Shannon with Cat and Liz, CJ with Trish, and Christine with Melinda, Shannon assigned a group of stalls to each team. Then she and the girls headed for a golf cart and the hay shed while the others went to the tool shed.

It didn't take long to see that the girls, Melinda, and Trish thought they had died and gone to heaven. Shannon's first stop with the girls was at Missy's stall, where they immediately fell under Missy's spell.

As they moved down their row of stalls, CJ and Trish kept looking over at Shannon's team. Each time, they found Missy, on lead, dragging both girls to the next stall.

Finally, Trish turned to CJ. "You do know they will be completely impossible to live with after this? I sure hope the price of gas comes down soon, because I see myself making *a lot* of trips out here."

375

Several times, CJ saw either Shannon or Christine hugging Cat, Liz, or Melinda as they explained what had happened to one of the horses and how they had ended up at the ranch. The same had been true with Trish as CJ explained how Ella and Jewel had found their way here and showed her cell phone pictures from when they first arrived.

All three teams finished their stalls and met up at the turnout corral. CJ led them all over to the turnout gate, and Milton started braying. "This is Milton, Shawn's puppy mule." she said, as she opened the gate and let Milton out. He immediately went straight to the girls and positioned his head between them so they both could pet him and each had an ear to play with.

"Milton and Shawn adore each other," CJ added. "When he's here, Milton never leaves his side."

"I'm surprised you're not jealous," Trish threw in.

"Are you kidding? He's training Shawn better than I ever could." Smiling, she added, "Besides, when Shawn and I are here alone Milton keeps him occupied, and I can... um... actually get something done."

Shannon looked over at Christine. "Why don't you let one of the girls take Missy back to her stall and the other can put Milton back? Then they can bring Ella and Jewel down to the turnout. Afterward, join us up at Deveny's stall."

Cat and Liz looked at each other, and Trish was afraid their faces would break from smiling so much. "Well, you just made their century."

After Liz put Milton back, she joined Christine and Cat, who had Missy in tow, and they headed for Missy's stall.

Shannon came over and put her arm through CJ's, then looked over at Trish and Melinda. "Well, don't just stand there. Grab an arm." Arm in arm, the four of them headed up the hill, laughing and carrying on like four schoolgirls who had been best friends forever.

"You guys are amazing." Melinda said, as they reached Deveny's stall. "I don't know what I admire more. The obvious love you have for each other or your passion for helping the horses."

Shannon smiled at her. "We're always accepting new members."

"I'd love to, but I don't know anything about horses."

"Neither did CJ or Christine when they first got here. All you need to do is be willing to help and have compassion for the horses. We'll teach you the rest."

Melinda looked over at CJ. "Are you kidding? You didn't know anything about horses?"

Shannon stared at CJ and started laughing. "She couldn't even *spell horse* when she got here."

Laughing, Trish said, "You three are a hoot."

"Thank you," Shannon said, as she winked at CJ. Two minutes later, Christine and the girls joined them.

Shannon explained to everyone how Deveny had been found wandering at the edge of the desert and what had been done to her, then asked, "Would everyone like to meet her?"

Christine walked over and opened the stall gate as Shannon reminded them to approach her slowly with their hand held out so she could smell them. Trish approached her first, followed by Melinda.

As Melinda stroked Deveny's nose, she turned to CJ. "Thank you," she whispered. She leaned her head against Deveny's and whispered, "I'm so sorry for what people did to you." Deveny moved her head to the side and looked into Melinda's eyes as if to say, *It's okay, I'm here now.* She laid her chin on Melinda's shoulder and snuggled against her cheek.

While everyone else stared in amazement, Deveny and Melinda stood like that for what seemed like forever. A single tear escaped and ran down Melinda's cheek as she asked Deveny, "Can I come visit you again?" Deveny stepped back and nodded as if she knew exactly what Melinda had asked.

Shannon and CJ came up beside Melinda as she gave Deveny another snuggle, and a few more tears escaped. Shannon and CJ led her from the stall toward the volunteer trailer. Halfway up the hill, Melinda stopped and pulled them in.

Smiling through the tears, she mumbled, "Thank you both for the best day of my life. Shannon, can I come out and volunteer at the ranch?"

Looking over at CJ, Shannon's face turned serious. "I don't know. What do you think, CJ? She already admitted she doesn't know anything about horses."

CJ broke into a big grin. "Yeah, tell that to Deveny. I've never seen anyone bond with a horse like that."

"Yeah, you're right. I guess if I let you come out to volunteer, I'll just have to put you in charge of Deveny. You okay with that?"

Melinda lit up like a Christmas tree. "Oh my God. I'll do anything. I'll even shovel horse poop."

"Oh, don't worry, you'll do plenty of that." Shannon chuckled.

While CJ and Shannon consoled Melinda up the hill, Trish couldn't help but notice Deveny's eyes follow them. Even when Christine introduced the girls to Deveny, she approached the girls, lowered her head to let them pet her, but not once did she take her eyes off Melinda.

Christine, Trish, and the girls finally moseyed their way back to the picnic bench, all talking at the same time about one horse or another.

As they reached the bench, Trish turned to Melinda. "You look like you just won the lottery."

"Even better. I'm going to volunteer here, and Shannon said I could take care of Deveny."

Trish smiled at her. "That horse adores you. When you left and came up the hill, she never took her eyes off you."

"Christine, can you go grab your calendar and let's set up a training session for Melinda. I'd like to get her trained as soon as we can." Turning to Melinda, Shannon asked, "You okay with that?"

Melinda was speechless and just nodded, all the while just staring at CJ.

"Can we get in on that?" Trish asked.

"Sure," Christine answered.

Trish continued, "Melinda, how about if we all come out and get trained together? The girls are out of school next week so you pick the day and we'll pick you up. How's that?"

Melinda just kept nodding her head and staring at CJ. Finally, CJ asked, "Are you okay, Melinda?"

"No," she whispered.

CJ walked over and sat next to her. "What's wrong?"

"If I tell you, you're all going to think I'm crazy."

Shannon joined CJ, lifted Melinda's chin, and looked into her eyes. "We're all crazy here, which is why you fit in so well. So what's wrong, and what can we do to help fix it?"

"That's exactly what's wrong. What you just said." They all looked at each other totally confused.

Finally CJ smiled and said, "Okay. Obviously you're a little crazier than the rest of us so why don't you help us catch up?"

"I'm just overwhelmed, in a good way, that's all. In less than one day, you *all* turned my life completely around. This morning, I was being my normal loner self, reading a book on my Kindle, ignoring the world. Then you all troop in, act like we've been BFFs forever, and invite me to the best day of my life." She looked over at Shannon and added, "I know. *BFFs forever* is redundant. So don't go there," to which Shannon stuck her tongue out, while everyone else cracked up.

"What's wrong is that one morning with you and I love you all like sisters. Then... I meet this horse, and I instantly know she's changed my life forever." Turning back at Shannon she added, "Then the icing on the cake comes from Ms. Mindreader over

380

here who says, '*Gee, I guess we'll just have to put you in charge of Deveny.*' So no. You can't help me fix my problem. You all *are* my problem. You're all crazy. This morning, I was normal, but now I'm crazy too and loving every minute of it."

Cat looked over at Trish. "Mom, I don't understand?"

Melinda called Liz and Cat over and wrapped her arms around both of them. "I know I'm not making a lot of sense right now. Someday, I hope someone or something will come along and leave you with a part of them that will change your life forever. If you're lucky, several of them will all come at once, like you all did for me, and you'll understand everything I just said."

She smiled at them. "Bet you didn't know you changed my life today, did you?" They both shook their heads. "Well, you did. It started with you, Liz, when you said there was plenty of room in the truck and asked me to join you. Then all morning long when I looked over at you two, you reminded me of how amazing everything here is. You made me see things through your eyes, with your enthusiasm and your wonder. And from now on, I'll do that every time I look at something new."

Cat looked up at Melinda. "You're neat."

"Well, thank you. You two are pretty neat too."

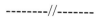

A small van pulled through the gate and parked in front of CJ's old trailer. Rob and Linda jumped out and walked hand in hand over to the picnic table. "Did we miss a meeting?" Rob asked.

"No, we just finished giving CJ's friends a tour of the ranch," Shannon said.

"Tour?" Trish said, looking around. "Did I miss something? All I remember is hauling horse poop all morning."

Linda looked at Shannon. "Suckered another group into the tour thing, did you?" They all started laughing.

Shannon went around the table and introduced everybody, then the whole group helped unload the van. While CJ went over the trailers utility turn-offs and quirks with Rob and Linda, Christine set up a training date for Melinda, Trish, and the girls. Afterward, they all met up at the picnic table.

As they sat down, CJ leaned over and whispered in Trish's ear. Trish nodded her head, then stood up. "CJ and I would like to invite you all to join us for Food Truck Friday in a couple of weeks." She went on to explain how the group at the station used it as a great excuse to get together every month and how she and CJ just knew they would all get along great with everybody.

Rob immediately apologized because he and Linda needed to keep an eye on the ranch at night. "No way. We'll take care of that," Shannon said. "I'll have Jason and his sheriff buddies keep an extra eye on the ranch that night."

"Great, and you can stay with us. That way, you don't have to worry about driving back late at night," Trish added.

CJ looked over at Christine and Shannon. "The same goes for both of you. The guest room is yours for the night."

"No way," Melinda piped in. "You two are staying with me. After Food Truck Friday, you can just leave your stuff at my place. We can all drive out to the ranch on Saturday and, afterward, make Saturday night a girls' night out in the Gaslamp."

Shannon glanced at Christine, who nodded. "We're in." She looked back at CJ. "Besides, that way the two lovebirds don't have to worry about trying to be quiet."

Trish looked over at CJ. "Well, I guess we should head back."

"Wait," Shannon said. "Melinda, would you like to say good-bye to Deveny?"

"Can I?"

CJ smiled at her. "Of course. Take your time." Shannon and Melinda turned and started down the hill.

Suddenly, Shannon stopped and looked back at the girls. "Well, are you two just going to sit there?" They both looked at each other, jumped up, and started running toward Deveny's stall.

Two steps past Shannon, they both jammed the brakes on and skidded to a stop. "Sorry," Cat said.

"Very good," replied Shannon.

Turning to CJ, Trish smiled. "Well, you did it again. Melinda thinks you walk on water." She turned to Christine. "You too. She and the girls are just in awe of all of you. As am I."

"Thank you," Christine said.

All the way back to Bonita, Melinda and the girls talked up a storm. They each picked their favorite horse—gee, guess which one Melinda picked—and their favorite *job* on the ranch. Finally, since the girls expressed concern about whether they would be able to *pass* the training class, CJ went over what would be covered and assured them they would have no trouble passing.

They pulled into the parking lot of Starbucks and everyone got out to say good-bye to Melinda. After she hugged the girls, they hopped back into the truck while CJ and Trish said good-bye.

As they turned to get back in the truck, Melinda stopped them. "I can't thank you both enough for today. I meant what I said at the ranch, all of you changed my life today. I've just kind of been floating through life, trying to figure out what I want to do. Now I know. I want to go to school and become a veterinarian. And I want to specialize in horses."

She took one of their hands in each of hers and smiled at them. "The vet part came from the ranch and Deveny, but the 'get off my ass and do something' came from you guys. Thank you for making me feel so comfortable. I hope we're all friends for a very long time. Oh, and Trish? If I ever have kids, I hope they turn out to be just like yours. See you guys next week."

After dropping Trish and the girls off, CJ headed to the station.

Chapter 32 - Fireman, Fireman, Light my Fire

CJ parked in front of the fire station and walked around to the open engine bay door. As soon as she turned into the bay, Shawn spotted her. "Hey, babe. You're back early. How did it go at the ranch?"

"Actually, it was fantastic," she answered, as Shawn wrapped her in his arms and drew her into a wonderful kiss. About the time she thought he would let go, his tongue found hers and her legs went weak. She fell into him, put her arms around his waist, and pulled him even closer.

Neither of them had any idea if anyone was around until Bert passed by and whispered, "Conference room, you two. You're bordering on illegal."

Shawn tried to break off the kiss, but CJ pulled him back in. Finally she let go, looked up at him, and smiled. "Wow. Did I ever tell you how hot you are?"

As Bert passed by going the other way, he smiled at CJ and said, "No, but I think we should wait till Shawn's not here before we have this conversation."

The three of them started laughing, and Bert started chanting, "CJ thinks I'm ha-ott. CJ thinks I'm ha-ott."

Shawn smiled at her. "Sorry. It's been a long uneventful day, and you're the first damsel we've seen. We did rescue a skunk and put a hummingbird nest back in a tree, though. Oh, and the golf-club lady clubbed her hubby again because he cancelled her Penny Saver ad for his driver."

Just then, Bert came by again. "You forgot our shopping trip to Vons."

"Wow," CJ said. "Another exciting day at Blackrock, huh?"

Smiling at Shawn, she said, "Milton says *Naaaay.* and... you have competition for Deveny. We took Melinda from Starbucks out with us, and she and Deveny have bonded like they were born for each other. Oh, and Missy has claimed Cat and Liz, so you better keep an eye on Milton before someone steals him too."

"I'm never letting you go out there without me again. I leave you to defend my harem while I'm doing skunk and hummingbird rescue, and now I've lost *both* of my girls and all I'm left with is a eunuch." Looking up to the ceiling, he added, "Sorry, Milton, I really didn't mean that."

Unable to keep from laughing, CJ spit out, "Sorry? He's a gelding... not a eunuch. And if he hears you, he'll be devastated. Besides, you still have me. And I'd be very careful how you continue with this conversation because you're about to step in deep doo-doo if you're not careful."

With his best Cheshire cat grin, he said, "I love you."

"I love you too."

Shawn pulled her back in and gave her another soul-searching kiss. "Stay safe, my knight," she whispered in his ear. "I'll be waiting with coffee when you get home."

"Hmm, think we might mess around a little tomorrow morning?"

386

"We'll see. I've got an appointment to set up my scholarship and stipend accounts at ten, but if you're good, I might just bring home dessert."

"Oh, you are so bad."

"I know… that's what makes me so good." She smiled back.

--------//-------

CJ did in fact bring home dessert, and she and Shawn spent the afternoon lounging around the condo, making love, and napping in each other's arms into the wee hours of the next morning.

On Wednesday, Shawn set off for the final shift of his go-around, and CJ met with her counselor to finalize her class schedule and complete registration. On the way home, she stopped by the station to update Shawn.

"Hi, Tim."

"Hi, CJ," the captain answered.

"I noticed the engine is gone. Are they out on a call?"

"Yup… house fire."

"Oh, I hope no one was hurt."

"No, everyone got out okay, but the kitchen didn't fare too well. They're on their way back if you want to wait. By the way, how's registering for school going?"

Her eyebrows went up. "How did you know I was registering for school?"

"Are you kidding? Do you have any idea of how proud Shawn is of you? You're all he talks about when he's on shift." He smiled, then added, "And it sure isn't hard to see how much he loves you."

CJ turned beet red, but Tim just smiled and added, "I think every single guy at the station is hoping you have a sister."

CJ snorted and started laughing, just as the engine pulled into the bay.

Shawn and the other firemen climbed down from the cab, and he shed his heavy jacket as he walked over to CJ. "Hey," he said.

"Hey back at ya," she answered. "The captain said you guys went to a *real* fire today."

"Yup, rescued two frying pans and one spaghetti pot but pretty much lost the kitchen." Pulling her into his arms, he gave her a quick kiss and smiled at her. "Did he ask you if you had a sister?"

"Yeah, sorta. But if I did, I'm sure she would have first dibs on your brother. Right after Shannon, that is."

The two of them started laughing and ended with another kiss. "Speaking of Shannon, I've got a safety class at Bonita High School on Friday morning. Do you think she might want to join me?" Shawn asked.

"I'm sure she would. I'll call her when I get home. If she does, is it okay if she spends the night with us?"

"Sure, how about if I do shrimp scampi with fettuccini alfredo, garlic bread, and a Caesar salad?"

"Stop it. You just made my stomach growl."

"Sorry. How did things go at school? Did you get your accounts taken care of, and were you able to get all the classes you need?"

CJ nodded. "Well, it's good news, bad news, and more good news. The first good news is my accounts are in place and I got all my classes. The bad news is I don't start until the spring semester, which begins next January. So that means the best news is we get to spend a lot of time together till then."

Smiling, he gave her another kiss. "Gee. I think I can manage that. I'm so glad you got all your classes... I had better get back to work, though. I'll see you first thing in the morning, and we can do breakfast before you head to the ranch."

"I hadn't really planned on going out, but if I do, aren't you coming with me?"

"I wish I could, but my safety lecture notes are in desperate need of updating, so I need to behave myself and work on them before Friday. Besides, I need to at least be able to hold my own if Shannon joins me. Not only is she smarter than me, I'm sure she's a lot better at presentations than I am."

"Not true," CJ said.

Just then the alarm in the firehouse went off and the dispatcher announced the call was to a four car pileup on the 805 Freeway at Bonita Road. Shawn gave her a quick kiss. "Gotta run," he said, as he slid his jacket back on and headed for the engine's cab.

"Be safe, my knight," she whispered, as he climbed in and the engine roared to life.

CJ waved as they pulled out, then she turned and headed for her truck.

-------//-------

As soon as she was inside the condo, she pulled out her cell phone and tapped Shannon's picture.

"Hi, CJ. What's up?" Shannon answered.

"Hi, Shannon. I just left Shawn, and he wants to know if you would like to help him do a safety lecture at Bonita High School on Friday morning?"

"Sure, I'd love to, but hold on and let me check the volunteer schedule and make sure we've got enough help. Hold on."

A minute later, she was back. "No problem. What time does he want me to meet him at the high school?"

"Actually, we were hoping you could stay with us tomorrow night. Then the two of you can ride over to the high school together. As a bribe, Shawn has promised to cook dinner. How does shrimp scampi, fettuccini alfredo, garlic bread, and Caesar salad sound?"

"I'm leaving right now. What's for dinner tonight?"

CJ chuckled. "Well, since I'm cooking, it'll be my famous Spaghetti-Os casserole. I've even got some leftover Swiss cheese I can throw on the top."

After a long pause, Shannon said, "Oh God, girl. Ugh. Where did you learn to cook?"

"I'll have you know I'm self-taught and attended the one hour Chef Boy-Ar-Dee Can-label School of Gastronomical Delights." Trying to keep from completely cracking up, she squeaked out, "More commonly known as the Burp, Fart, and Belch School of Cooking." Then she fell on the couch, holding her side.

Shannon, who was laughing almost as hard, composed herself long enough to squeak out, "I'll bet you make a mean chili," before she too completely lost it. The next few minutes were spent listening to each other laugh.

Finally, wiping the tears from her cheeks, CJ asked, "Were you serious about coming over tonight?"

"I was till you told me what you were going to make." To which, they started laughing again.

"Oh God. Stop already," Shannon finally said. "Do you want me to come over tonight?"

"Yeah, but don't you need to be at the ranch tomorrow?"

"No. It's Thursday, remember? Rob, Linda, Kate, Christine, and two volunteers will be here, and I've got the day off. I'll come over tonight *only* if you promise we'll go *out* for dinner."

Still chuckling, CJ asked, "Do you need directions?"

"Just the address so I can program it into my Garmin."

CJ gave her the address.

"Give me a few minutes to pack my notes and some clothes, and I'll head out. CJ, are you sure I'm not going to… ah… interrupt anything? With you and Shawn, I mean."

"Nope. Shawn's at the station tonight, and we'll try to be quiet tomorrow night."

"Gee, thanks. CJ. Can I ask you something personal?"

"Sure."

"Uh… Shawn doesn't let you cook for him, does he?"

CJ grinned and tried not to break up laughing again as she spit out, "No. Aside from scooping ice cream, I'm banned from the kitchen unless he's here."

"Smart man," Shannon said, and they both lost it again.

Finally, Shannon croaked out, "I love you. See you in an hour," and hung up.

Forty minutes later, the doorbell rang, and CJ found Shannon standing on the porch. She gave Shannon a peck on the cheek, reached over, and took the handle of her roll-on to guide her into the living room.

Shannon's eyes went wide. "Oh wow. This place is gorgeous." She turned and took in the rest of the living room, then stared at the serve-through into the kitchen.

"Come on, I'll give you the twenty-five cent tour." Smiling, CJ added, "You'll have to do the kitchen by yourself, though, since I'm not allowed in there."

CJ took her hand and led her down the hall, stopping at the guest bath. "This is your bathroom. There's soap and stuff in the basket. Feel free to help yourself to anything you need."

Shannon stood with her mouth hanging open. "You've got to be kidding me. This is the *guest* bath? Do you guys provide a boyfriend with the second sink?"

"Sure." CJ smiled. "You want red, blond, or brown hair?"

Pulling her out of the bath, she led her to the guest room. "Oh. My. God." Shannon pushed past CJ, threw herself on the bed, and went spread-eagle. "I'm never leaving. This is bigger than my whole friggin' apartment." she spit out. Then she noticed the sliding door. "My own patio? I've got my own patio." She looked up at CJ and smiled. "*Excusez-moi*, madam. Please wake me at eight. Oh, and I'll be having my breakfast on the patio. Eggs over easy, toast with jam, green tea, and bacon crisp, if you please."

It took her a few seconds to notice the look on CJ's face. "Oh shit, I forgot, you can't cook. Does Shawn do guests?"

CJ started laughing. "He better not if he wants to live."

"No. No. I meant for breakfast."

"And I meant for anytime."

"Oh crap, I'm just digging this hole deeper, aren't I?"

"Uh... Yeah."

Still laughing, CJ sat on the edge of the bed and pulled Shannon close. "It is so good to have you here. I really miss our laugh sessions when you and I get going."

"Me too," Shannon said. CJ pulled her up and toward the door.

"Come on, I'll show you the rest of the place." As they walked into the master bedroom, Shannon's eyes grew even wider, if that was possible. Aside from the size of the room, she immediately was struck by its warmth.

"Oh, CJ, this is unbelievable."

"Wait till you see the bathroom." CJ smiled, pulling her toward the bathroom door.

"Oh. My. God." Walking into the shower and sitting on the bench, Shannon put her feet up and leaned back. "If I lived here, I would never leave the shower."

"Funny, that's the same thing I said the first time I saw it."

Shannon stood, walked over, and hugged CJ again. "I'm so happy for you. I knew the minute I met Shawn that he was going to treat you like a queen, and this.... this is like your own modern castle. How do you manage to sleep at night? If I lived here I'd spend my nights staring at the ceiling and thanking the gods."

Smiling at her, CJ whispered, "I spend my nights staring but not at the ceiling."

Shannon laughed. "Ah... yeah, I'll bet you do."

CJ took Shannon by the hand again and started pulling her back toward the hallway. "Wow, you've got your own patio too."

"Yup... It's great to sit out there with coffee in the morning. Problem is, it's open to the golf course and the social circle, so we've got to put something on before going out there."

"Oh... bet that's a bummer," Shannon said, smiling. Then she added, "What's the social circle?"

"I'll explain later," CJ said.

As CJ led her toward the kitchen, Shannon snorted.

"What?" CJ asked.

"Sorry, you and Shawn sitting naked on the patio with coffee just flashed in my mind."

"If you move that to the shower, you've pretty much got the first hour of our morning," CJ whispered.

"TMI," Shannon shot back. "The first hour? An hour? Don't you two know there's a water shortage?"

"Ask me if I care," CJ responded, as they entered the kitchen.

Stopping to look around, Shannon was totally speechless. "No wonder he doesn't let you in here. I wouldn't let anybody in here. CJ, this looks like the set from Bobby Flavors cooking show."

"I think it's Bobby *Flay*—"

"Yeah... him too," Shannon said, laughing.

Walking over to the refrigerator, CJ reached in and pulled out two beers, opened them, grabbed Shannon's hand, and led her back into the living room. Sitting on the couch, CJ set both beers on the coffee table, turned toward Shannon, and held both of her hands.

"I'm so glad you're here. I miss you and our time together so much."

"And I miss you too. But I'm so happy for you. This is what you deserve. Shawn is what you deserve. And I want to move in with you. If I can't move in, you have to promise me I can shower in your shower before I have to go back to my dinky-ass apartment."

The two of them reached over, picked up their beers, and clinked bottles as CJ said, "To the most wonderful person I know and the sister I never had. Somewhere out there is your Shawn, just waiting to discover you. And no, you can't move in, but yes, you can use our shower for as long as you want." They both took a long swig of beer, set their bottles back down, and locked each other in a very long hug.

"Okay, what do you feel like for dinner?" CJ asked.

"Nothing fancy," Shannon said. "A Big Mac and some fries would work."

"Ugh... How about a really good burger and homemade fries?"

"That will work."

"Good. I've got just the place. You okay with outside by the water?"

"Are you kidding? That's perfect."

They finished their beers and headed out to CJ's truck. "You mind if I stop by the station real quick? I just want to let Shawn know you're here and that we're heading out to grab something to eat."

"Wow, can I get a ride on the fire truck while we're there?"

"I doubt it, but you can ask."

For the second time that day, CJ pulled into the station and parked. As they walked through the front door, Bert was just coming out of the dispatcher's office.

As soon as he spotted CJ, he smiled. "I knew it. You just can't—" Shannon stepped out from behind CJ. "—uh… stay away from… me."

CJ chuckled and was trying to think of a comeback when she realized Bert was no longer looking at her. He was, however, staring at Shannon. She looked over at Shannon who was staring back at Bert with the biggest grin she had ever seen on Shannon.

Stepping past CJ, Shannon stuck her hand out. "Hi, I'm Shannon."

"Hi, I'm Bert."

Shaking her head, CJ said, "Well, so much for introductions. Think I'll go find Shawn while you two *bashful* people get to know each other."

"Uh… he's in the engine bay, I think," Bert said without taking his eyes off Shannon.

"Thanks." CJ chuckled. Then she mumbled, "I didn't think you knew I was still here."

"Bye," Shannon said without looking at CJ. Then added, "Take your time."

CJ went down the hallway and out into the engine bay. Shawn was standing with his back to her, and she quietly walked up behind him, put her arms around his waist, and hugged his back.

"Hi, my knight," she whispered.

Turning in her arms, he bent down and kissed her. "Hi. Is everything okay?"

"Ah, at the moment. But that may change any minute."

Shawn just stood there, looking very confused.

"I called Shannon about helping you on Friday and staying with us, and she's was fine with it. Since she's off tomorrow, I suggested she come over this afternoon, which she did. So… I thought we would stop by on our way to the Galley and let you know."

Looking around, Shawn asked, "Did you lose her on the way here?"

"Kinda. Bert spotted us as we came in, and now he and Shannon are out in the lobby making googly eyes at each other."

"Anyway, she's here, and if I can pry the two of them apart, we're going to the Galley for dinner. I just didn't want you coming through the door in the morning and ripping your clothes off, only to find yourself staring at Shannon."

Shawn laughed. "I don't think we need to worry. If Bert is that interested in her, my guess is he's asking her out to breakfast right now, and he'll be right behind me in the morning to pick her up."

"Should I be worried?" she asked.

"About Bert? No. He's really a nice guy. I think he and Shannon would make a great couple. Frankly, she's just what he needs to finally get him out of the funk he's been in since his fiancée died two years ago. And he'll treat her with respect and care."

"His fiancée died?"

"Yeah, they were college sweethearts, had just gotten engaged, and moved in together. She was out on her morning run when some kid, stoned out of his mind, hit her and kept going. She died instantly, and when they arrested the kid two days later, he had no idea what they were talking about.

"Bert was devastated. He worshiped her, and it took him over a year before he would even look at another woman. We finally got him to start joining us on Food Truck Fridays, but he's had little interest in dating anyone. It frankly doesn't surprise me that it was Shannon that woke something up in him. And trust me, if he's interested in Shannon, she would be hard-pressed to find someone that would treat her better than he would."

"Thank you. That makes me feel a lot better." CJ reached up and pulled him into a kiss. "Stay safe, my knight. I love you." Then CJ turned and headed back toward the lobby.

As she turned the corner, Bert and Shannon were laughing and carrying on like they had known each other for years. Shannon saw CJ and smiled at Bert. "Gotta run. See you in the morning?"

"Is eight thirty okay?" he asked.

CJ glared at Bert. "So am I to assume you're dumping me for my best friend?"

"Sorry." Bert smiled back. "I'm a sucker for red hair, freckles, brains, and a wonderful personality."

399

CJ put her arm through Shannon's and continued to glare at him. "She's my best friend and very special, and you better treat her that way, or you'll have me to answer to."

Bert looked at CJ, then Shannon. "I wouldn't have it any other way."

Still arm in arm, they started toward the door when CJ looked back at Bert. "No Denny's," she said.

"No Denny's," Bert repeated, smiling.

They pulled into the marina parking lot and got a space right in front of the staircase to the Galley. As they got out, CJ heard her name and looked up to see Linda standing at the top of the stairs, waving.

Shannon smiled. "Wow, didn't take you long to become part of the *village*, did it?"

"That's Linda. She and Shawn dated for a while, but now they're just friends."

"Right," Shannon said. "And now you and she are friends?"

"Yup. She's really nice and so is her boyfriend, Jack."

When they reached the top of the stairs, Linda asked, "Where's Shawn?"

"On duty," CJ said. "This is my best friend Shannon, and she's spending a few days with us. Since I can't cook, she made me promise that we would go out for dinner, so here we are."

"Hi, Shannon. I'm glad to meet you," Linda said, then turned to CJ. "Inside or outside?"

"Outside, of course," CJ answered.

"I was just getting ready to leave, but I'll seat you first."

"No, just give us the menus and get out of here. We'll find a table. I assume you and Jack have something planned."

"No, actually, he's on a business trip, so I'm bacheloretting it tonight."

"If you don't have any plans for dinner, why don't you join us?"

"Oh, I'm sure you guys have plenty to talk about and don't need me hanging around."

CJ took the menus out of Linda's hand and put them back on the reception stand. She put her arm around Linda's shoulder, turned her toward the main seating areas, and flagged down a waitress.

"Table for three," she said when the waitress came over.

By the end of dinner, an observer would easily have believed that CJ, Shannon, and Linda had known each other all their lives. They laughed and joked. Talked about boyfriends, past and present, where each of them were from, things they liked and didn't like, and generally got to know each other.

Just as Linda finished a story about several drunken, rowdy boaters who had made fools of themselves earlier in the day, she realized they were the only ones left on the deck.

"Holy crap, it's ten thirty already," she said after looking at her watch.

Shannon looked at CJ. "We better get going. I need my beauty rest." Then she turned to Linda and added, "I've got a breakfast date with a hot fireman in the morning."

"Bert is taking her out for breakfast," CJ added.

Linda stared at Shannon. "Wow. How did you get a date with Bert? I think every girl at Food Truck Friday for the past year has hit on him with absolutely no luck."

"Skill and cunning," Shannon said.

CJ laughed. "Ah… there wasn't much skill or cunning involved. Shannon walked through the door of the station, and Bert went gah-gah."

Linda looked over at Shannon and raised her eyebrows. "Bert is one of the nicest guys you'll ever meet. You're going to be the envy of every single girl in Bonita and Chula Vista."

"Did you two date?" CJ asked.

"I wish," Linda answered. "Aside from running into him at Food Truck Fridays, his boat is the first one on the far right," she said, pointing to the boat. "He usually comes in whenever he's on the boat, and everyone here absolutely adores him.

"Bert treats everybody with respect and kindness and never fails to stop and chat with everybody. Even the busboys and the dishwasher. When he first bought the boat and was fixing it up, he started to come in, and all the waitresses fought over who was going to wait on him. It got so bad that we finally made a rotation chart. That way, no matter whose station he sits at, we know whose turn it is to wait on him. Since his fiancée died, we could see he was hurting terribly and angry at the world, but he was never short or took it out on any of us. We all felt so sorry for him and wished we could've helped."

"He had a fiancée?" Shannon asked.

"Yeah… I just found out. I planned on telling you about it when we got back to the condo," CJ said.

"She died about two years ago. I think she was out jogging and got hit by a drunk driver or something like that," Linda said. Then she added, "Shannon, I know it's none of my business, but please be careful with him?" She reached over and put her hand on Shannon's. "If he asked you out, he must really think you're special enough to finally open his heart back up."

Shannon nodded. "I promise I'll be very sensitive to what he's been through."

On the way back to the condo, Shannon turned to CJ. "I meant what I said about you becoming a part of the *village*. In the few short weeks you've been with Shawn, you've made more friends than in the five years you were at the ranch. And it's obvious that Cat and Liz think you're the greatest thing since Wonder Bread and PB&J sandwiches were invented."

CJ glanced over at her. "But you'll always be my best friend, you know."

"I've never thought otherwise." Shannon smiled back.

Chapter 33 - What Happens in the Stable, Stays in the Stable

CJ and Shannon were up at 5, and after explaining the social circle to Shannon, CJ talked her into going with her on her morning run. When they were across from the fire station, they noticed all the firemen outside milling around an old burnt-out car. Spotting Shawn, CJ called out his name and waved. Shannon, not to be outdone, saw Bert and did the same.

Within seconds all of the firemen were waving, blowing kisses, and yelling, "We love you, CJ and Shannon."

"Wow. No wonder you run every morning. Sure I can't move in with you?" Shannon panted out.

When they got back, CJ told Shannon to grab her body wash and shampoo and join her in the master bathroom. CJ showered first, and then Shannon stepped in while CJ dried off and got dressed.

"Showering will never be the same. This thing will spoil you forever," Shannon said, as she stepped out and grabbed her towel.

A little after 8, Shawn came through the door and, as usual, found CJ waiting with a kiss and a cup of coffee.

"Nice touch," Shannon said, as she turned and disappeared into the kitchen. Yelling out to Shawn, she asked, "How does Bert take his coffee?"

"Black," Shawn yelled back.

Five minutes later, the doorbell rang, the door opened, and Shannon said, "Good morning" as she handed Bert a cup of coffee.

Bert smiled at her. "Wow, first the greeting at the fire house and now coffee. I could get used to this."

Shannon smiled back. "Me too," she whispered.

Laughing, CJ said, "Okay, you two. You just met, remember? You'd think neither one of you had been with the opposite sex for months."

Bert and Shannon looked at each other and simultaneously said, "How did she know?" And they all started laughing.

"I'm going to be updating my safety presentation, and I'd like to get about an hour with you this evening so we can integrate our presentations?" Shawn asked Shannon.

"Sure," she said. "Let me give you my presentation and notes. Look over everything while we're gone and, if you want, take a shot at an agenda. After we get back, you and I can do a final integration and lock the agenda in."

While Shannon went to her room to grab her tablet with her presentation and notes, Shawn asked Bert if he wanted to join them for dinner. "Sure. But I don't want to get in the way of you two working on your presentation."

"No problem, I promise I need less than an hour with her."

Ami found the first gate open when she arrived for her 10 am appointment with Kate. For a change, after passing through the second gate, she got out, closed it, then pulled into the volunteer parking area.

Looking up the hill to the trailer, she saw three volunteers she didn't know and Christine come down the steps and head toward the stalls.

Just as she reached the steps, Kate came out. "Hi, Ami. You're right on time. Come on in."

Kate led her over to the kitchen area and directed her to one side of the booth then slid in on the opposite side. "I have to admit, Ami, I was pretty surprised to see you apply for the caretaker position especially after telling you that you were no longer welcome here."

Pasting on a grin, Ami shook her head up and down. "Yeah, I can understand, but all that was CJ and Shannon's fault. Those two hate me and set me up so that you would think I'm just stupid. But I'm not stupid, and you need to get rid of those two and get someone you can trust to run the ranch."

"Ami, I was the one who caught you on the ranch, twice, when you shouldn't have been here. How could CJ and Shannon have had anything to do with that?"

"You don't understand. They're both in this together and Christine's helping them. Both times you caught me, I came out to the ranch to get evidence to show you. But they must've somehow found out I was coming and they left, and well, you caught me trying to sneak up on them."

Disbelief was written all over Kate's face. "Ami, you're not making any sense. What evidence? Why would they set you up so I would catch you?"

406

"To get rid of me. Because they're selling drugs out here and I figured it out. After everybody leaves, people come to the ranch and CJ sells drugs out of her trailer. Haven't you ever noticed how the two of them are always together? Kind of weird, don't you think? I'm pretty sure Shannon is her supplier, and it wouldn't surprise me if she was her lover too. I haven't figured out how Christine is involved yet. She might just be another lesbo."

"Ami, why are you doing this? What could you possibly hope to gain by accusing CJ and Shannon of selling drugs and being lesbians? CJ is one of the few people who has defended you. If it wasn't for her, I frankly would have banned you from the ranch a long time ago." Kate stared at her. "Ami, am I understanding this right? You did all this just to get rid of CJ and get her job."

Glaring at Kate, Ami clenched her fists. "You're even dumber than I thought. They trashed the trailers and let the horses out. They made it look like I did it because I figured out where they hide their stash. I can show you. Those two bitches are using your ranch as a cover. I can prove it. Just go look in CJ's truck or under her mattress."

Kate stood up. "Okay, I've had enough. Jason, would you like to come out and arrest this young lady?"

-------//-------

Bert and Shannon left, and Shawn fixed breakfast for himself and CJ. Afterward, he buried himself at the serve-through with his presentation while CJ curled up on the couch with her course catalogs. Around 1 pm, they nibbled on snacks for lunch and then Shawn gave a dry run of his presentation for CJ. Just as he finished incorporating her suggestions, Shannon and Bert rang the doorbell.

CJ let them in, and holding hands, they headed for the couch. "How was breakfast?" CJ asked.

407

"It was great," Shannon said. "He tried to surprise me by taking me to this wonderful place at the marina called the Galley." She glanced over at Bert and smiled. "I think he was the one that was surprised, though, when Linda ran up and hugged me before him.

Anyway, breakfast was great; then he took me out on his boat. We sailed across the bay to Coronado Island and walked around the little shopping village by the marina. Afterward, we sailed out to Point Loma, turned around, came back, and here we are." She bent over and kissed Bert on the cheek, then smiled at him. "Thank you for a great day."

As Shannon was explaining what they had done, CJ sat quietly watching them. When Shannon finished, CJ looked at her, then turned to Bert. "This is serious between you two, isn't it?"

Bert looked at Shannon. "I hope so," he said.

Shannon looked at him and nodded. "Me too. But we both agreed that we need to spend more time getting to know each other." She turned back to look at CJ and Shawn. "Which is a perfect opening for me. Would I be imposing if I spent a few more days with you?"

"Are you kidding?" Shawn said. "You're welcome to stay with us as long as you want."

"Our casa, si casa," CJ added, smiling.

Shannon's eyebrows went up. "I think that's *mi casa, su casa*."

"Not in CJ Spanish." Shawn laughed. Looking at CJ, he asked, "By the way, did you remember to get your socks from the restaurant bathroom before we left the other night?"

CJ punched Shawn in the arm and glared at him. "If you tell them, you'll die in your sleep." Then she started laughing. "Okay, go ahead and tell them."

By the time Shawn had finished telling the story, everyone was holding their sides and trying to stay upright.

When they finally caught their breath, Bert smiled at Shannon and said, "If we get along half as good as Shawn and CJ, this is going to be a wonderful relationship."

Since Shawn had a captive audience, he quickly went through his presentation once more then put everyone to work helping to prepare dinner. After dinner, he and Shannon retreated to the living room to integrate their presentations while CJ and Bert cleaned up, then settled in at the serve-through with two Coronas. CJ told Bert about the ranch, how she and Shannon had met, and finally, about Shannon's promotion.

As soon as Shawn and Shannon finished, Bert stood up. "I know it's early, but I'm going to get going and let you all get some rest before your presentation in the morning. Shannon, I'll pick you up around six tomorrow for dinner?"

"That'll work," she answered. "Come on, I'll walk you to your truck."

Just as they reached the door, CJ's phone started buzzing.

"Hello? Oh, hi, Rob... Is everything okay?... Oh no." She turned to Shawn. "Go stop Shannon and Bert and tell her I need her right away."

Shannon overheard her, and she and Bert came back through the door. "What's wrong?"

"Hold on, Rob, I'm going to put you on speaker." CJ pushed the speaker button, and Rob's voice blared out of the phone.

"Missy was just bitten by a rattlesnake."

"Rob, this is Shannon. Is anybody there with you?"

"Uh... Linda. But she's down by Missy's stall. I had to come over by the trailer to get the phone to work."

"Okay, I need you to stay calm and listen to me carefully. You're going to stay on the phone and shout instructions to Linda. Got that?"

"Yeah... uh... let me tell her."

They all listened as Rob yelled out to Linda.

"Okay," Shannon said. "Where was she bitten and how long ago?"

"On the muzzle. We came out to feed Stanley, heard a ruckus down by the stalls, and turned to see a snake hanging from her muzzle. That was about five minutes ago, I would guess."

"Where is the snake now?"

"Dead. The snake finally let go and tried to get away, but Shakespeare stomped it to death."

"Okay, yell to Linda and tell her to go to the tool shed and grab the snakebite kit. It's on the shelf just to the left of the door."

"Will she—"

"Rob, just tell her what I said. It's clearly marked, and she'll find it... but she needs to go now. Time is critical, and she needs to tend to Missy right away."

Everyone stopped breathing while Rob yelled instructions to Linda.

While Linda was getting the kit, Shannon went on. "Okay. If the snake held on long enough for you to see it, this probably wasn't a dry bite. Since horses can't breathe through their mouth, we need to keep her nostrils open. As soon as Linda comes back, tell her to find the two straw like tubes in the kit, coat them with Vaseline, and gently insert one in each of Missy's nostrils. It's really important she get them in before Missy's face swells up and closes off her breathing."

They all listened as Rob once again yelled the instructions over to Linda. "Okay, she has them in."

"Good. Now tell her to find the tape in the box and tape the tubes so they don't fall out. Once her face swells up, it will help hold them in place, but till then, we need to make sure they don't fall out."

Shannon took a deep breath, as did everyone else. She looked over at CJ. "I need to take your phone with me. Okay?" CJ nodded. "Rob, I need you to call me back on CJ's phone in... let's say... ten minutes. Got that?"

"Uh... got it. Ten minutes."

"Good, I'm coming out there. While you're waiting to call me back, I need you and Linda to stay with Missy and keep her as calm as you can. When the ten minutes are up, come back to where you are and call me. Okay?"

"Got it," he said.

"And Rob? Thank you. Missy still has a long way to go, but if it wasn't for you two, there is no way she would make it."

Shannon hung up, and CJ started into the hall, calling back, "I'm going with you."

"No. You need to stay here," Shannon said, as she turned to Bert.

"I really need your help. Can you drive while I stay on the phone with Rob?"

"Of course. I'll go pull my truck up and meet you out front."

Next, she turned to CJ. "You… get to go with Shawn tomorrow and do my presentation. You've seen me do it enough times that you should have it about memorized by now. Just remember, you're defending my honor. But don't show Shawn up too much," she added, smiling.

Shannon ran into the guest room and came back with her jacket. On her way out, she called back, "I'll call you later… when I know how Missy is doing."

"I'll call the emergency number for the vet while you're on your way out," CJ said.

"Thanks. Talk with you in a little bit."

The passenger side door of Bert's truck was standing open, and Shannon jumped in, closed the door, and buckled her seat belt. As they pulled out, she turned to Bert. "Thank you. Not only for taking me out there, but for being with me. Right now, I'm scared to death and having you here means a lot."

"Shannon, I wouldn't want to be anywhere else. And no one would ever know you're scared to death. I've never seen anyone just automatically take control and stay so calm."

Shannon chuckled. "If only you knew. What do they call it? The swan effect? Calm on top and paddling like crazy below. That's me right now. My stomach is doing flip-flops... and look at me." She held out her hand, which was shaking.

"I don't know much about horses, but I remember from somewhere in my training that most horses don't die from a snakebite. They're just too big for the venom to have the same effect as it does with a human."

"You're right. But what you don't know is that Missy is a miniature horse. So she's only half the size of a regular horse. That, and the fact that the snake hung on and had enough time to pump a lot of venom into her. That's why I'm really worried about her surviving."

"Well, if she does survive, it will be because of you."

Shannon was holding CJ's phone and just about jumped through the roof when it rang. Bert reached over and took her hand as she answered. "How's she doing?"

"Not good," Rob said.

"Is she still standing and able to walk?"

"I think so, but I'm not sure for how long."

"Okay, walk her slowly to the next stall and put her in the shed at the back. You'll have to take Shakespeare too, or she'll refuse to

413

go. Don't worry about the horses in there. They all know Missy, and Buttermilk and Rose will be fine sharing their stall."

"Got it. I'm walking over to help Linda. If I—" The phone went dead.

Five minutes later, CJ's phone rang again. "We made it. She's in the shed, and Shakespeare, Buttermilk, and Rose are all trying to jam their heads through the door to see how she's doing. The vet's office just called. CJ gave them our cell number. I have no idea how they got through, but a Doctor Hoover? is on her way out, but it's going to be about twenty minutes before she can get here."

"Good. We're less than ten minutes away. I need you to go back into the snakebite kit and find one of the syringes labeled Banamine and give her a single injection. How is the swelling?"

"She's pretty swollen around the face area, but thanks to the tubes, she's breathing okay. And she's still standing, but she's not very steady on her feet."

"Okay. We just got off the freeway, so we'll be there in a few minutes. Go help Linda. Oh, and Rob?"

"Yeah?"

"Thank you."

Bert pulled up to the first gate. Shannon jumped out, unlocked the gate, and jumped back in, leaving the gate open for the vet. When they got to the ranch gate, her feet hit the ground before Bert even had a chance to come to a stop. After he drove through, she closed but didn't lock the gate and pointing to Missy and Shakespeare's stall, told him to drive over and park next to it. Once again, she was out the door and running before the truck came to a stop.

Linda came out of the shed. "How is she?" Shannon asked, as they both tried to push their way through the three horses' heads blocking the doorway.

"About the same. We gave her the shot, and I don't know how, but she's still standing."

Shannon walked over to Missy and gently lifted her chin. As she lightly probed Missy's muzzle with her finger, Missy looked at her with the biggest, saddest brown eyes Shannon had ever seen.

"I know, sweetheart. It hurts, doesn't it?" She finished probing and kissed Missy on the forehead. "It's going to be okay, young lady. You're going to be okay. You hear me? You're strong, and you're going to get through this."

Just then, Shannon felt Bert's arms go around her waist, and she took a step back into his chest. "Thank you," she whispered and pulled his arms tighter around her. Looking at Rob and Linda, she said, "We've done everything we can. All we can do now is wait for the vet."

The four of them spent the next ten minutes talking to Missy, telling her everything would be alright and that Shakespeare was right there waiting for her to get better.

Finally, Shannon turned to Rob and Linda. "Why don't you two go get some rest? We'll come up and let you know how she is as soon as Dr. Hoover looks at her. Rob, would you please call CJ and Shawn and let them know what's going on? She's got my phone."

As soon as Rob and Linda left, Shannon turned in Bert's arms and broke down. Sobbing, her head still against his chest, she turned and looked into Missy's eyes.

"Please don't die. Everybody loves you and needs you, damn it. You can't die."

Bert pulled her in tighter and hugged her as hard as he dared and stroked her hair.

A minute later, Dr. Hoover fought her way through the door. "Think you could get another horse in here?" she mumbled. "Well, she's still standing. That's a very good sign." She looked into Missy's eyes and smiled. "Hi, Missy. How you doing, young lady?"

As Bert and Shannon looked on they swore Missy's eyes brightened. Bert bent over and whispered in Shannon's ear, "I think she just winked at us."

"Yeah… she did, didn't she?" Shannon whispered back.

Dr. Hoover finished examining her and turned to Shannon. "So tell me what happened."

Shannon related Rob and Linda's description of the snakebite and Shakespeare's killing the rattler.

Dr. Hoover turned to the doorway and looked at Shakespeare. "Way to go, big guy."

They all chuckled, and Shannon went on to explain what they had done to treat Missy.

Dr. Hoover smiled at Shannon. "Well, if it wasn't for you, she likely wouldn't be here. I couldn't have done any better myself. Putting the tubes in kept her nasal passages open, and the Benemine helped keep her from going into shock. That, and the rattlesnake vaccine regimen we did with her last year are definitely why she's still here." Dr. Hoover looked over at

Missy, then Shakespeare. "That and her orneriness. Right, Shakespeare?"

Shakespeare snorted and nodded his head up and down, and all three of them started laughing.

"She's not out of the woods yet, though. I'm going to give her an anti-inflammatory to help reduce the swelling, along with an antibiotic and a tetanus booster. But you're going to need to stay with her tonight to keep her calm and make sure she stays hydrated."

Dr. Hoover looked over at Bert with a big smile, then winked at Shannon. "Not exactly how you planned on spending your evening, I'm sure."

Bert kissed Shannon on the cheek then looked back to Dr. Hoover. "I want to see somebody top this for a *first date* story."

Dr. Hoover's eyebrows went up and she smiled at Shannon. "If he's still here in the morning, he's definitely a keeper."

Shannon pulled Bert in tighter and smiled back at her. "He'll still be here..." She tilted her head back, looked at Bert and winked. "And I already know he's a keeper."

"Okay." Dr. Hoover packed her bag. "I'll be back in the morning to check on her." She walked over to Shannon, took her hand, and lightly squeezed it. "You did good. With the horse... and the guy." Then she turned and fought her way back through the doorway.

Shannon eased out of Bert's arms and walked over to Missy. She carefully laid her head against the side of Missy's neck. "First you scare the shit out of me, and now I have to sleep with you. You're going to owe me big-time when you get better."

417

"We," Bert said.

Shannon looked at him. "Huh?"

"We," he said again. "We… have to sleep with her. There is no way I'm letting you sleep out here by yourself." He paused, then added, "That is, if you're okay with sleeping with me on the first date?"

"I'm way okay with it… but no messing around in front of the horses." She chuckled.

"I wouldn't dream of it." He chuckled back.

Rob and Linda fought their way in, and Shannon filled them in on Missy's condition and everything the vet had said. "Bert and I are going to spend the night with her, but can you watch her while we go call CJ and go to the bathroom?" She looked at Bert, "I'm first. I really gotta pee. Outta my way, you guys," she added, as she tried to get out of the shed.

By the time Bert stepped into the volunteer trailer, Shannon was just coming out of the bathroom. "Next," she said with a relieved smile. While Bert was in the bathroom, she called CJ and Shawn and filled them in on what happened and Missy's condition.

Smiling at Bert as he came out, she laughed into the phone "So Bert and I will be sleeping together on our first date. But… it's okay. Missy, and three of her closest friends, will be chaperoning us." She hung up with both of them, still laughing.

Bert gave her a big hug and stared at her. "I'll sleep with you on one condition. You have to promise me I can tell this story at the station. Not that anyone's going to believe it."

"It is pretty funny, isn't it?" She smiled back. "Okay. But... if anything were to happen tonight... I'm not saying it will... but if it were to... you cannot talk about that part. Okay?"

He held his hand up, palm out. "What happens in the stable, stays in the stable," he said, and they both broke out laughing.

Chapter 34 - What's a Gelding?

Bert woke and looked around, wondering where he was. He glanced up and saw a horse, with two straws stuck in its nose, staring down at him. He turned his gaze to the doorway, and there stood three more horses, all staring at him. *Where the hell am I?* Then he felt Shannon's naked body snuggle closer to him.

He reached over and moved a large tangle of her thick red hair away from the side of her face. *She's so gorgeous.* His mind started to catch up with the events of last night.

Shannon turned, kissed him and asked, "Are you staring at me?"

"Uh-huh," he answered. "And I'm not the only one," he added, looking up.

"Missy," Shannon yelled, as she sat up and the blanket fell away. Missy lowered her head, and Shannon reached up and petted her neck. "Oh, Bert. Look. The swellings gone way down."

"Uh-huh," he said. Shannon punched his arm. "She's up there, not down here," she said, as he continued to stare at her chest.

"Sorry," he said, as she bent over and kissed him.

"Thank you for last night," she whispered.

"You're welcome. Has anyone ever told you how drop-dead gorgeous you are?"

"Only you... about fifty times last night." She chuckled.

"Think we can find some coffee around here?"

"Sure," she said. "Up at the volunteer trailer." Suddenly she turned serious. "Shit. What time is it?"

"Eight fifteen," he said.

"Oh crap. Get dressed." She pulled her panties on, then stuck her hand under the blanket. "Where the hell's my bra?"

"This what you're looking for?" he asked, holding her bra up.

"Thanks. Get dressed. You've got to get dressed," she hissed.

No sooner had she zipped up her shorts and he his jeans, than someone knocked on the side of the shed. "Brought you some coffee," Linda's voice said.

"We'll be right out," Shannon yelled.

"Good, cuz there's no way I can get in," came Linda's reply.

Bert and Shannon picked up the blankets, shook them off, and headed for the door. Shannon stopped and gave Missy a big kiss on the forehead. "You look so much better. You scared the holy crap out of us, young lady. But thanks to you, I have a new boyfriend. Missy, meet Bert. Bert, meet Missy."

She turned to Bert. "Uh… I do have a new boyfriend… don't I?"

He smiled. "I don't know. I've dated girls who like camping, but I'm not sure my back can take another night in a stable. But… then again, I've kinda taken a liking to all your furry friends."

He leaned over and whispered in her ear, "On the other hand, I'm not sure I can deal with having four sets of big brown eyes

421

watching me while I make love to the most gorgeous girl in the world."

"None of that seemed to bother you last night."

"You're right." He bent over and kissed her. "Okay. I'm officially your boyfriend."

"By the way, my friends are hairy, not furry. Horses have hair... not fur."

"Picky, picky, picky," he said, and kissed her again.

"You're as bad as Shawn. Do you know *anything* about horses?"

"Not much. Guess you'll just have to teach me."

"Okay, you guys. Out of the way. Come on. Move it. Move it. There's nothing else to see," she added, as she pushed Buttermilk back, looked over at Bert, and smiled. They both stepped out into the bright sunlight and tried to shield their eyes.

All of a sudden, they heard clapping, followed by someone yelling, "Our heroes."

When their eyes finally adjusted to the light, they saw Christine, several volunteers, and Rob and Linda watching them and clapping.

Linda handed each of them a cup of coffee, and Shannon bent over and whispered, "They didn't see anything, did they?"

"I doubt it. It's pretty hard to see anything with three horses jammed in the doorway." Linda chuckled.

Rob and Linda were amazed at how much better Missy looked and agreed to keep an eye on her till the vet arrived. Holding hands, Bert and Shannon headed up the pathway to the volunteer trailer. Once inside, they refilled their coffee mugs, and Bert offered to take her for breakfast as soon as the vet gave Missy the okay.

While they waited, Shannon called CJ. "Missy looks much better and as soon as Dr. Hoover confirms she's okay, we're going to stop for breakfast then head back to Bonita."

As she talked, visions of Shawn and CJ's shower flashed in front of Shannon's eyes. When they got back, they were going to spend at least several days in the shower so they didn't smell like they had slept in a stable. And, after that, a long nap in a nice soft bed sounded like the next order of business.

"I can't believe you two slept in the shed with Missy all night. He must really like you to have done that," CJ told her.

"Uh… I'd say I just had my first date with the brother Shawn didn't know he had," Shannon said, smiling at Bert. "CJ, is it okay if Bert showers and crashes with me at your place? I don't know how you and Shawn feel about that and I don't want to just assume it's okay."

"I think Shawn will be okay with it, but let me ask." A minute later, she came back on. "He's fine with it as long as you two are *quiet* during your nap. Oh, and he said you're both, *separate or together*, welcome to use our shower."

"Wow. Tell him I owe him big. See you after the presentation, if we're still up. If not, then after our *quiet* nap. Love you."

"Shannon?"

"Yeah?"

"I'll put my key to the condo in your truck, under the driver's side floor mat."

"Thanks."

Dr. Hoover came by and checked Missy out and, like everyone else, was amazed at her progress. The swelling was way down, but she suggested they leave the tubes in for at least the rest of the day. Christine and one of the volunteers led Missy and Shakespeare back to their stall. Shannon and Bert headed to the little mom-and-pop place for breakfast, and things at the ranch pretty much went back to normal.

Arriving in Bonita, they made a quick stop at Bert's apartment so he could grab a change of clothes. While he threw his stuff in his gym bag, Shannon took in his apartment. What met her was clean, neat, and apartment-beige boring. She was quite sure he had furnished the entire place at IKEA and aside from two very dull and ugly prints in the living room, there was absolutely no color, anywhere. Everything was tan, light brown, and blond wood.

"Pretty dull, huh?" he asked, coming out of the bedroom.

"Uh... do you have something against color?" Shannon said, smiling.

"I moved here right after Ann died, and honestly, the apartment kind of reflects my mood for the past two years."

Shannon took his hand in hers. "I'm very sorry she died."

"Me too," he said. "She was and always will be my first love. But she's gone, I've mourned her, and now, it's time for me to move on with my life." He kissed her. "Subject for another time and two or three six-packs."

"I'll be happy to just sit and listen anytime you want." Then she added, "I'll even buy the beer." She pushed him toward the door. "Come on. I have *got* to go shower."

They arrived at the condo complex and found the key in Shannon's truck, as promised. Once inside, she led him by the hand to the guest room. While he stripped out of his clothes, she went into the guest bath, grabbed two sets of towels and put them in the master bath. On her way back, she grabbed the laundry basket. Back in the bedroom, she stripped, threw all their clothes in the basket then took his hand and led him into the master bedroom.

"Wait till you see their shower," she said, but her eyes, and his, were definitely focused elsewhere.

They stepped into the bathroom, he looked around, and said, "Wow. Nice," but his eyes immediately went back to her.

Shannon put her arms around his waist, stepped into him, and laid her head against his chest. "You need to know how much I appreciate your being there for me and everything you did last night. If it weren't for you, I don't think I could've survived the night."

"Oh, I highly doubt that. All I did was provide a shoulder for you to lean on when you needed it."

"Bert, you were way more than a shoulder, and I'm not talking about the sex part. Your confidence in me and the way you knew when I most needed your support was what got me through the night." She stretched up, kissed him, and seconds later, their tongues were doing a very provocative tango. Finally, she broke off the kiss and led him into the steaming shower. "Enough of last night. Right now, I need my back—" Her eyebrows went up. "—and other parts washed."

They spent the better part of the next hour scrubbing and playing with various parts of each other. Finally, Bert whispered, "We're running out of hot water. Besides, if we don't get out soon, we're going to look like two Shar Pei puppies."

After toweling each other off, they padded into the guest room where Shannon ripped the towel from around Bert's waist and headed out the door. "Hey. Where are you going? Give me back my towel."

Bert pulled back the duvet cover and climbed into bed while Shannon hung their wet towels in the guest bathroom. He watched her as she closed the door and shook his head.

"What?" she asked.

"Have I ever told you how gorgeous you are?"

"Stop it. My head's not going to fit in the bed if you keep saying that."

"Okay. Have I ever told you how adorable you are?"

She jumped onto the bed, straddled him, bent down, and locked him into a very passionate kiss. "You're impossible."

"And you're still adorable." He smiled back.

She laid her head on his chest and asked, "Am I being too forward?"

"No," he whispered.

"Even when I just about ripped your clothes off in the stall last night?"

"Uh… I think we mutually agreed to rip each other's clothes off so technically you weren't being forward. And, for the record, I love having you rip my clothes off."

He could feel her smile as she snuggled closer into his chest.

"Will you be okay if I just fall asleep like this for a little while?" she asked.

"You're welcome to fall asleep on my chest anytime."

"Careful," she whispered. "I might just take you up on that."

He ran his fingers through her hair, bent, and gently kissed the top of her head. "I can't think of anything I'd like better."

Seconds later, they were both sound asleep.

Shannon woke to voices off in the distance. It took her a few seconds to remember where she was and that the hand cupping her breast belonged to Bert. Slowly turning under his arm, she kissed him and snuggled against him.

"Hi, sleepy" she said, then added, "Think we should get up?"

"Why? You got a hot date or something?" he mumbled.

"Actually I do. This really good-looking hunk promised me dinner and a ride on his boat."

"Didn't your mom ever tell you not to take boat rides from strangers?"

"Yeah... but I'm going to pretty much ignore her this time 'cause—" She slid up and kissed him. "—I'm horny as hell."

An hour later, they walked into the living room with two of the biggest grins Shawn and CJ had ever seen.

"Perfect timing," Shawn said. "We're just about to start working on dinner."

"Thanks," Shannon said as she hugged Bert's arm. "But this really cute guy promised me dinner followed by a moonlit boat ride under the stars."

CJ looked over at Shawn. "Okay then. Guess we know where we stand. Right behind dinner out and moonlit boat rides under the stars."

"Don't forget cute guys," Shawn added.

"Sorry?" Shannon said.

CJ chuckled. "Shut up and go have fun. One look at you two and we knew there was no way you were staying for dinner. We were just trying to be polite."

Shannon handed CJ her condo key. "Keep it. You'll need it to get in when you get back."

"Uh... I think we'll be spending the night on the boat," Bert said.

"Of course." CJ smiled at Shawn. "Add *night on the boat* to the list."

"How did the presentation go?" Shannon asked.

"Absolutely outstanding," CJ replied. "Your notes and slides were wonderful, and Shawn's presentation fit perfectly with yours. We even got a standing ovation when it was over. They also asked us if we, actually you and Shawn, would be willing to present it at all the schools in the South Bay District."

"That's great," Shannon said.

Shawn added, "Between the two presentations, we covered a lot more than they ever expected. They were also pleased that we tailored it to things the kids could relate to and understand. And the kids went nuts on the horse safety part. But listen, we can talk more about it tomorrow. You two get out of here and go have fun."

Before they started for the door, Bert walked over and pulled CJ into a hug. "I'll never be able to thank you enough for bringing Shannon to the station," he said.

"If I had any idea we were going to keep moving down the list, I would've left her in the truck." CJ chuckled. "I love you," she said and laid her head on Shannon's shoulder, then looked back at Bert. "I don't expect you to completely understand our friendship, but I'm trusting you with one of the two most important people in the world to me. I need you to promise me you'll protect her and treat her like the special person she is."

Bert pulled Shannon in close. "I actually do understand. I knew she was special the minute she stepped out from behind you at the station." He kissed Shannon's cheek and added, "I've been trying to tell her how special she is for the past two days." He looked back at CJ. "And I promise you that I would never do anything to hurt her and would give my life before I would let anything or anyone harm her."

"Thank you," CJ said.

Shannon went over and hugged Shawn. "The same goes for you," she said.

Shawn nodded and pulled CJ close to him. "I know. You would make me a gelding, and Kate would draw and quarter me if I let anything happen to her."

"What's a gelding?" Bert asked.

"I'll explain on the way to the boat." Shannon chuckled then winked at CJ.

Chapter 35 - If You Ever Want to See Your Mother Again

Winter turned to spring and spring to summer, but hardly anyone realized it. San Diego's cherished seventy-two degree average temperature had disappeared sometime around mid-March and was quickly replaced by temperatures in the mid to upper eighties along the coast. Even typically mild Bonita found itself sweltering in the low nineties and recorded a record number of days over one hundred, long before July arrived.

Inland at the ranch, it was a whole different story. Week after week, they sweltered as the temperature hovered at, or passed, the one hundred degree mark.

By the beginning of April, the California declared an early start to fire season and Cal Fire started moving aircraft, equipment, and supplies into Southern California in anticipation of a long and dangerous year.

Stations from the larger fire departments in the South Bay—San Diego, Chula Vista, and El Cajon—were constantly being dispatched to help Cal Fire fight brush fires all over the county. That meant the Bonita Station found itself on Move Up status, providing backup for the stations that were left unmanned, on almost a daily basis. This, in addition to their normal calls.

Shawn, Rick, and Bert were frequently on the same go-around, but long gone were the occasional opportunities to socialize or even catch their breath between calls. In fact, more likely than not, the next call came in before they made it back to the station. It got so bad that washing the engine became a luxury and often had to be done in the wee hours of the morning.

Life at the ranch had also dramatically changed. Shannon and Christine often found themselves the only ones showing up because of the heat. To help them out, CJ had committed to spend as much time at the ranch as she could, and Kate finally broke down and *hired* Rob and Linda as full-time ranch hands. Once school let out, Trish started bringing the girls out as often as she could.

When other volunteers did show up, Shannon, Christine, and CJ took turns providing hourly reminders about staying hydrated, making sure the horses and other animals had plenty of water, and being overly cautious about doing *anything* that might start a fire.

The economy and unemployment were improving at a snail's pace, and while San Diego was generally doing better than the rest of the country, the foreclosures continued. This was especially true for people that owned horse property and had finally run out of options for keeping their property… and horses. Thus, the ranch was still taking in new horses almost every week.

The worst months were March and April…. tax time. In those two months alone, the ranch took in twelve horses, two burros, and a variety of other livestock. The good news? Most of them had been abandoned, but not abused. The bad news was most were emaciated and had issues that required not only special attention, but often expensive medical care.

That didn't stop Kate, CJ, Shannon, Christine, Rob, Linda, and the volunteers from welcoming each of them as if they were the only horse on earth. It also didn't stop them from having their heart broken every time the CAS trailer gate was lowered.

As it turned out, the two new volunteers that were hit hardest were Shawn and Bert; the two firemen who thought they had seen everything. More than once, CJ and Shannon found themselves consoling the men they loved after a horse had been led out of the trailer.

While life at work had become more stressful for everyone, love and friendships abounded during spring.

The watering hole of choice had become 57 Degrees and the groups from the ranch and the station, as well as Linda from the Galley and Melinda from Starbucks, had quickly become good friends.

In April, Kate had declared Food Truck Friday a monthly ranch holiday. At the station, unless you were on your go-around, showing up for Food Truck Friday was considered a must. For those on shift, the girls had designated a committee to make sure a bundle of goodies was dropped off at the station on their way home.

In addition, couples or smaller groups often stopped by on their days off just to relax and watch the world go by. Mike and Carolyn regularly reserved the back corner for them and opened the two garage doors, giving them an unobstructed view of the bay and planes coming and going from San Diego International.

As for Shannon and Bert, after spending two weeks *bringing some color into his apartment… and life,* Shannon had moved in with him. She and CJ had become closer than ever and CJ often rode with her during her daily commute to the ranch.

If it was possible, Shawn and CJ were more in love than ever before. On mornings when Shawn was due home, CJ refused to leave for the ranch until she had welcomed him. Often, with more than just coffee. Shannon, loving CJ's ritual, adopted it for her and Bert. The result was, one or both of them often didn't arrive at the ranch until well after 10.

On days when Shawn or Bert were off, they would regularly join CJ and Shannon at the ranch, but both couples made it a point to frequently spend time alone or together, by *disappearing* for the day. On those days, Shawn and CJ would typically sleep in then spend the morning having a leisurely breakfast at the Galley. Afterward, they would take in a local attraction, then end up at 57 Degrees or C-Level, nursing appetizers and simply watching the world go by.

On days when they were joined by Bert and Shannon, which was more often than not, the four of them would watch a big yacht leave or a plane take off and speculate on where they were going. After they decided on who had the most exotic location, they would plan what they would do if they were going there.

By mid-June, everyone but Shannon knew Bert planned to ask her to marry him, and on Food Truck Friday, in front of everybody, he proposed. He never actually finished asking because halfway through she landed in his lap and almost suffocated him with a kiss that went on forever. At the end of the evening, Jason and Carol, Shannon's sister, had to drive them home and put them to bed. The following morning, Shawn, with CJ following him, delivered Bert's truck to their apartment before CJ dropped him off at the station to take Bert's shift.

July arrived, and with the exception of a few days, the heat and fire danger remained the same. On the Fourth of July, one of the station's busiest days, the department held a barbecue for the entire department and their families. The primary and backup engines were pulled out of the bay, and tables and chairs set up to keep everyone out of the sun. Outside, four large grills were set up and a variety of potluck salads, desserts, and condiments were spread out on two large tables.

Under the only two trees, an inflatable jumping chamber and other games had been set up for the smaller kids. Inside, several flat-screen TVs with video games had been put in the conference room for the teenagers.

As it turned out, Shawn and Bert were both on their go-around, and CJ and Shannon had to save then replace their food plates while they went out on two accident calls around noon. In the afternoon, they were called out again. This time to put out an out-of-control barbecue fire and rescue the owner who had tried to use gasoline as a charcoal starter.

While Rachel and her partner hauled the guy off to the hospital, the engine headed to assist Chula Vista with a small brush fire by the freeway. Around 4.30, the engine followed the EMTs back into the station parking lot. By then, most of the families with kids had left and the remaining group had formed a giant circle in the engine bay and were swapping stories.

CJ and Shannon had saved seats and dessert plates for Rachel, Shawn, and Bert and welcomed all of them back with big hugs and kisses for the guys. As Shawn explained how the homeowner they rescued had used almost an entire can of gas "to make sure I didn't have to keep relighting it", everybody just shook their heads.

"I can't believe he used an entire gallon of gas," someone said.

Bert laughed. "Uh… it was a five-gallon can, and it was almost full. He poured so much on, half of it leaked out before he ever lit it."

Shawn added, "By the time we put it out, the barbecue was nothing but a melted ball, and his deck now has a six-foot-wide hole in it."

Finally, CJ asked, "How can anybody be that dumb?"

Rachel said, "Wait. It gets better." She started laughing. "On the way to the hospital, he had us call Shawn and Bert… to make sure they *saved* the steaks."

While she broke out laughing, Shawn said, "After Rachel called, I put a pile of ashes next to his back door."

"And I put a Post-it above it that said *STEAKS,*" Bert added.

By now, everyone was roaring.

Around 7, it finally started to cool off. Other than those on duty, only a few of the firemen and their families were left, and everyone started to clean up. As the sun started to set, they began to hear fireworks off in the distance; first from the direction of the amphitheater, then the bay. Minutes later, sporadic fireworks, interlaced with occasional gunfire, much closer to the station, started up.

"God, they never learn," Tim said. "There's nothing but dry tinder and brush everywhere, and these idiots are out there shooting off fireworks and firing guns. Don't they understand that what goes up comes back down?"

Ten minutes later, the alarm in the bay went off and the dispatcher announced a child injured call. The engine followed the EMT truck out with sirens and horns wailing.

CJ and Shannon could tell they had only gone a few blocks before everything went quiet.

They finished clearing the tables and wiping them down and were just debating if they should head home when Tim came out into the bay. "Can I talk to both of you for a minute?"

"Sure," CJ said, looking confused.

She glanced at Shannon, who asked Tim, "What's wrong?" He was bleached-white.

"Oh my God. Are Shawn and Bert okay?" CJ yelled.

"They're not hurt, but they're pretty shook up. Rachel too," Tim said.

"The call was for a three-year-old who was shot," he whispered. "As I understand it, two neighbors fired off volleys from automatic weapons. Most of the bullets came down a couple of houses away and hit the little girl. Shawn, Bert, and Rachel were the first ones out of the trucks. The sheriff's deputy told me... half of her head was missing... the three of them ran up on her before he could get a sheet over her or stop them."

CJ reached over and took Shannon's hand. "Oh no. Oh my God."

"Whe-where are they? Shawn and Bert? And Rachel. We need to be with them," Shannon whispered.

Tim looked at them. "One of the deputies ran them to Sharp Chula Vista Hospital. A counselor is talking to them right now. I'll have someone take them home as soon as he releases them."

"No," said CJ. "We need to be with them. Please tell them we're on our way, and we'll bring them home."

"Okay. I'll have someone take Rachel home," Tim added.

"No," Shannon said. "She's coming home with us. There is no way we're letting her be by herself."

"Okay, I'll let the hospital know."

Tim gave them directions, and in less than fifteen minutes, they were at the hospital. They found the building that Shawn, Rachel, and Bert were supposed to be in, approached the receptionist, and told her who they were. The receptionist made two phone calls, confirmed the three of them were there, and said it would be over an hour before they were released.

Shannon and CJ took seats in the waiting area, and CJ reached over and took Shannon's hand. Neither of them said anything, but every once in a while, one of them would reassure the other by squeezing their hand.

An hour later, Bert was the first one to come through the door. He reached Shannon before she could stand and gently pulled her into a hug. She whispered, "I love you so much. I'm so sorry you had to see that."

He laid his head on her shoulder and whispered back, "Thank you for being here. I'm going to need your help to get through this. We're all going to need help."

He eased back from Shannon, reached over to CJ, and pulled her into the hug. "Shawn is going to need all the love and tenderness you can give him for the next few days."

"I know," CJ said, as Shannon pulled them both closer. "I'll be there for him... Shannon and I will be there for all of you."

"Shawn and I are really worried about Rachel. She's really taking this hard," Bert said.

"She's coming home with us. You're all coming home with us," CJ whispered, as she sobbed into his chest.

Ten minutes later, Shawn appeared in the doorway. CJ ran to him and hung on for dear life. "Oh my God, Shawn. I'm so sorry. So so sorry."

"I thought I'd seen everything until today," he said. "That poor child," he added as tears streamed down his face.

He reached up and held CJ's face in his hands. "Bert and I are really worried about Rachel. She passed out as soon as she saw the baby lying there. She's a total basket case. We need to protect her, CJ. She has no one."

"She has us, and we're not going to let anything happen to her. She's coming home with us. Everybody's coming home with us," she whispered. "We're all going to get through this together. All of us."

Another hour went by. Finally, a nurse wheeled Rachel through the doorway. She was as pale as a ghost. "We tried to tell her she needs to stay here, at least for a day or two, but she insists on going home," the nurse said. "Maybe you all can convince her she should stay."

"We're taking her home with us," CJ told the nurse. "She'll be with friends, people who love her, and we'll take good care of her."

The nurse glared at them, shook her head, and handed CJ a card. "Okay. Be gentle with her, but she needs to talk about what happened. She needs to deal with it, or it will haunt her until she does. We're here if you need us. Just call. There's an emergency hotline on there also. Don't be afraid to use it."

CJ pulled Shawn's truck up, and the nurse wheeled Rachel to the curb. Shawn and the nurse helped her into the back while Bert ran around and climbed in on the other side. Shawn slid in and sandwiched Rachel between them as Shannon jumped into the passenger seat.

"I need to go home," Rachel said.

"You're coming home with us," Shawn answered.

"Oh great. You two are as fucked up over this as I am. A lot of help we're all gonna be. I just want to go home. I want to get shit-faced and stay shit-faced. Never sober up."

Shannon turned and put her hand out. "I need the key to your apartment."

Rachel reached into her pocket, pulled her keys out, and put them in Shannon's hand. "Look, I love you guys, but you have no idea what you're getting into. I am going to wake up screaming every ten minutes with that fucking kid's face in front of me."

"Good," said Shawn. "We can all wake up screaming together."

Rachel's eyebrows shot up. "Oh, thanks. During my ten minute naps, I get to be woken up by you two. Maybe I should have stayed at the hospital."

"See, we're joking around already. That's a good sign," Bert threw in.

After a quick stop at Rachel's, then Bert and Shannon's, and a longer stop at the liquor store, they headed to Shawn and CJ's. Once inside, they all collapsed on the couch.

Rachel put her head back and stared at the ceiling. "God, I wish this day had never happened."

Shannon moved over and gave her a big hug. "We all wish it had never happened, but it did and we're all going to get through this."

CJ had gone to check the flashing light on the phone while Shawn grabbed a bottle of tequila, five shot glasses, salt, and several limes. Before he even set the stuff down, everybody was grabbing for a glass and slice of lime.

He poured a round and held his glass up. "To the best friends anyone could ever ask for. Here's to getting totally shit-faced."

"Best friends," they all said and downed the shot, then sucked on their lime slices.

"Oh that's good," Bert said.

While Shawn refilled shot glasses, CJ announced, "The phone message was from Tim. He said he doesn't want to see any of your ugly faces for the next week. Actually, I added the ugly." She chuckled.

"To ugly," they all toasted and downed their second shot.

Two more shots and everyone had a good buzz on. Finally, Shawn went where none of them wanted to go but knew they needed to if their nightmare day was ever going to end.

"Rachel, I'm going to start with you because this hit you the hardest," he said. "You and all of us, need to know there was nothing we could've done to stop what happened today. We can educate people, but we can't live their lives for them. We can't stop them from doing what they know is wrong and stupid.

"We need to concentrate on the good things we've seen and done. Think of the hundreds of people you've saved. How many we've all saved. The homes we've saved. The children who wouldn't be here if it weren't for us."

He looked around. "We're all in the business of saving things. CJ and Shannon save horses. The three of us save people. We win some and lose some. But we win a lot more than we lose."

441

Rachel stared at him. "Shawn, that doesn't make the losses any less painful. How can I ever forget the face of that child?"

"You can't," Shawn whispered. "And you shouldn't. Everyone in this world should see the face of that child. She should become the poster child of all that is wrong in this world. But what happened to her shouldn't stop us from saving the next child or the next one, or their parents. You can't give up, Rachel. I will not let you. Any of you."

He glanced over at Bert then back to Rachel. "You two are my partners. You have my back, and I trust my life to both of you every day. We trust our lives to each other. I don't want my life in anyone else's hands, I want it in both of yours because I know you love me. I know you care, and I know you would never let anything happen to me. I know you'll have my back, and I'll have yours. No matter what happens."

Rachel gazed at each of them. "I thought we were all good friends, but... it's a lot deeper than that, isn't it?"

Shawn nodded. "Next to CJ and my family, the three most important people in the world to me are right here in this room, Rachel. And I think everybody else here feels the same."

Everybody else nodded, and CJ crawled over and took Rachel's hands in hers. "You're family, Rachel. When you hurt, we hurt. When you're happy, we're happy." CJ took a big breath. "Rachel, you sat in my room and watched over me when you didn't even know who I was. When hardly anyone cared if I lived or died... you were there. Now... I'm here for you. We're all here for you."

Tears were rolling down Rachel's cheeks as she looked around. "Wow. This is all overwhelming. I always knew how I felt about all of you, but I was always afraid to even wonder if you felt the same about me."

Shannon smiled at her. "Now you know. Welcome to the family. I need to warn you, though. There may come a day when you want to disown us or… at least keep it a secret that you even know us."

CJ looked over at Bert, then Shawn. "Are you two okay? We've all been concentrating on Rachel, but you two saw the same horrible scene she did."

Bert spoke up. "I think I'll be okay. It's going to take a while, but I've got Shannon to lean on. Rachel, you're all alone, and I can't tell you how worried we all are about you."

Rachel looked around. "I'm not alone anymore."

"You okay, my knight?" CJ asked Shawn.

"I'm good," he said then added with a smile, "I will need some extra pampering, though."

"Uh… I think we can arrange that," CJ said, then added a wink.

CJ jumped up. "Okay, I've been thinking about sleeping arrangements. We don't have enough beds to go around, and we don't want any of the three of you far from a hug. So. We're having a good old-fashion campout, right here in the living room."

Bert put his hand up. "Can we build a fort out of couch cushions?"

"Uh… that would be a NO," CJ said, laughing.

Shannon glanced at Rachel. "And you thought I was kidding about not wanting to admit you know us?"

443

CJ came out of the hallway and piled pillows and blankets next to the couch while everyone else cycled through the bathrooms to change into their pajamas. Shawn and CJ were last to change, and when they came back out, Bert's hand was back up.

"Now what?" CJ said.

"Uh…. what if Shannon and I want to… uh… you know."

Everybody started laughing. "If you two want to do the… *dirty deed* just go in the guest room and close the door," CJ said, shaking her head. "But… you have to come back out when you're done." Snorting, she added, "Then… we all get to ask questions about what you did and how it was."

"If you go in there… you're going by yourself," Shannon said.

"You guys really are crazy," Rachel mumbled.

Two more rounds of shots, another round of bathroom trips, and Bert started telling jokes and campfire stories.

"The last time I camped out was during my two-week Cub Scout career," Bert said.

"Two weeks?" CJ asked.

"CJ, please don't encourage him," Shannon said.

"Yeah, my parents signed me up just before the yearly Boy Scout Jamboree. The following weekend, they shipped me off to the Poconos. I think that was the weekend my sister was conceived.

"Anyway, my two tent mates, who were veterans of the previous Jamboree, told me there was a tradition I had to uphold before I could become a full-fledged cubby. After everyone went to sleep, I had to take one of the hot bricks that circled the fire pit, pee on it, then slip it into the tent next to ours.

"Not wanting to be responsible for the tradition dying out, I did as I was told. The following morning, one of the pack leaders drove me home and informed my parents that I was not *Cub Scout material*.

CJ was holding a pillow up against her face and laughing into it hysterically.

In between snorts, Rachel looked over at Shannon. "Who is this? And what did you do with the real Bert? The one we have to beg to join the conversations on Food Truck Fridays?" she asked.

Shannon's eyebrows went up. "Beg to join a conversation? Bert? Surely you jest?"

Bert leaned over and kissed Shannon. "It's Shannon. She brings out the best in me."

"No way. No way am I responsible for him. He was like this when I found him," Shannon said, as she kissed him back.

Turning back to Rachel and CJ, Bert asked, "Did I ever tell you my birthday bicycle story?"

Simultaneously, Shawn and Shannon said, "Oh no... not the birthday bicycle story."

Completely ignoring them, Bert went on. "As you may have guessed, I was not the best kid in the world when I was growing up."

445

"No shit," Shawn mumbled in the background.

"On my tenth birthday I desperately wanted a new bike. So for weeks, I begged and pleaded with my parents. Finally, to shut me up, they told me that if I was good, God would let them know and they would get me the bike.

"Before they had finished, I ran upstairs to my room, pulled open my desk drawer, got out a sheet of paper, and started writing. *Dear God, If I promise to be a good boy for the next week...* Thinking about it, I realized there was no way I was going to make a whole week.

"I crumpled up the paper, pulled out another sheet, and started again... *Dear God, it's me again. If I promise to be a good boy for one day...* Once again, I realized this was just not going to happen. After crumpling up the second sheet, I sat there for the longest time trying to figure out how I was going to get my bike.

"Finally, it dawned on me. I got up from my desk, opened my closet, and took everything on the floor out. My football, my shoulder pads, my bat and glove, my hardly ever used Cub Scout uniform. I completely emptied the floor.

"After carefully checking the hallway, I silently snuck into the bathroom and pulled a clean bath towel out of the linen cabinet. From there, I slinked into my parents' bedroom, eased the door closed, and quickly went to their dresser.

"Checking to make sure I was still alone, I quietly spread the towel out on the bed. Then I reached over and gently picked up the statue of Mary that always sat on their dresser. I gently wrapped her in the towel, crept to the door, and rechecked the hallway. Finding the coast clear, I slithered back down the hallway and into my room."

446

By now, CJ and Rachel were hanging on Bert's every word, and neither of them were breathing. Shawn and Shannon just sat in silence, shaking their heads.

"I went to the closet and gently set Mary, protected by the towel, in the middle of the closet. Next, I carefully put everything back into the closet, completely burying her.

"Checking to make sure I was still alone—" Bert looked around. "—I went back to my desk and pulled out my last sheet of paper.

"Picking up my pencil, I started again... *Dear God, If you ever want to see your mother again....*"

Rachel and CJ fell over, rolling and snorting. Even Shawn and Shannon, who had each heard the joke several times, were laughing.

After she was finally able to speak, Rachel looked at Shannon and asked, "Is he always like this?"

"Are you kidding? In the morning, his eyes fly open, his feet hit the floor, and his mouth starts going. It's so bad that I keep a chip clip next to the bed so I can shut him up until I can at least get a cup of coffee in me."

By 3 am, they were all exhausted, as much from laughing as from the events of the day. They each claimed a pillow and blanket and staked out a spot on the floor in front of the couch.

Shawn found himself sandwiched between CJ and Rachel, while Bert was sandwiched between Rachel and Shannon. CJ asked if everyone was okay, and Shawn smiled. "Of course we're okay. Bert and I are surrounded by the three prettiest girls in the world."

As they were about to fall asleep, Rachel whispered, "Bert? Did you ever get your bike?"

"Nope," he whispered back.

For the most part, everyone slept much better than they expected, the tequila and exhaustion playing a large role.

Rachel woke up twice, the first time screaming and the second time with just a start. Both times, Shawn comforted her, and both times, she fell back asleep with her head on one side of his chest, CJ's head on the other, and CJ's arm around Rachel's shoulders.

Bert woke up once with a start. Shannon quickly pulled him into a hug, told him his bicycle was safe, and they both fell back asleep.

Chapter 36 - Firemen, Firemen, Save My Child

Shawn, Bert, and Rick were an hour away from their shift ending when the alarm went off. "House fire," the dispatcher announced over the PA. Bert climbed into the jump seat behind the driver as Shawn sat opposite him, pulling on his jacket. A second later, Rick closed the passenger side door, and the engine roared out of the bay. As they passed Starbucks and turned onto Central, the EMTs truck came up behind them.

It had been a really long shift. Two brush fires, three accidents, four medical calls, and now a house fire to round things out. Everyone had been preparing to head for home when the alarm went off, and if the next shift had been just a few minutes early, Tim would have sent them out instead.

The engine pulled up in front of a two-story house. Flames and black smoke could be seen rising from the back side of the house, but it looked like it hadn't reached the front yet. A young couple ran up to Shawn just as he stepped off the truck.

"Our baby is in there," screamed the woman.

"Try to stay calm," Shawn said. "Who else is in the house besides the baby?"

"No one," the husband said. "We were in the kitchen when smoke started coming out of the wall. I tried to get upstairs to the baby, but the staircase was full of smoke and the hallway at the top was on fire."

"Okay, where is the baby?"

The husband turned and pointed to the flat roof over the garage.

Shawn looked at him, confused.

"That's our bedroom on the right, above the garage. There's a patio on the left, and the baby's crib is on the other side of the sliding-glass door. The one right there... that you can see. She's right there," the husband screamed.

Bert and Rick were standing next to Shawn. "Where's the kitchen?" Bert asked.

"We don't care about the kitchen. You need to get our baby out."

"We understand, but where is the kitchen?"

"In the back. On the right."

A second engine from Chula Vista rolled up, and Rick ran over to the truck. "Everyone is out except for a baby in the master bedroom." He pointed to the rooftop patio. "We're going up to get her. It sounds like a kitchen electrical." Pointing to the electrical service panel, he said, "Box is right there, and the kitchen is back right. We're also going to need a hose on us."

While Bert and Rick pulled a ladder off the truck, Shawn pointed to the sliding-glass door and yelled to Rachel, "Baby upstairs. Opposite side of the patio door. She's probably going to need oxygen."

Shawn turned and followed Rick up the ladder. They climbed over the short wall surrounding the patio, and Shawn headed for the sliding door. Bert came up last, handed Rick an axe, and stayed at the top of the ladder.

Rick came up next to Shawn. "Baby's on the right behind the blinds. Take out the glass on the left, and I'll reach in and grab her."

"Make it quick," Rick said. "It's getting really hot under my feet."

Rick swung the axe and the glass door disintegrated. Shawn stepped past him, turned right, and pulled the baby and her blanket out of the crib. As he wrapped the blanket around her, flames from the hallway leapt through the bedroom doorway and engulfed the whole bedroom.

Shawn pulled the baby into his chest, turned his back to the flames, and started toward the ladder. Halfway across, the roof under him gave way. He turned and threw the baby at Rick, who was two steps behind him. As Shawn fell through the roof, he reached out and grabbed a beam.

Circling around the portion of roof that had collapsed, Rick reached the ladder and handed the baby to Bert. As Bert went down the ladder, Rick turned and headed back to where Shawn was hanging. Just as he reached out for Shawn, the whole roof collapsed.

Shawn reached out, and grabbed Rick's jacket and pulled him in with all the strength he had. A second later, he felt his left ankle snap as their combined weight landed on it. The two of them landed on a pile of flaming roof material on the garage floor, with Rick on top of Shawn. Before either of them could move, a flood of water drenched them.

-------//-------

The last thing Shawn remembered was being dragged by the collar of his jacket and everybody yelling.

A screaming siren and CJ whispering, "Wake up," interrupted his dream. He opened his eyes and found Rachel staring down at him. "Wake up," she said. "Shawn, you need to wake up." He looked at her and smiled. She smiled back, wrapped her arms around him, and bawled.

-------//-------

CJ was waiting at the door with a cup of coffee in her hand. A mile away, Shannon stood inside the apartment she shared with Bert, in the same pose. A few miles farther, Trish was telling the girls to stop arguing or they could forget going to the ranch after Rick got home.

-------//-------

An hour later, Shannon's phone rang. "Hi, hon. Where are you? They make you guys wash the truck before you could leave?"

"Shannon, I need you to go pick up CJ and Trish."

"What? What's wrong? Oh God, Bert, are you okay? Tell me you're okay." she said.

"I'm okay, hon, I'm okay."

"Shawn? Is Shawn okay? Damn it, Bert. Are he and Rick okay?"

"Shannon, take a deep breath… I don't know. We were at a house fire, and they fell through the roof. They're taking them to Scripps Mercy right now." He could hear Shannon softly crying. "Honey, I need you to keep it together. I need you to go get CJ and Trish. I don't want them hearing about this through a phone call, and they need to get to the hospital."

Her voice cracking, she managed to whisper, "Okay." He could picture her nodding her head. "I'll be strong," she finally said. "Where are they?"

"Scripps. Scripps Mercy. The trauma center. I know Shawn's leg is hurt, but that's all I know. Rachel is with him. She insisted she go with him and almost ripped the other EMT out of the back of the truck. I don't think Rick is hurt as bad as Shawn because they held him till the third ambulance got there."

By then, she had started to compose herself. "Oh God, Bert. I need to get myself together… Third ambulance? Did someone else get hurt?"

"The first ambulance was for the baby. Shawn and Rick rescued a baby," he said. "Shannon?"

"Yeah….I'm here."

"Listen, I need to go. Tell CJ that they took Shawn in an ambulance. You got that? Tell her if he was critical, they would have airlifted him. That's important. Can you remember that?"

"Uh… huh."

"Shannon? I love you. I'll meet you at the hospital."

She grabbed her keys and drove the short distance to the condo. By the time she got there, everything had started to sink in and tears were running down her cheeks again. She rang the bell and started shaking uncontrollably.

A minute later, CJ opened the door. CJ took one look at Shannon and grabbed the doorjamb. "It's Shawn, isn't it? Oh my God, is he okay? Shannon. Is he okay?"

"I don't know. He's at Scripps Mercy. He and Rick fell through a roof."

"Bert? Is Bert okay?"

"Uh-huh. He said they rescued a baby… and he said to tell you they used an ambulance."

CJ stared at her. "Who used an ambulance?"

"They did, they took Shawn in an ambulance. They didn't airlift him. That means he wasn't critically hurt." She put her arms around CJ, and they both held on for dear life. "He'll be okay, CJ. I just know it. He'll be okay."

"Rick?" CJ whispered.

"Bert said he wasn't hurt as bad as Shawn. They held him back till another ambulance got there." Shannon chuckled. "Did you ever think you'd be happy to know someone took an ambulance or which one they took?"

CJ grabbed her purse and pulled out her keys. She closed the door, locked it, and the two of them ran to Shannon's truck. Minutes later, they pulled into Rick and Trish's driveway.

Before either one of them could get out, Trish came out and walked up to Shannon's window. "We can't leave yet. Rick's not home and…" She looked at Shannon, then at CJ and knew something was terribly wrong. "What's going on? It's Rick, isn't it? He's not home. Why is he not home yet?"

Trish's legs started to collapse. She grabbed the windowsill to keep from falling just as CJ reached her. "Rick and Shawn were hurt on a call. We don't know for sure, but we don't think either one of them is critical. We need to get to the hospital."

"The girls, I need to get the girls."

CJ opened the rear door and helped Trish in. "I'll get them. Sit and take a deep breath. They're going to be okay, Trish. Everything's going to be okay."

Trish nodded, and CJ turned and went into the house. Two minutes later, she came out with one girl on each side of her and Trish's purse in her hand.

-------//-------

Bert met them at the entrance to the hospital. "How are they?" Trish asked.

"They're both doing good. They're both going to be okay." He took CJ's hand and squeezed it. "They just took Shawn into surgery. He's pretty banged up, but he's going to be okay, CJ."

He squeezed her hand again and whispered, "He's going to be okay. Let's get upstairs. The doctor said he would be out as soon as Shawn was out of surgery and give us the latest on his condition."

Shannon walked over, wrapped him in her arms, and kissed him. "I love you," she whispered, as he walked them all to the elevator. On the way up, he explained what he knew so far.

He looked at CJ. "Shawn took the brunt of the fall. As best we can tell, he pulled Rick on top of him as they were on their way down. Rachel rode in with him and said his leg is pretty well banged up. He's got at least two broken ribs and a bad gash on his head from when his helmet slammed the ground."

He turned to Trish and the girls and smiled at them. "Your dad's going to be fine." He turned back to Trish. "Trish, if Shawn hadn't pulled Rick on top of him... he might not be here. He was about to land on a piece of beam sticking straight up."

Bert paused and took a deep breath. "CV fire had ripped the garage door down and saw the whole thing. If Rick had landed on that piece of beam, it would have impaled him. Right through the chest." He took another deep breath. "He's fine, Trish. Very shaken up, but fine."

The elevator doors opened, and Bert led them to the waiting area across from the nurses' station. After they were all seated, he continued.

"Neither of them were burned. CV fire had the hose on them before they ever hit the ground." He turned back to CJ. "Rachel is in talking to her nurse friends to try to find out more about Shawn."

He reached out, took CJ's hand, then reached for one of Trish's. Smiling, he quietly added, "You both need to know something. If it hadn't been for them, that family's baby would never have made it."

-------//-------

Twenty minutes later, Rachel came into the waiting room. She sat next to CJ, took her hand, then leaned forward so she could see Trish and the girls. "This is all unofficial. Rick is fine. They're just about done patching him up, and he should be out soon. He's banged up pretty good, but nothing that a few Band-Aids and a six-pack of Corona can't fix."

She turned back to CJ and squeezed her hand. "Shawn is going to be okay. You hear me? Okay. He's a lot worse for the wear than Rick." She smiled at Trish. "The fact that Rick landed on him might have had something to do with that so Rick's going to owe him a couple of those Coronas." Trish reached over and took CJ's other hand.

"Anyway, he's got two broken ribs, a pretty good gash on his head, which I closed up on the way here, his leg is broken in two places, and he shattered his ankle." CJ sat completely dazed, and Rachel squeezed CJ's hand harder. "The good news is, the doctor said he's totally fixable."

She leaned over and kissed CJ on the cheek. "He's going to be okay, CJ. The doctor said it's going to be a while, but he doesn't see any reason why he shouldn't make a full recovery."

CJ leaned her head on Rachel's shoulder as the tears poured out. Someone handed her a tissue, which she quickly soaked, and they handed her another one. A second later, she sensed someone standing in front of her.

"Excuse me, are you, CJ?" She looked up and saw a woman with a baby in her arms. Next to her was a man with his arm around her waist looking for all the world like someone would steal her if he let go. CJ nodded. The woman looked over at Trish and the girls. "And you're Trish?" the woman asked.

"I'm Emily, and this is my husband Stan. And this wonderful bundle of joy is our daughter Lisa. Lisa is the one your husbands saved this morning." CJ and Trish just nodded and looked at each other. "They told us both of your husbands were hurt, and we wanted you to know that we're praying for their recovery. We would like to sit with you if we could? At least until you know they're okay." She smiled at them. "They will be okay, you know. They saved our daughter. God would never let anything bad happen to them."

Over the next two hours, Tim and everyone not on duty at the Bonita station had joined them. In addition, several Chula Vista firemen came by, as well as Kate, Christine, Linda, Melinda,

457

Carolyn, and Mike. By the time the doctor came out, the waiting room was standing room only.

He looked around at everyone and smiled. "Wow. Talk about a fan club. CJ and Trish?"

They both stood up, and he led them out into the hallway. "I'm Doctor Rashire, one of the head surgeons here." Smiling, he turned toward CJ and said, "Trish, let me start with you."

They both chuckled as Trish waved her hand. "Uh, over here, that would be me."

He turned to face Trish. "Sorry. Rick is going to be just fine. Aside from a broken finger and some cuts and bruises, he's in good shape. They're taping up his finger now, and he should be out in a few minutes."

"CJ? You are CJ, right?" They all smiled as she nodded.

"Shawn didn't fare quite as well as Rick, but he too is going to be fine. He had two broken ribs, a nasty cut on his forehead, his left leg was broken in two places, and he shattered his left ankle." He chuckled. "I left out a whole bunch of scrapes, cuts, and bruises, but who's counting.

"In any case, we taped up his ribs, stitched up his forehead, and reset his leg in two places. One of which required some glue and a small pin to keep things from coming apart. The ankle, I'm afraid, will require a little more effort." He smiled at her, reached down and took her hand. "I don't want to scare you. All this sounds really bad, but it's not. These are things we deal with every day. I can assure you, he'll be up and around in no time.

"He's going to need another operation to rebuild his ankle, but we're going to let his body rest for a few days before we take care of that. They should be wheeling him into his room right about now. As soon as they get him settled, a nurse will come get you and you can see him." He turned back to Trish. "The rest of you will have to wait a day or two. Any questions?"

She just shook her head. The doctor turned to leave, and Trish started to lead CJ back into the waiting room.

Suddenly, the doctor stopped, turned back to them, and smiled at CJ. "You can stay with him if you want. Just tell the nurse and we'll set up a bed and dresser for you. Oh… and, CJ, I hope you know you're married to a hero." His eyes went to Trish. "Both of you actually. If either of you need anything, just ask."

Rick came through the door at the end of the hallway just as the doctor was about to go in. They shook hands then hugged before Rick came over and put his arms around both CJ and Trish.

"It's so good to see both of you." Just then the girls rushed out of the waiting room, wrapped their arms around his waist, and hung onto him for all they were worth.

He bent down and picked Cat up while Trish and Liz continued to hug him. He looked at CJ and winked. "I know they're going to take you in to see Shawn any minute now. You tell that boyfriend of yours he's crazy and I owe him. If he hadn't done what he did, I wouldn't be here right now." He bent down and kissed CJ's cheek. "Tell him I love him."

"You tell him we *all* love him," Trish said. "And thank him for bringing my husband home."

The nurse came up to them, looked at everyone, and zeroed in on CJ. "You must be CJ. You're as pretty as Shawn described you. Will you be staying with us?"

CJ nodded. "I'm not leaving his side till he walks out of here."

"Well, I suspect you'll actually be pushing him out. I'm Marge, head nurse, by the way. I'll have a bed set up for you. If you need anything—and I mean anything—you just call me." She put her arm around CJ's shoulder. "Come with me," she said, as she turned her toward the doors.

"I'll bring you some clothes," Trish said.

"No. You and the girls spend time with Rick. Ask Shannon if she'll stop by and grab some stuff for me." She tossed her keys to Trish as she and the nurse disappeared behind the doors.

-------//-------

The door opened, and Marge stuck her head in. "There's a very lovely young lady out here who says she knows you." She opened the door all the way, and CJ stepped into the room.

She smiled at Shawn and said, "Hi, my fine knight."

She walked over to his bed, climbed in next to him, carefully wrapped her arms around him, and laid her head on his chest. Then the flood gates opened.

-------//-------

Marge eased the door closed and hung a Do Not Disturb sign on the knob.

Forty-five minutes later, CJ had cried herself out. Eyes all red and swollen, she looked up at Shawn with fear written all over her face and said, "I love you so much. I thought I lost you. Don't you know you're my life? You ever do that again and I'll kill you."

Shawn's laugh came out more like a cough. "I'll keep that in mind."

She laid her head back down and gently squeezed his waist.

"Oww… easy," he whispered. "I'm pretty much sore all over."

"Sorry." They lay there for the longest time, just holding each other, neither one of them saying a word.

At 6 pm, there was a gentle knock on the door. An orderly eased the door open and stuck his head in. "Okay if I set your bed up?"

Shawn glanced down at her, and she looked up with a smile on her face. "Ooops… Didn't they tell you? I'm moving in." She turned her head toward the door and said, "Come on in," but didn't get up.

The orderly pushed the bed in, and CJ saw her suitcase and toiletry case sitting on top of it. "Someone dropped these off for you," he said, as he put both bags in the closet. He set the bed up, put on sheets, and laid a blanket at the foot and a pillow at the head. He handed CJ a menu. "Just push eight on the phone when you're ready for dinner."

He started for the door, stopped, and looked back at them. "I should warn you. The news vans are camped out front. They're all trying to get in to interview you. You're kind of a local celebrity, not to mention a hero." He started to close the door, then added, "Thank you for saving that baby."

"My hero," CJ whispered and hugged him.

"Ouch."

"Sorry."

Shawn glanced down at her. "I'm starved. Can I see that menu?"

"Sure." She handed him the menu, but kept staring toward the ceiling above his knee.

He took the menu. "What are you looking at?"

"That contraption they have your leg in."

He smiled down at her. "Just don't pull anything."

She turned her head up toward him and he had a big grin. "Actually, I was thinking we could really have some fun with that, once your leg is out of it."

The next morning, CJ woke with a start. "Oh my God. Kim." She lifted Shawn's arm and slipped out of bed. Padding into the bathroom, she changed into a T-shirt and shorts, grabbed her phone, and started for the door.

"Where are you going?" Shawn asked.

"I need to call your mom. Your family has no idea what's going on. I need to call them and tell them you're okay."

"I'm up now, so you don't need to leave. Besides, I'd like to say hi."

CJ dialed Kim and spent the next fifteen minutes assuring her Shawn was okay and explaining what had happened.

Finally, she put Shawn on. "I'm fine, Mom… No. Please don't come out. Listen, I've been planning on a trip back so you can meet CJ. So give me a week or two. Once I'm able to get around a little better, we'll fly back and you can all meet her… Yes, Mom…. She's taking very good care of me. Actually, she's moved into the hospital room with me so I have twenty-four seven love and attention. And I'm sucking up every minute of it."

Shawn put CJ back on. "Hi, Kim. Yes, I promise I'll take good care of him. Uh-huh. I'll call you every day and let you know what's going on. I understand… if anything happens, I'll call you right away, but honestly he's really doing good." After a few more nods, she added, "I can't wait to meet you," and hung up.

As promised, the first thing CJ did every morning was call and let his family in New York know how he was doing.

For the next three days, CJ spent every waking, and sleeping, hour with Shawn. The only time she left his side was when she needed to use the bathroom, shower, or they came in to change his sheets. No need to change hers, she never used them. She spent every night, and a good part of each day, curled up by his side.

The morning of the fourth day, they wheeled Shawn back into surgery to rebuild his ankle. The doctor told her he would be in there for at least eight hours and to go home. He promised if anything happened, they would call her. When she looked skeptical, he raised his hand with his pinky extended.

"Pinky promise," he said. She laughed, locked pinkies with him, and let Shannon drive her home.

At 8 pm, they called and said Shawn would be out of surgery in about an hour. At 9.15, they wheeled him out of the operating room into the hallway. CJ grabbed his hand, kissed him, and walked with him back to their room.

The doctor came in as soon as they had Shawn settled back in bed. "The operation was a piece of cake. We glued, screwed, and taped him back together, and other than never being able to pass the airport security check, he'll be as good as new. You two get to play house here for another week then we're evicting you. Any questions?"

He looked at them for a moment. "I know I shouldn't meddle in your personal lives, but I will. I've never seen two people more in love than you two. If you want to get better soon, young man, I suggest you take a big dose of CJ every day for the rest of your life." He smiled, gave them the Vulcan salute, and said, "Live long and prosper." Then he left the room.

"He's crazy," CJ said. "But I love him."

The following week was a steady parade of people through Shawn and CJ's room. Everybody they knew had visited them at least twice.

On the morning before he was to be discharged, CJ left the room and returned with a wheelchair. "Mount your steed, my fair knight. Someone awaits you at yonder drawbridge."

CJ wheeled Shawn out the front door to where a truck with a horse trailer sat in the curved driveway. As they approached, someone on the other side lowered the ramp and Christine led Milton out.

Milton looked over, spotted Shawn, and let out a long bray as Christine led him over. He lowered his head and laid it on Shawn's shoulder. "How you doing, big guy?" Shawn asked Milton.

Christine gave Shawn a big hug as Kate came around the trailer and explained, "We were on our way to a fundraiser, and Milton just had to stop by and say hi. He and Deveny really miss you."

Within minutes, curiosity and Milton's charm drew a crowd. "It's not every day we see a donkey in front of our trauma center," said a nurse passing by. "Is he one of the therapy animals come by to cheer people up?"

Shawn smiled at her. "He's a burro, not a donkey. Right, Milton?"

"Well, whatever he is, you're going to have fun getting him in the elevator."

The next morning, Shawn was released, and CJ, along with Shannon and Bert, took him home.

Chapter 37 - Welcome Home, CJ

CJ pushed Shawn into the waiting area at Gate 4. They had a
little over an hour before their flight to New York boarded.
Never having flown from San Diego International, or any other
airport, and no idea how long it was going to take to get Shawn
through the security check, CJ had made sure they had plenty of
time.

For one reason or another, none of their friends had been able to
run them to the airport so they used one of the shuttle services.
Even though it was only fifteen minutes from Bonita to the
airport, the shuttle people had insisted on picking them up two
hours before their flight. Then when CJ told them Shawn was in
a wheelchair, they added another half hour. Adding that to the
hour and a half CJ had planned to get through the airport and she
wondered if having the shuttle drive them directly to New York
might not be quicker.

As it turned out, the four hours worked out perfectly. They were
early enough to be fifth in line to check their bags, get a gate-
check tag for Shawn's rented wheelchair and clear security. Once
inside the waiting area, CJ turned on her Kindle, tuned into the
airport Wi-Fi, and downloaded a book from Amazon to read.
Since word about Shannon and Shawn's safety presentations had
spread to every school in the South Bay, Shawn had brought his
tablet so he could fine-tune their presentation yet again.

"You okay?" she asked.

"Fine."

"If you need anything, just poke me," she said and started
reading.

A minute later, she started laughing. Shawn looked over at her as she went quiet. Another minute went by, and she burst out laughing again, then started shaking her head. "Oh my God," she said and snorted. Another minute and she was laughing so hard she had to put her Kindle down so she could swipe at the tears running down her cheeks.

Chuckling at her, Shawn asked, "What in the world are you reading?"

"Oh God," she said, still wiping her cheeks. "This book has to be the funniest thing I've ever read. It's by a Jenny B. Jones, and it's called *In Between*. It's told through the eyes of a sixteen-year-old girl who's been made a ward of the state. Her mother is in prison for selling drugs and her father is a no-show in her life, as she puts it.

"Anyway, she's in a girls' home called Sunny Haven when they ship her off to a foster family in the middle of nowhere, called In Between, Texas. Right now, Mrs. Smartly from Sunny Haven is dropping her off at the Scotts, her new foster family, in In Between."

CJ started laughing again. "They just passed a water tower with *Home of the Chihuahuas* on it. The girl says, 'There is no way I'm gonna be a Chihuahua. Maybe they can home-school me.'"

Cracking up yet again, she went on. "Now she's trying to convince Mrs. Smartly not to leave her, and Mrs. Scott not to take her in because she forgot her switchblade and rat poison collection, has a biker boyfriend named Snake, does dangerous and risky things, like sitting on public toilets, and anything else she can come up with."

Snorting, she smiled at Shawn. "You've got to read this when I'm done."

Sensing she was being watched, CJ looked up to find the woman from the check-in counter standing in front of her. "Since you're making such a ruckus over here, I guess I should board you two first. Please follow me." The woman said with a smile.

Still laughing, CJ put her Kindle in her messenger bag, plopped it into Shawn's lap, and started to push him toward the boarding ramp. As they reached the boarding pass scanner and the woman reached for their tickets and boarding passes, a guy pushed past them and got right in the woman's face.

CJ glared at him. "Uh… excuse us."

"Sorry, but I need to get on this plane," he said.

She looked at his suit and realized it was extremely expensive and perfectly cut. It also looked like he had slept in it for the last three days.

He tried to hand his boarding pass to the attendant and said, "Excuse me, ma'am, I'm a Platinum member and we're supposed to board first."

"Sir, we're not doing priority boarding yet," she answered. "These folks need assistance, and as soon as they're settled, we'll start our regular boarding process."

As a flight attendant came out to escort Shawn and CJ, the guy went off on the woman. "I need to get on this plane… now. I have to get to New York."

The woman smiled at him. "Sir, I assure you that as soon as these people are settled, we'll call for priority boarding. I also have to tell you, we have the whole back of the plane to board after you, and contrary to the belief of some passengers, the front of the plane cannot take off without the back. So the sooner you sit down, the sooner we'll get *everyone* boarded and the sooner we can take off."

She turned, handed the flight attendant Shawn and CJ's tickets and boarding passes, and said, "This is the couple."

The flight attendant walked behind Shawn's wheelchair. "Hi. My name is Brenda. I'll take him down the ramp for you," she told CJ. "Can he walk?"

CJ nodded. "As long as it's not far and he can use his cane."

As she released the brakes on the wheelchair, the guy in the crumpled suit said, "Excuse me," and tried to slip past them.

Brenda grabbed his arm as he tried to get by. "Sir, we're not boarding yet. As the gate agent told you, you need to wait till you're called." Two male gate agents appeared at the top of the ramp and started toward them.

"Look, I've got to get on this plane. It's an emergency."

Brenda stared at him. "If you go back up, I promise I'll come get you as soon as these people are settled, but we can't let you board until we call you."

She looked at the other agents, who had now reached them. "It's my fault," she said. "He thought I told him it was okay for him to board too. I'll be up to get him in a minute."

As they escorted him back up the ramp, CJ overheard one of the agents say to him, "This is your lucky day, pal. We were about to have security come get you. Behave yourself and you might just get on the flight."

"Wow. Is that typical?" CJ asked Brenda.

"He's a little bolder than most, but yeah, there's one on just about every flight. His emergency is probably he needs to get home and get his suit pressed."

At the bottom of the ramp, Brenda and CJ helped Shawn out of the chair and through the doorway of the aircraft. As CJ tried to steer Shawn to the right, Brenda pulled him to the left.

"Okay, one way or the other," Shawn said, laughing.

"This way," Brenda said.

CJ looked at her, shook her head, and pointed toward the back. "But our seats are in the back."

"Not anymore," Brenda said with a smile and led them to the very first row.

After putting Shawn's cane in the overhead and handing them blankets and pillows, Brenda went into the galley and came back with two glasses of champagne. "Guess I better go get our impatient friend… if they haven't arrested him by now. I'll be back as soon as we finish boarding everyone."

No sooner had she left than the captain stepped out of the cockpit and walked up next to their seats. "Good morning, folks. Our flight attendants taking good care of you?"

Overwhelmed that the captain was actually talking to them, all CJ could do was smile and nod her head.

"Good, you need anything you just let us know." Then he winked at CJ.

As soon as the cockpit door closed, CJ grabbed Shawn's arm. "He winked at me. Shawn. The captain of the plane winked at me."

"I'll talk to him right after we take off," Shawn said.

Brenda returned with Mr. Impatient and sat him two rows behind Shawn and CJ. Then she returned to the doorway to assist in seating everyone else. Twenty minutes later, everyone was on board and they closed the door.

As the engines started to whine and turn over, CJ had her nose glued to the window. "We're going. We're going," she exclaimed and hugged Shawn's arm.

The aircraft pushed out of the gate, and the captain came on the PA system. "Good morning, ladies and gentlemen. Welcome aboard Flight 212, nonstop service to New York's JFK International Airport."

CJ was still glued to the window, craning her neck every which way from Sunday as she watched their push back.
"CJ, you need to pay attention to the announcement. It's important you know what to do if something unusual happens."

"Sorry," she said, as Brenda came up beside their row and smiled at her.

The captain continued, "Before I welcome our Platinum and Bronze members, I want to let you know that it is our privilege have an injured hero and his fiancée flying with us today." CJ, who couldn't see over the seatback with her seat belt buckled, kept trying to look through the crack between the two seats so she could see the couple.

"Actually, I'm now told that she's not actually his fiancée... yet."

471

CJ looked up at Brenda, who was still standing next to them. "Where are they?" she mouthed.

CJ followed Brenda's line of sight to Shawn's hand and the small box he was holding. As he opened it, the most exquisite engagement ring CJ had ever seen sparkled at her.

Shawn never said a word. CJ's hand flew to her mouth, and tears welled up in her eyes. She looked at him and mouthed, "Yes."

Slipping the ring on her finger, he whispered, "Your heart and soul were already mine, and now, I have the rest of you."

The captain came back on. "Okay, it's official. She's now his fiancée. I also am told that they are *both* heroes. Shawn is a fireman who saves people, and CJ, his fiancée, saves horses. So if you get a chance after we land, please congratulate them as you leave."

The captain clicked off, then came back on. "One last thing. If you live in San Diego, you probably know that Shawn was injured rescuing a baby from a burning house a month ago. And the parents of the baby asked if we would all say a very special thank you to him and CJ for them."

Cheers and applause filled the plane, and CJ hung on to Shawn's arm as if someone would steal him if she let go.

Brenda smiled at her. "Your ring is amazing. I'm so jealous."

CJ held her hand out and looked at it. "It is… isn't it?" She looked into Shawn's eyes and smiled. "But then, so is my… *fiancé*."

"After your dinner, we have an engagement cake for you," Brenda said, then added, "Congratulations, you two… and thank you both… for all you do."

The plane taxied toward the runway, and CJ reached up, pulled Shawn's head closer and kissed him. "I love you so much, my fine knight, my hero, keeper of my heart and soul. You're my life, Shawn, and I will never stop loving you."

They broke their kiss just as the plane turned onto the active runway and the engines came up to full power.

As the aircraft shuddered and started to roll, Shawn smiled at her. "It's okay to watch out the window while we take off."

"Everything I want to watch is right here," she said and laid her head against his arm.

Following dinner and visits from everyone in first class, the flight attendants served them their engagement cake. Shawn and CJ snuggled and settled in for the rest of the flight. Just as CJ reached for her Kindle, Mr. Impatient arrived and leaned against the bulkhead in front of them. *Oh great. How to ruin the most wonderful day of my life.*

"Listen, I need to apologize to you," he said.

"It's okay," CJ said. "I'm sure you're under a lot of stress from… because of your emergency. No need to apologize."

"Actually *I am* under a lot of stress, but that doesn't excuse my behavior."

"It's really okay, we understand," Shawn said.

"Look, I want to make it up to you. My name is Bob Hall and I own a cruise line and a travel company. The cruise line is actually my emergency at the moment. We have a ship stuck in New York with two thousand people on board, and I need to get there and make sure we do everything we can for them. Selfishly, I also don't want to lose them as customers."

Shawn looked at him. "Wow, no wonder you're so upset. Honestly, we understand. It's over and forgotten. If you want to apologize to someone, it should be the flight attendant. If she hadn't jumped in and saved you, you'd probably be sitting in security at San Diego International right about now."

"I've already apologized to her, and I really do need to make it up to you too. So please accept my apology and take my card. When you're ready to go on your honeymoon, call the number I've written on the back. I've already told them who you are and given them instructions. You just tell them where you want to go, when you want to leave, and they'll take care of everything else. Your honeymoon is on me."

He turned and went back to his seat, leaving Shawn and CJ in total shock.

Five minutes later, Brenda came up with two more glasses of champagne and whispered, "My boyfriend and I got a cruise. What did you get?"

CJ smiled and whispered, "A honeymoon."

"Congratulations. That guy can harass me anytime."

Their flight landed in New York right on time. Brenda asked them to wait until most of the passengers were off the plane then she would help them exit. In the meantime, she would make sure Shawn's wheelchair had been brought up.

474

Bob Hall grabbed his carry-on out of the overhead, set it on his seat, and came back to them. "I am really sorry about making such an ass of myself. Congratulations, and I hope you two have a wonderful time in New York and a long and happy life together. Don't forget, call when you're ready."

Passengers waved to them and wished them luck as they exited, and finally the captain and copilot came out. They both hugged CJ and shook hands with Shawn.

The captain winked at CJ again and turned to Shawn. "Thank you for letting us be a part of your proposal. I take it you were surprised?" he asked CJ.

CJ said, "I had no idea that was coming. I kept looking around and asking Brenda where the couple was. Then she looked at Shawn, and I saw the ring. I almost had a heart attack." She hugged Shawn's arm tighter.

The captain smiled at her. "Good. You have no idea how many times we practiced that before you got on board."

"Thank you," both Shawn and CJ told them.

Brenda collected them and helped get Shawn into his wheelchair. After pushing him up the ramp, she turned him over to CJ. "I hope my boyfriend gets some ideas when I tell him what happened today. I wish you two the very best. Maybe I'll be lucky and be on your honeymoon flight if you leave out of San Diego. You two take care of each other."

CJ weaved Shawn through the maze of barricades opposite the security check for outbound passengers. "Vroom… Vroom…Wow, this is just like *Dodge-um Cars* at the carnival," she declared, as she pushed him faster.

She came around the last barricade, and a dozen chauffeurs stood in front of them; one had a sign reading *Mr. & Mrs. Shawn James*.

She pushed Shawn in front of him and smiled. "That's us."

"If you'll give me your tickets and baggage claim stubs and a description of your bags, I'll collect them for you. In the meantime, my limousine is right in front of the door. Please make yourselves comfortable. Just leave the wheelchair by the back door."

The doors to the terminal opened as CJ approached, and the longest stretch limo she had ever seen sat in front of them. "Oh my God. Are we picking up another twenty people on the way? I could get used to traveling like this."

Shawn smiled as she helped him into the limo. "Don't. Most of this is my parents doing. When we're paying for things, our seats will be against a bulkhead, but we'll be at the other end of the plane. We'll also have to strap our luggage and my wheelchair to the roof of our Car-To-Go Smart Car limo."

CJ looked around. "Hmm… Maybe we should butter up Mr. Hall a little more. I'm sure he could get us bumped up to a Prius limo. That way we can get at least one of our suitcases inside."

The limo drove out of JFK and headed for Southern State Parkway and Eastern Long Island. An hour later, they pulled up in front of Shawn's parents' house.

The chauffeur unloaded their luggage and the wheelchair, and Shawn went to tip him. "Already taken care of. You folks have a great day."

While Shawn settled into the wheelchair, CJ pulled something from the luggage then started pushing him up the walkway.

A woman wearing a giant smile stepped onto the porch above them as CJ looked up. "I have something of yours," CJ said with a giant smile.

"Sorry, he's yours now. I'm not taking him back."

"Not him. This," CJ said, as she held out Kim's casserole dish.

Kim hugged her and whispered, "Welcome home, CJ."

CJ rested her head on Kim's shoulder, looked up at the porch and straight into the eyes of Shannon, Bert, Christine, Rachel, Rick, Trish, Linda, and Melinda. In front of them stood Liz with a picture of Deveny and Cat with a picture of Milton.

-------//-------

THE END?

Author's note

The idea for my novel, *Horses of Tir Na Nog*, formed years ago during my first visit to the current ranch site of the Horses of Tir Na Nog. At the time, there were around 15 horses and several burros. As we walked around the ranch, Amy Pat, founder of Horses of Tir Na Nog and a good friend, told us the story of how each animal had found their way to the ranch.

During that walk, I remember three things: Looking at some of the most undernourished, thinnest and sickly looking horses I'd ever seen. I also remember constantly wiping tears from my eyes as I listened to the heart wrenching story of what each had been through before they arrived at the ranch. Finally, I remember looking into the beautiful eyes of each one of them and seeing love, hope and a smile!

Actually, I remember a fourth thing. I remember that each time I turned, I found Milton Burro standing next to me, with the most longing eyes I've ever seen, and looking for all the world like he'd just found the love of his life. Me! It was at that moment that I truly understood the meaning of 'love at first sight'.

As the economy grew worse, more and more horses found themselves at the ranch and unfortunately, the stories of how they came to be there grew worse and worse. I so badly wanted to tell their story yet, ideas for a book just rattled around disjointedly in my head. Each time we went out to the ranch new ideas popped up but somehow, I just couldn't connect the dots.

It finally took a movie about the sex trade ("Taken") and a news story about a young runaway found working as a prostitute in San Diego, to make all the pieces fall into place. Both of those events led to the creation and back story of CJ, the book's main character and a true heroine.

I want to stress that <u>none of the events or characters in my book are real</u>. They exist solely in my mind and their stories do not reflect any actual events. Any similarity to actual people or events is purely coincidental and unintended.

The ranch and horses however are as real as they can get. With permission from Amy Pat, I borrowed extensively from the back stories on the Horses of Tir Na Nog website. Horses who are now in a safe place, healthy and full of eternal warmth, love and care: This is what Tir Na Nog, and the ranch, is all about.

While the story of CJ's life before arriving at Tir Na Nog is pure fiction, I can't help but believe that it comes far too close to describing life for many of the young runaways on the streets of San Diego and other cities around the world. While writing book 2, I would discover that GenerateHope has created a Tir Na Nog for them. A place where they too can find a home full of care, warmth, love, support and safety.

I hope you've enjoyed book 1 of the trilogy and will follow CJ, Shannon and Christine through book 2, *The Sisterhood*, and book 3, *Dreams*, as they help each other through new hardships, rebuild their lives and bring new members into the sisterhood. All the while paying forward the love, warmth, caring, and support they share with each other.

Acknowledgements

My sincerest thanks to Amy Pat Rigney, Founder and Owner of Horses of Tir Na Nog. First, for allowing me to use Horses of Tir Na Nog as my book title and theme and for letting me tell the story of the ranch and just some of the horses. Thank you for all you and the volunteers do to rescue such amazing creatures, provide them with love and a safe, forever home and let the world know how truly majestic they are.

To the love of my life, my wonderful wife Sheryl, for not only being my greatest fan but for spending hours reading, re-reading and offering suggestions to make my book better. Her love for animals and life provided the inspiration for CJ's amazement, wonder and appreciation of even the smallest things in life and our love for each other the inspiration for Shawn and CJ's love affair. PS-I'm sorry for stealing your "If you ever want to see your mother again" joke and so many of the wonderful and loving jibes you throw at me each day.

Thank you to my sister-in-law, Virginia "Jini" Rasmussen, for the hours spent reading draft after draft on the train between Los Angeles and San Diego, even though love stories would normally be the last thing you would ever choose to read. Were it not for your comments and being so confused over my first draft of chapter one, my book would be very different and nowhere near as good as the one being published.

Sara Griffin. There are not enough words to thank you. Of all the people who agreed to read my drafts, you were the one with the busiest schedule. Yet, you managed to squeeze my book in week after week and spend Sunday after Sunday going over comments. Like Jini, love stories would be your last choice, yet, you offered suggestion after suggestion. Without your honest comments, Shawn would have come across as a sniveling wimp and CJ a teeny bopper. Thank you, thank you, thank you. (I am sincerely sorry if my book has made you into a love-story fan and sullied your reputation.)

To my ex-flight attendant and zoo volunteer buddy, Jacki Glascock, thank you for making sure every I was dotted, every T was crossed and every word used correctly. And for you and Sara beating me up at 57 Degrees for having Shawn and CJ jump into bed, way too early, in my first draft.

Thank you to Jenna Ramsey and Amanda Brewster for teaching me (or trying to) all about horses and what volunteering at the ranch is like. Were it not for the two of you, I would have had Shawn mounting Milton from the right side, riding off into the sunset, and banging his head on the The End sign, like the guy in the GEICO commercial.

A special thank you to Russ and Carly at 57 Degrees for letting me hold book review meetings there and for providing a wonderful venue for me to have Shawn and CJ and their friends (and our friends) meet and celebrate. I couldn't wait to get to the Food Truck Friday chapter and pour my heart into the so many wonderful Fridays we've enjoyed there. And make Mike and Carolyn soooo you two.

Another special thank you to Lesley Cohn of the Cohn Restaurant Group for providing so many of our favorite restaurants in San Diego and being thrilled that I took Shawn and CJ to C-Level on what was really their first dinner out. Where else could I have possibly taken them that would have had such a wonderful impact on them and my readers?

Finally, my sincerest thanks to Josh Krimston, my point of contact with the Bonita-Sunnyside Fire Protection District. Without your input, trying to make many of my book's characters and events seem real would have been next to impossible. To the EMTs and firemen and women of the Bonita Fire Station, my sincere thanks for inspiring so many of my characters. I hope my description of your counterparts accurately reflects the pride and appreciation everyone in Bonita has for all you do for our community. You truly are our heroes and heroines.

Before I get to my readers, I have one last person left to thank. Kelli Bavaro. You have no idea of the impact you have had on our lives and my book. So many of CJ's traits came from you. Her warmth, passion for life, and the fanatic value she places on friendship were all inspired by you. As well as the cherished pinky promise the doctor made to her.

-------//-------

To my readers. Thank you so much for buying my book. I hope I have been able to make you laugh, cry, and feel all the other wonderful emotions life has to offer.

Like most authors, I started out writing this for you. However, about halfway through (I'm a little slow), I realized I was writing it for me, and no one else. Once that lightbulb lit, I went back and rewrote a good portion of what I had already written and the remaining chapters flew off the keyboard.

Up until that time, only the horses and their stories were real. But once I stopped trying to make my characters appeal to everyone, they too became real. In so many ways, they reflect the things that are important in my life and the things I want to be remembered for. So how could they not be real?

About the Author

This is Bob Boze's first, but certainly not his last, book. Since a portion of the proceeds from this book are being donated to the Horses of Tir Na Nog, and GenerateHope, his fondest wish is that he will sell enough copies to make at least a little money to help the horses and women who have been rescued.

Bob was born in Queens, New York City and raised in Bethpage, Long Island, New York. While in the US Air Force, he fell in love with life in England, history in Turkey, and became fascinated with people and different cultures wherever he went.

Working with first the military and then the airlines, he has traveled the world with the love of his life, his wife Sheryl. While he would like to believe he has shown her the world, the opposite is in fact true. Not only does she glow with her contagious amazement and wonder in even the smallest things everywhere they go, the few people skills he has actually came from her.

Before finally settling in San Diego, Bob and Sheryl lived in several cities in central and southern California and owned a restaurant and a construction company. Since moving to San Diego, they have done too many things and traveled to too many places to list. Oh, and volunteered at the San Diego Zoo for over 20 years. (If you're bored in San Diego, it's because you're dead.)

If you're trying to find them, check: the Zoo, 57 Degrees, C-Level, the Galley, or any one of the Cohn restaurants. (Not necessarily in that order.)

-------//-------

I invite you to visit the horses and their stories at www.horsesoftirnanog.org and www.generatehope.org to learn about all the wonderful things that GenerateHope does to help the women they rescue win back control of their lives and become the most outstanding women you could ever meet.

Please purchase my books through the Amazon Smile program and designate GenerateHope or Horses of Tir Na Nog as your charity and think about matching the price of my book with a donation to either: It will cost you less than $10 total for the Kindle version, a little more for the paperback.

Finally, please, please, please leave a review of my books on Amazon.com and Goodreads when you have a moment. Good or bad, I read and take seriously all reviews and use them to try and help me become a better writer.

I love hearing from my readers. If you have questions about any of my books, or me, please check my web page https://bobboze.com, email me at bobboze70@gmail.com or contact me on Facebook at www.facebook.com/bobbozeauthorpage/ and I'll be happy to answer them.

Thank you for reading the Horses of Tir Na Nog. We hope the spirit, joy of life, and unending love of the magnificent creatures we care for has touched your heart as it has ours. In so many ways, they have changed who we are and who we will become. And it's because of them that we share such a wonderful bond of warmth and friendship between us. A bond that will stay with us forever. A bond that truly makes us sisters.

Shannon, CJ, and Christine

Made in the USA
Lexington, KY
28 September 2019